STELLAR FOX

BOOK TWO
OF THE CASTLE FEDERATION SERIES

STELLAR FOX

BOOK TWO
OF THE CASTLE FEDERATION SERIES

GLYNN STEWART

FAOLAN'S PEN
PUBLISHING
faolanspen.com

This edition published in 2018 by:

Faolan's Pen Publishing Inc.

22 King St. S, Suite 300

Waterloo, Ontario

N2J 1N8 Canada

ISBN-13: 978-1-988035-50-5 (print)

A record of this book is available from Library and Archives Canada.

Printed in the United States of America

2 3 4 5 6 7 8 9 10

Second edition

First printing: December 2015

Illustration © 2016 Tom Edwards

TomEdwardsDesign.com

Faolan's Pen Publishing logo is a trademark of Faolan's Pen Publishing Inc.

Read more books from Glynn Stewart at faolanspen.com

1

Midori System, Castle Federation
15:20 September 30, 2735 Earth Standard Meridian Date/Time
BB-155 Corona

CORONA WAS DYING.

Even the mightiest of the Castle Federation's battleships couldn't take multiple antimatter hits, and she'd been hit five times. Communications were down, and Vice Admiral Dimitri Tobin had no idea how the rest of the relief fleet he'd led to Midori was doing.

"Come on, sir!" his Chief of Staff bellowed. "Engineering tells me we have *minutes* at most until the positron capacitors fail. The entire ship is coming apart."

Tobin nodded and came to his feet. The immense, dark-haired Castle Federation Admiral met his Chief of Staff's gaze and nodded calmly.

"Any word?"

"No coms, no reports," the Fleet Commander told him. "We've got nothing – all I can tell you is that nobody is *shooting* at us anymore."

"It's not going to matter for *Corona*," Tobin noted calmly. "It's the fleet I'm concerned about. Let's go."

With a clearly audible sigh of relief, Fleet Commander Robert Brown gestured towards the exit from the flag deck. Even to the Admiral's implants, the room was dead – computers, networks, everything was gone.

"We're cut off from the shuttle bay," Brown told Tobin. "Escape pods are this way."

The Vice Admiral followed the younger officer, coughing as the smoke began to overwhelm the rapidly failing air control units.

They'd barely made it out of the flag deck before the entire warship lurched *again,* and a safety bulkhead slammed shut behind them. A moment later, the massive bulkhead flashed red as energy pulsed against it.

Tobin stared at the red hot wall for a moment, then sucked in a deep breath as his shipsuit automatically activated its helmet, the transparent shield extending over his head in a single motion. His implants confirmed that air was rapidly leaving the corridor.

"I guess I was wrong about them not shooting at us. We need to move," Brown sent over their implants. "Follow me."

Somehow, despite the beating *Corona* had taken, their deck still had gravity. It seemed everyone except for unusually stubborn old Admirals had evacuated already as the corridors were empty as they made their way to the escape pods.

The next explosion was clearly internal – a set of power conduits that over-loaded as the ship's network fragmented – and hit as they *reached* the pods. Brown was thrown backwards as debris hammered across the deck and gravity finally failed.

Tobin managed to catch his Chief of Staff and *barely* to brace himself against the explosion itself. Brown met his eyes, half of the officer missing and blood pouring from his torso in impossible quantities.

"It's all your fault," his loyal aide told him bluntly. "I shouldn't have still been here."

There was, Tobin noted in the back of his mind, no way someone missing that much of their body could speak that clearly.

And Brown had *survived* the *Corona*.

Before his mind could process that, the entire ship came apart in a shower of blood and fire, and Vice Admiral Dimitri Tobin woke up.

Castle System, Castle Federation
05:00 December 5, 2735 Earth Standard Meridian Date/Local Time
New Cardiff

DIMITRI WOKE up to his wife shaking him gently. Sasha Tobin was upright in bed, looking down at him in the soft light she'd turned on. She smiled softly at her husband as he shook himself.

She started to say something, but he held up a finger as he focused on his therapist's instructions for the dreams. With a simple command, he told his implant to access its picture-perfect memory of those last terrifying minutes aboard *Corona* and remembered.

The power conduits had exploded all right – Brown had caught the worst of the blast, losing half a leg and taking shrapnel damage across his body. Tobin's years-old first aid training had come in handy, as he'd thrown an old-fashioned tourniquet on the man's leg and dragged his Chief of Staff to an escape pod.

Whatever his *subconscious* might think, Robert Brown had survived – and survived because one Vice Admiral Dimitri Tobin had saved his Chief of Staff's life.

"The dream again?" Sasha asked as he opened his eyes and returned his attention to her.

"Yes," he said quietly. "It is… getting better." He checked the time and groaned. He wasn't due at Joint Command for another six hours, but he wasn't sure he would be able to get back to sleep.

"Are you sure you're ready?" she asked. After thirty years, he swore his wife could read his thoughts. "You did get an entire starship blown apart around you, Dimitri."

"And the war continues, Sasha," he answered, his voice still gentle.

"I put on the uniform, I took the stars they gave me. If Kane and Blake want to give me a new battle group, I can only obey."

"We both know you don't have to go," she told him. "The Federation isn't that short of Admirals, my love." She shook her head. "You went to one war for them, love, and almost didn't come home. What will I tell the boys if you don't come back from this one?"

With Dimitri away at war for most of the first few years of their marriage, they'd been late to have children. Their two sons were in their early teens, not yet ready to face a world without their father in it.

"I plan on coming home," he told his wife. "But if I don't..." he sighed. "It has to be me, my love. Someone else might get it wrong."

"I knew you'd say that," she told him, smiling. "I want you to stay, my love, but I know who I married. Now, go back to sleep!"

07:30 December 5, 2735 ESMDLT
Corona

CAPTAIN KYLE ROBERTS was a massive redheaded man, almost two meters tall with shoulders to scale. He had faced battleships and Commonwealth fleets and emerged victorious against the odds. He was, the media assured him, a Hero of the Federation.

He was currently being frustrated by an eleven year old boy.

"Yes, Jacob, you do still have to go to school today," he assured his son. On the other side of the kitchen table, his son's mother – who was *not* his girlfriend, hadn't been for twelve years in which they'd hadn't even spoken – laughed into her coffee.

"But Mom doesn't!" said Jacob Kerensky, who looked to one day grow into his father's height.

"That's because Lisa has *finished* her school, and gets to job hunt today," Kyle explained reasonably. He checked the time in his implant. While Jacob had to be at school in half an hour, the school was ten minutes away. *Kyle* needed to be at Joint Command in New Cardiff at ten hundred hours – and the main headquarters for the Castle Federation Space Navy was *much* further away.

He glanced at Lisa for support, and she just continued laughing into her coffee and gestured for him to carry on. She was *enjoying* subjecting him to his first tantrum ever. He had missed eleven years of them, after all.

The Marine Sergeant standing next to the door was no help. *That* worthy, in charge of the seven-person security detail assigned to an O-7 ranked Federation officer, was currently pretending to ignore the whole scene.

"Sergeant Rosenberg," he said, assuring himself he did not sound desperate, "when is the aircar due for me?"

"Corporal Heimdall reports they'll be arriving in about five minutes," the gaunt, shaven-haired man in a black uniform with green piping informed him calmly.

Kyle looked back to his son, who was momentarily distracted by the thought of the military aircraft he'd seen come round the house all of twice now. His neural implant wasn't what it had once been – lethal doses of radiation always left *some* scars – but it was enough for him to judge that he had extra time.

"If you eat your breakfast," he told Jacob, whose toast was cooling rapidly, "and promise to be *very* good at school today, we can drop you off in the aircar."

His eyes suddenly wide, Jacob dug into his breakfast with gusto, even as Lisa finally stopped chuckling.

"That's not fair," she objected. "I can't bribe him with military vehicle rides!"

"It would be improper tactics not to use every resource at my disposal," Kyle told her virtuously. Her response was a flung piece of toast, and he grinned.

Twelve years of hating and hiding might have killed any spark between them stone-dead, but they at least got along for more than just Jacob's sake now his existence had finally forced them to speak again.

As Jacob ran off to grab his school things and the sound of ducted fans suggested the arrival of the aircar outside, Lisa gave Kyle a hard appraising glance.

"You're going back out, aren't you?" she demanded.

"I don't know," he told her. "But... probably. They left me grounded longer than I expected after decommissioning *Avalon*. It's been three weeks since we stood her down. Kane has a job for me – hopefully a command."

The neurophysician his high school girlfriend had grown into shook her head.

"Good luck, then," she said quietly, as their son came pounding down the stairs.

2

Castle System, Castle Federation
10:00 December 5, 2735 Earth Standard Meridian Date/Local Time
Castle Federation Joint Command, New Cardiff

DESPITE THE DETOUR TO drop Jacob off at school – a detour Corporal Heimdall had taken completely in stride – Kyle arrived at Vice Admiral Mohammed Kane's office precisely on time. The head of the Joint Department of Personnel's aide was waiting for him and ushered him into the office at exactly ten hundred hours.

Kane, a tanned man with striking blue eyes under a plain white turban, rose from behind his desk to shake Kyle's hand and direct the young Captain to a seat. The room was cluttered with the mementoes of a long life of service – one wall was covered in pictures of the Admiral at different ages with various people and ships, though the rest were bookshelves stuffed to overflowing. About a third of the contents were books, the remainder were paper folios with names in tiny black print. It was more paper than Kyle had ever seen outside a library.

"Welcome, Captain Roberts. I trust the flight was uneventful?"

"Still getting used to being flown around," Kyle admitted cautiously. "I never made a particularly good passenger."

"From your background, I'm hardly surprised," Kane admitted. "We don't see very many officers transfer from the Space Force to the Space Navy – most would resign after an injury of the scale you took. Are you having issues adjusting?"

Kyle somewhat absently touched his temples. He had been a fighter pilot until a close encounter with an antimatter warhead had burned out his neural implant and left him unable to fly a starfighter. Shifting into the Navy had kept him in uniform.

"I'll never have what I had," he said quietly. "But I am adjusting. I prefer to be busy."

"We've seen what you regard as busy," Vice Admiral Kane replied dryly. "The Tranquility system remains free, Captain, and they thank you for it. You seem to have weathered the transfer between services well."

"Thank you, sir," Kyle told him, inclining his head slightly as he eyed the Admiral across the cluttered old wooden desk.

"You've made quite an impression in the media," Kane continued. "That's partially our fault – we needed a hero after the opening Commonwealth attacks, and you fit the bill. The 'Stellar Fox' is what they call you, isn't it?"

It was all Kyle could do not to roll his eyes in front of his superior.

"I am not fond of the nickname," he told Kane slowly. "Erwin Rommel, after all, *lost* his war and was forced to commit suicide by his government. I hope for a more positive fate."

"Our government is generally better than that," Kane allowed. "Though I don't know if you'll agree after we're done here today."

"I serve the Federation, sir," Kyle said automatically. Regardless of what else happened, his oath was to the Constitution and Senate of the Castle Federation.

"And in said service, you've put the CEO of one of our largest armaments manufacturers behind bars for a tad over sixty years," the Admiral warned him.

"Excelsior Armaments committed treason, sir." They had, in fact, stolen fighters from Kyle's previous command, *Avalon*, before he'd arrived. Fighters that he'd ended up flying against when they'd ended up in the hands of a Commonwealth black operation.

"They did, and Max Arthur deserves every second of his time in prison," Kane agreed. "Of course, you *also* put Joseph Randall's son behind bars."

Kyle didn't reply. James Randall had been a rapist and a thug, but he'd become the Judge Advocate General's star witness against Max Arthur and Excelsior Armaments. In exchange, he'd been spared the firing squad for his multiple capital offenses.

Unfortunately, between Kyle arresting James Randall and all of this becoming public knowledge on Castle, *Joseph* Randall had won a tight-fought election after his closest rival died in an air car accident. The elder Randall was now Senator for Castle, first among equals of the Federation's thirteen person executive.

"Senator Randall would like to see you beached and buried," Kane said flatly. "Absent that, he'd love to see you given enough rope to hang yourself. Others who were friends of Max Arthur – or at least business partners of the man – are in full agreement with him.

"Your *partisans*, on the other hand," the head of the Federation military's personnel department continued calmly, "think that a Hero of the Federation deserves better than a minor command. They want you given a command 'worthy of the Stellar Fox'."

Kyle winced. That was a lot more politics than he'd expected to go into selecting a ship to assign the most junior Captain in the Navy to.

"My impulse and preference, Captain Roberts, is to assign you to an older cruiser in one of the system defense Task Groups," Kane told him. "One with solid fellow captains to help you learn, and a Task Group commander willing to mentor an inexperienced officer.

"But while I could withstand the pressure from *either* your enemies or your friends, Captain, with all sides clamoring to see you given a 'worthy' command, my choices are constrained, and I am left with the impulse to throw a giant finger at *everyone*."

"Sir," Kyle said quietly. "A cruiser command such as you describe sounds appropriate for my experience. I would not object to such an assignment."

"No, but others would object on your behalf, or out of a desire to watch you fail," the Vice Admiral replied. "I am telling you this, Captain Roberts, so that you understand that the command you are receiving is *not* a reward. The gold planet on your collar was your reward for saving Tranquility. *This* is a political necessity you'd better not fuck up."

He presumably gave a mental command through his implant, because a moment later a hologram of a ship appeared above his desk, and Kyle inhaled sharply.

Kyle knew that ship. She'd been all over the news since he'd come home – the latest of the Federation's newest supercarrier class. She was an abbreviated spike in space, a kilometer and a half long and almost half a kilometer high at her base. Fighter launch tubes for ten squadrons – *eighty* starfighters, more than his last command had in her entire fighter group – marked her broadsides, mixed with heavy positron lances and missile launchers.

She was a *Sanctuary*-class deep space carrier, the biggest, most advanced class of warships ever built by the Castle Federation – which meant the most advanced warships ever built by anyone.

"She won't commission for another nine days, but it's time her Captain got aboard," Kane told him. "I have the paperwork here for you, Captain Roberts, and my aide will make the travel arrangements.

"I expect you take command of DSC-078 *Avalon* by this time tomorrow."

11:00 December 5, 2735 ESMDLT
Castle Federation Joint Command, New Cardiff

MOST PEOPLE who ended up in the office of the head of the Joint Department of Personnel had some degree of trepidation. Vice Admiral Mohammed Kane, after all, was ultimately responsible for all discipline that didn't fall into the hands of the Joint Department of Military Justice.

Vice Admiral Dimitri Tobin, however, had served with Kane during the last war. He'd happily arranged to insert himself into Kane's schedule and greeted the smaller man with a crushing bear hug.

When he released Kane, Dimitri turned the chair Kane put junior officers in around and leaned against it. He studied Kane carefully, noting the new lines in his old friend's face and the slight stoop to the shoulders that hadn't been there six months ago.

"You, my friend, need a vacation," Dimitri told the other man.

"Not happening," Kane replied crisply. "I won't pretend it isn't good to see you, Dimitri, but I do have a war to help run. You got yourself onto my schedule for this morning – what do you need?"

"It's not what I need." Dimitri leaned forward, meeting his friend's gaze evenly. "It's what the Federation needs. We don't have that many Admirals of any stripe, Mohammed, and we can't afford for me to sit on my ass getting fat."

"You got a ship shot out of from underneath you, and half a battle group blown apart around you," Kane said mildly. "There are those who'd say we don't need admirals who turn in performances like that – and I have psychiatrists who say you need time to recover."

"I lost three ships," Dimitri said flatly. "*Corona*, *Liberation*, and *Tara*. Two battleships, one carrier. The Imperium lost four ships, and the Factor two. The Commonwealth lost twelve and failed to take Midori. I will mourn my dead for the rest of my life, as I mourn those who died in the last war."

He shivered, old memories rippling through his mind.

"I will also take any man who dares suggest I should have done better into a dark alley and leave them wishing they'd been at Midori instead of meeting me there," he finished bluntly.

Kane chuckled and made a throwaway gesture.

"I agree," he admitted. "Though we have, as always, some mouthy politicians. Mostly MFAs, the Senators are better briefed than that."

Members of the Federation Assembly, drawn from all fifteen of the Federation's member worlds and its three Protectorates, were the democratically elected representatives of the Federation's people. They wrote its law and passed its budget and acted as a check on the power of the thirteen person Senate who ruled the seventeen star systems containing those eighteen worlds.

"I'm more concerned about the psych report, old friend," Kane told Dimitri. "They worry about you tearing open old wounds – Amaranthe. Trinity. Hessian."

"I read their report, Mohammed," Dimitri replied. "And, yes, I know I wasn't supposed to, but it's amazing what a Vice Admiral's stars open up.

"I'll add Midori to my ghosts," he continued, "but the psychiatrists cleared me for duty. And we both know the Federation has damned few experienced admirals left."

"We never had many, and most of them are dead," Kane admitted. "Are you certain, Dimitri? Let's be honest – we expected you to *lose* at Midori. You've already delivered one victory we didn't expect."

"Mohammed," the big Vice Admiral said sharply. "How bad is it?"

Kane swallowed and glanced at a paper report on his desk, its folder jet-black – marking the contents as Top Secret. The folder would contain tech that would check the identity of the user and destroy the contents if an unauthorized person tried to open it.

He leaned back and faced Dimitri, and the last of the mask dropped away. Kane looked *old* – well beyond what seventy years should do to a man with full anagathic treatments.

"We're losing," he said bluntly. "I know that's not what the news says – we aren't even controlling the media too much on that count, they're focusing on systems lost. They're quite cooperative in calling it a 'victory' if we still hold the system at the end of the day.

"So far as we can tell, Walkingstick's losses in the first offensives were, thanks to you and young Captain Roberts most prominently, far higher than he expected. He expected to hit Midori with twenty-five to thirty warships, facing ten to fifteen.

"Instead, you met his twenty with eighteen and kicked his ass six ways to Sunday," Kane concluded with some relish.

Fleet Admiral James Calvin Walkingstick had been declared 'Marshal of the Rimward Marches' by the Congress of the Terran Commonwealth. His new job description boiled down to 'conquer the Alliance in the name of unifying the human race'.

"So Walkingstick has a lot fewer ships than he expected for phase two, and we have more," Kane said after a few moments. "Unfortunately, the man is smart enough to have *planned* for that possibility, and he's currently engaging in a series of hit and run raids that aren't taking systems or even doing much damage – except to our capital ships.

"Every ship he destroys is one less mobile asset for Alliance High Command to shuffle," the turbaned Vice Admiral said grimly. "He's grinding us down, Dimitri. We're recommissioning the Reserve, but… they're still months away from deployment."

"He won't wait that long," Dimitri finished grimly. "Once he's stretched us thin, he'll concentrate his ships and hit the systems we need to fuel our war machine."

"Exactly."

"So you need me," the old Admiral told Kane. "My life is the Federation's, old friend. Tell me what we need."

With a sigh and a hand gesture, Kane brought up an image of a battle group. Dimitri's practiced eye picked out a Renaissance Trade Factor *Magellan*-class battleship, two Coraline Imperium strike cruisers – a *Rameses*-class and a *Majesty*-class – a Castle Federation *Last Stand*-class battlecruiser… and at the heart of it, the immense mass of a *Sanctuary*-class Federation supercarrier.

"Alliance Battle Group Seventeen," Kane said bluntly. "Being assembled around the new *Avalon*. It's a multi-national force, and will require an admiral both experienced in battle and in managing a multi-national force."

"*Avalon*, huh?" Dimitri said as he released the chair and walked a half-circle around Kane's desk, studying the hologram. "That's quite the strike force," he continued. "What's the catch?"

"A bunch," Kane told him. "The Trade Factor doesn't have a seventh-generation starfighter yet – hence them contributing a battlewagon. The Imperium *does*, and their cruisers are bringing the first wave of their *Arrow* type fighters. We've made sure both *Avalon* and *Camerone* have full wings of *Falcons*, but no one has built doctrine for *Falcons* flying with *Arrows* yet.

"Last, but not least, *Avalon* hasn't commissioned yet, *Horus* hasn't arrived yet, and Alliance politics mean at least your first mission is going to be glorified babysitting."

Dimitri eyed the force. *Avalon* was the biggest ship by far, but the battleship and all three battlecruisers were of a similar generation – which meant of a similar size. The only difference between a battleship and a cruiser, after all, was the role. Cruisers carried fighters, though *battle*cruisers still had battleship-grade guns – just not as many of them as a battleship.

"It sounds like I'll want to raise my flag on *Camerone*," he observed. "Let the new *Avalon* get their feet under them *without* the Admiral hanging over their shoulders."

"Normally I'd agree with you," Kane allowed, "but in fact, I'd regard it as a personal favor if you did fly your flag from *Avalon*."

Dimitri raised a questioning eyebrow at his friend.

"I ended up giving her to Captain Roberts," the head of personnel for the Federation's military told him. "The kid is good – the 'Stellar Fox' has more potential and more killer instinct that any other three Captains I could name, but he's also the most junior Captain in the fleet."

"You want me to mentor him," Dimitri said quietly. "It's… not my favorite task, Mohammed."

"You're good at it," Kane pointed out. "Those who *survive* your mentorship do well – and Roberts needs the crash course, unfortunately."

Dimitri grunted, looking at the six ship battle group again.

"My life is the Federation's," he repeated finally. "But you'll owe me."

"I don't have any appointments left till one," Kane replied. "May I offer lunch as a down payment?"

3

———————

"SO DOC, am I going to be able to dance after it's all said and done?"

Surgeon-Commander Adrian Cunningham was more than used to his patient's idea of a sense of humor, and the tall blond man looked down at Vice Commodore Michael Stanford with a sigh.

"That, Michael, will depend very much on whether you could dance before that door sliced off your legs," the Doctor told the newly promoted starfighter pilot. "From your reputation, I don't care to guess one way or another."

Stanford, a dark-haired man with pale skin and blue eyes, grinned incorrigibly up at the much taller doctor.

"And here I was hoping the door chopped off the extra left foot," he told Cunningham.

"Sadly, your new legs have the same genetics as your old ones," the Doctor replied. "You'll still have two left feet.

"In all seriousness, much as I know that's not your preferred state," Cunningham continued to a 'mea culpa' gesture from Stanford, "your new legs have grown in just fine. How's the PT coming?"

"Slowly," Stanford told him, shifting uncomfortably on the examination table. "I can walk on my own again at least." He'd arrived without a wheelchair, which was an achievement on its own after losing his legs in September. "But I won't pretend I can run a sprint. It's a good thing I don't need my legs to fly."

"Don't remind me," the doctor said dryly. "Remember, Vice Commodore, it was *my* order you ignored to fly at Tranquility."

"We needed me," Stanford said flatly. "We needed everybody."

"We did," Cunningham allowed. "But you aren't getting *back* in a cockpit, Michael, until I clear you." The Surgeon-Commander – promoted, like most of the old *Avalon*'s crew, after the Battle of Tranquility – blinked in a manner Stanford associated with neural implant usage.

"Which I have now done," he finished. "You are cleared to return to full active duty, CAG."

Michael smiled and inclined his head to the doctor. He'd been informed a full week ago that he would be taking command of Starfighter Group Zero-Zero-One and acting as Commander, Air Group for the new *Avalon*, but, technically, that appointment was dependant on him being cleared for full duty.

Which had in no way prevented him moving aboard the all-but-complete supercarrier and picking quarters and an office. He'd known he was only an appointment away from being cleared, and he'd *wanted* Cunningham, now the head surgeon on DSC-078 *Avalon* to sign off on him returning to duty. It had been Cunningham who had grounded him – correctly, as Stanford well knew.

Checking his own implant for the notification of the Surgeon-Commander's decision, he saw two additional messages. The first made him curse – the second made him curse again, with a very different tone.

"Vice Commodore?" Cunningham asked slowly.

"Bad news and good news," Stanford told him. "Mason didn't get assigned to *Avalon* – she's headed to one of Home Fleet's cruisers to serve as XO."

Senior Fleet Commander Kelly Mason had been Acting XO of the old *Avalon* at Tranquility – and was one Michael Stanford's girlfriend. The CAG was out of the XO's chain of command, so he'd hoped she'd be assigned to *Avalon*.

"That is unfortunate for you both," the doctor agreed. "I'm presuming that's the bad news?"

"Yeah. The good is we finally have a Captain," Michael said with a grin. "They're giving us Kyle back, Adrian."

Cunningham blinked as he checked his own messages and nodded slowly as he saw that one.

"I believe, Michael, I should get you on your way," the Navy officer murmured. "With no Executive Officer and no Chief Engineer aboard, I believe I'm actually the senior Navy man. I'll need to organize Captain Roberts' welcoming committee."

09:50 December 6, 2735 ESMDT
DSC-078 Avalon, *Shuttle One*

KYLE GREEDILY TOOK in every centimeter of his new command as the shuttle shaped its gentle parabola over the Merlin Shipyards. She was immense, over twice the size of the old *Avalon* she was replacing, a jet-black spike in space still nestled amidst the gantries and modules of the orbital dry dock she'd been built in.

"I can take us for another loop before we dock if you'd like, sir," the pilot offered, her eyes twinkling as she – and she alone, as Kyle had once again kicked the co-pilot out for an approach to a new command – watched his kid in a candy store glee.

Youngest Captain in the Navy or no, Kyle did still have a job to do, and he shook his head regretfully as he smiled at the pilot.

"That's fine, Lieutenant," he told her. "I'm sure I'll find other excuses to see her from the outside. Take us in."

With a nod, the young black-haired pilot slowed the shuttle even more, angling for the flattened prow of the carrier and the immense doors of her main flight deck.

The approach seemed silent, with no communication between the approaching shuttle and the carrier, but Kyle knew that even as he watched the massive supercarrier approach, the pilot was trading messages and information back and forth with *Avalon* at the speed of thought.

They approached the ship, their speed dropping as they came closer to the massive hatches. For a moment, despite having made this exact approach *hundreds* of times, Kyle thought the doors weren't going to open for them.

Then they whisked aside with a speed that belied their multi-thousand ton mass, frictionless super-conducting bearings carrying their mass smoothly out of the way.

The shuttle entered the airlock, slowing to a handful of meters a second relative to the carrier. The doors closed behind them, just as smoothly as they'd opened, and the inner doors opened an immeasurable fraction of a second later.

With a precision Kyle wasn't sure he could have emulated with his much reduced implant capability, the pilot settled the shuttle right next to the blast shield guarding the honor party. The tiny ship settled to the deck in the artificial gravity, and the thrusters shutdown.

"Everything checks out," the pilot told him. "We'll take care of the bird, Captain – sensors are showing the mid-ship exit should be cool enough to be safe."

"Thank you Lieutenant, I appreciate the smooth flight."

———

KYLE KNEW that *Avalon* didn't have anything approaching her full complement of crew and officers yet. She would be fully crewed before she commissioned, but that was still eight days away, and she was still short everything from Marines to pilots to an Executive Officer.

He hadn't been expecting a full honor party. At least he'd seen it on the way in, and was only mildly taken aback when the blast shield retracted leaving him facing a double file of Marines in green-piped black dress uniforms and the handful of senior officers aboard.

"Attention!" a familiar, hard-edged, woman's voice snapped out. Forty pairs of boots slammed together, and forty gloved hands snapped on the stocks of battle rifles as an entire platoon of Federation Marines came to attention, rifles on their shoulders.

Kyle took in the platoon of Marines, led by a small women with dark-haired and sharply angled eyes, in honor guard formation around the grand total of three officers, one each of Navy, Space Force and Marines, which awaited him.

"At ease," he ordered.

The tall blond man in the same uniform as Kyle, though with the Caduceus of the Navy Medical Corps under the two gold circles of his Navy rank, stepped forward and saluted sharply.

"Welcome aboard, Captain Roberts," the man greeted Kyle, who the Captain *finally* placed as they shook hands.

"It's good to be aboard, Commander Cunningham," he greeted the doctor. "Congratulations on the promotion."

"Thank you, sir," Cunningham allowed. "If I may present all of your senior officers who have made it aboard? I believe you know Vice Commodore Stanford."

Kyle shook Stanford's hand firmly, noting the twinkle in the other man's eye and suspected, quite strongly, who *hadn't* mentioned to Cunningham that an honor party wasn't necessary in dock.

"Michael, it's good to see you." He glanced at the Marine NCO and Lieutenant Major waiting for him. "We'll talk later," he promised, then turned to the others.

"Lieutenant Major Tyson McRory," the burly company commander, a fit and tanned young man with shockingly white hair, introduced himself. "I command your Third Company – Major Norup will be arriving tomorrow, I believe, to take up overall command."

"A pleasure, Lieutenant Major McRory," Kyle told the youth, then turned his gaze on the woman standing next to him. She'd clearly passed Castle Federation Marine Corps height standards by the skin of her teeth and potentially tricky hair arrangements, but she wore the uniform as if born in it.

"*Master* Sergeant Peng Wa," he greeted the woman, who had been a Gunnery Sergeant and the senior Marine Non-Commissioned Officer aboard the battlecruiser *Alamo,* his posting before the last *Avalon.* "I see the Marines have decided you're better at keeping me out of trouble than most?"

"I believe the exact phrase Colonel Armand used, Captain Roberts, was 'he didn't ram any battleships with us aboard, and I can spare you if I have to', sir," Wa said primly.

Kyle laughed and shook the NCO's hand warmly.

"It's good to see you too, Master Sergeant," he told her. "Dismiss your men," he instructed, then turned to Cunningham.

"What one of these worthies," Kyle glared, somewhat gently, at Stanford, "should have told you, Commander Cunningham, is that an honor party isn't necessary before the ship has even been commissioned. Nonetheless, I'll need the three of you with me on the bridge. Lead the way."

Cunningham only gaped like a hungry goldfish for a few seconds. Kyle *liked* his new ship's doctor.

10:15 December 6, 2735 ESMDT
DSC-078 Avalon, *Bridge*

KYLE LED THE THREE OFFICERS, currently the most senior officers aboard the ship, onto the new *Avalon's* bridge, and breathed deeply of the faint smell of ozone that made up the 'new ship' smell. As a starfighter pilot, he'd smelled that scent a few times – but it was far rarer for a *Navy* officer to smell it.

Avalon's bridge was significantly larger than the Secondary Control he'd used to con the old *Avalon* into battle. The layout was different from the bridge of the older ship as well, with forty more years of knowledge of the needs of a deep space carrier built into the new ship's design.

The screens that surrounded both the entire room and each console were entirely secondary systems. Most of the displays, and *all* of the control input, would be managed by the crew's neural implants. While the Navy didn't require the ninety-ninth percentile interface capability a starfighter needed, Navy officers still needed to have an above average ability to interact with computers through their implants.

The only thing identical between the old and new *Avalons* was the command chair. It sat on a raised dais in the exact center of the bridge, capable of three hundred and sixty degree rotation to allow the Captain to see over the shoulder of any of their officers.

Kyle walked over to the chair, stepping up onto the dais. He didn't sit in the command chair yet, but linked into its computer systems with his implant to activate the recorders for the logs.

Glancing back at his companions, he slotted a computer chip into the receptacle on the chair, and then removed a piece of archaic parchment from his dress uniform jacket. He turned to face the other officers, currently the only people on *Avalon's* quiet bridge.

"To Captain Kyle Roberts from Vice Admiral Mohammed Kane, Joint Department of Space Personnel, December Fifth, Year Two Thousand Seven Hundred Thirty Five Earth Standard," he read crisply. "Upon receipt of these orders, you are hereby directed and required to proceed to the Castle system and report aboard the Deep Space Carrier *Avalon*, hull number DSC – Zero Seven Eight, there to take upon the duties and responsibilities of Commanding Office of DSC – Zero Seven Eight *Avalon*. Fail not in this charge at your peril."

There was always some degree of noise aboard a starship, the hum of power conduits and air circulators. Even over that sound, though, he could hear the soft exhalation of his officers. Reading that paper made him the new master after the Senate of *Avalon's* crew.

"Thank you, gentlemen," he told his officers briskly. "I know we're all going to be busy over the next few days, so I won't keep you. Michael – if I can see you in my office?"

"Of course, sir," the CAG nodded calmly.

———

THE CAPTAIN'S office on *Avalon* was huge. Kyle had been expecting much the same as what Captain Blair had been given on the old *Avalon* – a small office with an attached break-out room that could handle meetings of half a dozen.

Instead, the office itself was larger than the old *Avalon's* break-out room, with the ship's seal of a gold circle around a hand rising from the waves emblazoned across the wall in what he was relatively sure was actually gold. The top of the seal had the new hull number, DSC-078, and the bottom the ship's name.

The break-out room was a full conference room, capable of handling the entire senior staff of the carrier's six thousand man and woman crew. Everything was slick and shiny, brand new chrome and leather furnishings.

"Damn," Kyle said softly. "If this is what my office looks like, I'm looking forward to my quarters."

"You should take a look at the flag deck before you get too enamored," Stanford warned him, taking a seat in one of the chairs facing the Captain's desk. "Not sure if we'll even be *carrying* brass anytime soon, but they built the *Sanctuary-class* to lead fleets, boss. The Admiral's office makes this," he gestured around the office, "look positively plebeian."

Kyle shook his head, running his hand across the smooth metal top of his desk as his implants queried the systems around him. Once, he would have simply *known* every system around him, and the lethargy of his implant's response still bothered him. It still took him only seconds to take in the wallscreens, the concealed filing cabinets and bookshelves, and the holographic projector concealed in the desk.

With a thought he activated the last, suspending a three-dimensional image of *Avalon* above the desk surface.

"Not sure if we'll be getting brass," he told his friend. "Though I did get the notice on the shuttle that Vice Admiral Dimitri Tobin will be taking command of Alliance Battle Group Seventeen. We may well get to host the flag – we have better facilities for it than *Camerone*."

"That's… quite the burden, for the most junior Captain in the Navy," Stanford pointed out quietly, and Kyle nodded.

He was, according to his research, the youngest officer ever promoted to Captain in the Castle Federation Space Navy. Not by as large a margin as he'd expected, at least – the next youngest had only been three months older, and promoted under very similar circumstances.

Of course, that officer had been killed in action two years later. Not a particularly auspicious omen.

"I suspect, though no one has said anything to me," Kyle told him, "that Tobin may well regard it as a mentorship opportunity. From his reputation… it will be an educational experience."

"Let me know when the fridge is installed in here," Stanford replied dryly. "I've heard about the man's idea of mentorship. Rather… make-or-break, as I understand."

"I'll deal," the Captain told him. "I owe you an apology, though – off the record, obviously."

"For what?"

"Up until Vice Admiral Kane made up his mind to assign *me* to *Avalon*, Commander Mason was supposed to be the XO," Kyle replied. "Instead, it looks like we switched with the cruiser *Sunset* in Home Fleet – *Avalon* was supposed to get her Captain while I took *Sunset* with her XO. Instead, *Sunset* gets Kelly, and we get their XO."

"Who do we get?"

"Senior Fleet Commander Mira Solace," Kyle told him. He'd barely had a chance to review the woman's file, but it was promising.

"She's older than I am, but one of Home Fleet's golden girls," he continued. "Four years as XO, a carrier before *Sunset* and now *Sunset*."

"Why's she not a Captain?" Stanford asked. A successful three to four year stint as XO was usually enough to get a Captain's gold planet.

"A… vicious personal assessment from the carrier Captain," *Avalon's* Captain answered softly. "Reading between the lines, she refused to sleep with the creep, so he tried to sabotage her career. Command gave her a second chance on *Sunset*, whose Captain isn't interested in women and has given her a rave review."

"That sounds like a fantastic recipe for a chip on her shoulder, boss," the CAG replied.

"My problem, not yours, Vice Commodore," Kyle told him, somewhat repressively. "What's our status?"

"Without a senior Navy officer aboard, there hasn't been much synthesis of data on the ship except by the yard dogs," Stanford warned. "My understanding is that everything is basically complete and they're just doing testing, but Hammond spent three hours *ranting* about the flight deck when he came aboard yesterday."

With a smile on his face, Kyle checked the records. The Flight Group's senior Non-Commissioned Officer, the man in charge of *everything* about the flight deck itself after the CAG, was indeed Marshall Hammond – now *Master* Chief Petty Officer Hammond.

"I'm glad we got Hammond," he allowed. "Other than his complaints about the flight deck, how's the Flight Group?"

"I've only got half our fighters aboard, and a quarter of my flight crews," Stanford observed. "What flight crews I have are imbalanced – I've more engineers than gunners or pilots, though that's working out as we need to go over every bird with a fine toothed comb."

"Think you'll have any issues being ready to launch in eight days?"

"Nah," the CAG replied with a cheeriness Kyle suspected Stanford had learned from him. "Should have everything and everyone aboard in three. If I can't whip them into *basic* shape in five days, I wasn't paying attention in New Amazon."

4

Castle System, Castle Federation
13:20 December 7, 2735 Earth Standard Meridian Date/Time
DSC-078 Avalon, *Main Flight Deck*

THE TWO WOMEN who stepped out of the shuttle onto the bare metal of *Avalon's* flight deck were a study in contrasts. Both wore the blue-piped black dress uniform of the Castle Federation Space Navy and carried standard issue duffels, but otherwise they had almost nothing in common.

Leading the way, looking fully recovered from her injuries in the Battle of Tranquility, was Kyle's new Chief Navigator, also his former Chief Navigator: Fleet Commander Maria Pendez. She was a petite dark-haired woman with faintly dusky skin and curves that Kyle had *seen* shutdown men's brains.

She was also a large part of the reason the Castle Federation had won the Battle of Tranquility, having navigated the ship into an insanely close emergence from FTL. Her promotion had been won the hard way.

Following Pendez, with an iron-straight back and flint-hard eyes, was Senior Fleet Commander Mira Solace. Solace was a tall woman with midnight-dark skin, only a few centimeters short of Kyle's own towering height, but slim and athletic with it. Her pitch black hair was cropped short to her scalp, and dark brown eyes gazed at Kyle levelly. She wasn't pretty or feminine in the same way as Pendez was, but she was... statuesque.

"Welcome aboard, Commander Pendez, Senior Fleet Commander Solace," Kyle greeted them warmly, extending his hand to first Pendez and then Solace. Pendez shook his hand warmly, gifting her Captain with a bright smile.

Solace's handshake was more perfunctory, her eyes continuing to measure him.

"It's a pleasure to be aboard, sir," Pendez told him. "She puts the old *Avalon* to shame, doesn't she?" she asked, glancing around the immense flight deck. Six hundred meters long and a hundred meters across, the deck couldn't, *quite*, swallow the entire old *Avalon*. It was more than sufficient to make the thirty meter long shuttle look like a toy.

"She does," Kyle agreed. "Clinkscales, Keller, take care of the Commanders' bags, will you?" he directed the two spacers he'd corralled up on his way to the deck.

"Uniform of the day is shipsuits until further notice," he continued. "We should have the entire crew aboard within a day or two, but I'm not insisting on jackets until the commissioning."

The two spacers stepped forward to take the officers' bags.

"We can show you to your quarters," Clinkscales offered, glancing at Pendez and Solace.

Solace had yet to say a word, and Pendez glanced quickly back at her superior officer over her shoulder, then met Kyle's gaze levelly.

"Lead on, Spacer," she told Clinkscales.

"I'll carry my own bag, thank you, Spacer," Solace then told Keller. "I do have a small container aboard the shuttle, I would appreciate it if you would see it transported to my quarters."

"Of course, ma'am," Keller replied crisply. She disappeared into the shuttle as Pendez and Clinkscales headed deeper into the ship – leaving Kyle alone in the cavernous flight deck with his new XO.

"Commander Solace," he said cheerfully, with his widest and brightest grin. "You have *no* idea how glad I am to see you."

"Sir?" the tall woman replied hesitantly.

"Have you been a keel-plate owner on a capital ship before?" Kyle asked. 'Keel-plate owners' were the first crew ever assigned to a starship – the ones who commissioned her, and to whom fell the duty of making her reputation and traditions.

"I haven't, sir," Solace replied, her voice still even.

"I was on *Alamo*," the Captain told her. "It's a lot of work, and there's more on us and the CAG than anyone who isn't in one of our offices will ever guess. You, Vice Commodore Stanford, and I are going to have our work cut out for us over the next few days."

At that, Keller emerged from the shuttle behind Solace, tugging a good sized cargo container. Kyle looked it over with a practiced eye, judging it in less than a second and confirming it well within tolerance for a senior officer, if more than most might have allowed themselves to take aboard a starship.

"I've been on Home Fleet duty for a while," Solace said quietly, a small flush lightening her cheeks. "The comforts of home are…"

"Available, and hardly a detriment," Kyle accepted, his cheer completely unfeigned. The instant of humanity from the woman helped – he'd been worried someone had slipped him a robot for a moment.

"Get yourself settled in," he ordered. "There's no rush – while I'm not joking about the workload waiting for you, it can all wait a few hours. Meet me in my office once you're settled."

"Thank you, sir," Solace told him quietly. "I look forward to it."

The moment of humanity was gone. Once again, his XO was a beautiful statue carved of onyx stone, and not a drop of warmth escaped.

He was going to have to work on that.

20:00 December 7, 2735 ESMDT

DSC-078 Avalon, *Captain's Office*

By the time Solace buzzed for admittance to Kyle's office that evening, he'd managed to make time to re-read her personnel jacket. He'd made a snap judgment on his first read of the file, and re-reading it after meeting the woman reinforced it. JD-Personnel had even added a code to one of the evaluations that he was familiar with – one that agreed with his opinion.

"Come in," he ordered with a sigh. Solace's last Captain had been married and gay. The Captain *prior* to that, however…

He gestured the statuesque black woman to the chair in front of his desk and stepped over to the side of his office. A command from his implant slid opened an alcove probably intended for a filing cabinet or some such mundanity. Kyle had better uses for it.

"Beer, Commander?" he asked.

"I don't drink alcohol, sir," she replied crisply as she took a seat.

"Fair enough. Coffee? Tea? Water?"

"Water is fine."

Fortunately, he'd installed a hot beverage dispenser on top of the mini-fridge. Its line to the ship's water supply was sufficient to produce a glass of chilled water. He passed it to Solace, and took a cup of tea for himself before taking his own seat, facing his new executive officer across the desk.

"Get your quarters setup to your satisfaction?" he asked after a moment. She'd taken longer than he'd expected to come by his office, though he wouldn't have had time to review her file again if she hadn't.

"I… wanted to get straight to work, sir," she replied, and he leaned back in his chair regarding her carefully. "I had a discussion with Commander Sadik in engineering with regards to some of the supplies we were short and raised that with Commander Hellet on the station. He seemed unimpressed, so we may need to escalate to get the parts we need."

Kyle raised his hand to cut her off before she continued. Apparently, some ground rules were going to be needed.

"Commander Hellet's lack of enthusiasm, Commander Solace, was likely due to the fact that he and I had an identical conversation this morning," he said dryly. "Your enthusiasm is laudable, but if you were that eager to get to work, you should have been *here*, not in engineering."

"Sir, I…"

"I am aware, Commander Solace," Kyle told her quietly, "that you were sent aboard this ship to help balance my own lack of experience. For that matter, I expect your experience to be an immense asset to this vessel.

"But a ship of war has one Captain. You have managed to make us both look like fools to the Merlin Yards, and while I have no objection to *being* the fool when I must, I prefer to be warned in advance. Do I make myself clear, Commander Solace?"

The statue was back. The woman could have been carved of black granite for all the emotion or humanity she showed as she met his gaze.

"You do, sir."

"Good. We have worse problems than looking like fools to Commander Hellet, so unless there's something *else*, the matter is dropped," he told her calmly, waiting for a moment for her to respond.

The statue was silent, hardly looking like a senior officer who'd just been upbraided for being an idiot.

"I have reviewed your file," he continued. "I presume you've seen Captain Haliburt's evaluation report?"

She nodded, once.

"Good," Kyle said after a moment. He smiled, a cheer the woman clearly didn't return. "Do you know what a JD-Personnel Administrative Code Seven Three is, Commander Solace?"

She blinked, a moment of confusion returning humanity to her face.

"I don't believe I've encountered that one, sir," she admitted.

"It was part of the briefing when an officer under my command was being considered for promotion," he told her. "It's not one they like to publicize. Code Seven Three, Commander, means that JD-

Personnel has assessed an evaluation report as being materially prejudiced.

"Captain Haliburt's report states that you are difficult to work with, arrogant, and many other minor and major complaints," he continued. The statue returned, and he barely suppressed a shiver at the thought of just how much pain it would take for someone to master *that* degree of control.

"His report is also marked with Code Seven Three," Kyle concluded. "The Joint Department of Personnel advises me that his report is prejudicial against you. Seven Three is generally used when we feel a senior is attempting to damage a junior's career.

"I don't always trust JD-Personnel's judgment, but I *also* have Captain Botteril's report," he told her. "Jowan, as compared to Captain Haliburt, states: 'Commander Solace is the epitome of professionalism. Her skills, integrity, and heart rank her among the best officers this Navy has.'"

Finally, the woman relaxed, a flush crossing her cheeks as she heard his words.

"Unlike Captain Haliburt, I have served with Jowan Botteril," Kyle finished. "I know which of these reports I trust, Commander Solace. Unless there's some reason I should distrust Captain Botteril?"

With a sigh, Solace released some of the tension locking her ebony skin together, and she graced him with a hint of a smile.

"Not that I am aware of, Captain Roberts."

"Good," he told her cheerfully. "Now, since you appear to have volunteered yourself to deal with Merlin Yards, *I* spent today going over our main positron lance batteries, and am *utterly* unimpressed with some of their work. I'm going to need you to…"

The woman sitting across from him was still stiff. Still cold. But she leaned forward as he spoke, and he had a spark of hope rise in him. He didn't need her to *like* him. He needed her to *work* with him.

5

Castle System, Castle Federation
11:30 December 9, 2735 Earth Standard Meridian Date/Time
DSC-078 Avalon, Bridge

"ALL RIGHT COMMANDER PENDEZ. Take us out – nice and slow now," Kyle ordered softly, watching through both the bridge screens and his neural implant as the last of the umbilicals and gantries finished retracting from *Avalon's* hull.

They had enough crew aboard that he had a full bridge shift gathered around him. Solace had taken one of the observer seats at the back of the bridge and was watching everything with a silent, measuring gaze.

Flipping open another mental window, he turned his attention to the faded brown skin and shaved head of his Chief Engineer. He wasn't sure how he'd managed to get Senior Fleet Commander Alistair Wong back after the other man's promotion, but he wasn't complaining.

"How's she looking, Commander Wong?" he asked, and the Engineer grinned broadly.

"Everything is clean and shiny down here," Wong reported crisply. "All primary zero point cells are online. Mass manipulators are showing green across the board. Can't tell you more without putting her through her paces, Captain."

"That's what we're here for," Kyle replied cheerfully, watching carefully as Pendez fired the immense ship's maneuvering thrusters. Thanks to the ship's dozens of mass manipulators of every size, it took far less thrust to move her than it should, but even so no one wanted to fire off her main antimatter engines remotely near a space station.

The Merlin Dry Dock slowly retreated from around the ship, still filling the entire view to the fore but no longer surrounding her on all sides. The station, one of six, was easily ten kilometers long and six high, holding bays designed to build, refit, and repair the immense starships that fuelled both the Federation's economy and its war machine.

Avalon moved slowly, but even under the light thrusters she would use this close to Merlin she felt more responsive and lighter on her feet than the last of her name. The Stetson Stabilizers that made Alcubierre drive FTL safe were limited by volume, not mass, and the old *Avalon* had been wrapped in a layer of neutronium armor. With new stabilizers, the new *Avalon* was over three times the size of her predecessor – but without the obsolete neutronium armor she only massed twice as much.

"Merlin Yards report us clear of the safety zone," Pendez told him crisply. "They have cleared us to initiate main drive."

"Then rotate us and make your course for the testing area, Commander," Kyle replied. "Let's see what this young lady can do. Take us to seventy gravities to start. Nice and slow still."

"Yes, sir," she replied.

The image of the world around them spun as the thrusters rotated the massive ship in space, aligning her with the testing area a full light hour clear of the yards. Then, with a rumble that rippled through the entire ship, the massive hydrogen-antimatter rockets at the rear of the ship flared to life.

Mass manipulators throughout the ship reduced her mass related to the exhaust blasted into space. More mass manipulators offset the acceleration – and yet *more* mass manipulators *increased* the mass of the superheated gas blazing out.

The combination of the three sets of manipulators brought the fuel usage down to almost zero. Seventy gravities was 'Tier One Acceleration,' most commonly used by civilian starships as it used almost no fuel.

It was still blisteringly fast by any absolute standard, and Kyle watched the Merlin yards rapidly drop behind them with a small smile. A ship, an engine and open space – what more was there to ask for?

"Well, Wong?" he asked the engineer after they'd been running for a full minute.

"What?" the engineer asked. "You mean we're moving? I could barely tell. Are we going to actually test the ship sometime today?"

"I'll take that as a 'the ship is fine,' shall I?" Kyle asked, his smile broadening. He turned back to Pendez. "Commander, take us up to two hundred gravities. Let's test her at flank speed."

"JD-Ships rates our flank speed at two thirty five," Pendez pointed out.

"And I suspect they underrated her," Kyle agreed brightly. "Let's take her to two hundred to start, shall we?"

He didn't feel a thing. If he hadn't been watching the dry dock on the screen and tracking the ship's speed, he wouldn't have realized they'd just nearly tripled their acceleration. He let the ship run for about thirty seconds and caught Wong's faked impatience in his window.

Kyle shook his head at the engineer.

"Behave, Alistair," he murmured. "Let's not act like children in the candy store, shall we?"

Wong looked mildly abashed, but smiled cheerfully. "She's just purring down here, Captain."

"I get the hint, Commander Wong," Kyle agreed, loudly enough for everyone on the bridge to hear him. "Commander Pendez – take us to two hundred and thirty five gravities please. Hold that for sixty seconds, then begin incrementing by one gravity every ten seconds until Senior Fleet Commander Wong tells us to hold.

"Wong," he turned back to the engineer. "Watch your scopes carefully. As soon as we clear the Tier Two plateau, let Pendez know."

Each tier represented a 'flat spot' in the fuel efficiency chart, unique to each ship's manipulator and engine setup though generally classifiable. Once they *left* that flat spot, they would start burning more fuel for each kilometer per second of speed – *fast*.

"Two hundred thirty five gravities, aye," Pendez replied, and the ship smoothly responded to her commands again.

Sixty seconds passed without incident, confirming, if nothing else, that the Joint Department of Technology and Design's Ship sub-department hadn't underestimated the ship's ability.

"Beginning increments," Pendez announced, and Kyle caught even Solace starting to hold her breath. He flashed the XO a quick smile, and she shook her head, ever so slightly, at him.

Seconds ticked by slowly.

"We have reached two hundred and forty gravities," the Navigator announced. "Still running clean."

Now *Kyle* caught himself holding his breath. It was rare for JD-Ships to be more than five gravities out on their estimate of a ship's acceleration tiers.

"Two forty-five," Pendez reported. "Wong?" she asked.

"Definitely in the tier," the Chief Engineer replied calmly. "Keep running her up, Commander. I'll let you know when we hit the line."

Ten seconds more passed. Then another ten.

"Two hundred and *fifty* gravities." Now Kyle *was* holding his breath – only to exhale quickly as Wong spoke.

"That's it, slow her back down," he snapped quickly.

Pendez instantly cut their acceleration by twenty gravities, and Kyle studied the numbers carefully, trying to hide the giant grin taking shape on his face.

"I think I owe some JD-Ship's designers a beer," he said loudly. "Ladies and gentlemen, we just clocked in at two hundred and fifty one gravities for Tier Two acceleration. That makes us, officially, *the fastest damn ship in the Navy.*"

"I have to object, sir," Mira Solace put in, and Kyle turned back to her observer chair with a raised eyebrow. "Based on my own analysis, that actually makes us the fasted damn ship... in the *Alliance*."

"She didn't even strain, sir," Wong interjected. "I'm comfortably rating our flank speed for two hundred and fifty gravities."

"Commander Pendez? Senior Commander Solace?" Kyle asked the others. "Any disagreement with Senior Commander Wong's assessment?"

"None, sir," Pendez replied, and Mira simply shook her head.

"Sir," Wong interjected slowly. "We passed Tier Two acceleration parameters, but... the ship wasn't even straining. I'd like to take her higher."

Kyle stopped, thinking for a long moment. There was, theoretically, no reason a starship couldn't make Tier Three acceleration – the five hundred gravities usually reserved for starfighters. Most starships weren't built to be able to do it, as the Tier 3 'flat spot' in fuel consumption was much, much higher.

It wasn't something he could justify on a regular basis, but knowing how hard they could push the ship in an emergency would be useful.

"That's a daring suggestion, Senior Fleet Commander Wong," he said very, very softly, glancing at Solace and Pendez. Pendez looked like a puppy who'd just had a bone waved in front of her face. Solace was... unreadable.

"If you see the *slightest* strain, we pull back to two fifty immediately," he ordered. "Commander Pendez – initiate a ten gravity every ten seconds increment. Let's see how fast we can go, shall we?"

There was almost no chance that any acceleration would leak through to the ship, but he saw several members of the bridge crew – including Solace – strap themselves in. He couldn't – it would show a lack of faith.

"Ready, sir," Pendez reported.

"Engage," he replied. As the ship began to leap forward, he hoped that no one else could see where his hands were clenching the sides of his chair. Despite his orders to Wong, this was still risky – risky enough he'd never try it any further away from the yards that could fix the ship.

The ship smoothly accelerated to two hundred and sixty. Then two hundred and seventy. Three hundred gravities passed without even a tremor, though the fuel levels being reported in one of his mental windows were dropping faster than he'd ever seen outside a starfighter.

Three hundred and *fifty*, and Kyle watched the numbers and metrics like a hawk. They were burning fuel prodigiously, but the ship seemed to be able to take it.

Then, just past four hundred gravities, his sensors went crazy.

"Zero thrust, *now!*" he snapped and Pendez obeyed. The ship's acceleration cut to zero but the chaotic mess across the ship's scanners remained. After a few seconds, it began to slowly dissipate, and he breathed a sigh of relief as he realized the sensors themselves weren't damaged.

"What happened?" Kyle demanded of Wong. The engineer had disappeared from the com screen, but returned after hearing Kyle's voice.

"Nothing permanent?" the Chief Engineer said questioningly. "We'll have to look into it, but it looks like several of the positron feeds opened all the way up. We had intact antimatter leaving the ship."

"Where it annihilated against the exhaust outside the ship, and lit up the sky like we were firing off nuclear fireworks," Kyle finished grimly. "How long is that going to last?"

"Depending on how many positrons got out… thirty, forty minutes?" Wong replied.

"All right people," the Captain said calmly, "we know we've got a four hundred gravity emergency sprint, and I think that's good enough. Let's see if we can make it through the tests without blowing up anything *else* we don't mean to."

Shaking his head, his grin returned. Despite its ending, it had been exhilarating to, even for a few moments, see the massive carrier fly like a starfighter.

"We're still on course for the testing zone, I presume?" he asked Pendez.

She nodded.

"All right. Take us over at two hundred and fifty gravities. It's time to reduce our surplus asteroid supply!"

––––––

14:00 December 9, 2735 ESMDT
SFG-001 Actual – Falcon-C *type command starfighter*

MICHAEL HADN'T BEEN on the bridge during their attempt at a sprint, but he'd been linked into the ship's network while reviewing his new Wing Commanders' files. It had been impressive to watch, though the 'fireworks' display at the end had been a little disconcerting.

Now, he was strapped into the cockpit of his starfighter, glancing around him with both his eyes and his starfighter's sensors. *Avalon* had two hundred and forty starfighters, all *Falcons*, with six *Falcon-C* command starfighters reserved for the CAG and the five Wing Commanders – each of whom led a six squadron wing as large as the old *Avalon's* entire Flight Group.

He sat inside his own command starfighter, one of the eighty already loaded into the big carrier's launch tubes. His starfighters made up the second part of the live fire test, and he watched Captain Roberts test the ship's main weaponry with interest while preparing for his turn.

First, an innocent asteroid was the target of all of *Avalon's* forward facing missile batteries. Eight Jackhammer capital ship missiles blasted into space at a thousand gravities to annihilate the poor planetoid in multiple gigatons of fire.

That test complete, the carrier aligned on a new victim, and twenty-four seven-hundred-kiloton-per-second positron lances rippled across space. Accelerated antimatter collided with the ice of the artificial target, and then the asteroid came apart in a glitter of debris.

Chunks of rock and ice continued towards *Avalon*, and her lighter beams opened up. Space glittered with the distinctive white flare of matter-antimatter annihilation as dozens of seventy-kiloton-per-second beams cleared a safe zone around the big ship.

Then an icon popped up on Michael's implant, highlighting a third asteroid.

"CAG, it's Roberts," the Captain said over his communicator. "It's your turn. Maximum turnaround launch, then melt that ice ball for me."

"Can do, Captain," Michael replied immediately, making sure all of his Wing Commanders got the target caret. He flipped to a different channel. "Chief Hammond," he addressed his Deck Chief, the senior NCO who ran the ship-side portion of the Space Force aboard *Avalon*. "Are we clear for a max turnaround?"

"First wave is locked and loaded, second and third are in their cradles," Hammond reported gruffly. "We are clear on your mark."

"JD-Ships says twenty-two seconds a cycle," Michael observed. "They underestimated the engines. Think they got the launch tubes right?"

"I wouldn't push them past twenty," the old Master Chief replied. "Let's not risk these kids just to make the Yards look good."

"Fair enough, Chief," the CAG replied. "Mark in five."

"Confirmed. Hold on."

Five seconds later, a massive weight slammed into his chest as the launch tube fired his fighter into space at five thousand gravities.

Eighty starfighters, most of two fighter wings, shot out into space with him.

"Alpha Wing, form on me," he ordered. "Bravo Wing, hold for your Five and Six squadrons."

"Sure, we'll float here looking decorative," Wing Commander Russell Rokos replied, and Michael shook his head.

He *heard* Alpha's Wing Commander, Thomas Avignon, try not to choke. Rokos had been with them at Tranquility, but none of his other Wing Commanders had. They expected – not entirely wrongly – that Rokos would get some extra slack for that. Honestly, though, *any* of his officers could get away with that. Stanford wasn't exactly going to flog people for a little humor.

Besides, the second wave – the rest of Rokos' Bravo Wing, Wing

Commander Carl Moriarty's Charlie Wing, and two squadrons of Wing Commander Adrianna Cortez's Delta Wing – was in space before Rokos had even finished speaking. Exactly twenty seconds for the cycle, Michael noted.

Twenty seconds later, the last eighty fighters were in space, and Wing Commander Lei Nguyen and her Epsilon Wing joined them.

"All right, since we don't want to use Commander Rokos as decoration, let's form up," he ordered. "The Captain has picked us a nice solid ball of ice, it'll take a few hits to break it up."

Vice Commodore Michael Stanford paused, reviewing the serried array of two hundred and forty starfighters at his command.

"Passes by the numbers people," he finished. "Sorry, Lei, but the rest of you *better* not leave Epsilon anything!"

He smiled with pride as his Flight Group lunged forward, hungry eyes and scanners already seeking the death of yet another ball of ice.

6

Castle System, Castle Federation
11:00 December 14, 2735 Earth Standard Meridian Date/Time
Orbital Dry Dock Merlin Four

THE OBSERVATION DECK on *Merlin Four* was nowhere near large enough to hold all six thousand members of her keel-plate crew. Once space had been allocated for the various political personages and reporters, only two hundred of Kyle's people had been able to attend.

Necessity meant that all of the senior officers were present, and he'd arranged a lottery for the rest. Now, those personnel formed a solid block of black uniforms in the middle of the observation deck. Mostly they were Navy, but he'd set the lottery list so thirty Space Forcers and thirty Marines joined them.

Most of the reporters were behind the block of officers and men, and then Kyle stood out in front with the VIPs. He'd met two of the three Senators standing with him, Senator Maria O'Connell of the planet Tuatha and Senator Madhur Nagarkar of New Bombay.

Senator Joseph Randall, Senator for Castle itself, he hadn't met. The man looked enough like his son that Kyle had no issues identifying the blue-eyed man with the fading blond hair when he arrived. The degree to which Senator Randall *completely* ignored him was a small hint as well.

The last two people standing on the little raised dais at the front of the observation deck were both flag officers. Kyle was familiar with Fleet Admiral Meredith Blake, the tall gray-haired woman who headed the Federation's Joint Chiefs of Staff. He'd reviewed Vice Admiral Dimitri Tobin's file after being informed the man would command the battle group *Avalon* was joining, but he didn't know the stocky man.

A band – borrowed from the station as *Avalon's* crew hadn't assembled the traditionally volunteer ship's band yet – played the brassy tunes of the Federation's *Call to Arms*, the battle hymn recognized as the anthem of the Federation's military.

Then a tall red-haired woman in a prim black business suit stepped crisply onto the dais, carrying a single sheet of parchment.

"Ladies, Gentlemen, I am Moira Anderson, Station Manager of *Merlin Four*," she said calmly. "It is my honor and my privilege to deliver deep space carrier number seventy-eight into the hands of the Castle Federation Space Navy."

For all that everyone knew her name, and they'd even cast her seal and mounted it in Kyle's office, *Avalon* was technically still only a hull. At this moment, she remained DSC-078, nothing more.

Admiral Blake saluted the Station Manager and took the sheet of parchment, officially taking possession of the carrier that hung outside the window, a sharp-edged presence with only minimal lights, ominous in the dark.

"Thank you, Miss Anderson," Blake said calmly and turned to face the cameras. "Naming a ship is always a challenge," she told the reporters. "Some ships are given new names as freshly forged defenders of our great nation. Others… others inherit names that carry history and legends.

"DSC-078 is our newest and most powerful carrier, a shield that will guard our worlds in these dark times. She is also the first carrier commissioned since this new war began, and it seems fitting that she bear the same name as the very first carrier Castle ever commissioned.

"Senator O'Connell, if you would do the honors please," Blake told the petite Senator with the flaming red hair.

The Senator bowed crisply and stepped forward. A control panel sat at the edge of the platform, linked to the pneumatic cannon outside the window – the cannon aimed directly at the carrier.

"Ladies and gentlemen of the media, officers and crew of the Castle Federation Armed Forces, my fellow Senators," the little woman said brightly. "I give you the Castle Federation's newest legend, reborn from the fires of the Battle of Tranquility to fight for us once more.

"I hereby christen this vessel *Avalon*." O'Connell hit the control, and the pneumatic cannon fired. A cask of champagne – traditionally exactly sixty liters – shot into space and smashed itself on the flat prow of the carrier.

In response to that signal, the ship's AI triggered the routine Kyle had carefully programmed before he left the ship. Starting from the point of impact, *Avalon's* running lights came fully online, rippling out in a growing sequence of lights that lit up every corner and edge of the ship.

Finally, the cloth that covered her name, invisible against the carrier's hull, was pulled away by a dockyard tug, revealing the ten meter high letters that spelled out her hull number and name on each of her four broadsides.

Blake allowed a few moments to pass for the media to get proper shots of the new carrier, then stepped back onto the platform.

"Captain Kyle Roberts, as per your orders and assignment, I hereby deliver to you DSC-078 *Avalon*. May you command her with honor for the glory of the Castle Federation."

Kyle stepped onto the platform and took that fragile sheet of parchment – *Avalon's* own commissioning orders – and bowed over them.

"I hereby assume command of DSC-078 *Avalon*," he said calmly.

Blake took his hand, shaking it firmly as the band begin to play again.

"Good luck, son," she murmured. "Stars above know you're going to need it."

———

DESPITE THE FACT that they were at war, Kyle had been unable to convince anyone not to follow up the commissioning ceremony with a reception for the politicians and reporters. A party was all well and good in his books, but reporters were like a bucket of cold water in his opinion.

Thankfully, he'd collided with the Coraline Imperium's ambassador at the buffet table, who turned out to be an ex-fighter pilot. The Ambassador had gleefully taken advantage of his exalted rank to monopolize Kyle's time for at least half an hour, discussing the comparative virtues of the Federation and the Imperium's seventh-generation fighters – the Federation's *Falcon,* an ECM-heavy craft, versus the Imperium *Arrow* which was primarily a missile platform.

Unfortunately, he hadn't checked the area around well enough before bidding the Ambassador farewell, and had barely made it ten steps towards the bathroom when the vultures stooped.

"Captain Roberts!" a reporter he didn't recognized said loudly. "Can you spare a moment to speak to our viewers?"

Kyle sighed, and turned to face the man. The speaker wore a badge identifying him as being from 'Federation Instant News', and looked the part of the steady anchor – muscular build, perfect hair, and a perfectly symmetrical face. Kyle couldn't help wondering how much of the man's appearance was natural versus surgery.

"Yes, Mister…?"

"I'm Brad Torrent, of FIN," the reporter said swiftly. A camera rose above the man's shoulder on a prehensile telescoping mount. "Please, Captain Roberts – what do you think of the new *Avalon*?"

"She's an incredible ship, a testament to her builders," Kyle said carefully.

"A perfect weapon to strike back at the Commonwealth, no?" Torrent asked. Kyle nodded slowly, hoping not to have let himself in for *too* much trouble. "Yet we sit on the defensive!" the reporter exclaimed. "Captain Roberts, the people want to know what the Stellar Fox thinks of the Senate's lack of action!"

For a long moment, Kyle wished breaking the man's arm and telescoping camera – in about that order – was an option as he glared at the man.

"Firstly, Mister Torrent, I have no enthusiasm for sensationalist nicknames," he said coldly. "If you're going to hang a damn stupid moniker on me, I'd prefer one that didn't link me to a man whose own government forced him to commit suicide!"

From the reporter's taken-aback expression, he didn't know the source of Kyle's nickname in the press. If he hadn't already been into negative points in the Captain's books, he'd have been sliding downhill.

"Secondly, as a Captain in the Castle Federation Space Navy, it is *not* my place to criticize or praise the Senate," he said firmly. "My duty is to follow their orders and complete the missions laid out in pursuit of their goals.

"Thirdly, Mister Torrent, the Reserve is in the process of being recommissioned. Between us and the rest of the Alliance, that's *eighty* more capital ships to enter our line of battle in the coming months. That boost to our forces will dramatically increase our strategic and operational options."

He'd moved forward into Torrent's personal space as he spoke. The reporter wasn't a small man, but Kyle was a very large one. The camera on its prehensile mount twisted backwards to keep Kyle's face in view, even as Torrent took an involuntary step backwards.

"In the end, your viewers should be reassured that the Senate does not rush to sacrifice the lives of their brothers and sisters solely to be seen to be doing *something*," he finished. "Smarter men and women than you and I are drafting the Alliance's war plans. I suggest you have faith."

He waited for a long moment to see if Torrent had more to say, then turned on his heel and disappeared into the crowd. He made it perhaps three or four meters before he was interrupted by a sardonic slow clap, and turned to see the stocky form of Vice Admiral Dimitri Tobin.

"Vice Admiral," he greeted his soon-to-be-commander with a slight bow.

"I'm impressed, Captain," the Admiral told Kyle. He was one of a very few men who could meet Kyle at eye level and he was, if anything, broader than the massive Captain. "Not many could turn Torrent's little ambush around like that. Well done."

Kyle nodded carefully, swallowing down the last vestiges of his adrenaline spike as he took in his new CO and the willowy blond woman walking next to him.

"I *hate* that nickname," he finally admitted, and Tobin laughed.

"Good," he rumbled. "It's probably a good sign. Captain Roberts, this is my wife, Sasha," he introduced the blond. "Sasha, you know Captain Roberts by reputation, if nothing else."

"Indeed," she murmured, bright blue eyes holding Kyle's for a moment. Those eyes were warm, caring – but he also felt like he'd just been appraised and measured thoroughly. "I need to grab some more food, I'll leave you gentlemen to it."

With a kiss firmly planted on her husband's bearded cheek, Sasha disappeared into the crowd. Tobin nodded towards the windows looking out over *Avalon* and led the way over.

"Sasha knows when to leave us officers to business," the Vice Admiral said softly, glancing after his wife. "You have no escort tonight?"

"I occasionally borrow my son's mother when it's made clear a plus one is non-negotiable," Kyle told his Admiral, "but that's… an account with limited credit."

Tobin nodded and let the matter drop. He clearly was at least passingly familiar with complex family situations.

"How were your space trials, Captain?" he asked.

"Smooth as silk, sir," Kyle told him. "Every metric JD-Ships rated her for, we exceeded. She's the fastest, nastiest, ship in the Navy, sir. We'll do you proud."

"You're clear to join the Battle Group then?"

"They'd cleared us for full operations prior to the commissioning," *Avalon's* Captain confirmed.

"That's how it's *supposed* to work," Tobin observed. "But it doesn't always."

"My intention is to move to BG Seventeen's orbit in the morning," Kyle continued.

"Good," the Vice Admiral told him. "My staff will contact you then with exact details. Barring something unexpected, though, I should be able to move my flag aboard tomorrow afternoon then."

Kyle swallowed, surprised.

"I... did not expect to be carrying the flag, sir," he confessed. "As the junior Captain, I assumed you would fly your flag aboard *Camerone*."

"There are many arguments as to what ship an Admiral should fly his flag from, Captain," Tobin told him dryly. "The largest. The one with the most starfighters. The one with the most positron lances. For some Admirals, it's the one with the prettiest junior officers.

"Why an Admiral picks a flagship should always remain a mystery to others though," he continued with a smile. "I will fly my flag from *Avalon*, the most impressive the Federation is contributing to BG Seventeen. Unless you have an actual *objection*, my dear Captain?"

"No, sir," Kyle told him crisply. Spotting Sasha returning, he gave the Vice Admiral a crisp salute. "I believe I will leave you to your wife," he told Tobin. "I was heading somewhere specific before our friend Torrent interrupted."

"Of course, Captain," Tobin agreed with a wave that approximated a return salute. "I wanted to let you know before the official notice arrived. A courtesy, if you will."

The two men parted and Kyle waited until he was well clear of the Admiral before pinging Solace's implant.

"Solace, once we're back aboard, check in with the Bosun. We're going to be hosting Vice Admiral Tobin's flag, and I *know* no one was focusing on the flag deck.

"Let's make sure it's prim and proper before he comes aboard. Let's not embarrass ourselves."

"*We're* carrying the flag?" she responded. "I expected him to fly from *Camerone*."

"So did I, Commander Solace," Kyle told her. "But one does not argue with Admirals."

7

Castle System, Castle Federation
18:00 December 15, 2735 Earth Standard Meridian Date/Time
DSC-078 Avalon, *Shuttle Three*

DIMITRI TOBIN REGARDED Alliance Battle Group Seventeen – now also designated Alliance Battle Group *Avalon* – with an appraising gaze. The immense abbreviated arrowhead of *Avalon* orbited below and behind the other ships, with the thirteen hundred meter spike of *Camerone* the only other vessel of the four to approach her length.

The Trade Factor's warships had originally been retrofitted merchant ships, and the *Magellan*-class battleship *Zheng He* showed that legacy in her design. She was a flattened sphere as wide as she was tall and only slightly longer. Only half a kilometer long, she was still three quarters of *Avalon*'s volume and packed twice the heavy armaments.

Horus was still missing, but the first Imperial contribution, the strike cruiser *Gravitas*, had already arrived. The *Majesty*-class strike cruisers were older ships, but still potent. The Imperium had purchased its original warships, a long time ago, from the Commonwealth and their capital ships were built on the same flattened cigar that had evolved into the Commonwealth's carriers. *Gravitas* was a kilometer long and a quarter-kilometer wide, with a wing of eighty starfighters and an armament only slightly heavier than the much larger *Avalon's*.

Combined with the Federation battle cruiser *Camerone*, which had another forty-eight starfighters and fell between *Gravitas* and *Zheng He* in terms of onboard weapons, Battle Group Seventeen was a powerful combat force, fully a third of the true capital ships in the Castle system.

All of that firepower – to be increased once *Horus*, an even newer Imperial ship, arrived – now answered to one Vice Admiral Dimitri Tobin. It was a sobering thought, and a responsibility he was determined to live up to.

Still wrapped up inside his implant, he considered the people on the shuttle with him. This was only the first load of 'flag staff' to come aboard *Avalon*, and he had fifty people coming with him. With his staff officers, their teams, the flag deck crew and its three shifts and officers to command those shifts, he was bringing over two hundred people aboard *Avalon*.

Too few of them were his team from *Corona*. Many of those worthies had died. A lot of others, like Robert Brown, were still in recovery from injuries sustained at Midori.

Most of his new staff and personnel had been put together by his new Chief of Staff based on JD-Personnel recommendations. He wasn't sure how he felt about Senior Fleet Commander Judy Sanchez, the head of his new team. She'd come highly recommended, but seemed a minor enigma.

This was only her second Staff posting. She'd spent most of her career working as a computer analyst with Navy Intelligence, with the kind of bland performance appraisals he'd have expected from a desk jockey… attached to a rate of promotion he would have expected from an officer in a combat zone. He could only wonder why Kane had sent him an ex-spy.

"Sir," the blond young woman interrupted his thoughts. "I'm getting traffic on the system defense net. You may want to check in."

The system defense net? Sanchez wouldn't have access to that except at the most rudimentary level until they were aboard ship. If she was seeing something via that connection, it was a high level alert.

Closing his eyes, Dimitri logged into the net, and immediately inhaled sharply. The map of the Castle system the defense net fed his implants had a glowing ugly red splotch out near the orbit of the gas giant Gawain – the marker for an unidentified Alcubierre emergence.

"Pilot," Dimitri linked into the shuttle's cockpit. "Get in touch with *Avalon* and let them know you're going to be coming in hot. I want to be on the deck in five minutes."

He *heard* the young man swallow. Junior Lieutenants, however, did not argue with Vice Admirals.

"I'll make it happen, sir," he promised.

Dimitri was already focusing his attention back on that red splotch, waiting for the nearby Q-Com equipped probes to let the net know just what had intruded into the Federation's home system.

The tiny robotic craft were scattered around the perimeter of the system, no more than a light minute or so apart. It took time for light to reach them and be processed and sent back to System Command. More time for System Command to assess the signatures and then update the map.

Then the splotch broke apart, settling into four crimson red icons. Commonwealth capital ships.

18:15 December 15, 2735 ESMDT
DSC-078 Avalon, *Bridge*

THERE WAS no time to get his flag staff organized. Dimitri boarded the ship to an appropriate lack of ceremony and charged directly to the bridge.

There, he found Captain Roberts in exactly the right place for the circumstances – directly in the middle of the bridge of his ship, preparing to engage the enemy.

"Give me an update, Captain," the Vice Admiral snapped. "What does System Command know?"

"Four Terran capital ships," Roberts replied promptly. "It's a somewhat unusual split for them – three cruisers and a carrier."

Dimitri nodded, considered Roberts' point. The Commonwealth regarded starfighters as a defensive measure, used to keep *other* people's starfighters away from the battleships that did the actual destroying. They tended to deploy in pairs of cruisers or sent a carrier to escort a battleship.

"Any idea of their objective?" Dimitri asked. "They dropped out of FTL way too far out to attack Castle itself, and they're outnumbered over three to one by the forces in-system."

"System Command is debating, but they're close to Gawain," Roberts noted. "That only leaves two real targets."

"Walkingstick isn't going for the cloudscoops," Dimitri said grimly, remembering his briefing from Kane when he'd accepted the command. "He's going for the Reserve Fleet."

"Agreed," his Flag Captain said instantly. "Home Fleet is preparing to move, but…"

"But, what, Captain?" the Vice Admiral demanded.

"I can't help but remember Puppeteer, sir," the younger man said calmly. "Walkingstick isn't above tricking us into pulling ships out of position. The Reserve Flotilla guardships aren't up to this fight, but…"

"Agreed," Dimitri said sharply. "Coms – get me a link to Admiral Blake."

Normally, he'd try to remember the officer's *name*, but he didn't have time. Nonetheless, the pitch black-skinned young woman running *Avalon*'s communicators got the channel for him in an admirably short time.

"Meredith, hold Home Fleet in place – our old friend Walkingstick may be playing games," he told her.

"We only have two ships and two hundred *Cobras* guarding the Flotilla, Dimitri," the old Admiral snapped. "*Someone* has to go."

"BG Seventeen's ships average newer and faster than Home Fleet, ma'am," Dimitri replied. "We've got that task group matched for ships and outmassed four to three. *None* of us can get there in time to save the Flotilla guard force, Meredith," he said quietly. "Let's not risk *Castle* as well."

The geometry had screwed them, badly. Of the thirteen warships in the Castle system, most were in orbit of Castle itself – *two light hours* away from Gawain and its dozen half-unmothballed ships. He ran the numbers in his head. Seventeen hours for Battle Group Seventeen, whose slowest ship could pull two hundred and thirty gravities. Home Fleet, with a maximum speed of two hundred gravities, would take over eighteen hours.

While the Commonwealth task group was still four hours from being able to attack the reserve ships, they'd still have fourteen hours to destroy an entire fleet's worth of ships, likely drop a few dozen missiles into the cloudscoops *anyway* and run.

"Sir, we may be able to make it," a soft feminine voice interrupted his thoughts. Tobin's gaze snapped up, glancing first at Roberts, and then at the softly attractive form of *Avalon's* Navigator.

"Finish your thought, Commander," Roberts ordered, his voice soft.

"The direct route is seventeen hours for the battle group," she said, confirming his math. "But that's staying in conventional space the whole way."

"The *star* is between us and Gawain, Commander," Dimitri pointed out, but his Flag Captain forestalled him with a raised hand. He fumed internally, but gestured for the Commander to finish.

"That's what they're counting on, sir," she told him, "but everyone's thinking in straight lines."

She threw a course up on the screen. It took them in the completely wrong direction for two and a half hours, and Dimitri was about to ask just what she was thinking, when the total flight time to Gawain came up. He shut up fast.

Two and a half hours to clear Castle's planetary gravity well to reach a space flat enough to engage the Alcubierre-Stetson drive.

But then an hour and a half to wrap an arcing course *around* the outside of the system that would drop them back into regular space on the *other side* of the Flotilla Station, heading straight for the Commonwealth task group with every centimeter of the velocity they built up before warping space.

They'd meet the Commonwealth ships with a combined velocity over ten percent of lightspeed – and they'd do it *before* the bastards reached the Reserve Flotilla.

"We're cutting the margins very tight," he rumbled softly, considering. "Can you do it?"

"I don't know about the rest of the Battle Group," Roberts told him, "but Commander Pendez can do it. She's the one that rode the needle all the way into Tranquility."

Vice Admiral Dimitri Tobin gave the crimson icons on his screen a predatory smile. He'd hoped he'd be lucky enough to get the Navigator that had taken Roberts into *planetary orbit* at Tranquility. He'd have to buy Kane a drink when he got back.

"Feed your calculations to them if you have to, Commander Pendez," he told her gently. "And let's get this Battle Group underway."

———

KYLE WAS GETTING sick of watching battles he couldn't influence. The delays on route to Tranquility had left him watching that system's entire fleet get blown away by a Commonwealth battle group, and it felt like he was watching a repeat as the two guardships of the Gawain Reserve Flotilla charged out to meet the attack.

The two older battleships defending the Reserve Flotilla, plus the two hundred fighters launched from the Flotilla station itself, deployed as soon as the presence and location of the enemy could be resolved. While BG17 was on its way, the Terran ships would be clear to launch missiles at the Reserve well before they emerged from Alcubierre.

"Sir, we've cleared all detectable gravity zones," Pendez reported. "Current gravitational force is beneath one pico-meter per second squared. We are prepared to warp space on your command."

"Admiral?" Kyle asked, glancing over at where Dimitri Tobin loomed in one of the observer seats at the back of the bridge.

"The rest of the Battle Group is following Commander Pendez's lead," the Admiral rumbled. "Carry on."

"How are our Class Ones looking?" Kyle asked his engineering officer. *Avalon's* five Class One mass manipulators were a good forty percent of the warship's price tag, and the only things capable of generating the singularities necessary for Alcubierre drive.

"We are clear and green," Wong reported over the ship's communicator.

"All right – Commander Pendez, initiate interior Stetson fields at your discretion," the Captain ordered.

A faint haze settled over the screens surrounding the bridge as hundreds of small emitters across *Avalon's* hull woke to life, stretching a field of electromagnetic and gravitational energy around the ship. Useless in any other circumstance, the only purpose of the Stetson field was to protect the ship from the immense forces it was about to unleash.

"Interior Stetson field active," Commander Pendez reported. "Exterior field on standby, mass manipulators on standby."

"How's the rest of the Group?" Kyle asked his new Tactical Officer, Commander James Anderson.

"I'm showing Stetson fields active on all ships, Captain," the pale redheaded man replied.

"All right," Kyle acknowledged. He spared one final glance at the seemingly impassive Vice Admiral, then turned to Pendez. "Commander, you may warp space at your discretion."

He felt the big ship hum as power fed to the Class Ones, and spotted the distinctive fuzz in the viewscreen of the A-S Drive's singularities.

On the tactical display his implant was overlaying on part of his vision, white stars marked the formation of the same singularities around the other ships. The distortions wavered, and then vanished in flashes of bright blue Cherenkov radiation.

"Warp bubble initiated," Pendez told him. "We are on route, ETA ninety-two minutes."

Kyle checked another set of numbers. His Q-Com-relayed display of the battle showed the Federation defenders already in missile range of the Terran ships, but still twenty minutes from positron lance range. Both sides were keeping their starfighters close as a handful of missiles probed each other's defenses.

By the time Battle Group Seventeen arrived, the two forces would have passed *through* each other, and the Terrans would be approaching weapons range of the Flotilla itself. Given the distance between BG17's initial space warp and their emergence, they wouldn't even know they'd gone FTL until the Allied battle group jumped them.

That would probably be enough to save the Flotilla, but everyone in the system already knew it wouldn't save the two *Indomitable*-class battleships charging out.

Even as Kyle watched, the Commonwealth starfighters charged out, followed by a swarm of missiles as the Terran starships fully opened fired.

He was taking mental notes and made sure Stanford was also receiving the footage. Coordination between the missiles and the fighters was poor. The missiles had twice the starfighters' acceleration, but their acceleration could be stepped down or up at will. It was an ability Kyle had used before to combine starfighter and missile attacks.

The Terrans didn't bother. The forty missiles of their salvo blasted ahead of their starfighters and, unsupported, ran into the Federation starfighters.

The Gawain Reserve Flotilla Defense Group might have been a secondary posting, but its starfighter flight crews were hardly incompetent. Not a single missile of the first four salvos made it past them.

Then they ran headlong into the Terran ships. Both sides had sixth generation starfighters – the Terran *Scimitar* versus the Federation *Cobra* – but the Terrans simply had more. Each of the three *Assassin*-class battlecruisers fielded thirty starfighters, and the *Safari*-class heavy carrier anchoring the task group deployed a hundred and eighty.

The last wave of missiles was also, finally, coordinated with the starfighters and was targeted at the Federation starfighters. The *Scimitar* was heavily optimized towards anti-fighter engagements, with multiple lighter positron lances and light missile launchers.

None of the Federation starfighters survived to interpenetrate. Six hundred men and women were wiped away in a matter of moments, and then the surviving Terran starfighters fell back. Commonwealth doctrine now called for them to act in a missile defense role while the battlecruisers did the killing.

The two Federation battleships had clearly realized they couldn't get missiles through the remaining hundred and fifty starfighters. They continued to fire them, but they were wide salvos – intended more to fill space with radiation and distort sensors than to kill starships.

Their own defenses shattered missiles by the dozens as they closed. Their heavy beams had a range that left a starfighter pilot like Kyle green with envy, with a chance of hitting their targets from almost a million kilometers away.

They almost reached that range intact. Missile salvo after missile salvo filled the space between the two forces, thoroughly demonstrating why no one regarded even capital ship missiles as ship killers as not a single missile hit.

Until one did. A laser cluster on one of the battleships didn't track in time. Three missiles slipped past and slammed into the Castle Federation battleship *Jackson*.

Three one-gigaton warheads flared within a second of each other. The battleship's massive armor shed some of the impact… but not enough. *Jackson* reeled, her engines flaring out as her mass manipulators failed and she tried to evade.

Without her sister to help stop missiles, *Kennedy* couldn't cover them both. Four more missiles from the next salvo made it through, and *Jackson* simply ceased to exist – and five thousand souls went with her.

Kennedy sought to avenge her. Moments after *Jackson's* death, the battleship reached her range of the Commonwealth ships – a range the cruisers and carrier couldn't match. Six hundred kiloton-per-second main lances spoke in anger, but at this range it took the lance beams almost three seconds to reach their targets.

That was enough to throw off accuracy, and the Terran *Assassin*-class battlecruisers had six hundred kiloton lances of their own. *Kennedy's* deflectors were stronger, but not enough to reduce the range by much.

Five ships danced in space, pirouetting like dancers as they dodged around beams of deadly antimatter. More missiles slashed in on both sides, and the Terran starfighters grimly stuck to their larger brethren's sides, picking off the robotic attackers.

Kyle watched in grim silence, convinced that it was all going to be for naught – and then one of the battlecruisers zigged when it should have zagged. Eight heavy positron lances slammed into the warship.

Where they hit, the matter of the ship's armor collided with the antimatter of the beams and annihilated. The starship's own armor turned into a devastatingly powerful explosive and ripped open vast gaping holes in her hull. The beams were only connected for half a second – and that was enough.

The battlecruiser came apart into pieces, its interior gutted by the beams of pure destruction that had ripped through her.

Any hope for *Kennedy* was short-lived. Even as her target died, the old battleship's defenses proved unable to handle the missile fire that she and her sister had withstood together. Five missiles made it through in a single salvo – and not even the mightiest battleship could stand that kind of fire.

Silence reigned on *Avalon's* bridge, and Kyle knew his crew had been watching the battle alongside him.

"Commander Pendez," he said quietly. "ETA?"

"We will arrive in forty-seven minutes, sir," she replied.

"Inform Vice Commodore Stanford," Kyle ordered. "Let's see if we can give these people a well-deserved shock."

8

VICE COMMODORE MICHAEL STANFORD looked over the data being relayed to him from the system defense net with an appraising eye. The Commonwealth fighter force had been hammered in their engagement with the defending fighters, but not nearly enough for his liking. They still had over a hundred *Scimitars* tucked in close to provide missile defense.

Someone in the enemy task group had also clearly been smart enough to guess at least the basics of Battle Group Seventeen's plan. As soon as the defenders had been destroyed, they'd altered their vector – now they were burning for open space.

Of course, that acceleration wasn't changing their vector towards the Gawain Flotilla. They'd waited after destroying the defenders and let themselves get close enough for a nice solid fix on the mothballed starships, and then started launching missiles.

A capital ship missile like the Commonwealth's Stormwind had a flight duration of a little over an hour. At an acceleration of over a thousand gravities, that gave them a range of roughly a light minute from rest and a terminal velocity over ten percent of lightspeed.

Of course, firing missiles through a defensive fighter screen was ineffectual at best, and the closer you were when you fired, the more accurate you were. The Commonwealth was still using a significant chunk of the Stormwind's range, leaving them with a thirty minute flight time.

Stanford ran the numbers through his implant and the starfighter's computers, but he knew the answer already. There was no way any of BG17's starships were going to get between those missiles and the Reserve Flotilla.

BG17's starfighters, however, were seventh-generation birds rated for five hundred gravities of acceleration. All of the battle group's three hundred and sixty eight starfighters could manage to get in front of the missiles if they launched immediately upon emergence from Alcubierre.

The Battle Group hadn't taken sufficient form, yet, for Stanford to be able to order that launch as senior CAG. Once the starfighters were in space, however, he would be in command as the senior starfighter officer on the scene.

Reviewing the statistics of the eighty Imperial *Arrows* under his command, he smiled grimly. Combining their extra missiles with his *Falcons'* powerful electronic warfare suite gave him an idea.

———

MICHAEL BARELY HAD time to register the wrenching sensation of the big carrier emerging from Alcubierre drive before he was slammed back into his acceleration couch as his fighter shot into space. It was refreshing after the improvisations they'd had to pull on the old *Avalon* to have a full set of fighter launch tubes.

Ten squadrons shot into space. Twenty seconds later, another ten followed.

Sixty seconds after exiting their Alcubierre, all of *Avalon's* starfighters were in space, forming up into a loose formation that left each starfighter the space to 'random-walk' to avoid incoming fire.

It took another ten seconds for *Camerone's* six squadrons and *Gravitas'* ten to join Stanford's people in space. All three hundred and sixty-plus little ships then turned as one and fired their engines – charging towards the enemy.

Michael triggered a mental command, linking him into the Federation Wing Commanders and the Lieutenant Colonel commanding the Imperial force.

"We can catch those bastards," Lieutenant Colonel Kai Metzger said immediately as the channel established. "There's no way they can reach a clear gravity zone before we can catch them."

"Negative," Michael told him. "We can't catch them *and* defend the Flotilla – we need those ships more than we need to catch the Terrans. The missiles are the priority."

"Three modern ships are worth more to the Commonwealth than six obsolete hulks are worth to us," Metzger snapped dismissively.

"That's not your call, Lieutenant-Colonel," Stanford replied bluntly, emphasizing the junior man's rank. "Castle command says we save the ships, so we go for the missiles."

"Do whatever the hell you want, Feddie," the Imperial officer said dismissively. "We're going to go kill us a carrier."

Even before the Coraline man had finished speaking, all eighty of his ships twisted away from the Federation fighters. Their vector would leave them completely out of position to intercept the missiles, but take them directly into the teeth of the Commonwealth task group.

"Get your ships back into formation," Stanford snapped immediately. Silence was his only response, and his implant calmly informed him that Metzger had dropped the link.

"What's the plan, CAG?" Wing Commander Russell Rokos asked after the silence stretched a moment too long. As usual, the phlegmatic pilot knew exactly what needed to be done.

Stanford shook himself physically, updating his plan for the *lack* of the Imperial fighters on the fly.

"I'm sending everyone positions for their fighter wings," he told the Federation officers. "With only our missiles, this could cut a lot closer than I was planning on."

"Our Starfires can't intercept Stormwinds," Wing Commander Andreas Volte, the leader of *Camerone's* Wing, objected. "Not without getting damn lucky."

"They don't need to," Stanford replied. "Get them close enough and the radiation wave will screw with their sensors royally – that'll make them sitting ducks. Trust me, gentlemen, ladies – some of us have done this before."

He carefully ignored the Imperial starfighters flying off on their own course as he structured the firing patterns for the Federation ships. That was a problem... but it was a problem for *after* there were Commonwealth ships in his home system.

————

THEY SWUNG WIDE around the Flotilla itself, Stanford taking a moment to mentally catalog the defense platforms and the main station weapons ready to defend the mothballed ships. There weren't as many as he'd have included with hindsight. Anything more than a dozen missiles was going to cause headaches for the remaining defenses.

Whoever was in charge of the station had clearly been watching for them. As soon as the *Falcons* passed the station, its massive radar arrays opened up at full power. While the missiles were capable of fuzzing their signatures and making them harder to *locate*, there was no way they could *hide* from the big stationary arrays.

Ten salvos burned through space, closing on the helpless ships behind him. Three hundred missiles.

"All Wings, fire missiles on my mark," Stanford ordered calmly as the information slotted into his plans and the computers returned the appropriate responses. "Detonation patterns downloading now."

A few moments passed as the computers talked to each other, and then confirmed to the CAG that everyone had the details of where to fire their missiles.

"All ships... maximum rate fire... MARK."

The rotary magazines attached to a *Falcon's* missile launchers could be emptied in twenty seconds. It was rarely the best use of the Starfire missiles, but in this case it had its advantages.

Over three thousand missiles launched into space in three waves. There were easily a dozen Starfires for each Stormwind.

If the Starfires had been faster, or smarter, or more maneuverable than the capital ship missiles, that would have been all that was needed. Unfortunately, the Stormwinds were just as fast and maneuverable as the fighter missiles – and a few tons worth of smarter.

Jammers flared to life and the suicidal robots began to dodge and weave. Entire regions of space dissolved into static, and Stanford watched it all with a practiced eye.

"Rokos," he said softly, opening a channel to just the Wing Commander.

"You need us to play targets, don't you?" the other man replied instantly.

"You got it," Stanford agreed.

"Just cover us, boss," Rokos replied. "Fifty asses in the wind, coming right up."

Ten seconds later, Rokos' six squadrons lit up as their ECM went to full power. The *Falcon* had fewer missiles than the *Arrow* in the same mass – and the Federation had used every gram of that mass for powerful computers and emitters.

Even *knowing* what was going on, Stanford's computers were still almost fooled. A ghost image appeared on his scanners – forty-eight starfighters pretending to be six mothballed starships.

Stormwinds were smart. They weren't fooled immediately, still focused on the Reserve Flotilla behind the starfighters.

But then the Starfires started detonating. The first wave only took out a half dozen missiles, but that was actually *more* than Stanford had expected.

The second wave of explosions wiped the entirety of the first two salvos, confused and lost in the radiation storm, from existence. The third and final salvo wiped over a hundred missiles away, making the missile strike *far* more effective than Stanford had dared hoped without the *Arrows'* extra launchers.

Of course, that meant there were still a hundred and twenty capital ship missiles bearing down on them – and over three quarters decided that Rokos' Wing were actually their targets.

Those missiles dove straight into the teeth of Stanford's squadrons, and never really stood a chance. Positron lances filled space with the glitter and fire of antimatter, and missiles died by the dozen.

The missiles Stanford was truly concerned about were the twenty-four that still went for the real ships. With ninety-odd weapons headed right at them, his people focused on defending themselves. Once they were clear, they turned their fire on those last few missiles.

The angle sucked, and the missiles were in final acquisition mode – dodging and dancing across space. Missiles died as Stanford's fighters took them from behind. Two, three – five.

Then the Flotilla defenses opened up. Lasers and positron lances filled space, and more and more missiles died. For a single heart-wrenching moment, Stanford thought they'd succeeded.

Two missiles broke through, dodging past everything thrown at them. Still in communication with each other, their suicidal brains picked different targets – and struck home.

Two *Commandant*-class carriers vanished in separate balls of fire.

22:40 December 15, 2735 ESMDT
DSC-078 Avalon, *Bridge*

VICE ADMIRAL DIMITRI TOBIN spoke four languages fluently and had learned to curse in three more. It took a full minute for him to finish swearing after watching the *Commandants'* destruction. The two carriers represented over a hundred trillion Federation Stellars of investment – a full *tenth* of a reasonably wealthy system's Gross System Product.

Even for the Castle Federation, two carriers was not a loss they could easily afford. Thankfully, there had been barely anyone on board, but the loss was still more than painful. The only question was…

"Captain Roberts," he said loudly, though far more calmly than his previous string of quietly muttered curse words. "A moment of your time, please?"

The big Captain blinked, probably checking the tactical display where the Imperial starfighters were busily scattering away from their abortive and failed strike on the Commonwealth ships, and then stepped over to Tobin.

"Sir," Roberts said quietly. He sounded far calmer than he could possibly be, and Tobin was impressed at his self-control.

"You've flown with Stanford," Tobin stated. "You taught him that trick?"

"In a manner of speaking," the Captain replied. "I'd used it before I met him, but he came up with it on his own in an intentional high-loss scenario I threw at him."

"Given the additional missiles from the *Arrows*, would it have worked?" the Vice Admiral asked bluntly.

Roberts glanced back at the main screen, showing where search and rescue shuttles were fanning out through the wreckage of the Reserve Flotilla.

"Just given their positron lances alone, it would have worked," he said calmly. "The Lieutenant Colonel just cost us two carriers, sir," he finished.

"And at least twenty of his own people," Tobin agreed grimly, his implant showing him the state of Metzger's fighter group. "This isn't acceptable, Captain."

"I'm not sure what more Vice Commodore Stanford could have done, sir," Roberts said stiffly. "He had the authority and the plan."

"Agreed." The Admiral nodded, his eyes cold as he pulled up Lieutenant Colonel Kai Metzger's file. "I'll have my Chief of Staff assemble an all-Captains meeting for the morning. Can you make sure your people are ready to receive them?"

"Of course, sir," the Captain replied.

"I'd suggest pinning down your JAG officer as well," Tobin continued. "Section Twenty-Six of the Alliance Treaty of Mutual Defense, Captain. Make sure you know our options. I'm not certain Captain Anders will see things our way."

Section Twenty-Six of the Alliance Treaty covered the interactions between the codes of military justice of over a dozen star nations, and the circumstances under which officers of one nation could demand charges of an officer of another nation. Disobedience in the face of the enemy was high on that list.

The big Captain nodded his acknowledgement, his face thoughtful.

On the screen behind him, the three remaining Terran warships vanished in bursts of bright blue Cherenkov radiation.

9

Castle System, Castle Federation
10:00 December 16, 2735 Earth Standard Meridian Date/Time
DSC-078 Avalon, *Flag Deck Conference Room*

LORD CAPTAIN HENDRICK ANDERS, in Kyle's considered opinion, did not look nearly concerned enough for a man whose subordinates had just completely messed up the defense of an ally's home system.

The Lord Captain, the grandiose title equivalent to Kyle's own rank, was a muscular man of medium height with bright blue eyes and short-cropped blond hair clad in a white and gold dress uniform with red shoulder lapels bearing the paired gold planets of his rank. He looked completely calm as he took a seat directly across from Kyle at the conference table.

Kyle did his best to ignore the man, turning his gaze to the other two Captains at the table. Captain Miriam Alstairs was *Camerone's* commanding officer. She was a slim woman with graying hair, and was one of the more senior Captains in the Federation Space Navy.

The fact that Alstairs hadn't been transferred to one of the Federations newest and shiniest warships was a sign she was probably due for a star any day now.

The fourth of Battle Group Seventeen's COs was Captain Lora Aleppo, a very small, pale-skinned woman with a shaven head who commanded the battleship *Zheng He*.

Vice Admiral Tobin was waiting at the head of the table with his Chief of Staff. That worthy seemed unimpressed with Kyle, though he couldn't think of anything specific he'd done to upset her. He could, at least, follow Tobin's hesitancy towards an inexperienced Flag Captain.

Anders was the last to take his seat, and the moment he did, a holographic image appeared in the middle of the room, hovering above the twelve-foot long black wood conference table.

Everyone in the room was provided a ringside seat to a perfectly detailed visual of the two *Commandant*-class carriers – and then, moments later, to the video of them exploding as that last pair of missiles struck home.

"So this was a fucking disaster," Tobin said bluntly into the silence as the image faded. "Would anyone care to explain to me just what the hell happened?"

"The inevitable consequence of deploying the battle group before it had been properly organized," Lord Captain Anders said calmly and precisely. "Confusion ensued, aggravated by an under-qualified senior officer. While unfortunate, the results were to be expected."

The room was silent. Kyle wasn't sure if everyone *else* was staring at Anders in horror, but he certainly was.

"I'm sorry, Lord Captain," he said slowly. "Are you saying that this was somehow Vice Commodore Stanford's fault?"

"Of course, with his lack of experience it was all too easy for an experienced officer to be confused as to why an obviously unqualified individual was attempting to give orders," Anders replied. "Given the uncertainty, Lieutenant Colonel Metzger utilized his best judgment as to what the correct priorities were. If Vice Commodore Stanford had supported his more experienced juniors, none of the Commonwealth ships would have escaped."

"Vice Commodore Stanford has been in uniform since Kai Metzger was in *high school*, Captain," Kyle said bluntly. "He has, last time I checked, vastly more combat experience – especially seeing as how last night was Colonel Metzger's first actual combat experience.

"Are you seriously sitting here, telling me that your officer did not fuck up? Thanks to Metzger, sixteen of your people are dead, a hundred and seventeen yard workers are dead, and we've lost two entire *carriers*.

"Section Twelve of the Alliance Treaty clearly states that in the case of any lack of clarity around command, the senior officer on the scene takes command," Kyle continued. "Even if Metzger was somehow confused, his computers were perfectly capable of informing him that Vice Commodore Stanford was the senior officer.

"In short, Lord Captain, your Colonel is guilty of disobedience in the face of the enemy," the big captain said flatly. Somehow, he managed to *not* yell or swear at the Imperial man, but he knew he was leaning forward, his bulk looming over the other man.

"That is *my* judgment to make," Anders snapped. "Look to your own house, Captain Roberts – the Federation seems to be making a habit of over-promoting its officers."

Kyle noted that Tobin seemed to be staying out of the argument, leaning back and watching with unreadable eyes. Aleppo was leaning back, clearly staying *out* of a fight that wasn't hers. Alstairs was fuming, but she made a small 'go ahead' gesture towards Kyle, leaving the Imperial Captain to his tender mercies.

He smiled coldly.

"Did you *miss* the video the Admiral played at the start of this meeting?" he asked Anders conversationally. "Your Colonel's actions directly resulted in the destruction of more firepower than many systems ever command. While you have the right to choose how he is disciplined, you do *not* have the authority to cover this kind of action up."

Anders lunged to his feet, the smaller man trying to make up some of the height difference between him and Kyle.

"I will *not* be lectured by an unqualified *boy*," he snarled. "I am Metzger's Captain, and I fully agree with his decision – in the absence of a qualified commander, he had as much right to choose his own targets as any senior officer."

Kyle slammed his palm down on the table. The crack echoed through the room, and the table itself shivered, several fine fracture lines rippling out from the impact point as Kyle glared at the Captain.

"This is my ship, Hendrick Anders," he ground out. "Sit. The fuck. Down."

For a seemingly eternal moment, the Imperial man met his gaze. Kyle didn't rise, didn't twitch, but he stared the other man down coldly. Finally, Anders sat.

"It seems I have been insufficiently clear," Kyle continued, still holding Anders' gaze. "If you do not prosecute Lieutenant Colonel Metzger, I will resort to the full powers available to me under Section Twenty-Six of the Alliance Treaty, and *I will make you shoot him*."

Avalon's Captain smiled coldly at his fellow officer.

"Discipline your damned dogs, Captain, or I will make you put them down."

The staredown resumed in silence, and for a few moments Kyle suspected he may have gone a few steps too far.

Then, Anders slowly bowed his head.

"I will make certain that the Lieutenant Colonel understands the full scope of his dishonor," the Imperial captain stated simply.

"Thank you, Lord Captain," Tobin said, someone *finally* stepping in now the immediate confrontation was over. "Now that… matter of protocol is resolved, I suggest we take a short break. I understand Captain Roberts' people have put on a light brunch, and I think we could all use a chance to let moods cool."

———

WATCHING his Captains file back in, Vice Admiral Dimitri Tobin smothered the grin he'd indulged in while they'd been out. Anders and Roberts were carefully giving each other a berth as they returned, but the confrontation between them had gone about as well as he could have hoped.

Roberts' *courage* had never been in doubt – this was, after all, the captain who'd intentionally set a ramming course at Tranquility. Tobin wasn't sure if the man had actually intended to follow through – the

Commonwealth ship had surrendered before it had got that far – but no one thought he lacked for courage.

Courage in battle, though, was very different than having a backbone interacting with other officers, especially an officer absolutely determined to protect a subordinate who'd made a bad mistake. Roberts appeared to have that as well.

His experience was still a concern for the Admiral, but Tobin's Flag Captain was starting to look more promising than he'd expected.

"All right," Tobin said as they all re-took their seats. "So last night's incident has increased Alliance High Command's concern level over the security of many of our systems. That was a deep strike, gentlemen – deeper than the Commonwealth ever launched in the last war.

"Walkingstick knows he can't risk a head-on assault on Castle or another central system, but he is clearly willing to push the edge of what's *safe* in the interests of cutting down our starship strength. He can afford to trade us ship for ship, and he'd come out ahead in the end. When he can trade us four for one, he's giggling all the way back to Earth."

Tobin grimaced and brought up the pictographic report he'd extorted out of Command the previous night. The graph showed a series of stylized stars with names and dates attached. Under each was a set of ships – one with multiple colors, different for each Allied nation, and one colored bright red for the Commonwealth.

"These are our losses in each system since the war began, matched against Commonwealth losses in each action," he told his people. "Looking at it on this scale makes the issue clear, doesn't it?" he asked.

Silence was his answer as the two men and three women in the room took in the chart. The initial exchange had been roughly even, though the Commonwealth losses had been disproportionately at Tranquility and Midori.

Since then, there had been no major actions, but the Commonwealth had initiated a series of small actions, single task groups hitting lightly or moderately defended systems. They hadn't brought along transports or made any attempt to take control of anywhere, but they'd been inflicting heavy ship losses.

In over a dozen minor actions, including the previous night, the

Alliance had lost twenty-two capital ships – and only taken out nine Commonwealth ships along the way.

"For those of you who weren't cleared for this," Tobin said quietly, "the current judgment of Alliance High Command is that we are losing this war."

With a mental command to his implant, he cleared the graph and dropped a three-dimensional hologram of a ship into the middle of the conference table.

"This is part of the Alliance's answer to our problem," he continued. "Designed roughly a year ago as part of a joint Imperium-Federation research project code-named Plowshare, this is the *Gallant*-class heavy gunship."

The ship was a saucer shape, maybe twenty-five meters thick and a hundred and twenty across. Parts of it were highlighted as he continued to speak.

"It's built around a single big gun – like the old *Avalon*," he nodded towards Captain Roberts, "the original weapons fit was born out of trying to find a use for the megaton-range lances built for the *Titans* before we discontinued our battleship programs."

Originally authorized to be a new class of twelve battleships, the *Titan*-class had been short-stopped by the Federation Assembly after only two were built. The Navy had received funds for ten battle-cruisers and two carriers in exchange, though, so no one had complained too loudly. They had, however, ended up with a stockpile of battleship-grade positron lances they had no use for.

Clever people had found uses for them.

"The *Gallants* aren't starships," he explained. "They're sublight guardships: two hundred thousand tons apiece, with one big and six small guns, backed by two capital ship missile launchers. And thanks to the some not-so-subtle bloody shirt waving when the design was finished, the facilities to *mass produce* them were completed six months ago.

"They cost half again as much as the same mass of starfighters, but can be crewed by retrained in-system spacers," he concluded. "Between facilities in Castle and Coraline, the Alliance has eighty-seven of these nasty little buggers ready to go, and they're all being staged through Castle.

"To help reinforce our allies, the Federation has also gathered every *Cobra* that's been pulled out of Home Fleet's carriers and the other core systems – roughly a thousand starfighters – and thrown them on the same transports, along with more missile launcher satellites than I thought we *had*."

With a wave of his hand and a mental command, he switched the screen from the schematic of the *Gallants* to a floating image of six spherical freighters, each exactly five hundred meters in diameter.

"Given yesterday's stunt by Walkingstick, High Command took a look at the convoy forming in Castle orbit this morning and had a collective panic attack over its lack of security," Tobin noted dryly. "These six ships contain the defenses intended to cover three star systems against an attack like today's. For anyone wondering, that means those freighters and their cargo are worth, roughly, a third of *Castle's* Gross System Product."

"I take it we're being assigned as their escort?" Roberts asked, the big Captain the first to break the silence as everyone regarded the six heavily laden starships.

"A bit of overkill, isn't it?" Captain Aleppo asked quietly. The Trade Factor captain probably knew the value of the freighters even better than Tobin did – even forty years after the Factor had been born out of a mutual defense pact between corporate-owned planets, the Factor's captains were expected to be very aware of the mercantile affairs of their nation.

"I would agree in principle," Tobin admitted – he had, in fact, argued that point strenuously – "except that we are seeing seemingly random raids by task groups of two to four starships. If one of those jumped this convoy in an outer system and it only has a single cruiser for an escort… it would be an expensive oversight."

He moved the ships to one end of the table, not-so-coincidentally hanging the hologram directly between Anders and Roberts. Above the other end, he lit up a map showing Alliance space, with Castle and three other systems highlighted.

"Since even such elevated individuals as I eventually shut up and follow orders," he told his Captains with a grin, "we're not going to waste too much time arguing over it. The convoy is hitting three systems and we'll be accompanying them all the way.

"From Castle, we go to Amaranthe, then Dis, then Kematian."

Looking at the stars, Tobin shivered slightly. Kematian and Dis were single-system members of the Alliance – small star nations with fleets of three starships apiece. Augmenting their defenses from Federation and Imperium resources would free up more of those ships for offensive operations – a win for all involved.

Amaranthe was a different story. They no longer had ships. Amaranthe had suffered badly in the last war, and both Castle and Coraline felt themselves obliged to make *certain* the battered people of that planet were safe.

Tobin found himself in full agreement on that point. He had, after all, been there.

10

Castle System, Castle Federation
13:00 December 16, 2735 Earth Standard Meridian Date/Time
DSC-078 Avalon, *Vice Admiral Tobin's Office*

DIMITRI WAS in the middle of reviewing the files of the three women, two men, and one hermaphrodite – a common affectation among those who'd traveled further along the path once called 'Transhuman' than the rest of humanity – who commanded the six ships being entrusted to his protection when Judy Sanchez knocked on his office door and entered.

"Senior Fleet Commander Solace is here to see you, sir," she told him crisply. "I setup the appointment with her as you requested."

The Vice Admiral paused, regarding his Chief of Staff levelly. "I don't recall requesting an appointment, Commander," he said mildly.

"You said you wanted to get a feel for Roberts' subordinates," Sanchez replied cautiously. "Part of your concerns about his inexperience, sir."

He paused. He really didn't remember saying exactly that, and even if he had, it was quite a jump to go from that to setting up an appointment with his Flag Captain's XO. He *had*, though, probably expressed some sentiment along those lines. It appeared he was going to need to be careful just what he suggested to his new Chief of Staff.

"Since she's here, you may as well send her in," Dimitri finally allowed. "Please make sure to run appointment requests through me first in future? Not every casual thought requires a formal meeting with the Admiral, after all," he said gently.

"Of course, sir," Sanchez said with a small, hopefully somewhat abashed, bow of her head. She stepped out and returned a moment later with the slimly elegant black woman who served as Dimitri's flagship's XO.

"Thank you, Commander Sanchez," the Admiral told her. "If you can have a steward bring us coffee? Or would you prefer tea, Commander Solace?"

"Coffee is fine, sir," Solace said primly. "Black, please."

"Of course," Senior Fleet Commander Sanchez agreed before bowing herself out of the Vice Admiral's office.

Dimitri gestured for Solace to have a seat. After a moment's hesitation, the Commander obeyed.

"Commander Sanchez wasn't clear why you wanted to see me, sir," she said after a moment. While Sanchez and Solace were both Senior Fleet Commanders, and Solace could certainly tell *Sanchez* to take a hike, she couldn't do the same to the Admiral.

The steward thankfully arrived before Dimitri had to answer Solace's implied question, delivering two cups, a carafe, and a small jar of the wildflower honey the Vice Admiral himself preferred. After the young man withdrew, Tobin picked up the cup – sweetened to the perfect level as the young man was one of the few carry-overs from *Corona.*

"May I be frank with you, Commander Solace?"

"You're the Admiral, sir."

Translation: I can't tell you what to do, but this whole interview is making me uncomfortable. Solace communicated better with intonations on the word 'sir' than Dimitri had seen some people manage with hundred page essays.

"What is your impression of Captain Roberts?" Dimitri finally asked, figuring that cutting to the chase was probably easiest. "Having reviewed both of your records, well, it would appear that you are more qualified for his role than he is."

"It is not my place to speak to my Captain's qualifications, sir," Solace told him, her voice calm.

"Commander, I'm not asking you to speak to his qualifications," he replied. "Just... your impressions. I've been asked to take a Flag Captain who's on his first major command. I am... concerned."

Solace was quiet for a few moments. Dimitri couldn't read her. He knew he wasn't as intuitive as some other officers he'd served with, and for a moment he wished he had a little bit more of that gift. He could have just accidently offended one of his key officers.

"Sir, your question skirts the limits of what is appropriate to ask of an officer," she said finally. "I understand your concern. I will admit to sharing it, as this is a powerful vessel, an unusual first command.

"But while I may have concerns about Captain Roberts' experience, I do not question his *qualifications*. Captain Kyle Roberts earned his planet winning a battle I do not believe another could have. He is a hero, and earned a command the hardest way possible."

Dimitri smiled grimly. Apparently backbone wasn't going to be in short supply aboard his flagship.

"All of that said, Commander," he said quietly, "do you think he's worthy of *Avalon*?"

"I don't know if he's worthy, Admiral," Solace replied, "but I do know this: he's earned the right to be judged for his actions and not your fears, sir."

Dimitri raised his coffee cup in the ancient *touché* symbol. She had a point. There were those who blamed him for the extent of the losses at Midori – and *his* superiors judged him to have done the best he could. Roberts was owed a similar allowance.

"Thank you, Commander," he told her. "Your sense of loyalty is appreciated – and I think you may be wiser than I. I appreciate your insight."

She nodded stiffly.

"Is there anything else, Vice Admiral?" she asked. "If we are to leave with the convoy in seventeen hours, there are munitions and supplies we need from the surface. Captain Roberts and I are pulling together a list, but our time is limited."

Dimitri gestured her out, and returned her salute crisply as the tall woman exited his office as stiffly as she'd entered.

The Vice Admiral shook his head. It was hard to be certain if Roberts had managed to inspire his XO's loyalty in a week, or if Solace had had the stick inserted before she arrived. Either way, she was *right*. He shouldn't be judging Captain Roberts based on fear, but on the man's actions.

With a sigh, he glanced at the coffee tray. Shaking his head with a chuckle, he returned to his work.

Solace hadn't even *touched* her coffee.

11

FOR A MAN USED to riding fire at four or five hundred gravities, the current pace of the convoy was excruciating. While the capital ships of Battle Group Seventeen could maintain two hundred and thirty gravities or more, the civilian ships were uniformly rated for Tier One acceleration – barely sixty gravities.

At this pace, it was going to take most of a day to reach a space where the convoy could bring on their Alcubierre drives.

The only positive of the convoy's lack of speed, in Michael Stanford's considered opinion, was that since they were still in-system when his last note from Senior Fleet Commander Kelly Mason had told him she'd be going off duty. Of course, they were already far enough away to need to use the Q-Com, but the Navy had always been generous with access time outside of combat operations.

Entering his request into the system flipped the orientation of the array of quantum-entangled particles in the heart of the ship linked to a matching set of particles aboard the switchboard station orbiting Castle. The first signal sent was a routing instruction, and the station linked up that sub-set of *Avalon's* entangled particles to another set, linked to a set of entangled particles aboard the cruiser *Sunset*. A reinvention of the ancient concept of the switchboard allowed the inherently two-point communication method of quantum entanglement to connect any points linked into the network.

The voluptuous blond woman who'd snuck into his heart on the old *Avalon* answered as soon as his call connected.

"Michael," she greeted him with a smile. "How's *Avalon*? The rumor mill had you in that whole mess at Gawain."

Michael shook his head. Of course, that was going to be the first thing to come up.

"We were," he admitted. "It was definitely a mess. None of our pilots were lost, though the Imperials took some hits. I can't say much more, and you know it."

"Fair enough, love," she told him with a smile. "I'm glad you're okay. Any chance of grabbing dinner before you guys ship out?"

A spike of disappointment hit Michael, and he sighed with a shake of his head.

"I see the rumor mill isn't *entirely* perfect," he observed. "We got ordered to escort a freighter convoy – urgent enough we aren't even getting our fifth starship! We're already shipping out."

"Damn," Kelly frowned. Her obvious disappointment, oddly enough, made Michael feel a bit better, and he smiled softly at her.

"We knew this was coming," he reminded her. "We are at war, after all."

"I hoped we'd both be assigned to *Avalon*," she admitted. "But then it makes sense you'd get Kyle or me, not both." She shook her head. "Solace left this ship in pristine condition. All I'm doing so far is following in her shoes – half the time, if I have a question, she has a note somewhere. The woman is *brilliant*."

"So I should not try to sneak anything past her?" Michael asked brightly.

"If she missed it, Kyle wouldn't," Kelly pointed out. "Do try not to get yourself in too much trouble."

"They sent me Rokos," *Avalon's* CAG replied. "If I get in any trouble, he'll get me out of it."

"Lucky you. Though we had some luck of our own – guess who our newest Flight Commander is?"

It took Michael a moment to think of who among the Flight Commanders they'd both worked with would make Kelly specifically call them out, and then he remembered a certain promotion.

"You got Williams?"

"We got Williams," Mason confirmed. Flight Commander Michelle Williams had flown under Michael on *Avalon* and, among other duties and missions, had saved Kyle Roberts' life. Michael figured he still owed the pilot for that.

"Did a certain Nurse-Lieutenant come along then?" Nurse-Lieutenant Angela Alverez, at Michael's last contact with Williams, been the younger officer's girlfriend.

"Nurse-Lieutenant *Commander* Alverez has apparently been sent back to school by the wisdom of the Navy," his girlfriend replied. "Apparently, she came out of the drive failure bound and determined to upgrade herself to doctor. Not something the Navy pushes people to do, I don't think, but no one is complaining either."

"Good for her," Stanford said cheerfully. "I guess you and Michelle can commiserate about being away from your lovers." He paused. "In public, perhaps?"

Kelly just laughed at him. He gloried in that laugh and smiled cheerfully at her.

"Keep an eye on her for me, will you?" he finally asked. "I'll admit to still feeling a bit paternal her way."

"I will," she promised. "*You* keep an eye on Roberts. I want to see both of you back here soon, you hear me, Vice Commodore?"

"Your wish is my command, Senior Fleet Commander."

20:00 December 17, 2735 ESMDT
DSC-078 Avalon, *Captain's Office*

"MASTER CHIEF, HAVE A SEAT," Kyle instructed his carrier's senior non-commissioned officer as the woman entered his office. "With everything going on, we really haven't had time to sit down and chat. Beer?"

"Sure," Cardea Belmonte replied. The Bosun was a hefty woman rivaling Kyle's height and width with pure white, short-cropped, hair. There was only one higher non-commissioned rank in the Castle Federation Space Navy, and Belmonte had been a Master Chief Petty Officer for twelve years.

He was lucky to have her, and gladly slid one of the beers from the mini-fridge he'd setup in his office across the desk as she took a seat. Belmonte, Marshall Hammond, and Peng Wa were the three senior NCO's aboard the ship, and Belmonte was the only one he didn't know well. He eyed her carefully as she opened the beer and leaned back.

"How are you finding *Avalon* so far, Bosun?" he asked.

"She's a damned fine ship," Belmonte replied. "You lucked out with Wong, I'd say – that man seems to have a gift for getting more out of everything than even I would expect."

"He always did," Kyle agreed. "Without that man, I'm not sure we would have managed to fly the old *Avalon* home under her own power. He pulled a few miracles out for me on the old lady."

"I was surprised they split the old crew up as much as they did," the Bosun told him. "Rumor had the plan being to use them as cadre."

"Timing was everything," he admitted. "We decommissioned early, for obvious reasons, so that left her crew available at a point when Vice Admiral Kane needed people to back-fill holes on a dozen ships. I think Command also didn't want both an inexperienced Captain *and* an inexperienced XO."

He wouldn't have explained that much to most NCOs, for obvious reasons, but as the Bosun Belmont was the Captain's left hand as much as the XO was the right hand. The smallest thing could be relevant to her job.

"How's morale?" he asked after taking another sip of his own beer.

"Our response to that attack… we did everything right, but we still lost four ships."

"Rumor spreads fast on a warship, Captain," she replied dryly. "I doubt there's anyone aboard who doesn't know *exactly* how large a strip you ripped off the Lord Captain. That probably helped morale more than the Imperials' screw-up hurt it."

Kyle shook his head. "That's really not something that should be common knowledge," he observed.

"This is true," Belmonte admitted. "I'll admit it did enough for crew morale I didn't look too hard into how it leaked."

"Fair, I suppose," he allowed. "While I think I will refrain from taking *official* notice, I would ask that you have a quiet word with the source. Leaking details of the Captains' conferences isn't something I can turn a blind eye to, Bosun. This was relatively minor, all things considered, but…"

"I agree. I will make sure a word lands in the right ears," she promised. "I was more concerned about morale, to be honest. Stopping rumors on a warship isn't easy."

Kyle took another drink and considered Belmonte.

"How's the ship's crew dealing with the Admiral's staff?" he finally asked. There was always some friction, but he needed to be sure it didn't impact efficiency.

"Better than usual," she replied. "By and large everything's running smoothly, though there has been a couple of fistfights. Broken up before we had to get the Marshall involved, thankfully."

"Fights, Bosun?" Kyle asked carefully. "That's not 'running smoothly'."

"Well…" she paused and shrugged. "Some of the Admiral's people *may* have made derogatory comments about *you*, sir, to which our people took offense. No one was injured, and the crew being willing to defend *your* honor is generally a positive thing."

With a laugh, Kyle shook his head again.

"Then I shall refrain from official notice again," he told her. "No other issues I should be aware of, unofficially or otherwise?"

"None so far," Belmonte said firmly. "I've got a good handle on our people, both Wa and Hammond are easy to work with, and JD-Personnel got a relatively good crew."

"Working well with the XO?" Kyle asked. He wasn't quite sure what to make of Solace himself. She was competent enough, but he still got the statue a lot more often than the woman. Part of him wanted to know her story – but the rest of him was all too aware it was *her* story, and he had no right to it unless it impacted the ship.

"Commander Solace is one of the better executive officers I've worked with, sir," the Bosun replied. "We've been working together closely to get everything in order. The woman has a wicked sense of humor that's been a joy while dealing with the rush to commission."

"She does?" Kyle asked in surprise.

The look Belmonte gave him in response was one he'd seen from senior NCO's before. It was the 'you're being an idiot, sir, but I can't tell you that' look.

"You are her Captain, sir," she pointed out finally. "Some decorum is probably needed."

Kyle could also tell that Belmonte wasn't telling him everything. He trusted the Bosun, however, to tell him anything actually necessary to run the ship.

He half-saluted the Bosun with his beer.

"Despite appearances, Master Chief, I am *somewhat* aware of decorum. Another beer?"

12

Deep Space, En route to Amaranthe System
04:30 December 19, 2735 Earth Standard Meridian Date/Time
DSC-078 Avalon, *Bridge*

KYLE HEARD feminine laughter coming from the bridge as he wandered down the corridor. It was roughly two hours short of when he was supposed to be on duty, but he hadn't been able to sleep. They were only a day and a half out of Amaranthe, and while he'd never *been* there, he had history with the system.

He wasn't entirely unused to nightmares, but that didn't make it easier to sleep.

In the middle of the ship's night, while under Alcubierre Drive, there were minimal demands of the watch on duty. He wasn't overly surprised to walk in and find Commander Maria Pendez and Senior Fleet Commander Mira Solace sitting together at the navigation station with their heads together like schoolgirls.

Technically, there was supposed to be at least a Petty Officer on duty with them, but his implant had already informed him that Solace had sent Petty Officer Second Class Helena Sheach to the Infirmary with a bad case of stomach cramps.

He paused for a moment, taking in the unaccustomed sight of Solace acting like something *other* than a completely professional officer. Kyle had no idea what the two women were looking at, but it was clearly amusing both of them.

Pendez said something, causing Solace to laugh aloud, then glanced back at the door and saw Kyle. She was immediately on her feet, reaching for the uniform jacket casually thrown across her console.

"At ease, Maria," Kyle told her with a laugh. "It's not even five in the morning, you can relax."

Solace stood up slightly less precipitously than her junior, but both women were on their feet facing him and he sighed.

"I couldn't sleep," he told them. "I can also do my paperwork from here, so if one or both of you wants to get some sleep early, you can consider yourselves relieved."

"Are you all right?" Solace asked. She looked more relaxed than he'd seen her yet, and her dark eyes seemed warmer than usual as she regarded him.

"I'm fine," he said, somewhat more shortly than he meant to. "Won't impact the ship, just couldn't sleep."

Solace stiffened at his dismissal. Still more human than ebony statue, but still...

"Get some sleep, Commander," he said quietly. "I just... I have history with Amaranthe. It's personal."

"Understood, sir," she answered, some of the stiffness leaking out of her. "With your permission, Captain, I think I will take you up on your offer. I have a meeting with Commander Wong at eleven hundred, and I'd like more than four hours of sleep before discussing fuel requirements for antimatter reactors."

"Dear gods, I let you schedule yourself for that?" Kyle asked, his concern only partially feigned. "Go, go! Sleep!"

That seemed to buy him a little bit less statue, and Solace was smiling as she nodded to both of them and slipped off the bridge.

Kyle interfaced with the computer as he carefully walked over to the command chair, checking the status of all the systems. If more was going on, he might have asked Solace for a report, but deep in warped space, very little could happen.

And the bad things, well, there tended to be very little anyone could do. Everyone on the old *Avalon's* bridge had died when their Stetson stabilizers had failed and flooded the outside of the ship with deadly radiation.

He glanced over at Pendez, who'd returned her gaze to her console.

"Sorry for interrupting, Commander," he said quietly. "That offer does apply to you too, you know. I think I can handle an FTL dark watch on my own."

His Navigator turned in her chair, leveling a set of soft brown eyes he'd seen leave a trail of broken hearts across an entire ship on him. Kyle was mostly immune to Pendez's charms, if not unaware of them.

"It was just girl talk. She," Pendez nodded to the door where Solace had disappeared, "has no idea what to make of you, you know?"

"Talking about the Captain behind his back? I'm that funny?" Kyle asked dryly.

"No," she chuckled. "You interrupted us looking at the latest fashion show in Castle City. Some of the outfits they brought out this year…" she shrugged. "Let's just say with my boobs and Mira's height, *neither* of us could pull them off."

"Fashion show?" Kyle asked, looking askance at Pendez. He could see her following fashion in the Federation's capital, but the thought didn't fit with his experience of Mira Solace.

"We spend ninety-plus percent of our time in uniform," Pendez pointed out. "A girl's got to feel pretty *sometimes* – and with her height and skin, the Commander can pull off some outfits that would make me look short and fat."

Kyle arched an eyebrow at his Navigator, who was in near-perfect physical condition under her curves, and she shook her head at him. They both knew he had no interest, and they both knew there was no appropriate response for him to make.

The conversation itself was a gray area, but it *was* an FTL dark watch after all.

"I'll admit, Commander Solace and I have not had much…

personal interaction," Kyle said softly. "I am pleased with our professional relationship, though, and we hardly need to be friends."

"She'll get that eventually," Pendez told him. "But… well, you know her first Captain tried to screw her – in multiple senses, right?"

"That took surprisingly little reading between the lines, yes," Kyle admitted. "I can also guess that she didn't report it, since Captain Haliburt still has a ship."

"Hard to rock the boat when dealing with the Master after God of where you live, boss," his Navigator told him. "She hasn't told *me* much, but I can tell the bastard made several years of her life a living Void. Her captain *after* that was, well…"

"Jowan Botteril is a skilled, capable officer," *Avalon's* Captain observed dryly. "He also *delights* in some of the most ancient stereotypes of his orientation in a way that skims the bounds of propriety aboard a warship. He would have been completely unthreatening to her in that sense."

"And then she has you," she said softly. "You're not exactly Navy Standard Issue as Captains go and, like I said, she doesn't quite know what to make of you."

"I can't go easy on her, Maria," Kyle replied, his voice very soft and serious. "She's my Executive Officer – and Gods know, she's *damn* good at the job."

"Don't think you need to go easy on her," his Navigator replied. "I think you just need to remember where she's coming from. You may not need to be friends, but from where I'm sitting, you *should* be. Even…"

She trailed off and then dodged away from Kyle's glance.

"Even what, Commander?" he asked.

"Partners, sir," she said finally, though Kyle wasn't sure that was what she'd originally meant to say. "You need to be partners, sir – because if you are, the Commonwealth is never going to know what hit them."

13

Amaranthe System
12:00 December 21, 2735 Earth Standard Meridian Date/Time
DSC-078 Avalon, *Bridge*

EVEN FROM A FULL light minute away, the planet Amaranthe looked sick. Diseased. The glass plains that had once been cities glittered in the starlight as Battle Group Seventeen approached from the outer system.

It had been beautiful once, a blue-green jewel of a world that had drawn immigrants from across the galaxy. At the beginning of the last war, the Republic of Amaranthe had been wealthy and powerful with the third-ranked Navy of the Alliance bringing over a dozen starships to the war against the Commonwealth

And then it had been the site of the single largest battle of the war. Fifty-seven capital ships had clashed in orbit while four billion souls watched. The Commonwealth had *shattered* the Alliance Second Fleet and seized control of Amaranthe orbit.

No-one – including the Commonwealth – seemed to be entirely

sure what had happened after that. During the invasion, a series of deadly nano-weapons had been unleashed that had *eaten* the planet's largest cities – and over two *billion* people.

After the Alliance kicked them out of the system in the *Second Battle of Amaranthe*, a massive relief effort had been launched. One of the sources of the supplies and money that had fuelled it, even before the war ended, had been the Commonwealth.

The Terrans had sworn blind after the war ended that their invasion force hadn't been equipped with weapons of that type – that the Commonwealth arsenal didn't even include mass-scale nano-weaponry.

As Kyle understood it, though, they'd basically said 'we invaded the system, so everything that followed is our fault' and formally taken responsibility for the atrocity. *Billions* of Commonwealth Dollars, Federation Stellars, and Imperial Marks had been poured into Amaranthe after the war.

Twenty years later, they had still barely begun rebuilding. The vast fields of nano-forged glass that had once been cities had resisted any attempt to break them up. The orbital infrastructure, destroyed by its own crews and workers to prevent it falling into Commonwealth hands, had only been partially replaced.

Amaranthe had no fleet now, but it didn't lack defenders. Twelve massive capital ships, six from the Coraline Imperium and six from the Castle Federation, orbited the world. Despite Commonwealth declarations that Amaranthe's neutrality in the war would be observed, the Alliance would take no chances.

"Sir, the Black Watch has requested our IFFs and approach codes," Kyle's communications officer reported.

"Send them over," Kyle confirmed. "They're expecting us."

Thanks to the Q-Com, even with a light minute between *Avalon* and the warships of the Black Watch it only took a few seconds for the exchange to complete.

"Admiral Kato sends his greetings to the Battle Group," he was informed. "I'm setting up a direct channel between Vice Admiral Tobin and Admiral Kato at their request."

"Understood." Kyle continued to watch the ugly splotches on the beautiful planet below.

"Sir, they're asking if we would like to setup a visit to the Memorial?" his com officer continued. "They can close it to the public for a while if we want."

A shiver ran through Kyle, and he bowed his head for a long moment.

"Tell them we'd like that, and inform the other ships' crews once you've received confirmation of the timing," he ordered, slowly raising his head. He thought a command, opening a channel to the Bosun.

"Master Chief, we're going to have an opportunity for those of the crew that want to visit the Memorial," he told Belmonte. "Can you check in with the section chiefs and make sure that anyone who wants to be on the list is on it?"

"Yes, sir," she replied crisply. "I'll make sure we have enough shuttle flights scheduled."

"Thank you, Master Chief." Kyle paused, then sighed softly. "Make sure I'm on the first shuttle, Bosun. I… need to see this."

Amaranthe System
22:00 December 21, 2735 ESMDT
The Memorial (what had been Verdant City)

DIMITRI TOBIN HAD BEEN to the Memorial before, but it still blew his mind. Once, a long time ago, it had been the Republic of Amaranthe battleship *Invictus* and the harbor of Verdant City, the Republic capital.

Invictus had crashed into one of Amaranthe's oceans in the battle over the planet, however, and Verdant City had been the site of one of the nano-weapon strikes. So the city had turned into a hundred-kilometer wide plain of gray glass, broken only by the harbor.

After the War, Amaranthe's leadership had towed the kilometer-long navigation hazard that was the hulk of *Invictus* into the harbor, anchored it down against the edge of the glass, and removed the handful of zero point cells and positron capacitors the Commonwealth hadn't ripped out to study. Decontaminated and safed, the hulk had then been used as the backdrop for plaque upon plaque of names. Every individual confirmed dead in the battle. Every individual confirmed or believed dead in the nano-weapon attack.

The names were in a very small font. For all that a kilometer-long hulk provided a lot of space, there were over two billion names listed.

With the Memorial being a kilometer long, it also left a lot of space. They'd shuttled down over four hundred crew members from the Battle Group's ships in the first wave, but the Admiral had found himself alone as he'd walked further along the glass plain, looking for a specific name.

There. It was where he remembered it from the last time he visited, and Dimitri laid his fingers on the etched letters of Flight Lieutenant Karl Michaels-Tobin. The old wound was mostly healed over now – twenty-plus years, a second marriage and multiple children could do that – but he still remembered.

Dimitri kissed his fingers, then pressed the kiss to the name.

"Never forgotten, my love," he said quietly. "Never forgotten."

Looking up from the name of his long-dead husband, Dimitri realized he wasn't the only member of the crew who'd walked well away from the rest of the party. Kyle was standing near the end of the Memorial, looking away from the wrecked battleship across the featureless glass plain that had been Verdant City.

Curious, Dimitri approached his Flag Captain. The other man seemed to be looking for something… but there wasn't much out there. The nano-weapon had eaten Verdant City's famous stone-work along with its people and its skyscrapers. Everywhere the City had stood was just glass, as was a good chunk of what had been the surrounding area.

He found the sight even more depressing than the Memorial itself, so the Admiral tended to avoid looking at it when he visited the Memorial.

"Captain?" he said questioningly, stepping up behind Roberts. "You look like you're looking for something."

"I am," Roberts replied, his voice unusually sad for a man.

"Matching up landmarks with some old photos." After a moment, he pointed. "There, I think."

Following the line of the Captain's fingers, Dimitri picked out one of the few features visible around the glass plain – the point where a line of hills ended, cut off by a sheer cliff where the nanites had eaten the soil and stone.

"The hill?" he asked.

"It fits the description," Roberts said softly. "I think that's where my father died."

Dimitri nodded slowly.

"My husband died in orbit," he confessed quietly. "A suicide strike by the last of our starfighters to try to stop the Commonwealth landing. They failed, obviously."

"You were here?" Roberts asked, turning back to face the Admiral.

"I was. Junior Tactical Officer aboard the battlecruiser *Samson*," Dimitri confirmed. "Karl was one of our pilots – we got married just six months beforehand. We were young, and in love, and determined not to let the war steal it from us."

The Admiral felt very old and shook his head slowly.

"I didn't know your father had died here," he admitted. "I... didn't realize he was killed in action."

"It took a few years for his body to catch up," Roberts said bitterly. "But he died here – died when he watched the nanites eat the people he'd been evacuating along with his entire company of Federation Marines.

"His body caught up the day the war ended, and he swallowed his own gun."

Tobin looked back to the cliff, and a vivid image of standing just past that line and watching the men and women you commanded and the innocents you were trying to protect dissolve into glass.

"My god," he whispered.

"They quote the number a lot," Roberts said softly, "that we only had seven post-traumatic suicides out of *seventy million* men and women sent to war. Only seven. It doesn't sound so wonderful when it was your family."

"I'm sorry, Kyle," Dimitri told him. He laid his hand on the other man's shoulder and squeezed gently – a moment of compassion neither would have allowed anywhere else. "I didn't know."

"You're not supposed to," the Captain told him with a snort. "You know, I've never been here. Twenty and more years since he died, and I've never been here to see where.

"But with the war back on…"

"I've visited here before, to remember Karl," Dimitri said quietly. "But I agree. It seemed… necessary to come by again."

Across the glass plains where a city had died, the two men watched the sun set, each alone with their grief – but stronger for facing it together.

14

Amaranthe System
08:00 December 21, 2735 Earth Standard Meridian Date/Time
DSC-078 Avalon, Main Flight Deck

STANFORD WATCHED the four *Falcons* of the overnight Carrier Space Patrol make their landings with a practiced eye. All four flight crews had done a good job of reducing velocity before entering the deck, and the carrier's carefully positioned mass manipulators did the rest of the job of bringing them to a halt.

They floated in the center of the deck, outside the gravity field, for a few seconds before telescoping arms reached out to grab the six thousand ton craft and drag them to their bays. Even as the old ships returned, his implant informed him that the new CSP had been launched from the forward launch tubes.

Avalon's relatively paltry commitment to Amaranthe's defense remained intact. Those four fighters would hold station on the big carrier, watching for anything unusual and adding another set of eyes to the net.

Between the Black Watch's three carriers and orbital launch platforms, the Watch had almost sixty starfighters in space at any moment. None of the starfighters in the convoy's freighters were headed here – though his implant was also showing him the engine tests of the *Gallant* the Republic Defense Force had chosen to check out before firing up all thirty.

Once the fighters were down, the deck was quiet. Stanford stood on the edge, watching the limited bustle of necessary maintenance checks and preparations while drinking his coffee. It was quiet enough he spotted the stocky, gray-haired, shape of Master Chief Marshall Hammond approaching him from over a hundred meters away.

The old Chief was well past sixty, and had been in the Castle Federation Space Force for as long as the Force had existed. There was no sign of age or wear to the man as he ably dodged his way down the deck to join the CAG in his quiet corner.

"Ekaterina took a micro-meteorite hit," he said gruffly. "Nothing serious, but Bravo-Five-Four is down for at least a day while we check it out for hidden damage."

"Understood," Michael said quietly. He had no doubt that the starfighter could fly and fight even with a small hole in it – *Falcons* were as tough as the rest of the breed – but there was no reason to risk it in a system as well-defended as Amaranthe.

"Anything else I should know, Marshall?" he asked. He'd learned to rely on his senior NCOs to have a pulse on the officers and men of his starfighter group. Learned it, in fact, from Kyle Roberts before injury had taken away the other man's ability to fly.

Hammond sighed.

"All the ships are checking out except Bravo-Five-Four. No *more* fights – the flag staff seems to have figured out insulting the Captain where anyone who flew for him can hear them is a dumb idea. Everything seems perfectly ship-shape, boss."

Michael waited. He recognized the opening sigh,

"There's rumors," the Chief finally said. "Nothing I've been able to pin down or even find specific people involved, but rumors."

"Am I going to have to drag this out of you, Chief?" the CAG asked calmly.

"*Rumor*," he emphasized the word again, "is that the Admiral's Chief of Staff is sounding out people. Specifically, new people – ones who didn't serve on the old *Avalon*. Not a morale-check mission, not… anything like I've ever heard of."

"Sounding them out about *what*?" Michael asked. For the Admiral's staff to be talking to his people without even informing him was concerning, though rumors were hardly enough for him to raise a complaint over it.

"I can't be certain," Hammond warned. "But it sounded like she was trying to find people who… were more loyal to the Federation than to the Captain, if you catch my drift, sir."

Vice Commodore Michael Stanford inhaled sharply, turning to face his senior Non-Commissioned Officer squarely for the first time since they'd started speaking.

"That's a dangerous accusation, Master Chief," he told Hammond.

"That's why I can't say I'm certain," the older man said gruffly. "No-one she's spoken to has come to me – I'm only getting rumors of what other people have seen and overheard. Reading between the lines, sir, I'd say that she's checking to be sure that our pilots would follow the Admiral's orders over the Captain's."

That, Michael reflected, was at least not outright *mutiny*. It was out of line, but it wasn't *quite* a crime.

"That's you giving the benefit of the doubt, isn't it?" he said aloud.

"Yes, sir."

"And if you were feeling more cynical?"

"I'd say the Admiral was trying to recruit a starfighter force that would follow his orders *against* the Captain."

Hammond was surprisingly calm for having announced he suspected the Battle Group's Commanding Officer of fomenting rebellion aboard his flagship.

"Right," Michael said quietly. "If you have any appointments for the next few hours, Chief, clear them."

"Sir?"

"We're going to see the XO."

"I can't prove *anything*, boss," Hammond warned.

"I know," Michael admitted. "That's why we're going to see the XO, not the Captain."

08:30 December 21, 2735 ESMDT
DSC-078 Avalon, *Executive Officer's Office*

THE COMMANDER, Air Group in charge of a carrier's flight group and the Executive Officer in charge of the carrier itself were the two swords of a carrier Captain. They were often the only O-6 ranked officers on the ship, though both *Avalon's* Chief Engineer and the Admiral's Chief of Staff shared that distinction aboard *Avalon*.

The CAG and the XO had to work together, which meant that it took less time for Michael to get onto Solace's schedule for the meeting than it took him and Hammond to travel the full kilometer between where he'd been loitering on the flight deck and her office.

When they arrived, Solace was waiting for them. She'd already laid out coffee – and Michael noted that not only was *his* coffee made exactly as he liked it, *Hammond's* coffee was as well. He and Solace had spent enough time in each other's company that she knew his preference, but she would have had to ask someone – or have Belmonte ask someone – to find out Hammond's choice.

A small thing, but a sign of respect for a senior NCO he found promising.

"Please, both of you, have a seat," Solace told them. She remained sitting behind her desk, everything about both herself and the room precise and perfectly according to regulation. There was none of the books, datapads, or physical paperwork that Michael knew littered his own office.

"Thank you for seeing us on such short notice," Michael replied as he took a seat. He took a sip of the coffee before continuing and smiled. The Captain's stewards always had the best coffee, and the XO clearly had access to their services.

"Master Chief Hammond brought something to my attention that I felt you and I had to discuss," he continued. "It's only a rumor, but it's a rumor of something sufficiently serious…"

"I see," Solace said calmly. She leaned forward slightly to focus on Hammond. "Would you care to explain, Chief? I understand," she continued, her voice softer, "that these are only rumors, and I won't hold you to them."

"Thank you, ma'am," Hammond responded. He laid out, quickly and precisely, exactly what he'd told Michael earlier.

The XO leaned backwards in her chair, drinking coffee in a somewhat obvious attempt to buy time to think.

"You have no idea who these conversations Sanchez allegedly had were with?" she asked finally.

"No, ma'am," the Chief admitted. "I can guess who they *weren't* with – any of the old *Avalon* hands would have told me or the Commodore. But… that's all."

"That's meaningful on its own," she told the two men. "You were correct to bring this to me, gentlemen," she continued. "Even rumors of this would need to be acted on if they reached Captain Roberts' ears.

"I will reach out to the Bosun and the Gunny," she promised. "If there is more to this than barracks imagination, I imagine Belmonte and Wa have heard things, though likely of even less weight.

"If you can give me a written note detailing what you have heard and been told, Master Chief, I would appreciate it," she continued. "It will *not* go past my office, you have my word. Kyle needs evidence before he can yank the Admiral's Chief of Staff up."

Apparently, when the XO was deep in thought, 'Captain Roberts' became 'Kyle'. Michael filed that note away with a mental smile.

"We'll keep our ears to the ground and let you know if anything else comes up," Michael promised. "If nothing else, I'll quietly lock the starfighters down so that only the Wing Commanders, myself or the Captain can authorize launches." He shook his head. "If Sanchez co-opts one of the Wings, we'll have bigger problems than preventing fighter launches."

"I appreciate that, Commodore," Solace told him. "I hope this is all paranoia, but I have some idea of what Tobin might be thinking. If I'm right, this is likely to explode at the worst possible time. We can't let that happen, gentlemen," she assured them.

Nodding, Michael finished his coffee and stood. "We should get to making sure that lock is in place," he told her.

"If you would stay a moment, Vice Commodore?" she requested. "I have a somewhat less pressing matter to discuss."

"Of course," Michael allowed, gesturing to Hammond to leave.

The Master Chief saluted them both.

"Thank you, sir, ma'am," he told them quietly. "The rumors were leaving me with an itch I couldn't scratch. Not sure I'm feeling better, but at least I've shared it."

The NCO slipped out, leaving Michael alone with Solace. She seemed to relax, slightly, with only her equal in the room. Michael wasn't sure the woman *ever* truly relaxed, there was a stiffness to her he found uncomfortable. She was always professional, always personable, but… never warm.

"What can I help you with, Commander?" he asked.

"You've served with Captain Roberts before," Solace stated. "It… falls to the XO to organize what little recognition of Christmas we allow aboard a warship. Do you know what traditions he favors?"

Michael laughed. That was *not* what he was expecting – he'd almost forgot the holiday was coming up. Like many religious days, it had been absorbed into the Federation's aggressively secular culture as a main event, despite Christianity's perennial duel with Reformation Wicca for second-largest religion on Castle.

"I honestly haven't served with the man at Christmas," he admitted. "I have no idea."

"Drat," Solace replied, the excessively mild curse word shocking another chuckle from Michael. "General Navy Tradition it is, then."

That meant holographic trees in the mess halls and emergency lights set to red and green throughout the ship, plus turkey as the main course for dinner. Gift exchanges aboard a warship tended to be small and personal, and very separate from the main celebration.

"We'll be back under A-S then?" Michael asked.

"Yes, we'll be on our way to Dis shortly, as soon as the Republic's Defense Forces are comfortable with the *Gallants* and the repair stations we've provided," she confirmed. "Christmas in deep space. I'm getting sadly used to it."

15

Deep Space, En route to Dis System
06:00 December 25, 2735 Earth Standard Meridian Date/Time
DSC-078 Avalon, Captain's Quarters

WHILE CASTLE'S rotation was close enough to Earth's twenty-four-hour day that there was little *date* discrepancy between the Earth Standard Meridian Date/Time used aboard starships, Corona City was roughly six hours ahead of Great Britain on Earth.

That meant Kyle was unsurprised to wake up on Christmas morning to a notification on his implant that he had a video message from Castle. Up well before his watch, he took his time cleaning up, noting that the floor level lighting had taken on cheerfully festive shades of green and red.

Once showered and dressed with a fresh cup of coffee, Kyle turned *off* the cheerful lights and made a note to let Solace know that he found that piece of Navy tradition utterly trite. If they were going to decorate the ship, they could pick up real garland on a planet somewhere. The ship might have dozens of kilometers of corridors, but it also had hundreds of often-bored Spacers and Specialists.

Shaking his head at his own wool-gathering, he settled down at his desk with his coffee and flipped the message to his wallscreen. The familiar, though time-fogged, image of Christmas in his mother's house lit up the screen, with Lisa Kerensky waving at the camera in the foreground.

"Merry Christmas Kyle," she told him with a grin. "Your mom is taking Jacob out to visit his grandparents for breakfast in a few minutes, they'll be down in a moment. You can see the aftermath of the gifts behind me."

She gestured at the strewn chaos of boxes and wrapping paper, the inevitable leftover of centuries of tradition. Sitting in pride of place on *top* of a pile of paper was a massive 1:1000 scale model of the old *Avalon*.

"I'm not even going to *guess* at who bought Jacob the meter-long starship model," Lisa said repressively. "I think *whoever* it was should realize he didn't have space in his room for it."

She heaved a long-suffering sigh, but there was a twinkle in her eye. A moment later, the thundering cavalcade of a single eleven year old boy rushed down the stairs and tackle-hugged her.

"Say Merry Christmas to your father, Jacob," Lisa instructed.

The redheaded boy, already reaching Lisa's shoulder and starting to look like he'd equal Kyle's own height, turned to face the camera with a bright smile.

"Merry Christmas Dad!" he half-shouted. "I got the ship! It's *so cool!*"

Kyle smiled helplessly as his son carried on in that vein for half a minute while his own mother came quietly down the stairs. Mrs. Roberts looked as spry and healthy as ever, but her careful steps always sent a twinge of guilt through him. When he'd stepped out of Lisa's and Jacob's lives for over a decade, his mother had filled the gap. He hadn't seen much of *her* either.

"Come now, Jacob," she finally interrupted. "We need to get to your grandparents. You can tell *them* all about it."

The video paused, then cut to an emptier home with just Lisa in it.

"I'll confess I'm glad for the time difference today," she told him, and her voice was quieter. Almost sad. "I have… good news, I think, but its awkward.

"You remember introducing me to Daniel Kellers?" she asked. He nodded, though he knew she couldn't see him.

Kyle had convinced Lisa to accompany him to a few affairs where it had been strongly implied he was *not* to show up without a guest. Since his love life had been nonexistent since he'd left her to join the military, he had a shortage of alternatives.

At one party, thrown by the Senator for Tuatha, they'd run into Member of the Federation Assembly Daniel Kellers, a local businessman of his and Lisa's age. While Kyle had been being shown off by the Senator, Kellers had kept Lisa company.

"We've… well, we've been seeing each other since then," Lisa admitted. "He helped me write my application for the position I just got at Corona City Hospital. And, well…" she paused, a smile flitting across her lips.

"It's pretty serious, Kyle," she told him. "Not expecting dresses and wedding bells, mind you, but…" She trailed off. "Jacob likes him."

"I know neither of us really felt there was anything – or *should* be anything – between us now, but I still feel like I'm telling you something you may not want to hear," Lisa continued. "He's never going to come between you and Jacob, but he's good for *me*."

The video was silent for a long moment.

"I know Christmas is a bad time for this," she finished, "but I needed to tell you sooner rather than later. If nothing else, to help you get your head back up and realize that *you* should be dating. Michael told me about that Phoenix officer!"

Kyle laughed, and the spell of him staring shocked at the screen was broken. He hadn't forgotten about the officer who'd propositioned him after his wing had beaten hers in exercises, but he also hadn't realized Stanford had told *Lisa* about it.

"Write me back when you get a minute, okay?" she asked. "I… well, I need to know you're okay with this."

The video ended, and Kyle let the positive bubble from the memory of Sub-Colonel Jenaveve LaCroix carry him for a few moments before letting it fade and considering Lisa's news. He poked at it mentally, like a sore tooth.

He was a little surprised to find he was okay with it. While any spark between them had faded, if someone had asked him yesterday, he'd have said Lisa dating would have bothered him.

Turned out he'd have been wrong. It... made him feel better.

13:00 December 25, 2735 ESMDT
DSC-078 Avalon, *Captain's Office*

CHRISTMAS DAY WAS GENERALLY a day for light duty unless the ship was likely to see action. Since Battle Group Seventeen wasn't scheduled to arrive in the Dis system until late on the twenty-sixth, Kyle had seen no reason to change that tradition.

He wasn't surprised that it took until after lunch for Solace to poke her head into his office. Since the ship was in FTL anyway, there was little that was likely to happen to need his attention. Another tradition was that the Captain wasn't out and about on Christmas – there tended to be a bit more drunkenness than the Commanding Officer wanted to take official notice of.

"Merry Christmas, sir," Solace greeted him.

"Merry Christmas, Commander Solace," Kyle replied. "Everything staying quiet?"

"So far so good, sir," she replied, taking the chair opposite him. "I am specifically *not* aware that there is a large party taking place on the Atrium with punch that is most definitely spiked with engineering's vodka."

"Then I shall also remain unaware," the Captain agreed cheerfully. "Drink, Commander? Since we specifically do not know our crew is getting drunk, I don't think anyone will begrudge us a beer."

She shook her head.

"I don't drink alcohol, sir," she reminded him. "Tea?"

Kyle grabbed a beer from the mini-fridge for himself and ran a tea out of the hot beverage dispenser for Solace.

It was a strangely awkward meeting, both of them trying to have the personal conversations normally allowed on Christmas while not really having that connection.

"Any news from home?" he asked as he passed her the tea.

"Cliath is a few hours behind Standard Meridian today," she told him. "My sister is probably only just now chivvying her kids out of bed."

Cliath was the capital city of Tuatha, one of the Federation's main member systems. The planet had a twenty-two and a half hour day, so its alignment with the Earth Standard Meridian Time used on starships shifted.

"Yourself, sir?"

"Got a video from my son and his mother," Kyle replied. "*Someone* gave the boy a meter-long replica of the old *Avalon*. He's ecstatic, and his mother is... tolerant." He shrugged. "She also apparently has a new boyfriend, which she seemed to think she was 'Dear John'ing me by telling me."

Solace seemed taken aback.

"Your son's mother...?"

"We dated in high school and she had an implant glitch resulting in an unplanned pregnancy," Kyle said quietly. "I ran off and joined the Navy, my mom helped take care of Lisa and Jacob. We're on good terms, but we're not *together*. Honestly happy for her – he's a good man."

"I didn't realize you had a son, sir," Solace admitted. "Your reputation is, well..."

"Chaste?" Kyle observed with a chuckle. "Celibate? Trust me, Commander, it only takes completely messing up one relationship to figure you aren't cut out for them. Besides, once I started ending up in command, the options got a lot more complicated."

"I see," his XO said. She was still stiff. Opening up about his family wasn't breaking down barriers, and Kyle mentally sighed. At this point, it was up to *her* to sort out her issues – so long as she kept doing her job.

"In any case," he said, realizing that they would both be more comfortable if he brought the conversation back to work, "I had some thoughts on exercises once we get to Dis…"

16

Dis System
20:00 December 26, 2735 Earth Standard Meridian Date/Time
DSC-078 Avalon, *Bridge*

"WHERE DID *THEY* COME FROM?!"

Solace's explanation echoed through the bridge without response for a long moment, then the XO regained her composure.

The two cruisers that had just lit off their drives were the center of attention on the bridge, and Kyle leaned back in his chair as he studied the situation.

Solace had kept a single Wing, forty-eight fighters, back to protect the carrier while sending the other four at the pair of battleships deeper in-system threatening the planet of Dis. That had seemed a logical decision at the time, almost conservative with no additional apparent threats.

Now, two *Hercules*-class battlecruisers, each a match for *Avalon* in mass though less maneuverable, charged towards her. Sixty *Scimitars* led the way, and Wing Commander Rokos' fighters slashed out to meet them.

His screen also showed Stanford trying desperately to turn the rest of the Fighter Group around. They were already millions of kilometers away with a significant velocity towards the battleships. They might get back in time to *avenge* the supercarrier, but they certainly weren't going to save her.

Nonetheless, Senior Fleet Commander Solace's orders were quick and firm. The carrier started accelerating away from the cruisers as her heavy beams began the almost futile attempt to help the starfighters engage the Commonwealth attack.

It was bad luck more than anything else that made the final difference. Lucky missile strikes in the first exchange took out Rokos and two of his squadron commanders. Disorganized, and with the firepower of the three capital ships filling the battlespace, the remainder of Delta Wing were annihilated.

Only a handful of the Commonwealth fighters survived, but they hadn't needed to. The *Hercules* had fewer beams and lighter deflectors than *Avalon* did, but their beams were almost half again as heavy as *Avalon's*.

They outranged her by over a hundred thousand kilometers, and the lights dimmed on the bridge less than thirty seconds after they entered their range. The 'Simulation Ended' message popped up on both the screens around them and everyone's implants.

Kyle quickly glanced at the mental 'screen' where he saw Vice Admiral Tobin's side of the engagement, and then at the other one showing the nine ships of the battle group and convoy peacefully dropping down Dis' gravity well.

"Well, that was... fun," Solace said flatly as Tobin's image popped up on the screen. "You are *sneaky*, sir," she told the Admiral.

"So is Walkingstick," Tobin said bluntly. "Thankfully, if the Commonwealth had been attacking Dis, those two cruisers would have run into *Magellan*, *Gravitas*, and *Camerone*, and there would have been a very different result."

"And if *Avalon* was operating alone, as fleet carriers do, my mistake would have just killed six thousand people," the XO replied bitterly.

"Learn, Commander, do not beat yourself up," the Admiral said bluntly. "Captain Roberts?"

"Admiral," Kyle acknowledged. He was making mental notes on what he'd seen on both sides of the exercise.

"I leave the critique to you," the big bear of an Admiral turned his gaze on the bridge crew and finished gruffly. "Your bridge crew's performance was acceptable given the odds. Let's aim for 'victorious' next time, shall we?"

The Admiral's image disappeared, and Kyle looked around his bridge with a small smile. He had his full Alpha Watch on duty for this exercise, and they were all looking abashed.

Commander Pendez had done *her* part beautifully, though she still looked concerned. Senior Fleet Commander Solace, on the other hand, had gone full black statue; and Commander Anderson, the Tactical Officer, was looking down at his console with a sallow expression.

"All right," Kyle said crisply. "Commander Solace, you were in command. Where do you think we went wrong?"

"I sent too many fighters after the battleships," she admitted crisply, her face frozen in the mask that he still found vaguely disturbing. "The error was mine, sir."

"It's an easy mistake for ex-cruiser officer to make," Kyle pointed out. "I've been guilty of it myself in exercises – it's the 'my last ship had less than a Wing of fighters, a Wing of fighters is therefore a *lot* of fighters' thought process.

"And," he continued sharply, "given what you were seeing, it was a relatively accurate assessment. Commander Anderson's horrified expression is suggesting that he has realized exactly where the main issue arose from. Would you care to elaborate, James?"

The redheaded officer was even paler than usual, but he swallowed hard and raised his head to meet Solace's gaze levelly.

"We had a pair of sensor ghosts where those cruisers came from," he said quietly. "Barely above detection thresholds; computer and human analysis suggested it was an old thermal trail from deeper in the system, so I didn't mention it. We saw them – and dismissed them – before you sent the fighters ahead.

"You didn't have enough information, ma'am," Anderson finished. "My fault."

"That… seems relatively reasonable, actually," Solace told him gently, the frozen statue fading slightly as she realized it was at least partially a junior's fault not her own. "I'm not sure I would have made a different call, James."

"Lessons for both of you, then," Kyle told them firmly. "Anderson – *never* assume the CO doesn't need to know something. It would have taken you ten, maybe fifteen, seconds to let Commander Solace know what you'd seen and how low the threshold was. There was almost ten *minutes* between the ghosts showing up and Vice Commodore Stanford's fighters passing the point of no return.

"What you see might not seem relevant – but you don't always know all of the Captain's plans.

"And Solace," he turned to his XO. "*You* can't assume that your bridge officers will pass on everything you need to know. They may not know all of your plans," he repeated with a grin, eking a chuckle from his officers.

"You have the ability to mirror anyone's displays into your implant," he continued. "Outside of combat, using without care can be rude. *In* combat, it's a necessity. I generally have the sensor feed from CIC, our ammunition status, and the primary navigation display either on my implant or on my console.

"There's no *time* for you to watch over everyone's shoulders in combat – but having the displays mirrored will give you more situational awareness – and help you realize when there's a question you *should* ask."

Both Solace and Anderson were nodding abashedly, though they'd both stopped looking like they were about to fall on their swords.

"Now," Kyle told them cheerfully, "we're going to do this all over again. I'll be running the Op Force this time – and, well, you just made me look bad to the Admiral."

Someone actually groaned aloud. He pretended to not notice, but he was reasonably sure it was Solace. That was a good sign.

DIMITRI REVIEWED the results of the follow-up exercises from the previous night with a grin. With his people now over-sensitive to sensor ghosts due to Dimitri's contribution, Roberts had used decoy drones to try to lure Solace into under-committing fighters to a strike.

Instead, the XO had decided to hold back all of her fighters and use sensor drones to validate her targets – and then dropped the full two hundred and forty fighter strike on the poor trio of strike cruisers Roberts had been trying to lure her into attacking with too little force.

The Admiral had also eavesdropped on the critique of the exercise he'd run the opposing force for. Roberts was doing quite acceptably though he still had some concerns around the man's experience and aggression.

At least Dis wasn't going to be an issue for anyone. Despite the paranoia-inducing exercises they'd been running, the system was completely secure. Three heavy fleet carriers – the entirety of the Dis Security Force's capital ship strength – hung in high orbit over the planet. His screens showed at least twenty guardships running escort on various industrial complexes, and easily two hundred starfighters flying patrols and escorts.

The DSF was a capable defensive force, one that didn't really *need* the carriers but had refused to deploy them out-system after Walkingstick's first wave of attacks. The twenty *Gallants* and three hundred *Cobras* coming here were more of a bribe than a necessity, in his opinion.

He shook his head. Their visit here would be short. Unlike Amaranthe, there was no reason for anyone to visit the surface, and there was no partial unloading – the ships that had carried supplies for Amaranthe would be emptied here. The convoy was going to drop three of the ships it had brought here, and the rest would head for Kematian.

"Sir, I have that analysis of the exercises you asked for," Sanchez informed him, sticking her head in.

"Bring it in, Judy," he ordered.

His Chief of Staff brought in one of the Navy's ubiquitous datapads and slipped it onto his desk.

"That second series of exercises mostly went Solace's way," she noted. "I would have expected the Captain to do better."

"Success in training exercises is not always measured in who has more victories, Judy," Dimitri reminded her. "They were intentionally one-trick exercises – if Solace saw through the trick in time, the odds were actually slightly in her favor. If she missed the trick, she got stomped."

Sanchez shook her head.

"Roberts seems overly enamored with those kinds of tricks," she told him. "Seems dangerous."

"It is," Dimitri allowed. "On the other hand, when they work, they can pull out a victory for an inferior force. It's how he won at Tranquility. It's a question of judgment on whether tricks are called for."

"I see, sir," Sanchez allowed. She glanced at the pad, which showed an assessment of Solace's performance. "And Solace, sir?"

"Solace underestimates the value of those tricks," the Admiral replied, skimming the data. "That doesn't appear to be a weakness that will survive serving as Captain Roberts' XO."

"Do you trust her judgment or Captain Roberts', sir?"

Dimitri looked up at Sanchez, eyeing his Chief of Staff carefully.

"Both are experienced officers," he said slowly. "Solace has more experience in Navy command, though Roberts has more combat experience. Having seen neither in action, I'd hesitate to judge one over the other."

"Of course, sir," Sanchez said promptly.

Dimitri couldn't quite shake the feeling the Senior Fleet Commander was fishing for something. The longer he served with Judy Sanchez, the more he was beginning to wonder about the woman. She was efficient, competent and took initiative – sometimes too much initiative, but better to restrain the courageous lion than prod the lazy mule.

But there was just something about her…

17

Deep Space, En route to Kematian System
01:00 December 29, 2735 Earth Standard Meridian Date/Time
DSC-078 Avalon, *Main Flight Deck*

AMONG THE MANY varied and entertaining duties of the Commander, Air Group, was surprise inspections. As a squadron leader, Michael had always found it useful to make those inspections with no one around, and he saw no reason to change the habit now that he was in charge of an entire Fighter Group.

Starting the inspection in the middle of the night also meant he might get through at least a full wing of ships before the day watch started and people began to realize the CAG was inspecting.

In the middle of an FTL dark watch, the flight deck was creepily silent. The lighting was a little bit dimmer than usual, not much but enough to throw shadows into stark relief behind and underneath the multi-thousand ton delta-shapes of his starfighters.

His Chief NCO and the squad of techs and Flight Engineers he'd dragooned into the task with less than ten hours' notice seemed less enthused with the whole idea than he was, but that was normal for *any* midnight duty.

"All right folks," he told them, gathering them around, "we're going to start with my ship first. In theory," he grinned, "this should be the example of what the starfighters *should* look like, but reality may differ."

The truth was that he'd gone over his ship with his Flight Engineer the previous day, and if it wasn't a perfect example, something very strange was going on.

As if the universe was listening to him, the lights in that corner of the flight deck promptly went out. That was, while not impossible, extremely unlikely to happen by accident.

"Hold position!" he snapped. "Hammond, what's going on?"

He flipped a check command into the net as he was speaking, and saw that the lights had been turned off. A blink and a thought, and the lights came back up – only to go down again as someone slammed an override command into the net.

The deck was filled with flickering light and shadow as he pushed the rest of the lights to maximum and he and Hammond charged forward.

There.

The shadows were moving. There were people there, using the shadows to hide as they tried to disappear from his deck. As he spotted them, *all* of the deck lights went down.

That *definitely* couldn't happen by accident, and worse, Michael was now locked out of the lights for his own flight deck.

"What the *fuck*?!" the Chief exclaimed.

Before Hammond had even finished swearing, Michael had gone for a different option – and the running lights on two hundred and forty starfighters lit up simultaneously.

Designed to be visible from hundreds of kilometers away in deep space, the deck was *brighter* with those running lights than with its regular lighting. With everything finally clear, Michael caught a glimpse of a figure disappearing into a side access door, and another figure turning back towards them.

"Stop!" Michael bellowed. "Stand the Void down!"

He had a moment to process what he was seeing as the ship-suited figure drew a weapon – and fired!

The first bullet whipped past his shoulder, shattering against the hull of one of the starfighters, and Michael froze. He was a *starfighter pilot*, not a Marine!

The second bullet sent his tech team scattering and Michael diving for cover, dropping behind one of the many robotic vehicles used for transporting munitions across the deck – this one thankfully without a cargo.

A third and fourth shot fragmented against his cover, and then a loud thud and an exchange of cursing began. That was when Michael realized that *Hammond* had kept going.

Finally shocked into motion, the CAG jumped over his cover to find the Master Chief struggling with the gunman. The gun fired twice and Hammond jerked as the bullets sank home, but then the gun was sliding across the floor.

The assailant went for a knife, but the big Chief got his hands on the other man's head and there was a sick snapping noise. The knife slid to the ground from boneless hands, and the gunman followed it.

"Dammit!" Michael swore. He activated his implant com as he ran to his Deck Chief's side. "Emergency Medical Team to the flight deck, by fighter SFG-One Actual. We have gunfire and men down. Emergency Medical to the flight deck!"

"Your fighter, sir," Hammond told him, pressing his arm over his chest to help his shipsuit exert pressure on the wounds. "They were in your ship."

"Dammit Marshall, let's worry about that after you're okay," Michael snapped.

"Fuck you sir – I'll live, but you make *damned* sure nobody touches that fighter without a forensics…" The Chief's words were lost in a fit of coughing, some of which came up bloody.

"You heard the Chief," Michael snarled at the techs. "Lock down my bird. Simpson, Aramir – draw arms from the Flight Control weapons locker. You're on guard until the Ship's Marshal gets here."

He knelt next to the Master Chief and prayed that the Stars would bring the Medical Team *fast*.

———

CAPTAIN ROBERTS and Commander Solace joined Michael on the deck shortly after the Medical Team arrived. Both stood back while the medics did a quick and dirty patch job on Hammond's wound, then slipped him onto a stretcher for movement to the Main Infirmary.

Once Hammond and the tech who'd taken a flesh wound from the ricochets had been carried away towards medical attention, *Avalon's* other two senior officers approached Michael.

"What happened?" the Captain asked simply. Glancing around the deck, still lit by starfighter running lights, he added: "Where are the lights?"

"Give me a second," Michael replied. Now that he'd done every-thing he could for Hammond, he could return his attention to the lights. Whatever override code had been used had been de-activated, and he managed to bring up the deck lights again. A moment later, he shut down the running lights on the fighters, and fully focused his gaze on Roberts.

"We were doing a midnight inspection," he explained quietly. "Starting with my fighter as an example – but the lights went crazy when we approached the bird. I tried to keep them on, but whoever was screwing with me had an override code that shut *me* down on *my own Void-cursed flight deck.*"

"Commander?" Roberts said questioningly, glancing over at Solace.

"There's no record, sir," she replied, surprise leaking through even *her* self-control. "I can see where the Vice Commodore was locked out. I can see the commands – but there's no user record, and there's no record of the code."

"That shouldn't be possible," the Captain replied, his own eyes distracted as he accessed the files himself.

Michael followed suit, and since he hadn't lost the starfighter pilot's bandwidth, he confirmed before the Captain finished.

"But it's true nonetheless," he said softly. "Sir, we have a dead tech – one of *mine* – who was armed with a weapon with no serial number."

They'd identified Specialist First Class Oscar O'Madden by the time the medics had arrived. He'd also, unfortunately, been very dead by the time the medics arrived. Spinal injuries were still deadly in the twenty-eighth century.

"Not from our armory then," Roberts observed, glancing up as the Ship's Marshal, Lieutenant Major Sirvard Barsamian entered the deck – followed by both her forensics team and a full platoon of Marines, led by Peng Wa herself.

"I see we're waking everybody up," Michael observed as he spotted the Gunny. It was a relief to see her – he knew the Captain trusted her completely, which meant she was a point of safety in a night that was getting very, very, scary.

"Someone *shot* Master Chief Hammond," Commander Solace observed before the Captain could speak. "And the camera records are also gone, so the only evidence we have is your people's vague impression of a disappearing person, and whatever was left in that starfighter." She pointed at his ship as Michael gaped at her.

"The cameras missed it?" he demanded.

"No, the cameras were shut down by an invisible override code, the same as the lights," the XO told him grimly. "Major Barsamian," she greeted the dark-eyed young woman leading the Marines. "I think this is now your area."

"Indeed," she observed calmly. "The combat area clearly was contaminated to allow medical rescue. We can work with that," she stated, "but if everyone would please move away from the immediate area, I would appreciate it."

Michael and the other senior officers got her hint and started shuffling everyone else away from the corner of the flight deck where everything had gone to Starless Void.

"Has anyone entered the starfighter?" she asked Michael as the space began to clear for her people to work.

"Simpson and Aramir have been guarding the door since this all went down, and I've locked it down to my implant codes," he told her.

"Please open it up for my forensics team," Barsamian replied. "Everything here is now being recorded by lapel-cams. Nothing is going to happen without record – and we *will* find out what happened."

12:00 December 29, 2735 ESMDT
DSC-078 Avalon, *Captain's Break-out Room*

THE LAST FEW hours had passed without sleep for Kyle and his senior officers. They'd pulled Tobin and Sanchez in at the end, and now the five of them were sprawled around his break-out room in various stages of exhaustion and concern as Barsamian, looking completely unbothered by her midnight wake-up, faced them calmly.

"Firstly," Kyle told everyone as he glanced around the room, "I've heard from Surgeon-Commander Cunningham. It was touch and go for a while, but it looks like Hammond will live. He is going to require significant internal reconstruction, and Cunningham's recommendation is that we transfer him to a base or groundside facility as soon as possible. The procedure will take months.

"Sorry, Michael, but it looks like you're out your Deck Chief – but he'll live."

"Stars know that's a trade I'm perfectly happy to make," the CAG replied, his eyes bloodshot and weary after the shock of the night's events.

"I think we can all agree on that," Solace chimed in. As usual, Kyle's XO was perfectly turned out, showing barely a tremor from the long night.

"As for why and *what*," Kyle continued, "I leave that to Lieutenant Major Barsamian."

Barsamian nodded at his words and faced *Avalon's* leadership.

"We don't have a lot to go on," she admitted. "O'Madden is dead. We are reviewing his movements since coming aboard, but during the most useful period, last night, vast swathes of the ship's cameras were disabled.

"The reason that no one was able to identify the override code used is that there wasn't one," she continued. "All of the apparent 'overrides' were actually a remotely directed, self-modifying, eventually self-*deleting*, computer program. A tailored virus, if you will."

"Is that even *possible*?" Kyle demanded. A virus capable of seriously impacting the ship was a deadly threat.

"Yes, but only for secondary systems like cameras and lights," the Marshal explained. "The ship's computers have highly capable defensive routines designed to prevent just this, but to help protect their code their use is restricted to high security systems.

"Similar viruses, I am told, are in the hands of Alliance Special Operations," she continued. "It is very definitely a tool of espionage, and one that has rendered us entirely unable to identify who O'Madden's accomplice was."

"Surely we can identify who came in and out of the blackout zone," Sanchez objected. "It would at least give us a place to start."

"The virus shutdown cameras on the entirety of the two decks the flight deck links to," Barsamian replied calmly. "It also shutdown cameras in randomly selected chunks of the ship, across what could have been seven separate continuous paths. I ran an analysis, Senior Fleet Commander. Of *Avalon's* six thousand crew members, four thousand, seven hundred, and eighty five could have been on the flight deck during the attack without us knowing."

The petite woman looked around her seniors.

"That number includes everyone in this room," she finished calmly. "Though, of course, we know for certain where Vice Commodore Stanford was."

"What about implant downloads?" Tobin asked. The big Vice Admiral sounded strained – fatigue and stress, Kyle presumed.

"We tried to download O'Madden's. Something – probably another virus – had corrupted his entire in-head storage. We'd require a warrant to force downloads of everyone else on the list," the Marshal replied. "While issuing said warrant is within the power of both you and Captain Roberts, the Code of Military Justice requires us to restrict said downloads to cases where we have probable cause.

"Bluntly, sir, we don't have probable cause to order five thousand implant downloads, and it would take us two weeks to process the paperwork and downloads anyway.

"With O'Madden's death and the virus screwing with our cameras, everything outside Commodore Stanford's fighter is effectively useless to us."

Kyle caught the codicil there, and from the look in his CAG's eyes, so did Stanford.

"What did you find in my fighter, Major?" the pilot asked softly.

"Our initial sweep turned up nothing other than O'Madden's fingerprints and some evidence to suggest someone with proper gloves was in there," she admitted. "I… deemed that unlikely, and we commandeered your Flight Engineer and took a second look.

"We found this."

She pulled a small black box, less than six centimeters long, from inside her uniform jacket and dropped it on the conference table.

"I'm trusting what your Engineer told me," she continued, "but it agrees with my own review of the schematics. This was placed on the power conduit to the mass manipulators used for inertial compensation. The assessment I was given was that it was designed to do two things: shut off power to those manipulators, and prevent the fail-safes from engaging for at least half a second."

The room was silent, and Kyle felt ill. You always knew there were risks to riding fire at five hundred gravities – it wasn't really a sane man's game, and few flight crews would pretend it was. You relied on the fail-safes to keep those gravities from crushing you. Your starfighter could lose half of its mass manipulators, and while it would guzzle fuel like water, it would still keep you safe because the failsafes prioritized compensating for acceleration over anything else.

Half a second of five hundred gravities was, roughly, half a second more than a human would survive.

"That's murder," Tobin said into the silence, the Admiral's voice a growl. "You're telling me that someone just tried to assassinate the Battle Group CAG?"

"My people ripped into its code," Barsamian said quietly. "It was designed to trigger after a sustained four minute sequence in excess of four hundred and fifty gravities. There would have been no survivors.

"O'Madden had the skills and knowledge to build this," she continued. "But… he was a ten year man, a loyal spacer, a loyal citizen of the

Federation. There is *nothing* in his background to suggest he would want to murder Commodore Stanford."

"You said there was someone else in the fighter?" Kyle demanded.

"There was," she agreed. "And they were a *professional*. O'Madden's fingerprints and DNA were everywhere. The person with him… they wore the right type of gloves, they had a DNA-cleaning nano-field, the works. I'm guessing they were the source of our virus, and the instigator of the assassination attempt.

"Sirs, ma'ams," the Ship's Marshal told them all, "I only see one conclusion: we have a Commonwealth spy aboard *Avalon*."

Kyle sighed. He'd drawn the same conclusion himself already, and everything Barsamian had said only confirmed that.

"All right, Major," he told her. "I want you to take the ship to Counter Intelligence Level Three. No communication leaves or arrives without your office being aware of it. All classified communiques can be reviewed by the Admiral's staff," he nodded towards Sanchez.

"My intelligence officer will take care of it," Tobin agreed grimly. "We need to do more, though, Captain – we can't have a spy on the Battle Group flagship!"

"We will do what we can, Admiral," Kyle replied. "Major, I want your people to go through *everything* O'Madden has done since he reported aboard. You said he could have built the device himself – I want to know if he actually did. I want to know who he spoke to, what he did – I want to know every time he *sneezed*. Understand me?"

"Yes, sir," she confirmed.

18

DIMITRI TOBIN WAS *NOT* happy with the discovery of a Commonwealth spy aboard *Avalon*. Since this wasn't an unhappiness he could actually direct *at* anyone, he was grumpier than usual as he sat on his flag deck drinking his coffee.

They were still six hours outside of Kematian, where the convoy would make their last delivery, and he hadn't yet received orders for where he was supposed to take Battle Group Seventeen from there. His last communique instructed him to take several days in the system for shore leave and Battle Group level exercises while Alliance High Command apparently sat around debating what to do with their most powerful available mobile formation.

That High Command didn't have a mission for his group yet told him that there was a debate going on – and probably a political one.

Different elements of the Alliance wanted different things – not just a split between defensive and offensive action, but between different kinds of offensive action.

There were six Alliance systems currently in Commonwealth hands. Alizon, Cora, Frihet, Hammerveldt, Huī Xīng, and Zahn were all single-system star nations. None had heavy industry, none had built their own starships, and in truth, none were strategically vital. Many officers and politicians felt their liberation should be the priority regardless.

Dimitri was in agreement with the *other* faction, one usually spear-headed by the Imperium – the destruction of fleet bases and re-fuelling depots had to be a priority. If the Alliance eliminated or reduced the Commonwealth's ability to deploy forces in the region they called the Rimward Marches, then the conquered systems could be liberated with ease.

When an alert popped up on his implant that he was being requested on a Q-Com call, he hoped it was finally news.

"I'll be in my office," he told Lieutenant Commander Lisa Snapes, his Intelligence Officer. "Ping me if anything comes up I need to be aware of."

Flag decks had a much less strict transfer of responsibility than the main bridge. In practice, the Senior Lieutenant in charge of the team running the consoles held 'the watch' on the flag deck, but most Admirals – Dimitri included – preferred to have one of the senior officers of the Admiral's staff on the flag deck, just in case.

Closing the door to his office, he mentally connected the Q-Com channel to the wallscreen. It quickly popped up a series of videos – the central one was Fleet Admiral Meredith Blake of the Castle Federation Space Navy, but there were a *lot* of secondary channels.

This definitely wasn't his orders. This… wasn't good.

"Ladies, Gentlemen, we're waiting on a few more," Blake said calmly. "A recording of parts of this message will be forwarded to your capital ship commanders. Distribution of this information beyond that is at your and your captains' discretion, but everything is classified Red Two."

Dimitri took his seat, suddenly paying a lot more attention. Red classification was the level below Top Secret, and Red Two was the second highest level of it. The entire convoy mission he was currently on was only classified Red Four.

Another half dozen windows popped up on his screen, and Tobin realized that he was seeing every Alliance Admiral who was currently awake. This was big.

"We're still sorting out the details," Blake told them finally, "but six hours ago a major Commonwealth Task Force, fourteen ships under Walkingstick himself, entered the Midori system."

Avalon's Admiral clenched his fists, his knuckles turning white as he remembered Midori. A lot of friends had died there… if they'd lost the system… he found himself plotting how quickly he could take Battle Group Seventeen there.

"They *exited* the system thirty-seven minutes ago," Blake, who had stepped up from Chief of Staff for the Federation to Chief of Staff for the *Alliance*, told them.

Dimitri sighed in relief. A suicide charge probably wouldn't have saved the system if Walkingstick *had* taken it – and it could easily have ended his career either way.

"They lost one battleship and between two and three hundred fighters. *We* lost the cruisers *Horus, Diamond,* and *Thermopylae*, along with the carrier *Michelangelo*," she finished grimly, and Dimitri winced.

That was an Imperial strike cruiser, a Federation battlecruiser, and *two* Trade Factor ships. A full quarter of the warships left at the big Alliance base in Midori.

"Reports are coming in from multiple systems of Commonwealth attacks," Blake warned them. "We have confirmed three other incursions in at least battle group strength. Be advised, we have confirmed at least one of these attacks was accompanied by troop transports.

"Some of these attacks appear to be the same kind of attritional raids we've been seeing for the last few months, but at least some of them are real attempts at conquest. Watch your frontiers, people," she ordered. "I have no intention of yielding any more ground to Walkingstick's people!"

The video dissolved into a cascade of what could be tentatively called 'discussion' – there were definitely some productive offers and requests of assistance between the Admirals, mixed in with the panic and the shouting.

Before Tobin could intervene, his implant pinged him and he muted the Q-Com.

"What is it, Lisa?"

"Sir, we've just received a message from Kematian," his Intelligence Officer informed him, and he cursed silently. He knew what she was going to say before she even said it.

"A Commonwealth battle group has arrived. Kematian is under attack."

————

"ARE we getting a data feed from the Kematian Navy?" Dimitri asked as he returned to his flag deck. The quiet morning of a few minutes ago was gone now, and his people were busily pulling up channels and linking into the other ships of the Battle Group.

"We are," Snapes confirmed. "They're vectoring Q-probes in closer and moving their fleet out to intercept."

"Get me a display," Dimitri ordered. "Make sure Roberts and Solace are seeing this, as well as the other Captains."

"They're already on the link, sir," the Lieutenant Commander confirmed. Moments later, the big display in the center of the flag deck lit up with a tactical view of the Kematian system.

Kem, Kematian's star, was a K9 orange dwarf with five planets. Kematian itself was the closest planet, with two cold and rocky worlds orbiting outside it that provided raw materials for its industry. Two massive gas giants marked the outer perimeter of the system and helped to extend the gravity well outwards to make the planet hard to reach.

Two of the KN's trio of cruisers were in orbit of the planet itself. The other orbited the second planet, Sumber. The display listed numbers of smaller ships, and he noted with a grimace that there were no guardships in the system.

There were, thankfully, almost a thousand starfighters – but they were an old design. The *Kavaleri*-type fighter was a *fifth*-generation design, notably inferior to the *Scimitars* the Commonwealth would be fielding.

"What do we know about the Commonwealth's strength?" Dimitri asked, stepping over to the red splotch on the edge of the display and studying it.

"We've confirmed nine ships," Snapes told him. "The Kematians are still sorting out details, but it looks like four are hanging back while five move in." As she spoke, the red splotch resolved into slightly more detail, tags on the individual ships resolving as the group split apart. "Their guess is we're looking at three transports and a battleship in Force Two on a slow gravity-assist course towards Kematian."

"And Force One?" Dimitri eyed the five ships. They were moving quickly for Commonwealth ships, at two hundred and thirty gravities.

"Acceleration makes them modern units," she agreed with his own silent assessment. "They haven't deployed starfighters yet, but Commonwealth doctrine would suggest a roughly even split between starfighters and heavy weapons.

"Given accelerations, we're likely to see a mix of *Hercules* battle-cruisers, *Saint* battleships and *Volcano* heavy carriers," she noted. Those were the Commonwealth's most modern units, twenty million tons and sixty-five million cubic meters apiece. *Avalon* was bigger and more massive than any of them, but the *rest* of the Battle Group was the same size or smaller.

The Kematian Navy, on the other hand, had three *Majesty*-class cruisers purchased from the Imperium, equivalent to BG 17's *Gravitas*. They were ten percent smaller than the Commonwealth ships, with barely three quarters of the mass and firepower.

Dimitri opened a channel to Roberts.

"Captain, are you seeing what I'm seeing?"

"Yes, sir," Roberts confirmed. "It looks like Force One is intentionally maneuvering to allow the KN to concentrate before engaging. Given what they know, it makes sense, and it helps draw the KN to a position where they can't intercept Force Two."

Looking back at the display, Dimitri realized his Flag Captain was correct. The Kematians would consolidate their forces in about four hours, and unless the Commonwealth launched fighters in the next twenty minutes, Force One wouldn't engage until after that. If they meant to keep their missiles and fighters together, that clash would likely take place in about six hours.

But Force One represented the main threat, so the KN *had* to maneuver to block them. And while they were doing that, Force Two would drop past them and intercept the planet in *eight* hours, where if Force Two went in with Force One, no landing would take place for half a standard day.

What the Commonwealth commander *didn't* know was that Battle Group Seventeen was on the way – and would arrive in the system in... just over six hours.

13:00 December 31, 2735 ESMDT
DSC-078 Avalon, *Bridge*

KYLE WAS GETTING sick of watching battles he couldn't influence. At least this time, Battle Group Seventeen would arrive before the action was likely to be concluded. Their arrival could – and hopefully would – make a difference in how the Commonwealth forces reacted.

Tobin had sent up a virtual conference with himself and Sanchez for all of the Group's Captains and Executive Officers, plus Vice Commodore Stanford as the Group CAG. All ten of them were reviewing the same tactical display of the system, watching the icons of the various forces in play.

The Kematian Navy was completing its rendezvous, with just under twelve hundred starfighters forming into a defensive sphere around the three cruisers. They were now vectoring away from both their homeworld and Force One, trying to draw the Commonwealth into a stern chase.

It was a stern chase the Commonwealth force's faster, more modern, ships would win. Three *Volcano*-class carriers and two *Saint-*

class battleships followed the Kematians, and they'd already deployed over six hundred *Scimitars* between them.

For the moment, both fleets were keeping their starfighters close to hand, though that would likely end before *Avalon* and her companions entered the system.

Meanwhile, Force Two had accelerated its approach towards the planet. A single *Resolute*-class battleship – a last-generation ship, but still modern – escorted the three assault transports as all of them made an easy hundred gravities toward Kematian.

It was pretty clear Force Two believed Force One could take the Kematians, and Kyle had to admit they were probably right. The *Scimitars* were more than a match for the *Kavaleris* one on one, and while they couldn't take them at two to one odds, they could definitely keep them from closing with the Commonwealth ships.

Once those two *Saints* with their megaton-range positron lances ranged on the Kematian ships the battle was over. With the newer ships' heavier weapons *and* heavier deflectors, they had the locals outranged by the best part of a light second.

Of course, Battle Group Seventeen could change that entire calculation – and they would arrive in slightly less than an hour.

"We need to concentrate our forces, combine with the Kematians and pound Force One into debris," Lord Captain Anders concluded. "With their heavy space power destroyed, Force Two will run – there's no point in landing troops when we control the skies."

"I agree," Captain Aleppo said after a moment. "Kematian's orbital defenses are not impregnable, but it would take time for the battleship to wear them down – time our presence denies them."

It *sounded* right, but the thought bothered Kyle. With a mental command, he highlighted the planet's orbital platforms.

"If we focus on Force One," he pointed out, "the entirety of Kematian's orbital industry and infrastructure are at risk. If they avoid the civilian habitats, it's a legitimate military target, and one whose destruction would leave us committing even more resources to this system's defense.

"While a *Resolute*-class battleship lacks the firepower to bring down the defenses without time, if they don't decelerate they'll pass the planet at a velocity that will make their weapons even more dangerous.

"If we ignore Force Two, they could destroy Kematian's economy," Kyle warned. "I recommend splitting our forces, sir," he told Vice Admiral Tobin. "We can send two, even three, of *Avalon's* Wings after the landing force without compromising our ability to destroy Force One.

"We could even deploy decoys to make our fighter strength seem larger, and leave them doubting which fighter force is real," he continued. "It would achieve the goal of making Force One nervous and threatening Force Two."

Alstairs whistled softly.

"That's not bad, sir," she added. "Play the cards right, we could leave them guessing to the last minute – might even get both Force One and Force Two to run."

"Or we could find ourselves flying right into the teeth of two super-modern battleships without the starfighter strength to press home the assault," Sanchez objected. "We don't have a lot of data on the capabilities of the *Saints*. If Intelligence's estimates are off, even two fighter Wings could make the difference between a comfortable victory, and a tight-fought one that loses us more ships than we can afford!"

"You raise a good point, Captain Roberts," Tobin interjected before he could reply. "It's a risky plan, though – the kind that looks fantastic on paper but that reality tends to shred."

Kyle *might* have been falsely maligning his Admiral, but he was pretty sure there was a factor of 'a more *experienced* officer would know that' in his words. Though *Camerone's* Captain Alstairs was the most senior Captain in the group by at least two years.

"The Commonwealth is also unlikely to launch the kind of attack you're predicting," Tobin continued. "There is a not-insignificant risk of hitting the habitats or even the *planet* in that kind of rushed bombardment, and the Terrans tend to *shoot* officers who hit planets – however accidentally.

"The simple fact ladies, gentlemen, is that we *know* Walkingstick is prioritizing inflicting capital ship casualties over anything else. We can sadly afford to lose Kematian's orbital industry better than we can afford multiple starship losses.

"We will keep the Battle Group and Commodore Stanford's fighters together," the Vice Admiral ordered. "This is a chance to punch out five of the Commonwealth's shiniest warships. If the Marshal is willing to give me this chance, then I am by God going to take it!"

19

Kematian System

14:00 December 31, 2735 Earth Standard Meridian Date/Time

SFG-001 Actual – Falcon-C *type command starfighter*

ALMOST AS SOON AS the warp bubble around *Avalon* collapsed, acceleration slammed Michael back into the command seat of his starfighter. The Kematian system resolved into reality around him, and he started checking in with his fighter Wings.

It took roughly a minute for all of the Battle Group's fighters to launch into space, and he scanned the numbers. Two hundred and forty from *Avalon*, eighty from *Gravitas* – they'd replaced their losses and their commanding officer before BG 17 had left Castle – and forty-eight from *Cameron* gave him almost three hundred and seventy of the little ships, all seventh-generation spacecraft.

"Wing leaders, check in," he ordered.

"*Avalon* Alpha here," Thomas Avignon reported.

"Bravo on your left," Russell Rokos chimed in.

"Charlie's locked and loaded."

"*Avalon* Delta is looking pretty."

"Epsilon online."

"*Camerone* Wing in position," Wing Commander Andreas Volte told him.

"Attack Wing *Gravitas* online and awaiting your orders," Lieutenant Colonel Annika Schmidt reported last. She'd been yanked from another Imperial ship in Castle – the one escorting the Ambassador, no less! – to replace Kai Metzger after the Imperials had finally admitted the previous commander had screwed up.

Michael took a quick moment to review the tactical display now feeding directly to his optic nerves. The Kematian Navy was now outright running in front of the Commonwealth force. The Terrans, unfortunately, edged them by about ten gravities overall – and had a velocity edge of almost ten percent of lightspeed.

They were in missile range now, and the starfighters had *just* been sent into the attack. The missiles would follow, though with twelve hundred Kematian starfighters providing cover, they weren't likely to get through.

The Commonwealth force seemed willing to play the long game. Every minute that passed got Force Two closer to the planet and, in the end, if the Kematians didn't get offensive with their starfighters, they couldn't win.

Whoever was in charge had to be wondering what the defenders were thinking – the position they'd taken was buying them time, but at the cost of their best chance for victory.

Of course, the Commonwealth commander didn't have the advantage of being linked into the system's sensor net and the Kematian Navy's sensors by Q-Com. He had to wait for light to reach him at its age-old pace of three hundred thousand kilometers a second.

Which meant the Terrans would know about Battle Group Seventeen's arrival roughly… now. Almost as soon as the light would have reached them, the acceleration of the starfighters cut to zero. Moments later, they resumed acceleration – at a rate that would bring them back into company with their warships.

The Terrans were still going after the defending fleet – but they were being a *lot* more careful about it.

"They know we're coming," he told his Wing Commanders. "Let's go say hello, shall we?"

Moments later, three hundred and sixty eight starfighters fired off their drives and charged the enemy at five hundred gravities.

––––––

OVER THE NEXT FIVE HOURS, Michael had a front row seat to a display that would have made any ancient Spanish matador proud.

Force One's commander had clearly decided to try to finish off the Kematian Navy before engaging BG 17. Unfortunately, his ten gravity edge in acceleration wasn't enough to *force* the three cruisers into range of his battleships, not when they kept adjusting vectors.

By now, the defenders' fighter strength had been gutted. Of the twelve hundred four thousand ton ships Kematian had sent out to defend herself, barely three hundred survived – but they'd *annihilated* the Terran *Scimitars*.

It looked like the Kematians' luck was running out. With most of their fighters gone, the Commonwealth opened up with every missile launcher they had. Fifty missiles blasted into space, followed by fifty more twenty-one seconds later.

Flight time for the Stormwinds was over fifteen minutes still, but that steady metronome of incoming salvos could easily be too much for the remaining starfighters.

Of course, Battle Group Seventeen had fired *fifty* minutes ago, and sixty-five missiles were now burning up behind Vice Commodore Stanford's starfighters – and with less than fifty starfighters left, Force Two was about to have a very bad day.

"On my mark," Michael said calmly. "All fighters fire two salvos. First is to detonate at one hundred thousand kilometers to screw with their sensors for the starships' missiles. Second is to close and kill."

He smiled.

"We'll be right behind them."

He waited. At the speed they were closing, milliseconds would make the difference – but he was fully linked into his starfighter, and milliseconds were all the time in the world.

"*Mark,*" he snapped.

The rotary launcher the Federation had developed, and the Imperium had 'borrowed' – mostly with permission – had a cycle time of a little over four seconds. By the time those seconds had passed, his three hundred and sixty odd ships had thrown over three thousand missiles into space,

They shot ahead of his ships at a thousand gravities and the Battle Group's Jackhammers came up behind them, their higher velocities closing the gaps between the three salvos.

Seconds ticked by like years. Positron lances started to flash in space around them, the battleships and their carrier charges lighting up space as they tried to destroy missiles and starfighters at maximum range. In theory, the *Saint's* one megaton main guns could hit them at this range – but the whole purpose of having a pilot in the expendable little spacecraft was to make them too unpredictable for that.

Force One had started accelerating directly away from Michael's people. Not enough to change anything, but enough to allow their lances and defense lasers to have a chance. At the speed they were closing, it changed the time frame by only seconds – but at these speeds, seconds were everything.

The first salvo detonated exactly on cue, a hundred thousand kilometers clear of the Commonwealth force. The interlaced shockwaves and radiation clouds shot forward, maintaining the velocity of the missiles and filling space with natural jamming.

On the heels of that chaos came the *Falcons* and the Battle Group's Jackhammers. Decoys and even more jamming filled in the space behind the radiation cloud, rendering the empty space a chaotic hell that rivaled the heart of a star for discord and chaos.

Sixty-five Jackhammer missiles struck from the heart of that cloud of chaos.

They met the starfighters first. Fifty-four *Scimitars* remained, and they charged the missiles, lances and defensive lasers flashing into space. The missiles were designed for this, weaving and dodging and scattering electronic signatures across thousands of kilometers.

Thirty missiles passed through, and then the Terran starfighters passed into range of Stanford's starfighters. He hadn't given orders for what to do – he hadn't needed to. Moments after the Terrans entered his people's range, they were dead, shredded by four or five positron lances apiece.

Two of his *Falcons* died with them, but he forced those feelings aside as the seconds ticked away.

Three seconds after the first missiles detonated, the Jackhammer salvo hit home. Of the sixty-five missiles launched almost an hour before, one made it through everything the Commonwealth could throw at it, and collided head-on with the lead *Saint*.

Traveling at almost twenty percent of the speed of light and carrying a one-gigaton antimatter warhead, the Jackhammer hit with *two* gigatons of force. The twenty million ton battleship *visibly* lurched backwards, debris scattering into space from the point of impact, fire blasting out of the hull to disappear as the oxygen fuelling it was exhausted.

Michael Stanford *knew*, intellectually, that battleships were the toughest things ever built by human hands; that modern meters-thick ferro-carbon ceramic armor was almost as tough as the old thin shells of neutronium. It was a far different affair to watch the *Saint* take that missile on the nose and *keep firing*.

It changed nothing.

Two seconds after the sole Jackhammer impact, the second fighter missile salvo charged in on its heels. Hundreds of missiles had been deceived by jamming and other countermeasures. Hundreds more of the less-capable fighter-launched missiles died to the defenses that had killed dozens of capital ship missiles.

'Only' one hundred and twenty missiles made it through. The already-damaged *Saint*, with its weakened defenses, was the target of over half of them, and vanished in a ball of fire.

The other four ships survived, somehow, dancing and pirouetting in the cataclysm of fire that embraced them. Half-gutted, barely functional hulks, but they survived, and were still firing.

Vice Commodore Michael Stanford and Battle Group Seventeen's starfighters were barely two seconds behind their missiles.

15:00 December 31, 2735 ESMDT
DSC-078 Avalon, *Bridge*

KYLE HAD NEVER SENT starfighters into battle without accompanying them before, and it was a far more nerve-wracking experience than he'd expected. When the battle was finally joined, everything disintegrated into a chaos even the Q-Com links to the fighters and accompanying drones couldn't sort out.

It probably wasn't any clearer when you were in the middle of that chaos, but it *felt* clearer. You knew what you had to do.

From the outside, you just watched a thousand people disappear into a ball of hellfire, and prayed to the Gods that they came out alive.

He knew from the speeds and firepower in play that it would be over in less than twenty seconds. Those seconds passed, and the computers still struggled to resolve anything from the debris and radiation. Another twenty seconds passed.

Finally, over a minute after Stanford had detonated the first wave of missiles, the computers combined the data from the starfighters and the probes and reported the results of the fighter strike.

Force One was *gone*. Where a minute before, fifty-plus starfighters and five of the Terran Commonwealth's newest warships had charged through space, only wreckage remained. As Kyle watched, a handful of escape pod beacons began to light up. Not many – not nearly enough.

Fifty thousand people had just died in less than a minute.

Thirty-six of Battle Group Seventeen's fighters had gone with them. Glancing over the numbers, Kyle saw they'd been lucky – twenty-five of the ships had ejected their emergency capsules, saving their crews.

Seventeen of the thirty-six lost starfighters were Imperial *Arrows*, a disproportionate loss. The Imperium would tear the result apart in their review sessions, but he suspected it was as simple as the Coraline fighters' lower powered electronic warfare suites being less able to keep them alive in the middle of the fray.

"Get me a status on the Kematians and Force Two," he heard Tobin order, and pulled his thoughts back to the living.

"The KN has six salvos, three hundred missiles, inbound," Anderson reported onto the squadron net.

Kyle caught a quick glance over from his Tactical Officer and gave the young man a reassuring nod. He didn't need Kyle's permission to share that data, though some Captains might object to the junior officer taking it on themselves to respond to the Admiral's query.

"What's the ETA on those missiles?" he asked Anderson himself. The loss of their motherships made the missiles less deadly, but by no means helpless.

"First salvo arriving in eight minutes, final in ten," the young man reported crisply. "Our fighters don't have the vector for intercept – it's all on the locals."

"Damn," Kyle whispered. Anderson had answered his next question before he asked it. "Gods protect them."

"Force Two is accelerating again," Sanchez reported, answering the second half of Tobin's question. "They are vectoring away from the planet. The battleship will make their closest approach at two million kilometers at roughly five percent of light speed, the transports at ten million. Both will be in roughly twenty minutes."

If there was nothing Stanford could do for the Kematian Navy, maybe…

Kyle opened a channel to the CAG.

"Michael, do your ships have missiles left?"

"Half-load on everybody," Stanford replied. "What do you need?"

"I want you to vector towards the planet," Kyle told him. "There's no way any of us can intercept Force Two, but I want to make them nervous – make them think about running, not making precision attacks on the orbital infrastructure."

There was a pause.

"Not any *less* helpful than chasing missiles I can't catch," the CAG observed. "Making it happen."

Kyle realized, *after* giving the order, that it was probably Tobin's call not his. He glanced at the window in his implant showing his link to the Admiral, though, and got a quick thumbs up directed at him and Stanford.

"Good call," the Admiral agreed. "Let's make them sweat."

"Kematian starfighters are intercepting the missiles," Anderson reported quietly. "Ninety seconds to first wave impact."

Intercepting missiles with starfighters was only moderately effective and dangerous – being too close to a *successfully* intercepted missile had nearly killed Kyle and was responsible for the NSIID that had permanently grounded him.

But when you had three hundred fighters to hand, and over three hundred capital ship missiles headed your way, you used the tools you had.

Even on their own, the Stormwinds were smart enough to activate and run most of their electronic countermeasures. Jamming and false images filled the scanners – but unlike the missiles, the starfighters *did* have their motherships behind them.

The cruisers' massive computers interpolated data across the hundreds of *Kavaleris* and dozens of Q-probes circling the battlespace, and fed the exact locations of the missiles back to the starfighters in near-real-time.

The first pass was a resounding success. Only five missiles cleared the fighters and were easily shredded by the cruisers' defenses.

As the lead time decreased, the success degraded. Four survived of the second salvo. Six of the third. Ten of the fourth, and fifteen of the fifth and sixth.

Twenty-five starfighters died along the way, victims of unlucky direct hits or just too close to the explosions of missiles that were caught.

Behind them, the Kematian Navy's three cruisers danced in the fire. Missiles died as lasers and positron lances lashed out. For over a minute, as everyone on *Avalon's* bridge held their breath, every missile died.

One solitary missile, a glitch-induced straggler from the fourth salvo launched barely four seconds ahead of the fifth, dodged under and around everything. As the targeting computers switched to the clump of missiles behind it, most missing the singleton.

It took precious seconds for a human to see the gap and re-direct defenses. Antimatter beams and lasers retargeted, but it was too close.

They caught the missile a quarter-kilometer from the hull of the lead cruiser. Too close to be safe – but far enough away to save the ship.

Fire hammered across the cruiser's hull, stripping away sensors, stabilizer emitters, and all tools that necessity placed outside a starship's massive armor.

When it passed, the cruiser was battered and burnt, but it remained.

Cheering echoed *Avalon's* bridge as Kyle's people let their collective breath go. The Kematian Navy's fighter losses were brutal, but its starship strength was intact – and in a cold final analysis, the main purpose of starfighters was to die so that starships didn't.

"All right," Tobin said loudly, cutting into the cheering on both the flag deck and the bridge. "Get me a channel to the Kematians – we'll need them to pull Search and Rescue.

"As for us, get us on a course after Vice Commodore Stanford," he ordered. "It's time to send that last ship running back to Walkingstick!"

———

KYLE WATCHED the single remaining battleship carefully. The assault transports were clearly giving up the attack as a lost cause, all three of them heading for the system perimeter at two hundred gravities. They'd pass well outside of even missile range of the planet's orbital defenses.

The battleship, on the other hand, was courting a missile duel with the closest of the orbiting battle stations. The stations had, in fact, been firing on her for about thirty minutes now, with the first salvos closing in as Kyle watched.

Still with ten minutes to go before their closest approach, the Terran warship continued to bat down the individual salvos with ease. While the orbital platforms were throwing seventy missiles at the ship at a time, they were being launched from multiple platforms in salvos of ten.

Without starfighters to distract and add to the chaos, there was no way seventy missiles were going to penetrate a modern battleship's defenses. Whatever the Commonwealth Captain's plan was, he was clearly willing to weather the platform's fire until he was close enough to make precision attacks.

They were barely five minutes from their closest approach when they finally opened fire, and it was almost a relief. Watching them close through the defensive missiles without firing, like some unstoppable juggernaut, had been nerve-wracking.

Twenty-four missiles shot into space, a tiny answer to the over seven hundred the defensive platforms had thrown at the single ship but fired in a single salvo and targeting much less heavily defended prey. Twenty-six seconds later, another salvo entered space.

In the five minutes it took the battleship to reach its closest approach, the Terran warship launched eleven salvos. The twelfth was launched just after the ship passed the nearest approach, and then the battleship ceased fire.

The first salvo hit the defensive platforms ninety seconds after the closest approach. Lasers and defensive positron lances slashed through space, lighting up Kematian's sky with explosions as antimatter missiles died.

Three of the seven platforms on the battleship's side of Kematian died with those missiles, though, and a thousand people with them. Those larger explosions sent shivers down Kyle's spine – the weapons platforms represented half of the anti-missile defenses covering the planet's orbital infrastructure. He was starting to get a sinking feeling.

With the reduced defenses, the second salvo took out the remaining platforms. Another thousand-plus people dead, and the anti-missile defenses protecting the planet were gutted.

The third salvo had clearly been targeted on the platforms as well, detonating in the space where the battle stations had orbited, illuminating their wreckage and filling the space above Kematian with static and radiation.

The fourth salvo split on its way in, wrapping around the planet to hit the other defensive platforms as they neared the horizon. Only two platforms were destroyed, but that was enough to remove any chance of further missile fire on the battleship as she ran.

Kyle closed his eyes as the fifth and sixth salvos struck home. Even without the platforms, the missile defenses were ripping the heart out of the salvos, but a dozen missiles from each salvo still struck home. Even with his eyes closed, his implant continued to relentlessly feed him the sensor data, and he watched as orbital manufactories, sublight shipyards, and transfer stations died in balls of fire.

The seventh salvo was the first time a habitat died. It wasn't specifically targeted – it was just too close to a smelting platform and was caught in the fireball. By the eighth, it was clear that no safety allowance had been made around habitats as three more were caught in explosions and half-incinerated.

Avalon's Captain opened his eyes, querying his implant. There had to be *some* way they could bring the battleship down. The computers calmly informed him that even using their missiles' ability to fly ballistic and re-activate their drives, there was no way they could hit the battleship. Even Stanford and his starfighters were fourteen hours away from Kematian at this point.

By the eleventh salvo, sixty percent of the planet's orbital infrastructure was gone. The debris fields would finish off the rest as they orbited into each other. Tens of thousands were dead or would soon die, no matter how desperately they scoured space for life pods and sections with atmosphere.

It was a callous attack but, just barely, short of an atrocity. *Most* of the habitats had been far enough away from the industrial platforms to be spared. The losses could be argued as collateral damage. Kyle watched the last salvo close grimly, burning every detail in his mind.

Then *Avalon's* bridge crew, including himself, gasped in horror as the missiles ducked through the fields of debris their sisters had created. There were no defenses left to stop them as they charged further and deeper than the other salvos – and dove into Kematian's atmosphere.

There was nothing any of them could do but watch in horror as every city on half a planet vanished in balls of antimatter fire.

15:30 December 31, 2735 ESMDT
DSC-078 Avalon, Flag Deck

DIMITRI TOBIN WAS SURROUNDED by silence. No one in a command position in the Battle Group would ever forget those moments. The realization that the Terran commander had gone past atrocity into outright mass murder.

It had been almost a hundred years since the invention of small enough stable antimatter containment units to allow for antimatter warheads. Almost a hundred years, which had seen dozens of wars both large and small across human space.

Kematian was only the second time they had ever been used on a planetary target.

"Recall the," he coughed, clearing the surprising lump of phlegm in his throat. "Recall the starfighters," he repeated himself.

"Sir, they…" Snapes trailed off as he turned a level gaze on her. Dimitri wasn't sure how much of the burning anger and hate he was feeling showed in his eyes, but his Intelligence Officer shut up.

"They can't catch that battleship," he snapped. "No-one in this system can catch that ship before it reaches FTL."

Again, he had watched the Commonwealth destroy without mercy. He'd watched Amaranthe die, and while no one had ever been sure what had happened there it had happened *after* the Commonwealth landed. He'd watched when an outnumbered Commonwealth battle group had *completely* destroyed Hessian's orbital infrastructure, intentionally targeting civilian habitats – and he'd helped wipe every last ship in that battle group from existence.

A sickening sense of failure and helpless rage sank deep into his bones. Every major atrocity of the last war had happened on his watch, and now the first atrocity of the new war joined them. Maybe he *should* have stayed home. It certainly appeared his presence was a curse for the innocents of the worlds he tried to defend.

"You were right," he told Captain Roberts bluntly on a private link. With no sound, the implants carried only text between them.

"*Nobody* predicted this," the Captain replied instantly. "Even the *Kematians* thought Force One was the threat."

"We're going after the bastard," Dimitri told Roberts, the decision made as he said it. There was nothing else he could do at this point. He couldn't let the *bastard* who'd just burned half a planet go home. Even if Command ordered him to stay…

"Walkingstick will hang him for us if we let them go," Roberts pointed out.

"I will not rely on the Commonwealth to provide justice for *our* dead," the Admiral snapped.

"Agreed," his Flag Captain said calmly. "I think we can push *Avalon* above the light year a day squared mark," he continued. "It might be a strain, but I don't think they'll see it coming."

A vicious snarl spread across Dimitri's face. It had been fifty years since anyone had managed to reliably get an Alcubierre-Stetson drive to accelerate more than one light year per day squared. He knew JD-Tech had been experimenting, and that the results of some of those experiments had been included in *Avalon's* engines. Even a tenth of a light year of extra velocity each day would make running down Kematian's murderers easy.

"Move our Q-probes in closer," he instructed Roberts. "I want to know everything about that ship – its name, its engine signatures, what the Petty Officer running Lance Six had for breakfast. *Everything*, Captain Roberts."

"Done and done."

Looking around at his flag deck crew, the Admiral realized his cold snarl had caught his staff's gaze, and they were all looking at *him*.

"Get me Captain Alstairs on a private implant link," Dimitri ordered harshly. "Inform me as soon as Vice Commodore Stanford and his people are aboard.

"I think we're going to be taking *Avalon* hunting."

20

Kematian System
03:00 January 1, 2736 Earth Standard Meridian Date/Time
DSC-078 Avalon *Main Flight Deck*

IT HAD BEEN a long and emotionally exhausting flight home.

Michael had set the computer to fly the simple course back to *Avalon* and tried to sleep, but it wasn't happening. Victory had turned to ashes in his mouth, and when he closed his eyes, his mind insisted on replaying his implant's picture-perfect record of the missiles striking home.

Having a good idea of what was going to be waiting once he returned to the ship, he'd eventually ordered his implant to force him to sleep. It wasn't as restorative as natural sleep, for reasons he was assured were as much psychological as anything else, but it let him feel somewhat rested as he settled his *Falcon* into its docking cradle and exited into the flight deck.

He was completely unsurprised to find Senior Chief Petty Officer Olivia Kalers waiting for him. His Acting Deck Chief with Hamond on medical leave was an older woman with a shaven head and a perma-nently sour expression.

"The Captain wants to see you," Kalers said quickly. "He wants me to make sure we have a detailed list of everything we need to bring the Group up to full strength by the time we hit orbit."

Stanford winced. They were still in the process of retrieving fight-ers, and the Kematians still hadn't retrieved all of his people's emer-gency pods. They would soon, he was assured, but there were a lot of escape pods in the debris of Force One's running battle with the Kema-tian Navy and subsequent destruction.

"Do your best," he told Kalers quietly. "Pull whatever resources you need – Stars know the crews coming back in could use a distraction."

"Wasn't their fault, sir."

"It wasn't anyone's fault but the Commonwealth's, Chief," Michael replied. "Keep an eye out for anyone who'll need to see Cunningham's people," he added after a moment's thought, shaking his head. "This isn't something everyone is going to be able to compartmentalize."

His only response was silence, and the CAG looked over at his Acting Deck Chief. Kalers's gaze was focused on the floor, and the woman looked old.

"Not sure I'm going to be able to compartmentalize," the Chief admitted. "My God, sir – *half a planet?!*"

"It's evil, Chief," Michael told her, very softly. "It's evil, and we will hunt down the bastard like the sick dog he is. But put yourself on that list for Cunningham," he ordered. "I need you fully functional."

"Will do, sir," Kalers acknowledged.

03:15 January 1, 2736 ESMDT
DSC-078 Avalon *Captain's Office*

MICHAEL ENTERED the Captain's office to find Solace and Roberts clearly in the middle of a video conference. Solace shushed him with a finger to her lips as he opened the door, then gestured him to a seat waiting for him.

Avalon's Executive Officer looked shattered. She was in full dress uniform – Michael was suddenly all too aware that he was still in his combat flightsuit – but the collar was askew and she'd spilled coffee on it at some point.

Roberts, on the other hand, looked as unflappable as ever. He gave Michael a small wave, but his attention was focused on the wallscreen showing a dozen other senior officers, and one old, exhausted, man in a business suit.

"I assure you, Mister President," Vice Admiral Tobin was saying, "we have no intentions of leaving Kematian unprotected! I am breveting Captain Alstairs to Force Commander and leaving all of Battle Group Seventeen except *Avalon* behind."

Force Commander was an odd rank, one that didn't appear on the tables and was never permanently granted. It acted as an O – Seven point Five, a brevet-only rank between the Federation's Captains and its Rear Admirals. The only reason for its existence was to allow an Admiral to designate a specific Captain to command a sub-force.

"Only *Avalon* has the upgrades to the Alcubierre drive that make a pursuit even remotely possible," Tobin told the President of Kematian.

"We need all the help we can get," the man told him. "With explosions of this size, my advisors are warning of catastrophic ecological damage, even on the side of the planet that was untouched."

"We have at least a partial solution to that," Captain Aleppo of the *Zheng He* told him. "The Factor had a terraforming expedition going on in an uninhabited system we'd claimed. Given the circumstances, we'd already ordered them back the Rembrandt system – but they can and have been re-directed.

"I am advised by my government that the terraforming vessel *Mona Lisa* should be arriving here within three days," she concluded. "They have the equipment and the specialists to be able to minimize the long-term damage."

The old man visibly slumped in relief.

"I will pass my thanks to your government," he said softly. "Whatever this service costs, we did not think such a team would be available in time."

"The Factor Board has already decided that we will carry the cost," Aleppo told him. "There are times and services when friends are more valuable than profit. This is one of those times."

"Vice Commodore Stanford has joined us," Roberts interrupted as everyone was silent for a moment to digest the somewhat unusual generosity of the Factor. Born of a union of corporations that owned planets rather than planetary governments, profit was always at least second or third in the Board's thought processes.

"Ah, good," Tobin replied, turning his gaze on the screen linking him to Roberts' office. The Admiral's eyes belied his energetic words and motions – they were bloodshot, surrounded by wrinkles Michael was certain hadn't been there before.

"*Avalon* cannot leave until your starfighter group is fully up to strength," the Vice Admiral told him. "I want to be on our way within two hours of making Kematian orbit – every hour, every minute, that passes runs the risk of that ship escaping us."

Before Michael could say anything, the Captain dropped a note onto his implant.

"We identified the battleship," he said. "*Triumphant*, one of the last *Resolutes* built. Intel is digging into the Captain."

"My staff are already working on a list," Michael told them. "Off the top of my head, we could use a munitions resupply, but our biggest issue is fighters and crews. I lost sixteen starfighters in the battle, and while half of those crews are fine, they won't catch up to us in that time frame."

"Force Commander Alstairs," Tobin said briskly, glancing at *Camerone's* commander. "Once we're in orbit, I'll want you to transfer pilots and crews from your own group to make up Stanford's strength."

"Understood, Admiral," the newly breveted Force Commander replied. "I presume you'll want complete squadrons?"

"If you've got them," Michael said cautiously. His own losses were scattered through his Wings, but he'd have a more functional weapon if he integrated two complete squadrons into his Group than if he tried to insert new fighter crews into his existing squadrons.

"Two of my squadrons took no losses," she confirmed. "I'll have them aboard *Avalon* as soon as we're in orbit and they've managed to catch some sleep."

"What about pursuit vectors?" Roberts asked. "Did we get a line on where *Triumphant* went FTL?"

"We did," a shaven-headed man in a dark burgundy uniform unfamiliar to Michael replied. A quick implant query informed him the man was the Fleet Admiral commanding the Kematian Navy – and currently aboard one of the cruisers sweeping the debris for survivors.

"We got our drones into position before the *bajingan* warped space," he continued. "Both *Triumphant* and the transports are on a vector for KG-779. It's a brown dwarf system, nothing there, but it makes a useful navigation relay."

"Captain Roberts," Tobin directed his attention back to the Captain. "Have you had a chance to discuss the Alcubierre upgrade with Commander Wong?"

"I have," the Captain replied. "And he and I both managed to raise Rear Admiral Klein, who's running the upgrade project back on Castle.

"The reasons the upgrades aren't being pushed to the entire Navy is that the speed boost is minimal," he continued. "We're talking one point one light years per day squared instead of one. It'll add up, though. We won't catch them at 779," the Captain warned. "But we *will* catch them."

That reassurance seemed to hit home as Michael saw a lot of nods and grim expressions that could charitably be called smiles on the wall.

"We'll be in orbit of Kematian in five hours," Tobin told the President. "We'll transfer fighters and munitions as necessary, and drop most of *Avalon's* small craft to assist in the search and rescue. By then, the convoy will also be inbound and set to rendezvous.

"I suggest that those of you who can get what you rest you can," the Federation Vice Admiral told his people, then glanced back to the Kematians. "Once we hit orbit, we're all going to be very busy."

Slowly, with a series of acknowledgements and final orders, the various screens winked out. When the screen faded back to plain metal at last, Roberts heaved a huge sigh of relief and turned his gaze on Stanford.

Somehow, despite everything, Roberts still looked energetic and engaged.

"Mira, go get some sleep," he ordered, taking in the shattered state of the XO. "Belmonte should be back on duty in an hour, I can hold the fort down until then. I'll need you fresh when we hit orbit."

"What about you, sir?" she asked, and Michael was surprised by her gentle tone.

"Rank hath its privileges – in this case, stimulants – and its detriments – in this case, too many duties," he replied cheerfully. "I'll sleep once we're en route out of the system. Go."

With a quick nod to both men, the exec slipped out of the room, leaving the two friends sitting together.

"Starless Void, what a disaster," Michael said quietly. "How bad, Kyle?"

"Twenty-four cities," Roberts replied, his voice equally quiet. "Average population fifteen million. But that's… being ignorant. One-gigaton explosions don't just hurt what they destroy. Ash. Acid. Debris. The regions for a hundred kilometers around each impact are toxic death zones. Including the countryside and smaller cities in the debris zones and those overlaps…"

The big Captain sounded more tired than Michael had heard him since they'd thought they were going to die at Tranquility.

"Current estimates are at half a billion dead and rising," he said simply. "If *Mona Lisa* arrives in time, they should be able to minimize the damage, but…" Roberts' hand closed on an empty coffee mug, and threw it against the wall in a convulsive motion.

"Even *minimized* Kematian could see a billion dead from this *massacre*," the big Captain snarled. "I could have stopped it. Should have argued harder. Dammit, Michael, we *failed*."

"We couldn't see this coming," Michael objected. "The Commonwealth's worst are usually the true believers, the ones willing to sacrifice anything for Unity – this is as Voids-cursed anathema to them as you or I.

"Even if *Triumphant* eludes us, the fucker won't survive," he told his friend. "Some of the higher ups might be willing to let it slide, but Starless Void knows Walkingstick *is* a true believer. This kind of blood doesn't help their cause, and he knows it."

"It changes nothing, Michael," his Captain replied. "Half a billion and more dead. What's revenge to that? What's *justice* to *that*?"

"You're not sleeping because you can't, aren't you?" Michael demanded. "This isn't your Voids-cursed *fault*, Captain Kyle Roberts," he snapped. "It isn't even Vice Admiral bloody Tobin's fault, though I bet you diamonds to donuts he's fighting the same demon you are."

Roberts quirked his lips in something that might have been a smile and bowed his head.

"I *also* have work to do," he said. "But you're not wrong."

"Then let's get to that work, boss," Michael told him. "Because one thing I do know – justice may be a frail shield against something like this, but by all the Stars, I still plan on killing the son of a bitch who did it."

21

Kematian System
10:00 January 1, 2736 Earth Standard Meridian Date/Time
DSC-078 Avalon *Bridge*

AVALON SPENT LESS than two hours in Kematian orbit, which was, in Kyle's opinion, about three lifetimes too long.

About the only positive of antimatter warheads used on a planetary target was the lack of radiation. When cities powered by fusion and fission reactors were the target that was a moot point. Combined with the immense craters blasted most of the way through the planetary crust, the continent that had suffered the brunt of *Triumphant's* anger was an uninhabitable hell-hole.

Hundreds of shuttles and aircraft braved the vicious hurricanes already forming across the entire planet to enter that hell-hole and bring people out. Unavoidably, not all of those craft survived their trips – which didn't stop any of them.

There were still hundreds of millions of people in the affected zone. The massive effort being launched by Kematian's people, now joined by the shuttles from Battle Group Seventeen, could save hundreds of thousands. Perhaps millions.

They couldn't save everyone.

There was *nothing* Kyle could do from orbit to help, either. *Avalon* had sixty-four non-starfighter small craft of various sizes, almost all of them capable of search and rescue. He'd kept eight of the mid-sized twenty thousand ton rescue tugs and sent the remaining ships down to help the planet. The desperate attempt to rescue *anyone* could use everything from the dozen five thousand ton SAR shuttles to his pair of hundred thousand ton drone tenders.

"All the fighters from *Camerone* are aboard and locked down," Stanford told him over the implant com. "Alstairs' people dropped off a munitions reload on their way down to the planet, too. We are fully stocked and prepared for operations."

"Thank you, CAG," Kyle acknowledged and glanced around his bridge. "Anything anyone hasn't mentioned to me yet?" he asked.

There were chuckles at that. Solace had rejoined him ten minutes after they'd hit orbit, and his people had done a fantastic job of getting everything moving and down to the planet. Any resource they could spare for Kematian had been loaded onto the shuttles heading out – everything from portable infirmaries to medical supplies to generators and decontamination units.

A Deep Space Carrier was designed to single-handedly fill the role of a wet navy carrier group, which meant it had a *lot* of seemingly random equipment aboard. It was rare for a carrier to find a situation the crew didn't have a tool for – and now thousands of tons of those tools had been deployed to the surface of Kematian.

Kyle had reviewed the ship's entire equipment list before they'd reached orbit and given most of the orders for deployment himself. He knew he'd micro-managed the process, his fingers far deeper into his senior officers' departments than he usually went, but this time, no one seemed to mind.

It was a poor sop against all of their consciences.

"Admiral, *Avalon* is prepared to move out," he told Tobin quietly. "Your orders?"

Operating as a Battle Group of one ship was always an awkward situation, but Kyle agreed with the Vice Admiral's logic. They only needed one ship to take down *Triumphant*, and *Avalon* was the only one that could catch her. The rest of their ships would be better used helping Kematian.

"No change, Captain," Tobin replied simply. "If we're ready, take us to KG-779. Do we have an ETA yet?"

Kyle glanced over at Pendez. "Commander?"

"We are four hours from warping space," she reported. "From there, to travel the nine light years to KG-779, we're looking at one hundred and thirty-seven hours. It will take *Triumphant* six full days, so we'll have a seven hour advantage and will enter the system five hours behind them.

"That's dependant on us being able to sustain one point one light years per day squared for the full period," Pendez warned. "We haven't tried this before, and it may not hold together for six days."

"Understood, Commander Pendez," Tobin rumbled. "Don't worry, Commander Wong gave us the same warning."

"In fact, Maria," Kyle interrupted, "I want you or your deputy in constant communication with engineering so long as we're pushing the drive. As *soon* as there is an issue, pull us back to one light year a day until Wong approves something different."

Vivid memories of the morgue that had been the bridge of another *Avalon* flashed through his mind, and he glanced over at Tobin's image on the screen.

"We won't do anyone any good if we die before we catch *Triumphant*," he reminded the Vice Admiral. "And one Alcubierre failure in a career is enough for anyone!"

"Agreed, Captain." The big Admiral looked tired, blinking heavily against bloodshot eyes. He was likely on the same stims as Kyle, but while they could keep you awake and reduce the functionality loss, they didn't stop you *feeling* tired.

"And if we're on our way," the Admiral continued after a moment, as if reading Kyle's mind, "*you*, Captain Roberts, should get some sleep. Commander Solace looks bright eyed and awake beside you."

Kyle glanced over at his XO, who did look *much* better after five hours sleep. There was the same haunted look in her eyes as everyone else on the ship, but she didn't look like she'd been run through a meat-grinder.

She turned a smile on him, and a shock ran through his system. For the moment at least, the statue was gone, and he was tired enough that what registered in his mind was that the woman sitting next to him was absolutely gorgeous.

He shook his head to clear the fuzz, and very carefully returned his gaze to the Admiral. "You're not wrong sir," he allowed, "though I would suggest a mirror as well."

Tobin laughed, a loud surprised rumble that shocked the entire bridge.

"You're also not wrong, Captain," he replied. "We'll talk once we're in FTL."

11:00 January 1, 2736 ESMDT
DSC-078 Avalon *Admiral Tobin's Quarters*

CORONA BURNED AROUND HIM. *A power conduit burned through, the resulting explosion throwing debris across the hallway. Shrapnel cut through Brown's torso, cleaving his Chief of Staff in two. Blood poured impossibly from the man's torso as Dimitri caught him.*

"It's all your fault," his aide told him, his bright blue eyes meeting his Admiral's gaze. "Look at it."

Somehow, the half of a man in Dimitri's arms gestured widely, and Tobin realized that the entire side of the ship was gone. Outside, he could see the blue-green skies of the planet below. He didn't recognize it for a moment, then the ugly splotches of immense mushroom clouds erupted from the surface.

"You're doomed, Dimitri," a softly accented voice told him. "Everything you try to protect will die. Like me."

Flight Lieutenant Karl Michaels-Tobin was dressed exactly as he had been the last fateful day Dimitri had seen him. The lanky blond man looked sad, with no sign whatsoever of the antimatter blast that had ended his life with no chance for his family to even see a body.

"You failed me," Karl snarled. "You failed Amaranthe. You fail everyone you try to protect – why do you keep trying?! Others would do better."

"Your arrogance killed me," Brown joined in the chorus. "It killed Kematian. Why, Admiral, why?!"

Behind him, more explosions marched across Kematian, a world he'd been supposed to save dying in fire as his lover and his friend repeated the same question:

"Why?"

———

DIMITRI FINALLY AWOKE with a start to his darkened cabin, sweating and cursing aloud as he fumbled for light. It was several seconds before he managed to marshal his brain into a coherent enough shape to issue an implant order.

Finally, the room lit up with a bright stark light that chased away nightmares. The Admiral sighed, stumbling from his bed to desk and pulling a bottle from the bottom drawer.

There were no real memories to play to shield against this kind of nightmare, he knew that from long ago. He poured himself a shot of vodka and considered the dream.

"Happy fucking New Year, Dimitri," he whispered to himself.

Downing the shot, and then a second one, he tried to steady his nerves. It had been *years* since his subconscious had dragged Karl's memory up as part of its attacks on his sanity. His husband was long dead. Karl's parents were god-parents to his and Sasha's children – they'd helped him move on and *find* Sasha after Karl's death.

The nightmares had been getting worse after Midori though. With Kematian... he shivered. He was afraid sleep was going to be hard to come by until he brought *Triumphant* to justice. He *needed* to avenge Kematian – he doubted anything less would let him sleep at night.

There was a quiet knock on his door and his implant informed him Commander Sanchez was outside.

"Enter!" he snapped. "What is it?"

His young blond aide saluted crisply, her precise uniform a sharp contrast to his own rumpled shipsuit.

"I had an alert set for when you woke up, sir," she told him. "Are you all right? You didn't sleep very long."

"I'm fine," he said shortly, slamming back a third shot of vodka. "I'll be back asleep in a few minutes. What do you need?"

"New dispatches came in from Alliance High Command, sir," she told him. "Not urgent enough to wake you, but they are your eyes only and require your authentication code so they may be important."

"Give them here," he ordered. He yanked the pad out of her hand, downloading his implant code.

"That's the wrong pad, sir," Sanchez said quickly, snatching back the datapad and replacing it with another. "That's my report on the Kematians' long-term logistical needs. It's not ready yet."

Blinking blearily against the alcohol and incipient exhaustion, Dimitri grabbed the new pad and unlocked it. This one did open up the list of dispatches, and he exhaled as if struck.

Kematian had held, though the price was beyond imagination or acceptance.

Two other systems hadn't. Battle Group Seventeen and the Kematian Navy had destroyed five Commonwealth capital ships without starship losses of their own.

The Toledo and Arsenault systems had bled the Commonwealth, but had fallen. Seven more Commonwealth capital ships had been destroyed, but so had nine Alliance ships.

His pursuit of *Triumphant* was authorized, but with a very strict time limit – if they hadn't caught up to the battleship in two weeks, they were ordered to return to Kematian and reassemble Battle Group Seventeen.

Alliance High Command couldn't let more systems fall without trying to retrieve them. It appeared that Battle Group Seventeen was to be part of that operation.

Regardless of the cost to Dimitri Tobin's soul if he had to let *Triumphant* go.

22

Deep Space, En route to KG-779
11:00 January 2, 2736 Earth Standard Meridian Date/Time
DSC-078 Avalon, *Executive Officer's Office*

IT WAS a depressed group of senior officers and NCOs that gathered in Solace's office the day after entering FTL. Michael had brought Kalers along to help speak for the Space Force personnel aboard the ship, and was pleased to see that Solace had invited Belmonte – and that Major Caleb Norup had brought Peng Wa.

Michael hadn't interacted much with the commander of the short battalion – four companies with no heavy weapons element – of Marines embarked aboard *Avalon* but the broad-shouldered man seemed solid enough. Master Sergeant Wa seemed to think so, anyway, which was enough for the CAG.

The seventh person in the room was Ship's Marshal Barsamian, and she looked at the collection of more senior officers and more experienced non-commissioned officers with a calm Michael wasn't sure he'd possess in her place.

"We have completed the process of taking the ship to Counter Intelligence Level Three," she said calmly. "Per the Code of Military Justice, we are required to inform all personnel inside a full communication review zone within twenty-four hours of the review commencing. Delivering that notice falls to the senior officers and NCOs of each service branch."

"I downloaded the message template before everything came apart at Kematian," Michael told the others. "This isn't my first go around with potential spies."

"It is mine," Solace replied grimly. "I'll take a copy of that template if you will, CAG."

"Of course."

The XO turned back to the Marines.

"For some reason," she continued calmly, "second-rate carriers and Home Fleet cruisers don't see many spies. I haven't been involved with any sort of counter intelligence sweep. What do we do next?"

"First, we monitor all communications and watch for *anything* suspicious," Barsamian explained. "This is honestly the part most likely to turn up something useful. Even knowing that messages are being monitored, conspirators have to communicate home somehow."

"What if they have a Q-Com linked to the Commonwealth network?" Solace asked. "That would bypass any attempt on our part to intercept, wouldn't it?"

"In theory," the Marshal allowed. "In practice, the *containment fields* necessary to maintain an entangled particle have a distinct energy signature that can be detected at distances of up to five or six hundred meters. Shipboard sensors automatically scan for them – and private Q-Coms are not permitted aboard warships."

"What else?"

"There are some smart programs we will run in the ship's surveillance systems to check for suspicious behavior," Barsamian told them. "They're notorious for false positives and not likely to turn out anything incredibly useful, but they may point us to something we might have missed."

"All of this is very vague and circumstantial at best," Solace noted. "Is there… something more active we should be doing?"

"Counterintelligence work is almost never active," Michael pointed out quietly. "Last time I went through this, we never caught the spy. It was peacetime, so we don't even know who they might have been working for. Void knows, there might have not even been a spy."

"This time, we are quite certain some form of enemy agent is aboard," Barsamian replied. "But the CAG is right, Commander. At this point, there is very little we can do to bring this agent into the open. All we can do is wait for them to act and be ready."

Peng Wa shook her head, the senior Marine NCO looking frustrated.

"Is there anything I can shoot in all of this?" she demanded, only half-joking from her tone of voice. "For that matter, are we sure this isn't tied into those rumors we were hearing about Sanchez?"

The office was silent for a very long moment, and then Michael finally spoke, very quietly.

"I don't think anyone in this room *likes* Sanchez," he said bluntly. "And I definitely think she is stirring up trouble in ways that are at the least… questionable.

"But her record and her history speak for themselves. Senior Fleet Commander Sanchez is a decorated officer with twelve years in Navy Intelligence. I don't *like* her," he repeated, "but I don't think her loyalty to the *Federation* can be questioned."

"Nonetheless, we need to keep an eye on that situation as well," Solace pointed out. "Sanchez speaks for Vice Admiral Tobin. It's possible that what we're hearing is exaggerated, a cynic's view of an attempt to get a feel for the officers under his command.

"But with one thing and another, my shoulderblades are feeling itchy," the XO told them all. "Worse, I don't think I'm the one being measured for the knife. We need to keep poking, people. If Sanchez *is* trying to put together some kind of fifth column of our crew and Marines, we need proof we can take to the Captain."

"Tobin's the Admiral," Norup objected. "Even if we can prove something, what can the Captain do?"

"This is Kyle's ship, not Tobin's, Major," the XO replied harshly, to a sharp nod of agreement from Michael. "Even Admirals have things they cannot do."

"If what rumor suggests is correct," Marshal Barsamian explained, "it would be within Captain Roberts' rights to arrest and detain both Sanchez and Vice Admiral Tobin for mutiny."

The room was silent again as everyone considered the firestorm that would ensue from that action.

"Mostly, I think *that* worry falls on you, Marshal," Michael said quietly. "The rest of us, well," he shrugged. "We need to worry about catching a battleship."

22:00 January 2, 2736 ESMDT
DSC-078 Avalon, *Captain's Office*

TECHNICALLY, Kyle was holding down the FTL dark watch, back-stopping Commander James Anderson.

Since, like many of *Avalon's* crew, Commander Anderson was an experienced and competent officer, Kyle had ordered the younger man to advise him if anything came up, setup a video link to the bridge, and settled down in his office to do paperwork.

While no one was going to question anything that had been dropped off on Kematian, or the starfighter transfers, or any of the activities of the scant hours they'd been in the system, all of it still needed to be recorded, tracked, and approved.

When Solace stepped into his office without bothering to buzz for admittance, he was glad for the interruption. He closed his files with a thought and an unnecessary gesture and regarded his executive officer as she closed the door behind her and took a seat in silence.

The shock in Kematian which had awoken his awareness of her attractiveness had faded, but the awareness hadn't. Tonight, though, she looked utterly drained. Her hair was uneven, looking in need of either being recropped or a *very* good stylist to make growing it out look good. She hadn't bothered with a uniform jacket, though her ship-suit had the distinctively perfect creases of one pulled directly from the refresher.

"Couldn't sleep?" he asked gently. His own dreams were starting to feature the destruction of Kematian alongside the memory of flying the old *Avalon* through a battleship and the wreckage inside *Ansem Gulf* after his old crew had retaken her from pirates. He couldn't imagine that Solace, for whom this had only been her second ever combat, was dealing any better.

"We just watched a world die, Captain," she replied, her voice soft and sad. "How... how could I even *begin* to sleep?"

"Your implant is perfectly capable of forcing you into dreamless sleep," he pointed out. "It isn't great in the long-term, but trust me, it's better than not sleeping at all."

Solace blinked, it clearly taking a minute for what he was saying to sink in.

"You too?"

"After *Gulf*," he agreed. "Then again after Tranquility. And now Kematian added in. Have you talked to Cunningham yet?"

She shook her head.

"Feels... weak," she confessed.

"There's a reason every Doctor on this ship is as rated for counseling as they are for trauma surgery," Kyle told her. "There's a lot, even ignoring counseling, that the Surgeon-Commander can do for you. Our implants have some useful functions for this – functions that are even better than we had in the last war."

He hadn't realized his bitterness over that had leaked into his voice until he saw her eyes narrow.

"That sounds personal, sir," she replied.

"Mira," he said gently, "it's the middle of a dark watch and we're in my office. You can call me Kyle."

"Very well... Kyle," she accepted. "But... what happened in the last war?"

He sighed and stood. The wallscreen behind him was blank, but he faced it and brought up an image of Amaranthe as he turned to face it.

"My father was in command of the Marine garrison assigned to the Federation Embassy on Amaranthe," he said quietly. "As the Terrans were landing, he was evacuating the Embassy personnel and anyone who'd come with him.

"He was leading from the front, with a company of Marines and almost two thousand civilians behind him, when the nano-weapon went off."

Kyle stared at the splotchy planet for a long moment.

"He escaped," he said finally, the memories rushing back of the official inquest after the suicide, and the recordings and reports he'd desperately watched and read as a teenager to try to find some kind of answer. "Most of his company, and almost all of the civilians they were escorting, didn't.

"Somehow, he held it together for years. Came home. Had me." He wasn't sure how Solace was taking this. She was silent behind him, and he was focused on the world that killed his father.

"Then, on the day the war ended, Major James Roberts blew his brains out with a service pistol, leaving behind a wife and an eight year old son. One of seven post-traumatic suicides from the Federal forces in the war."

"I'm sorry, Kyle," Solace said behind him. "I really didn't know."

"It's very specifically *not* in my service file, Mira," he replied. "We are shaped by what we survive, but I don't need or want pity for it. I do my job."

"How?" Solace's voice was torn. He turned to see her face was in her hands, but she looked back up at him. "We just watched a world die," she repeated. "Somewhere on this god-damn ship is a spy. The Admiral's staff is playing political games, and I'm not sure who I can even trust. How do we do the job like this?!"

"Because we swore an oath, and we put on the uniform," Kyle said gently as he crossed over to her. "We can't control the politics. We can't magically find the spy. So we go on. We factor them into our decisions, we remember who we can trust, and we do our job."

"I don't even know who I can trust," she admitted. "I've never dealt with a spy, or this kind of political *bullshit!*"

The shouted curse echoed in the office, and Kyle turned his best shit-eating grin on his executive officer. Apparently, there was *definitely* a human being in the statue. He stepped over to his fridge and dragged a pair of cups of tea from the dispenser.

"We can trust the crew to do their jobs," he told her. "Beyond that? I trust Michael, I trust Belmonte and Kalers – because Hammond recommended her, if no other reason – and I trust you. Everything else is chain of command – I can't not trust my crew because there's one bad apple. I *need* them – and they need me to trust them."

"I haven't exactly been giving you excuses to trust me," she pointed out, taking the cup gratefully.

"You've given me no reason not to, Mira," Kyle said softly. "So you haven't been the friendliest or warmest officer I've ever worked with – so what? You've being doing your job, and you've been doing it well.

"You were dumped on this ship with no warning, told you were expected to fill an inexperienced Captain's holes, and then handed your third male Captain in a row. When the previous list includes one of the most flamboyantly homosexual Captains in the Navy and a man who tried to use his position to *rape* you, a little distance was inevitable."

"That isn't in my file either," Solace replied, looking down at her tea.

"I read between the lines," Kyle said. "And I've heard stories about Captain Haliburt. Any Captain who has JD-Personnel marking his reports as of questionable worth should be drummed out of the Navy."

"He's always on the right side of the line," his exec said quietly. "Just barely. He knows just where it sits."

"It won't save him in wartime," Kyle promised. "Mira, I understood why you needed distance. I needed you to work with me – and you did. So I trusted you. Anything else..." he made a throwaway gesture and spilled tea on himself.

"Crap."

That seemed to work. Senior Fleet Commander Mira Solace disintegrated into schoolgirl *giggles* as he dabbed desperately at his uniform with a napkin.

Once he'd finished cleaning himself up, and she'd regained composure, she leveled the same smile that was causing him issues at him again.

"Thank you for understanding, Kyle. It shouldn't have been necessary, and it is *very* appreciated."

She offered her hand across the desk and he took it, feeling the firmness of her grip and the warmth of her skin.

"Partners, then?" he asked aloud, remembering Pendez's words.

"Partners," she agreed. "Gives me a starting point for who to trust."

He lifted his teacup in a mock toast: "To partners – and *damnation to the Commonwealth!*"

23

Deep Space, En route to KG-779
09:00 January 5, 2736 Earth Standard Meridian Date/Time
DSC-078 Avalon, *Main Engineering Bay*

THE MAIN ENGINEERING bay of the new *Avalon* was smaller than her flight deck by a significant margin. There was no other open space on the ship that rivaled it, though it hardly *felt* as immense as it was. Machinery ran along every side of it, and *Avalon's* array of primary zero point cells ran along the center of the bay.

The bay, and the warrens of tunnels, capacitors, fuel tanks, antimatter reactors and engines that wove through the entire ship like veins and muscles, were the domain of Senior Fleet Commander Alistair Wong.

"I see you finally made your way down to the dungeon," that worthy told Kyle as the Captain entered the bay, as if the inspection hadn't been scheduled for two weeks.

"I *still* think the dungeon is Barsamian's brig," Kyle pointed out, glancing around at the gleaming equipment and reporting stations at

Wong's command center. "Everything ship-shape? I believe there's some kind of *inspection* scheduled."

"Oh crap, I *knew* there was something I was supposed to tell my crew!" Wong exclaimed.

Kyle shook his head and grinned, looking *past* his Chief Engineer to the neatly drawn up ranks of those members of the current engineering shift not doing anything critical. He *knew* engineers – there was no way this many of them were clean an hour into their shifts by *accident*.

"As it happens," Kyle told the crew, "Commander Wong and I have a little bet. He tells me that he's pulled together the cleanest, most efficient engineering department in the Navy. I think you're *good*, don't get me wrong, but I served on *Federation* herself back when I was a fresh Space Force pilot. I really don't know if you're better than the Navy flagship!

"But since I always put my money where my mouth is, there's a *very* large case of beer – conveniently, enough for everyone in engineering – riding on this inspection. Shall we get started?"

"Right this way, sir," Wong gestured for Kyle to head into the center of the engineering center. Displays surrounded him, permanently fixed to show the energy densities of the zero point cells, temperatures of the antimatter secondary plants, and capacity of the positron capacitors.

Everything critically important was instantly visible. More information was easily available to the engineering team via their implants, but this was still the nerve center of engineering, which made it the beating heart of *Avalon* to the bridge's brain.

"How're the engines holding up?" Kyle asked quietly. Three days of pushing the ship ten percent past its rated faster-than-light acceleration put an extra edge on the importance of this inspection.

"Not as well as I'd hoped, not as poorly as I'd feared," Wong replied. "We'll make it to KG, but…"

"I don't like 'buts' with the Alcubierre Drive, Wong."

"We'll be fine," the Engineer replied sharply. "But I don't think we're going to want to do a full ten points over again. She can *take* it, but... well, she can *take* a mass driver hit. Doesn't mean it's good for her."

"We need to catch that battleship," Kyle pointed out. "If it isn't possible, I'll take that hill for you, Commander, but..."

"I didn't say we can't go faster than that ten year old hunk of rust," Wong snapped. "I said we shouldn't go ten points over after this trip. *Five* should be perfectly safe."

"All right," the Captain allowed with a sigh of relief. "Not a hill I want to die on with the Admiral. I *want* that fucker."

"So does the entire crew," Wong replied. "My best guess is that we can run at ten points for about fifteen days, after which we'd need to recalibrate the stabilizers and the Class One manipulators. That's a *three week* process, Captain. We're burning most of those days getting to KG, but we should be good for almost as long as normal with re-calibrating at five points."

"Should be good enough. If we can't catch them with a five percent acceleration edge..."

"That's your problem, Captain," the Engineer replied quietly. "I'll guarantee that five percent edge. Anything more..." He shrugged.

Kyle glanced over the displays. They were similar to, though far more complex than, the equivalent displays and implant feeds on a starfighter. The difference was more a matter of scale than anything else, so he really could tell at a glance that everything on the ship was running well within tolerances.

"Shall we get to that tour, then?" he asked. "I need to at least *look* at your people's work before I agree with you and give them the beer."

"Let's start with the main zero point cells," Wong agreed, leading the way down the row of immense spherical power cells, each sixty meters in diameter. Inside each, incredibly powerful magnetic fields spun through the 'quantum soup,' extracting the charged particles from the constant creation and destruction of particles that formed the background of the universe.

"Every cell is running at one hundred percent efficiency," the Engineer told Kyle. "Obviously, we're not running at a hundred percent capacity – we would only ever go past ninety-five percent if we were under heavy missile attack and firing every laser aboard."

Only *Avalon's* missile defense lasers would actually draw from the ship's main reactor. Her positron lances were zero point cells all on their own, and actually fed power *back* into the ship's grid when they fired – the electrons pulled out of vacuum to offset the positrons they shot into space.

"Any problems down in engineering?" Kyle asked as they walked up to and checked over each of the massive cells. "I'm leaving the hunt for our spy to Solace and Barsamian, but I hear rumors."

"I know the ones," Wong said grimly. "None of my NCOs or juniors have said anything, but that doesn't mean much if someone's talking... trouble. It's not like Stanford or Hammond suspected O'Madden."

Kyle nodded as he stepped around the cell. A work-cart, loaded with tools, sat in the way. It was the first item out of perfect place in the tour, and he frowned slightly. If someone was working on the big zero point cell, where were they?

He was stepping forward to investigate when Wong came out from behind the cell.

"What the hell?" he demanded. Spotting Kyle's motion, he slammed a heavy hand on his Captain's shoulder and *yanked* Kyle back. "That should *not* be there," he snapped.

"It's just a work-cart," Kyle pointed out.

Before Wong even finished opening his mouth, the cart exploded. Kyle instinctively used the momentum from the Engineer's pull to charge backwards, slamming into the other man and bringing them both to the ground.

A moment later, what he *thought* was a wrench ricocheted off the extremely powerful reactor next to him, centimeters above his head.

Silence reigned for a long moment. Then the screaming started.

16:00 January 5, 2736 ESMDT
DSC-078 Avalon, *Captain's Break-out Room*

"WHAT THE FUCK IS GOING ON?" the Admiral demanded from the head of the table.

Arguably, internal security of the ship was Kyle's problem, but having just had someone try to assassinate him, he was a little less willing to argue than usual. This time, at least, Sanchez was busy somewhere else and Tobin had only inserted himself into the meeting.

"Someone appears to be attempting to assassinate key senior officers aboard this ship," Barsamian told the Admiral calmly. "First the CAG, now the Captain. We were lucky today – the bomb was next to a major positron cell, and those are armored to withstand *anything*. We have four injured people, but no significant damage to engineering itself.

"Whoever this is, they are extremely professional with a full suite of modern intelligence tools," she continued. "We pulled the camera from the engineering bay. The footage is all there. That work-cart isn't."

"That's not possible," Wong objected. "That would require…"

"Some sort of program or macro actively editing in real-time, most likely," she agreed.

"Another virus, then," Tobin rumbled.

"There is no sign of a virus," Barsamian told him. "After the prior incident, it was the first thing we checked for. So far as we can tell, there are no signs of any kind of intrusion, back door use, or viral infection in the computer systems in engineering.

"It appears that someone with full authority to edit that footage loaded a semi-intelligent macro that followed a specific item of some kind and removed any object that item was attached to. From the moment the object – whatever it was – was attached to the work-cart, that cart was invisible."

She shook her head. "We tried to validate when it disappeared, but it appears to have been at some point while the unit was in storage with several dozen other carts. Given that we can't detect the exact moment of it disappearing from our systems, we suspect it was obscured from the camera – and that is likely why that specific cart was chosen."

"There's only so many people with that authority, Major," Kyle pointed out. "Does that help us restrict down our list of suspects?"

"Sir, *nobody* with that authority is aboard this ship," the Marshal said flatly. "Shipboard surveillance is coded as read only, it should not be editable, and there is a physical, uneditable backup."

"Like I said, it's not possible," Wong pointed out. "They're intended to provide an unquestionable record of events for inquiries, reviews and courts martial."

"Nonetheless, the soft versions have been edited," Barsamian said quietly. "The hard backup is corrupt. The last three *days'* worth of footage in the disks is gone. We didn't notice because we normally use the soft copies, and the failsafe to inform us the data was corrupting had been disabled."

"By who?" Tobin demanded.

"*That* footage is gone," she admitted. "I understand this does not look good on my department, but, again, we are clearly dealing with an extremely well equipped professional.

"In theory, you could use high enough level access to create a root account on the ship's systems that would allow you to pull this off and look like a legitimate user," she concluded.

"How high, Major?" Kyle asked. He was tired, his shoulder hurt where Cunningham had extracted shrapnel, and he figured he could guess what the answer was.

"Yourself or the Vice Admiral," Barsamian said flatly. "You were the target, and, well, to be blunt sirs, neither of you have the technical skill to pull this off."

"I'd feel insulted, but since your judgment is that I didn't commit treason, I'll live with it," Tobin grumbled. "But you're telling me that we have *no* idea who has now tried to assassinate *two* officers on this ship?"

"That is correct, sir," the Marshal sighed. "I wish we were having more success, but to be honest, my people's skillset is closer to small town cops than counterintelligence operatives."

"Sir," Kyle said quietly, "Unless you object, I intend to take the ship to CI Level Two."

Counter Intelligence Level Two meant *no* personal messages left the ship. Even the more non-essential portions of the ship's communication with the Navy were suspended. It also involved personnel on Castle filtering and reviewing even those messages.

Level Two was an active presumption that the ship was compromised.

"Very well, Captain," the Admiral said softly. "Take us dark."

24

Deep Space, En route to KG-779
17:00 January 6, 2736 Earth Standard Meridian Date/Time
DSC-078 Avalon, *Flight Country Mess*

THE SOUND of crashing furniture from the main officer mess in Flight Country wasn't really a surprise to Michael. The only real question was who was fighting whom.

"What is going on here?" he bellowed, channeling as much of Roberts' energy and volume as he could as he burst into the mess hall. It had a gratifying quieting effect on the occupants of the room, two of whom froze in the act of trying to put each other through the remnants of the table they'd already snapped in half.

Michael surveyed the frozen scene, trying to put enough disdain into his movements to make clear how badly his people had screwed up. The mess hall wasn't an overly decorative portion of the ship – that was reserved for the ship's three carefully maintained 'Officers' Lounges' – and the long tables and uncomfortable chairs were cheap plastic.

One of those tables had clearly had someone body-slammed onto it, and said cheap plastic had snapped under the impact. Two men, both Flight Lieutenants with, he sighed, pilot's wings insignia were half-crouched in the middle of the debris field as the rest of the room's occupants were gathered around.

The situation had not yet degraded into a mass brawl at least, and it didn't even look like blood had been drawn or bones broken. That opened his options up a *lot*.

"Well?" he demanded, walking into the room and carefully stepping over the shattered remnants of a chair. "Does *someone* have an explanation for this mess?"

Flight Lieutenant Ivan Kovalchick was an old *Avalon* hand. The big blond kid had served under Roberts as Wing Commander before the Captain's transfer to the navy, and he'd spent most of the last two years under Michael's command.

The other combatant was Flight Lieutenant Antonio Zupan, a whipcord-thin snake of a man with black eyes, black hair and tanned-dark skin marked with tattoos where his sleeves were rolled up. He had, until a few days ago, served aboard *Camerone*.

"This lying… jerk," Michael *heard* Kovalchick censor himself, "says we've got a spy aboard and it's one of us," the youth gestured to one side of the room.

The CAG didn't sigh aloud when he realized the room was clearly split between the original *Avalon* flight crews and the new squadrons transferred from *Camerone*.

"And?" he asked patiently.

Kovalchick flushed.

"None of us are traitors!" the youth snapped, directed more at Zupan than his CAG. "More likely this new bunch have a *snake* in their midst!"

The ex-*Camerone* pilot started to open his mouth, but Michael held up a hand.

"Ivan," he said quietly, "we had a spy aboard before these boys and girls came aboard. We *know* that. So Mister Zupan is correct in that it's more likely to be one of the old hands than the new."

Michael turned to Zupan and leveled a hopefully cold gaze on that pilot.

"On the other hand, I would *hope* my pilots had enough Voids-cursed *sense* not to be picking fights," he snapped. "You were about to say Ivan here swung first?"

Zupan nodded.

"Tell it to the Starless Void. You provoked him, he hit you. Sounds about fair in my books," Michael told the pilot.

To his surprise, the man laughed, and nodded.

"Can live with it," he said, and offered Kovalchick a hand.

Hesitantly, the younger man took it. Despite being at most two thirds of the blond's size, Zupan easily hauled the other to his feet and out of the mess of the table.

Michael nodded to them both and took the *immediate* issue as settled. He turned back to face the crowd and shook his head. Sixty people in this room, most of them pilots, though he spotted a few gunners and engineers.

All of the ex-*Camerone* pilots, he noted, but the old hands were a mix from all his wings. Anything he said was going to get back to everyone, and damned fast too.

"Look around you," he told them. There were a lot of sheepish faces obeying him, but he needed to drive his point home, and hard.

"Everyone around you is starfighter flight crew. That means if we go into real action, between a tenth and a third of the people in this room won't come home," he reminded them flatly. "You all took this job because you don't think it'll be you.

"But do you really think a Commonwealth spy would be willing to ride fire alongside you?"

The chuckles and denials and headshakes took a moment, but they came. His people were fighters – they *knew*, in the sort of bone-deep certainty that would deny even obvious evidence, that no spy would fly alongside them. That no spy could do what they did.

"These people will be riding fire beside you when we catch Kematian's killers," Michael told them. "You need to trust them – because whether you trust them or not, your life will be in their hands.

"There isn't a pilot, a gunner, or an engineer in this fighter group I wouldn't trust behind me in a starfighter. That ought to be good enough for all of you."

The room was quiet, but he could tell he'd made his point.

All he could do now was hope that the spy really *wasn't* one of his.

17:00 January 6, 2736 ESMDT
DSC-078 Avalon, *Vice Admiral Tobin's Office*

DIMITRI SHOOK his head as he reviewed the sheaf of reports on the latest datapad Sanchez had given him.

"The first is my assessment of the action in Kematian," she told him. "I have reviewed the suggestions laid out by Captain Roberts and the others."

"And?" he asked.

"Had we followed Roberts' suggestion, the Kematian Navy would have been destroyed, with potentially no difference to the fate of the planet," Sanchez laid out. "*Triumphant* could have launched before the fighter group caught them, ending in the same result for the planet. Bluntly, sir, his stratagem would have sacrificed the Kematian Navy for nothing."

Dimitri laughed and shook his head again.

"You really don't like him, do you?" he asked.

"Sir?"

"Captain Roberts was *right*," he snarled. His self-loathing *wanted* to believe her, but he knew she was wrong. "*Triumphant's* attack was almost certainly a direct response to the destruction of Force One. By the time we engaged, the KN had demonstrated that they were able to drag the fight out for *hours* – more than long enough for us to neutralize *Triumphant* and return to Force One.

"We – I – ignored the vulnerability of the planet, and half a billion civilians paid for it," he said grimly. "I can't imagine what kind of mental gymnastics it took to try to make Captain Roberts look in the wrong there."

He tossed the datapad back to her, part of him *enjoying* her taken aback look. While she'd earned that strip the hard way, he knew he was mostly unleashing his self-hatred at her. It felt disturbingly good.

"So, like I said, you really don't like Roberts, do you?" he snapped. "Is it going to be a problem?"

This obviously hadn't been the response she'd been expecting to her report. Sanchez was gaping at him like a shocked goldfish.

"Sir, he is an inexperienced youth, promoted past his competence or proven capabilities," she said sharply. "He has no respect for you, your rank or your people!"

"As Commander Solace pointed out to me a while back, Captain Roberts earned his planet the hardest way possible – winning a battle no one else could have," Dimitri replied harshly. "He may not have experience at sitting in orbit dealing with bored spacers, but he's one of the most combat-experienced officers we have. The only person on this ship with *more* combat experience, in fact, is me."

His Chief of Staff was silent, and he glared at her for a long moment. Finally, she glanced aside, and he continued flatly.

"He has not exerted any privilege with regards to you and the rest of my staff that is not the prerogative of a Captain. I will *not* stand for you attempting to undermine him with me – and yes, Commander, I know what you're doing. I came by the gray hairs honestly, and I've seen this bullshit before."

Sanchez looked back up, and her eyes were hard and fierce.

"He won at Tranquility by being *reckless*," she snapped. "He is too familiar with his officers, too unthinking in his aggression. That man is *dangerous* to have in command of a warship of the Federation!"

That rocked Dimitri back in his chair. He hadn't expected Sanchez to be quite so… vehement in her opinion of Roberts.

"Commander, I'm only going to say this once," he said, his voice flat, cold, and quiet. She had to lean into hear him, and he met her ice blue eyes calmly. "*I* do not agree with you on this. Alliance High Command does not agree with you on this.

"If you continue to attempt to undermine my Flag Captain with me, or if I discover that you're, God-forbid, trying to undermine him with his *crew*, you will be off my staff and out of the loop so fast you'll be wondering what planet fell on you.

"Am I clear?"

She dropped her gaze to his desk, but said nothing.

"I said, Commander: *Am. I. Clear?*"

"Yes, sir," she ground out.

25

Deep Space outside the KG-779 System
06:30 January 7, 2736 Earth Standard Meridian Date/Time
DSC-078 Avalon, *Flag Deck Conference Room*

KYLE HELD his steaming cup of coffee carefully, warming his hands as he watched his and Tobin's senior officers enter the briefing room. It was early in the ship's day, but with barely forty-five minutes until they emerged in KG-779, anyone with complaints was keeping them to themselves.

Once Wong and Anderson trickled in, the last of the ten senior officers aboard the ship to arrive, Kyle rose to get their attention.

"If everyone has their caffeine of choice to wake up, we can begin," he said crisply. "We're coming up the KG-779 system. If we're lucky, we'll find *Triumphant* somewhere in system where we can intercept her.

"Unfortunately," he warned the others, "the likely situation is that the Commonwealth is only using KG as a waypoint. It is possible that *Triumphant* has already left, and even if she is still in the system, she's likely to be far enough out that she can initiate Alcubierre before we can bring her to into weapons range.

"While catching *Triumphant* would be preferable, our *objective* is to find where she went from here," Kyle concluded. "We will not be able to sustain the same acceleration advantage that has brought us here so soon after *Triumphant* going forward. Commander Wong's assessment," he nodded to his engineer, "is that we can safely sustain one point zero five light years per day squared. A five percent edge adds up fast – but a ten percent edge added up faster.

"We will be deploying Q-Com equipped probes as soon as we enter the system, and if necessary, I intend to self-destruct those Q-probes rather than retrieving them," Kyle concluded. "I do not intend to remain in KG-779 any longer than we have to."

He looked around the room.

"Any questions?"

When no one responded, he nodded to Tobin's Intelligence Officer. "Intelligence has, as usual, cut things down to the wire. Commander Snapes received an update on *Triumphant* less than an hour ago. If you could update us, Commander?"

The Lieutenant Commander, a tall and slim woman with jet-black hair and Asiatic eyes, stood and activated the hologram in the middle of the conference table.

"While we keep at least some information on file on all Commonwealth ships, *Triumphant* wasn't deployed anywhere near us six months ago," she told everyone. "Central Intelligence had to dig deep into their archives, and see what data they could beg, borrow, or steal from our allies.

"In the end, we identified Captain Jonah Richardson as the commanding officer of *Triumphant*."

An image appeared in the middle of the table. Richardson was a pudgy man of just below average height, with thinning and faded brown hair. In his Commonwealth Navy file photo, he had a mildly bemused expression.

He looked like somebody's favorite uncle, not a mass-murdering lunatic.

"Captain Richardson was promoted to O-6 five months ago, and given command of *Triumphant* when she was transferred to the Rimward Marches," Snapes continued. "For those who aren't up to date with Commonwealth policy, they assign starship commands to O-6s instead of the O-7 most Alliance navies feel is necessary."

Kyle, for all that he had the same *title* as Captain Richardson, actually outranked the man. The Federation had long ago felt that the scale of a starship's independence, firepower, and crew numbers meant that the ship needed a senior officer with an experience level older navies would have required of their most junior flag officers.

"Richardson has served in their Navy for fifteen years," Snapes continued. "His last duty prior to command of *Triumphant* was commanding a guardship squadron at the New Krishna Navy Base. While on assignment there, he picked up no less than three reprimands for the use of excessive force to keep civilians away from the Navy Base."

"Before anyone leaps to conclusions, by Commonwealth standards that basically means he fired a warning shot," Tobin pointed out. "At least in their own territory, they're damned careful of their force levels."

"Indeed," Snapes allowed. "The most important detail of his service at New Krishna for our purposes, however, is that is where he met his wife."

Kyle had a sudden sinking feeling as he realized where this was going, and the Intel Officer nodded as she saw the officers catching the hint.

"He and Commander Janet Richardson were married a little less than a year ago," she said quietly. "Commander Richardson was the Executive Officer of the battleship *Saint Christopher*, which was destroyed at Kematian. At the last information from Kematian authorities, we have definitely identified all officers retrieved from the escape pods.

"Commander Richardson was not one of them. She died with her ship."

"That justifies nothing," Tobin snapped, the Admiral then looking somewhat abashedly around the room.

"No-one is saying it does, sir," Kyle said gently. "But understanding what drove our enemy to this kind of vicious stupidity helps us catch him."

"Agreed," Snapes replied. "My guess is that what we saw in Kematian was the result of a moment of bloodlust, revenge, and mob mentality on the bridge of a modern warship.

"Our reports are that Walkingstick has been apprised of what happened by the transport captains. It is extraordinarily unlikely that he will let this stand."

"I have no intention of trusting *Walkingstick* to handle justice for Kematian," Tobin said grimly. "We'll burn this Richardson before he makes it home."

"We need to be prepared for Richardson to react in ways we might not regard as rational, sir," Snapes told the Admiral. "We can all-but-assume he had some form of psychotic break – and his crew went along with him.

"This is a man who has already demonstrated a willingness to commit mass murder, with a crew that has already followed him into the worst crime they could commit.

"What is that man going to do when we call on him to surrender?" she asked softly. "Hell, what is he going to do if the *Commonwealth* calls on him to surrender? He'll know as well as I do that anyone who takes him is going to shoot him."

"This could get very ugly, very fast," Solace said softly. "If he decides he can't go home, and the Alliance is to blame for his wife's death… *Triumphant* is a modern battleship. With nothing to lose, they could do a *lot* of damage before we bring them down."

"Then let's make damn sure we bring him down first," Tobin rumbled. "Starting here, in KG-779."

KG-779 System
07:15 January 7, 2736 ESMDT
DSC-078 Avalon, *Bridge*

"WE HAVE FULL SHUTDOWN," Pendez reported. "Class Ones are on cooldown, all stabilizers are powered down and safed. We have entered the KG-779 system."

"Thank you," Kyle told her, studying his implant and the screens around him. They were currently showing the computer's estimate of where the system's trio of lonely planets were and not much else.

KG-779 was an old, dying, star. It had one rocky planet too close in to be of use, and two massive gas giants who had, according to the astronomers' best guess, eaten each other's moons over the eons.

"Commander Anderson?"

"Passives are pulling in data now," his Tactical Officer replied. "We'll have updated details... now."

The data being fed to his optic nerve by his implant updated, a ripple spreading through the image of the solar system as the computer processed the light it was receiving. As ships appeared, the system tagged each one with the age of the light they were seeing – without Q-probes they were limited to old-fashioned speed of light.

"What are they *doing*?" he heard Solace ask aloud.

He was wondering the same thing. There were four ships on the screens – *Triumphant* and the three assault transports she'd been escorting at Kematian. The three transports were together and moving *fast*. They were already a full light hour into the system and dropping into the gravity well at almost three hundred gravities.

Triumphant was well behind them, still in a region where they could enter Alcubierre Drive if they wanted, but also on a vector that would stop any attempt by the transports to *leave*.

"If I didn't know better, and I'm not sure I do right now," Kyle responded brightly, "I'd say the transports are running from *Triumphant*, and that Richardson is trying to keep them trapped in the system while keeping his options open."

"Well, he's a lot closer to us than the transports are," Solace pointed out. "They won't see us for an hour – he'll see us in ten minutes."

"Anderson. If we fire *now* how close will our missiles be when he sees us?"

"Still basically ten light minutes away, sir," the redheaded officer replied. "To hit him at this range, we'd need an extended ballistic leg –

we're talking multiple hour flight time." Anderson shook his head. "I'm sorry, sir, but unless they *want* a fight, there's no way we can engage them before they jump out."

"I figured," Kyle noted. "Commander Pendez, take us after him anyway. Let's not push the engines though – let's save our sprint for when we have a chance of catching the bastard."

The big carrier smoothly set into motion, a soft trembling running through her hull as the mass manipulators offset her acceleration.

"Vector our probes in as close as possible, Commander," he told Anderson softly. "I want the best sensor data we can get when he goes FTL."

"On it. We've got six Q-probes heading his way at five hundred gravities, and two more dropping in on the transports."

"Should we be doing something about those, sir?" Solace asked quietly.

"I'd love to," Kyle acknowledged, "but there's nobody closer than Kematian, and they're a little busy. We could force them to surrender with Stanford's fighters, but then we'd have to fly escort to take them anywhere useful."

"Which is not happening, Captain, Commander," Tobin interjected. "Those assault troops are useless without starships to clear their way into a system. I'm more concerned about taking out a modern battle-ship and avenging Kematian than neutralizing a few dozen thousand troops, when the Commonwealth has literally *millions* of soldiers to send."

"He's right, Commander," Kyle told her. "The Commonwealth is far more restricted in terms of transport and spaceborne firepower than they are in ground troops. Some of their occupation garrisons are over a million strong. Those *transports* almost have more strategic value than the thirty thousand troops aboard."

"Besides, let's be honest, this whole trip is about revenge, not strategy," the Admiral pointed out. "Our job is to blow *Triumphant* to hell and make it *damned* clear no one gets away with what they did."

That was enough to silence both the bridge and flag deck for several minutes. Then, finally, Anderson sighed aloud.

"There we go," he said. "Right on schedule – emergence plus twenty minutes."

A moment later, Kyle saw what his officer had seen. *Triumphant* had – roughly ten minutes ago now – rotated in space and set course outwards at two hundred plus gravities.

"How close do our probes need to be for us to nail down his escape vector?"

"We either need a probe within two light minute for an exact reading, or three at least a light minute apart from each other to triangulate," Anderson told him. "Close or wide – we need another thirty minutes for wide – or almost two hours to get a probe close enough."

"You've got Q-probes going for both?"

"Of course," the Tactical Officer sounded almost offended, which Kyle gave him. He *was* micro-managing.

Seconds ticked away as Kyle watched *Triumphant* on the display. The battleship was flying directly away from them, which wasn't going to take them anywhere. It was almost as if they weren't quite sure *where* to go.

"He's running scared," *Avalon's* Captain said quietly. "No idea where to go."

"Ten more minutes," Anderson replied. "I hope he stays…"

"Damn," Solace cursed, interrupting the junior officer. "There he goes."

On the screen, *Triumphant's* crew had made up their mind where they were going. Her headlong flight from *Avalon* stopped as she rotated in space. A moment later, she vanished in a bright blue blast of Cherenkov radiation.

"Anderson?" Kyle asked softly.

"They jumped too soon, sir," the other man admitted. "I don't have an exact vector."

26

"THAT'S NOT ACCEPTABLE, COMMANDER," Dimitri snapped, staring at the screen showing him the bridge in shock. "We did not chase them this far to lose them now!"

"I didn't say we'd *lost* them," Anderson objected. "I said we don't have an *exact* vector. I'm running the analysis of where they could be headed now."

Dimitri waited impatiently. They'd been prepared to pursue if *Triumphant* had already left; how long could it take to track them when they'd been *right there*?

"This isn't good," *Avalon's* Tactical Officer finally admitted. "Depending on how far they're going, the vector gives me twenty-two systems – most in Commonwealth space."

Opening his mouth to start cursing, the Admiral paused, took a deep breath, and forced himself to count to ten. By the time he was done, Captain Roberts was speaking.

"What I'm hearing is: we need more data," the Captain said far more cheerfully than Dimitri found believable. "Tell me what you need, James – we are bringing this bastard down."

"Old light, sir," Anderson replied instantly. "We need to jump out ahead of the light of their Alcubierre jump and setup a set of widely dispersed probes. It... will take some time."

"We still have a five percent edge in FTL acceleration on them," Roberts pointed out, as much to Dimitri as Anderson, the Vice Admiral suspected.

"Better we're late to the right system and have to chase them again, then we end up a dozen light years or more away from them," he finally rumbled. "Get on it, Roberts. I *want* these sons of bitches."

"You and everyone else on this ship, sir," Roberts replied.

Dimitri grumpily allowed the Captain and his bridge crew to get to work, pulling up Anderson's data himself.

The Tactical Officer wasn't wrong on how wide a net they'd cast. With the Q-probes and *Avalon* as distant as they'd been, there was a fifteen degree by fifteen degree cone in which *Triumphant* could have actually jumped to FTL.

Most of that cone was in Commonwealth space. There were systems in the list whose defenses they couldn't risk taking *Avalon* in against – though those were all weeks and weeks away.

He didn't like the delay, but Roberts was right. They needed more data. There was no way in Hell he was going to let Richardson get away.

———

"WE ARE LAUNCHING a new set of Q-probes now," Anderson announced.

A forty-five minute Alcubierre jump had put *Avalon* two light hours out from *Triumphant's* exit point. Dimitri watched as another set of four Q-Com equipped probes shot into space.

This set wouldn't be any more retrievable than the last set, putting the cost of just the self-destructed Q-probes into the hundred million Stellar range. Cheap compared to even a starfighter, the Q-probes still cost more than capital ship missiles.

All four probes shot away from the carrier at five hundred gravities. With an hour and a quarter to get into position, the little robotic ships would give *Avalon* a set of triangulation points over twelve light minutes apart.

Time ticked by slowly. The top shift was on both the bridge and flag deck, and they went about their tasks quietly, despite the ratcheting tension.

Dimitri tried not to grumble openly, though he was certain his ill-concealed impatience wasn't helping anyone's tension. He kept reviewing the list of potential systems that Anderson had identified, trying to guess which system Richardson would have fled to.

Even assuming he'd stay inside the operational zone of the fleet fighting against the Alliance, there were still too many options. They needed this data.

His understanding was that, knowing the exact time and place of the *Triumphant's* entry jump to faster-than-light, this process was now only a question of time. They knew where and when they could pick up the energy signature of the battleship's Alcubierre-Stetson activation, and they had the drones spread wide enough to triangulate.

The thought of failure, however, was unacceptable. Dimitri Tobin had seen too many atrocities over the years. Justice had been done for most of them, but he was sick at heart from what he'd seen, what the Alliance had lost to the Commonwealth's determination to unify humanity.

If they didn't identify the *Triumphant's* destination, he would take *Avalon* and start sweeping *every* possible system. There was only so far the Commonwealth ship could go, after all.

"We should be picking up their jump signature shortly," Anderson murmured, loud enough that everyone in both rooms heard him. The tension instantly ratcheted up, with everyone focusing on the sensor displays around them.

"You're not going to see much, people," Captain Roberts told his crew with a laugh. "From this far away, it's a pretty small burst of light."

Even as he finished speaking, there it was. Dimitri had the section of space it would appear in marked on the display in his implant and it highlighted the flash as it appeared.

Dimitri's attention focused on Commander James Anderson. Everyone else was looking at the redheaded young man as well, but he was ignoring them all, focusing on both the physical console in front of him and the information running through his implant.

Finally, Anderson leaned back and flashed a bright smile back at Captain Roberts.

"We've got them, sir," he announced. "They're en route to Alizon. ETA six days, twenty hours."

"Pendez?" Roberts asked immediately.

Dimitri turned his attention to the Navigator, who was already working through the course.

"If we get underway ASAP, *our* ETA at one point oh five is six days, eighteen hours," she announced.

"Are we certain they're headed to Alizon?" Dimitri asked, the risk of losing his prey still top of his mind.

"Changing vector while under A-S drive is functionally impossible, sir," Pendez replied. "You can change your acceleration, but not your direction."

"There's nothing on their direct line for about two hundred light years, and that star is an uninhabited red giant system past the other side of the Commonwealth," Anderson added. "Alizon's our system, sir."

"Snapes," Dimitri turned to his Intelligence Officer. "What do we know about what the Commonwealth has done since taking Alizon?"

The system was an Alliance member that had fallen in the first wave of attacks Walkingstick had launched. While it had been taken by a task group of two battleships and two carriers, all of those ships were known to have been at the Battle of Midori.

"Not much, sir," Snapes admitted. "We know they have an occupation garrison and have moved in a number of orbital platforms. We only have visual on the exterior of the platforms, though, and Intel isn't sure if they're fighter bases or just a logistics depot."

"What about starships?" Roberts asked.

"No idea, sir," she told him. "Walkingstick has been moving his forces around to keep our intelligence guessing – it's unlikely Alizon has more than one warship in the system though."

"A logistics depot and at most a single ship and some starfighters to protect it," *Avalon's* Captain murmured. "I think Richardson is playing for time. If the Commonwealth will take him back, it lets him find that out without his risking his ship."

"And if they won't, he can take the supplies he'll need to operate independently by force," Dimitri concluded. "Captain Roberts?"

Roberts flashed a brightly cheerful smile at his Admiral.

"We're on our way," he told Dimitri. "Anderson, blow the Q-probes. Once we've confirmed destruction of the probes via lightspeed scanners, you may warp space at your discretion."

27

Deep Space, en route to Alizon System
19:00 January 9, 2736 Earth Standard Meridian Date/Time
DSC-078 Avalon, *Atrium*

KYLE HAD READ the pages and pages of text, across hundreds of design and engineering articles, in which Castle Federation warship designers justified, excused, and allowed for the green space atrium they insisted on installing on their ships.

It served as a reserve source of oxygen. It added a clean feel to the air that no artificial filters could replicate. It was necessary for the crew's morale.

Most of these arguments had some degree of truth to them, but he suspect it all boiled down to one key factor those articles carefully didn't mention: tradition.

The colony ship *Guinevere* that had carried the first colonists on their two-year Alcubierre-Stetson drive voyage to the Castle system had been built around an atrium to keep the colonists sane, so all large ships built by Castle and her daughter systems would have an atrium.

The new *Avalon's* atrium was smaller than some he'd seen, but was still a forty meter wide, ten meter tall, and hundred meter long green space in the heart of the warship. Most of the maintenance was done by the crew on a volunteer basis, which had never stopped the atrium on any ship he'd served on being perfectly arranged and maintained.

He took a moment to take a deep breath of the air. Surrounded by trees and greenery, there was definitely something fresher about the air in the atrium. He was probably going to need the energy.

Peng had asked to meet him here, near the small, tree-shrouded, shrine tucked away in one corner for the crew's Stellar Spiritualists. The single largest 'religion' both on Castle and in the Federation, despite its lack of formal structure, always had a similar shrine on Federation warships.

While the Navy followed a policy of almost always approving requests for space for worship, most of the Federation's largest religious groups tended to setup shrines in the atriums. The volunteers shaped the trees and greenery to conceal them from the main open areas, but everyone always knew where to find the Spiritualists, the Wiccans, the Christians or the Buddhists. Smaller groups might have spaces as well, but those four were almost always present on a Federation warship.

"Captain," Wa greeted him, the Master Sergeant materializing out of the bushes with a suddenness that shocked him. "Thank you for coming."

"What's this about?" he asked, but she shook her head and gestured for him to follow her.

Hidden behind the trees was a small auditorium, assembled from Navy-issue furniture and a few specific pieces brought in by the Spiritualists themselves. At the center was a slowly rotating hologram of the galaxy, a view onto the stars the Spiritualists venerated. They didn't, as he understood it, *worship* the stars. They just recognized the stars as both the natural beginning and the natural end of all life.

Kyle didn't pretend to understand it. What he did recognize was that the dozen non-coms and junior officers waiting in the auditorium had all served aboard the battlecruiser *Thermopylae*.

Waiting at the front was Chief Hammond, in a wheelchair and

wrapped in a full-torso medical cast. He nodded slightly to Peng and turned his ever-stolid gaze on his Captain.

"With the com restrictions, there isn't much reliable news making it through the ship," he said hoarsely. "But rumors spread regardless, and I guess we needed to hear it from you, Captain. *Thermopylae…* was she lost?"

"I'll have to talk to the department heads," Kyle noted, trying to marshal his thoughts and emotions. "News *should* be getting through – especially to the senior NCOs."

He sighed and took one of the nearest seats. From the expressions around him, they all guessed what he had to say now.

"The Commonwealth raided Midori," he told them gently. "Another one of Walkingstick's attritional attacks, though on a larger scale than the rest. The Alliance lost four ships – and yes, *Thermopylae* was one of them.

"There *were* survivors," he continued. "I will make certain that the list is propagated." He shook his head.

"I hadn't considered that impact of the coms restrictions," Kyle admitted. "I'll make arrangements – news *will* make it out."

"It's an intentional part of Level Two restrictions, boss," Hammond pointed out. "Information that doesn't make it onto *Avalon* can't be betrayed by someone on *Avalon.*"

"I know," the Captain agreed. "But while we may need delays or to limit information, data that *is* reaching us should be distributed. I'm sorry," he told them. "I can't tell you if your friends aboard *Thermopylae* are among the survivors, but I will make sure you can find out as soon as possible."

"Thank you, sir," Peng said softly. Her gaze went to the series of candles around the hologram of the galaxy. "We suspected. But with the lives of friends… we wanted to know. We will light a candle for the fallen."

Kyle bowed his head slightly in acknowledgement. He'd put word in a few ears himself. The Stellar Spiritualists weren't the only ones with lost friends, and there'd be more than one candle lit once the news spread.

21:00 January 9, 2736 ESMDT
DSC-078 Avalon, *Executive Officer's Office*

"In short, sir, ma'am, we have completely failed to find any evidence of the spy," Barsamian reported calmly. The young Lieutenant Major sat at attention in the chair in Solace's office, and Kyle watched her with some amusement.

The focus of the Major's attention was *mostly* on him, as the recipient of the report, but her gaze kept drifting to Solace. It was a nervous twitch he normally saw in inexperienced *male* officers… usually dealing with Commander Pendez, who tended to disable young male brains.

"I have to admit," he said after a moment, focusing his attention on the matter on hand, "that having someone who's tried to kill both myself and Stanford aboard and not having the slightest clue who they are makes me… twitchy."

"I'd suggest we could upgrade the security on your quarters, sir, but…" the dark-skinned Ship's Marshal shrugged. "Your quarters, the Admiral's, the CAG's and the XOs are the most secure on the ship. Unless you want me to provide guards on your quarters and a twenty-four-hour MP escort, I'm not sure what else we can do, sir."

Kyle grimaced. He wasn't entirely comfortable with the level of distance a Captain required as it was – adding an armed guard to that did *not* sound appealing.

"I doubt we're likely to see armed assassins in the corridors," he said mildly. "We'll pass on the guards for now. Let me know if *anything* breaks, Major."

"I will, sir. With your permission?"

"Of course, be on your way," Kyle ordered cheerfully.

With a nod to Kyle and a nod that was almost a slight bow to Solace, the Ship's Marshal bowed out of Solace's office.

"I think our young Lieutenant Major has a bit of a crush on you, Commander Solace," Kyle told his exec with a brilliant grin.

"Wait, what?" Solace demanded, her cheeks flushing. It was a good look on her dark skin, and Kyle's smile widened.

"Either that, or she thinks you're the assassin, and it didn't seem like *that* kind of distracted look," he pointed out.

The flush was even brighter.

"There's nothing wrong with a crush," his XO managed to say levelly, "so long as no violation of the chain of command or anything else inappropriate occurs."

Kyle laughed aloud. Solace's responding smile was good to see, and it helped loosen some of the tension that filled the office after Barsamian's briefing.

"She's *married*, Mira," Kyle told her. "Her wife is an accountant on New Bombay, all she's going to do is look. But she's definitely looking."

Solace shook her head repressively at him.

"In less relaxing news, though," he continued quietly, "I realized we – as in you and I, specifically – missed something when we went to CI Two."

"Void," she cursed. "We went through the whole process, sir. What did I miss?"

"I said 'we,' Mira," Kyle pointed out, "and I meant it. As two of our three NCOs pointed out to me today, there's currently *no* news getting to the crew about anything going on outside *Avalon's* hull."

"*Starless* Void," Solace repeated.

"There is an intentional security factor involved," he continued, "but we do have an obligation to let our people have some idea what's going on. Not least," he concluded sadly, "to let them know about lost ships and fallen friends."

Solace sighed. That hit her as hard as it had hit him.

"I'm sorry, sir, it didn't occur to me."

"It's my mistake as well, Solace," Kyle told her. "I'm more concerned about fixing it than laying blame anyways. I want you to sit down with Sanchez and put together a plan for a daily news update to the crew – you and she will review and approve what news we can release considering we may well have a Commonwealth spy on board."

"Delegating dealing with Sanchez, I see?" his XO pointed out.

"The woman is convinced I was promoted to the level of my incompetence," he told her. "She's rather more bitter than I would prefer, and since I have such high-quality minions to fob her off on…"

"If she thinks you're incompetent, she might be the last one left on the ship," Solace observed.

"She's not wrong about my inexperience," Kyle noted. "If I'd spent longer as an XO, I might have realized we had to do something to keep our people informed when we went dark."

"I *have* spent longer as an XO," Solace replied. "I didn't think of it. "Don't worry sir – I'll deal with it."

"I'll consider this one a personal favor, Mira," he said quietly. "She's starting to be *very* uncomfortable to work with."

"Have you raised it with the Admiral?"

"Not yet," he admitted. "But… if she doesn't shape up, I will. For now we're a long way away from a replacement Chief of Staff, so I'll play nice.

"For now."

28

Deep Space, en route to Alizon System
01:00 January 14, 2736 Earth Standard Meridian Date/Time
DSC-078 Avalon, *Captain's Quarters*

KYLE AWOKE WITH A START.

His room was dark and empty. *Avalon* had the cubage to allow surprisingly large quarters for her commanding officer, but since he spent most of his time in the office he hadn't bothered to put much in his rooms. Like, say, lamps.

The back of his neck tingled as if someone was watching him. The last time he'd felt this nervous for no reason, he'd turned out to be flying towards a hidden Commonwealth battlecruiser.

He heard a soft unfamiliar sound, and sat up, looking around his room. There *should* have been some light in the room, enough that setting his implant to night vision mode would allow him to see, but it was pitch black. His implants couldn't process light that wasn't there for his eyes to receive.

Feeling paranoid, he flipped a command to the ship to turn on the lights.

Nothing happened.

That moved the paranoia to spasms of panic. The last time he hadn't been able to contact the ship's computer, the old *Avalon* had suffered a critical Alcubierre failure. He breathed carefully, feeling the vibration of the ship around him.

Avalon was still running normally. He just couldn't talk to her. It was almost as if…

The realization he was being jammed caused him to leap to his feet, dodging out of his bed moments before *something* slammed into the space he'd occupied. There was a horrible tearing sound as metal slashed through the sheets and mattress, but he couldn't see *anything*.

Kyle didn't carry a sidearm, but he *kept* one – and kept it right next to his uniform, in case he'd ever need it. Dodging against the wall, letting memory guide him, he found his uniforms just as a metallic *mass* slammed into the wall where he'd been standing with a crashing noise.

Just what was in the room with him?

His hand finally fell on the roughened metallic grip of the pistol. That same skittering sound headed towards him, and he dropped to the floor – dragging the pistol with him.

This time, he wasn't fast enough, and fire seared across his shoulder as some kind of blade sliced through his shipsuit and into his skin.

Rolling away, wincing as the fresh wound hit the floor, he linked his implant into the pistol, checking its ammunition load, charge – and most importantly, *light*.

The tiny light buried in the tip of the barrel was astonishingly bright for its size, and it lit up his entire bedroom in stark relief. In the middle of the floor was a creation out of someone's nightmares. It was dog sized, but resembled a mechanical cockroach more than anything else – a metal dome about seventy centimeters across, from which emerged all *kinds* of legs and blades.

It saw the light and charged him, blades flashing out on the end of long, articulated arms. Rolling aside again, he opened fire.

His first shots went wide, hitting the walls and fragmenting exactly as the frangible anti-personnel rounds were supposed to do. He still managed to put two shots on target, but they shattered on the metal shell in the same way.

Dodging another robotic charge, he slammed the manual release panel for his bedroom door. It ignored him, and then came apart in a shower of sparks as a telescoping arm slammed a metal blade into it, barely missing his head.

Then the robot slammed bodily into him, hammering him first into the wall and then onto the ground. He somehow managed to keep hold of the pistol and slammed it into the gap between arms as the thing reared up to strike.

There were seven rounds left in the magazine, and he emptied the gun into the inside of the thing. Spasming, its arms lashed forward again. His uninjured shoulder flared in agony as one of the blades went clean through muscle and bone to slam into the deck… and stop there.

A moment later, pinned to the deck by both the blade and the dead robot's weight, Kyle's implant *finally* linked back into the ship's network.

"Medical and security to Captain's quarters," he ordered. "Medical and security to Captain's quarters *right the fuck now!*"

02:30 January 14, 2736 ESMDT
DSC-078 Avalon, *Main Infirmary*

KYLE WASN'T EVEN *PRETENDING* to be a good patient, so when Lieutenant Major Sirvard Barsamian entered the section of the Infirmary where Cunningham was treating him he waved her right over.

"Could you at least hold *still?*" the doctor hissed. "Yes, this is a very clean, very neat hole – but if you *move* while I'm working on it, it won't *stay* that way!"

The Captain winced at the thought. His right shoulder had only

GLYNN STEWART

been sliced open and was neatly stitched up, but the Surgeon-Commander had his left shoulder immobilized as he cleaned the wound and ran automatic nano-sutures down into the depths of the cut muscle.

Modern nanotech nerve-blocking, however, made it easy to forget that you were badly injured.

"Please tell me you have something, Sirvard," he told the Marshal. "I don't care to repeat tonight's experience."

"We don't have much," she replied. "But we're pulling together data. We're, uh, tearing your quarters apart, sir."

"That's fine," he agreed quickly. "I'll bunk in my office for now – lock my quarters as long as you need. Besides," he glanced at the doctor beside him as he checked the time, "we are barely ninety minutes out of Alizon. I'm not going *back* to sleep.

"What do you know?" he finished.

"No-one exactly distributes assassination drone schematics," Barsamian told him dryly. "So we can't be certain of much about the drone. What I *can* tell you already is that we weren't supposed to be able to say anything about it – it had a thermite-based self-destruct that would have incinerated the entire thing after you were dead."

"Why didn't it destroy itself when it failed then?"

"At a guess, the computer core had to order the self-destruct," she explained. "You put four bullets through it, so it wasn't ordering much of anything. Since the only weapon you had to hand *shouldn't* have been able to kill it, I guess whoever sent it didn't expect to fail."

"Wonderful, I'm luckier than my intended murderer hoped for," Kyle replied.

"What I can tell you so far is that drone was built aboard *Avalon*," Barsamian said grimly. "Probably in one of the auto-fabricators engineering uses for small and mid-sized parts. Suffice to say, the *design* isn't in our systems, but one of our people built the damn thing."

"Our spy is appearing more and more like an assassin every day," he grumbled. "Anything *else*?"

"It's a nasty piece of work," she allowed. "The shell would resist any small arms fire that isn't armor piercing. No poisons or anything on the blades, but the blades allow for a silent kill that won't trigger ship's sensors – as soon as you started shooting at it, my people were on their way.

"We have no idea how it got into your quarters, and, shock, all of the cameras in your section of the ship were down for the seventy minutes prior to the attack," she concluded grimly. "The latter is aggravating, since I had an alert added to the system for if we had camera issues... and the cameras happily reported they were working until we checked them.

"I *do not* like the degree of control this *person* has over our ship."

"It's pissing me off," Kyle cheerfully admitted. "Unfortunately, right now we're about to enter a system we *know* the Commonwealth controls, in hot pursuit of a madman who blew up half a planet. The disgustingly competent spy trying to kill me comes in at, oh, number three or four on my priorities."

"You'll forgive me if it's the top of my list," the Marshal replied. "We'll dig into where the drone came from – it's the best piece of evidence we've had so far."

"Unless someone is actively shooting at us, let me know as soon as you find anything," Kyle ordered. He paused and then sighed. "Get together with Master Sergeant Wa as well. I want a list from the pair of you of Marines you both completely trust to act as bodyguards. I don't *like* it, but it looks like I need to concede on that point."

"The Gunny already has guards on your office, your quarters, and this Infirmary ward," Barsamian told him. "She and I will sort it out. And I *will* catch the son of bitch trying to kill people on my watch."

"Whatever resources you need are yours, Marshal," the Captain told her. "I don't need to be watching my back when we go to war."

He cringed as a moment of pain flashed through the nerve block, and he looked over at Cunningham.

"Are we done yet, Adrian?" he asked.

The doctor grimaced, and pulled the trigger on one last dose of nanotech filled foam covering the last piece of the wound.

"We're done," he confirmed. "Now, what you *should* do is lie down and not move for about twenty-four hours while the nanites work."

"Ninety minutes from a Commonwealth-held system, Adrian," Kyle said quietly.

"Right. So I'm immobilizing your shoulder," Cunningham said bluntly, pulling an uncomfortable looking clamshell cast out from a cupboard.

"Hold *very* still."

29

SOLACE WAS WAITING for Kyle when he returned to the bridge. His exec looked tense, as if ready to spring into action or escape some kind of trap. When she saw him, some of that tension released – only for her face to freeze up when she saw the shoulder brace.

"Are you okay?" she demanded.

"I'll be fine," he told her, carefully loud enough for the rest of the bridge crew to hear him. "Adrian was just being very pointed about the fact I shouldn't move my shoulder."

"Sorry I couldn't check in on you," Solace said quietly, so the rest of the bridge crew couldn't hear her. "Someone had to be on the bridge."

"Agreed. You did the right thing," he reassured her, though the thought that she had *wanted* to check on him gave him a warm feeling he carefully did not examine closely.

"I'll need you down in Secondary Control," he continued. "We have no idea what's going to happen in Alizon, and I want to be sure someone I can trust is in position to take command."

Solace nodded, stepping out of the command chair.

"Are we expecting it to be that bad?" she asked softly. She was closer to him than usual, and something to do with almost dying made him more aware of that he expected.

"More than anything, every attack our assassin has launched has been more and more blatant," he admitted. "I wouldn't put it past our spy to manage to somehow blow up the bridge in the middle of a battle. No matter what, Mira – I want our people safe, and I want the mission complete."

"Understood," Solace replied crisply, stepping back as if she realized she'd done something wrong. "I'll plan to not be needed then, sir," she continued with a wink.

"If I find footstools and fruity drinks in Secondary Control later, there will be hell to pay," he told her loudly, startling chuckles from several members of the bridge crew. "Be on your way, Commander. We're running low on time."

He traded salutes with his XO and dropped into the command chair. The shoulder brace didn't, *quite*, hurt – but he was pretty sure Cunningham had dug up the most uncomfortable way possible to immobilize his injured limb.

"Admiral," he greeted Tobin as he linked into the flag deck. "I have us emerging from Alcubierre in ten minutes. Any updates?"

"Negative, Captain, we proceed as planned," the Vice Admiral replied. "Are you all right?"

"I've never been stabbed before," Kyle observed. "Blown up, yes. Irradiated basically to death, yes. Stabbed is a new one. I'll live."

The big man on the other end of the channel shook his head.

"Someday, Captain, your sense of humor is going to be what kills you."

"I look forward to it, sir," he replied. "If my sense of humor kills me, our assassin friend and the Commonwealth have failed.

"We will arrive in Alizon roughly two hours prior to our ETA for *Triumphant*," Kyle continued. "If everything goes well, they won't even know we're there until it's too late."

"It's always possible they've dropped a probe on the other side of the gas giant to stop someone doing just this, sir," Pendez warned from her station.

The Alizon system had an absolutely *giant*, barely sub-stellar, gas giant in its outer system. The massive planet had swept everything outside the third planet's orbit into its own orbit and Trojans, which had left the second planet – the habitable one – almost completely lacking in the normal array of impact craters.

It also meant that emerging with the gas giant between *Avalon* and Alizon gave them a decent chance of evading detection. It also, unfortunately, meant they would have almost a full light hour to fly. *Triumphant* would arrive two hours after them, but it would take *Avalon* a full twelve to make a zero distance, zero velocity rendezvous with the planet.

Of course, one of the best ways to avoid detection in space was to hide your acceleration in the signature of something large and highly energetic – like a barely sub-stellar gas giant.

"We'll have to see," Kyle warned Tobin. "This could be very sneaky – or we could end up looking very silly.

"Either way, we'll know if the Commonwealth's force in Alizon is more than we can handle long before we're past our final point of no return."

———

EMERGENCE.

One moment, all of *Avalon's* screens and implant feeds were showing either the strange, super blue- and red-shifted view of the inside of her warp bubble or a computer simulation of the world around them.

The next, the screens were rapidly updated with the reality outside. Alizon IV filled the main screen, its surrounding cloud of collected debris a navigation hazard. Radiation pulsed out from the gas giant, rendering any attempt to see directly past it hopeless.

"Scanning for artificial objects," Anderson announced immediately. "I'm not seeing anything. No probes, no sensor stations – if there's anything out here that has picked us up, it's being damned sneaky."

Which was, Kyle reflected, entirely possible. Active sensors weren't needed to pick up an Alcubierre emergence, and no sensor in the world could detect the quantum entanglement link that allowed a Q-Com to work at any significant distance. Alizon IV's debris field would do handily for hiding a passive-only probe.

"We'll deal with that if it's the case," he said calmly. "Commander Pendez, set your course. Coordinate with Commander Anderson and watch your angles – we need to keep the gas giant behind us at all times."

"Yes, sir," she replied, with exaggerated patience. "I'll also make sure there's fuel in the engines before I fire them, and that the mass manipulators are on."

He laughed aloud.

"All right, I deserved that," he admitted. "We don't sneak very often in a twenty million ton starship – I'm a little out of practice."

Kyle leaned back in his command chair, allowing the information on the status of his ship to flow through him as Pendez expertly maneuvered *Avalon* into the orbit that would take her around Alizon IV without being seen.

"We'll clear the debris cloud in forty-five minutes," she announced. "We will be ballistic at that point in time and for about forty-five minutes after that, then we should be able to bring the drive up at flank acceleration without being detected."

Nodding silently, Kyle continued to review the status reports from throughout the ship. Everything was reporting fully ready for battle. Positron capacitors were charged to feed the positron lances. The warheads for the starfighter missiles had been charged, and the missiles themselves loaded carefully onto the starfighters. The special capacitors setup to rapid-charge the warheads of the carrier's own capital ship missiles were fully loaded, and the missiles themselves were in position to be charged and fired.

It was good to see, but also left him feeling nervous. They had a Commonwealth agent of some kind aboard – one who'd tried to assassinate both him and Michael – but that agent didn't seem to have carried out any other kind of sabotage.

Almost regardless of what *Triumphant* was doing here, they were going to attack Alizon at this point. If there was ever a moment for a saboteur to strike, it was today.

But all he could do was wait. Barsamian was carrying out her investigation even as *Avalon* shaped her course deep into the enemy held system.

Waiting was all he could do for today's battle as well. With stealth at least the initial priority, he'd ordered no probes or starfighters launched until they were much closer. The smaller craft's engines were less likely to be detected than *Avalon's*, but this stunt was risky enough as it was.

The engines cut out, and the big carrier continued her motion now, her course a fast orbit that would bring them around Alizon IV without going too deep into the debris cloud. Unlike the positron lances her electromagnetic deflectors were built to defeat, very little of the debris had any kind of magnetic charge.

Normally, they'd clear their path through this kind of field with lasers and light positron lances, reducing the larger debris to dust and pebbles the ship's massive ferro-ceramic armor could absorb. This was also *very* detectable, not quite as bad as the engines but close.

He felt his ship shudder as the first of the debris crashed into her armor. They'd run the numbers. They weren't going deep enough to hit densities that would cause serious damage, but their speed made even small particles dangerous.

It was going to be a bumpy ride.

05:00 January 14, 2736 ESMDT
DSC-078 Avalon, Flag Deck

DIMITRI WATCHED his implant feed carefully as *Avalon* swung around the planet, carefully reviewing each piece of information about the system as it came available. He'd also carefully used his authorization codes to setup a heavily secured connection funneling all of the sensor data back to the Alliance.

His codes should suffice to keep the spy from getting any value of the connection, and the Alliance needed to see everything they could about Alizon. If, for whatever reason, *Avalon* wasn't able to secure the system while dealing with Richardson, the intel she gathered could still allow the Alliance to make plans.

If nothing else, *Avalon's* presence would draw Commonwealth forces to Alizon, and weaken the defenses at more valuable targets.

Alizon I was visible before its habitable sister. A close-in, star-scorched chunk of rock with no value except for some esoteric science studies, its only recognizable feature was a small science station inhabited by the kind of people for whom unusual rock formations were fascinating.

Apparently, the Commonwealth found said geologists no more worthy of attention than *Avalon's* Vice Admiral did, as the station was still there and didn't even have a guardian fighter squadron or other watchdog.

The habitable planet, Alizon itself, was inevitably more protected. As it came into view, everyone on both the flag deck and the bridge focused on what the sensors showed, even if it was an hour out of date.

It looked like the vast majority, if not all, of the civilian orbital infrastructure had survived. There were notable gaps in the orbital tracks, though – places where civilian platforms had been shifted by tugs to clear them out of the path of debris from the orbital battle stations that *hadn't* survived.

Alizon had a single medium-sized moon, and like most planets with a single significantly size moon, its LaGrange points were clusters of high orbit activity. One of the points had been cleared of civilian stations, however. Instead, a series of recognizable prefabricated Commonwealth platforms occupied the space.

Studying the Commonwealth base, Dimitri realized either he'd underestimated what Snapes had meant by 'a number of orbital platforms' or that the Terrans had dramatically expanded their presence since the last Alliance Intelligence sweep of the system.

There were easily eighty or ninety platforms, the smallest a disk a hundred meters across, the largest a series of linked modules and girders almost two kilometers long. Not only were there *definitely* fighter launch platforms in the mix – two of the Commonwealth's ten ship squadrons were flying a close security patrol – the Terrans had brought in and assembled a complete capital ship repair dock.

"I think that answers the question of what they're setting up here," he observed, loudly enough to be sure Snapes, Roberts and Solace all heard him. "That's a forward repair and logistics base. A cool couple hundred billion Terran dollars."

"Commander Snapes," Solace addressed the Intelligence Officer. "I'm seeing at least two squadrons worth of fighters flying escort, but the warbook doesn't have enough data to pick out the launch platforms. Before we send Vice Commodore Stanford's starfighters in, can you tell the size of the hornet's nest?"

"We have some intelligence that isn't solid enough for the warbook," Snapes replied. Two of the platforms highlighted in green. An even dozen more highlighted in yellow. "The green are definitely launch platforms, roughly equivalent to one of our Wings – five of their ten ship squadrons.

"The yellow *might* be launch platforms or have squadron bays," she admitted. "I can't be certain – but I'd guess we're looking at about twenty squadrons – two hundred fighters, as the Commonwealth organizes them."

"Regardless of the launch platforms, I'm betting there's at least one more factor in play," Roberts added cheerfully. "That dock may be empty right now, but I doubt the Terrans left her undefended. As the Admiral pointed out, that's a *lot* of money's worth of supplies and prefabs. My guess is there's a starship hiding on the light side of Alizon's moon – if they're between the moon and the planet, we wouldn't see her unless we dropped a probe right into orbit."

"That... makes sense," Sanchez admitted, and Tobin smiled to himself at her strained tone.

"I'm not going to stop you dropping whatever drones you want,

Captain," he told Roberts. "*Avalon's* your ship. Let's just make damn sure *Triumphant* doesn't make it out of here."

"Right now I'm enjoying the unusual feeling of sneaking up on someone in space," *Avalon's* Captain replied brightly. "Once *Triumphant* arrives in an hour or so, I may reconsider. But for now, let's play it nice and safe."

"Do you even know the meaning of the word, safe?" Sanchez demanded, and Tobin's smile faded.

"Right now, Senior Fleet Commander," Roberts said levelly, "'Safe' means I'm presuming there's enough force hiding behind that moon to destroy *Avalon*, and I don't want to attract their attention until I know I can take out *Triumphant*. Safe enough for you?"

30

Alizon System
06:30 January 14, 2736 Earth Standard Meridian Date/Time
DSC-078 Avalon, Bridge

"THERE SHE IS," Anderson announced into the anticipatory quiet of *Avalon's* bridge as *Triumphant* appeared on the screens.

The image was most of an hour old, *Triumphant* having emerged on a very different approach track than *Avalon*. The Commonwealth battleship wasn't trying to hide from the logistics depot, after all.

The big carrier's own approach seemed to be going unnoticed. It was hard to be absolutely certain, though, as the light from their drive activation was still fifteen minutes from the base – and it would be another hour still after that before *Avalon* saw their reaction.

"What's your assessment of her approach?" Kyle asked his Tactical Officer. "That's a bit closer in than I expected."

Anderson paused to think for a second, highlighting the battleship on the feed going to the entire bridge crew and dropping vector data in on it.

"She didn't exactly thread the needle," the Commander replied after a moment. "Came in a few minutes late, carved half an hour off of her approach. It's risky, but not too dangerous... but it's an *assault* profile, sir, not a friendly system arrival profile.

"And look," he flashed the vector data, "she's going in fast – two hundred and thirty gravities. *Resolutes* are only rated for two hundred, so either they upgraded her engines and manipulators at some point, or she's burning fuel like water."

"So she's not planning on showing up for hugs and kisses," Kyle observed. "What's the Marine complement of a ship like that?"

"Depends on the mission," Anderson replied. "Their default is a single eight hundred man battalion, but they can *carry* a full regiment – and since she was escorting an assault group..."

"Richardson probably has over two thousand Commonwealth Marines aboard." Kyle regarded the layout of the system calmly. "With, if I remember their table of equipment correctly, at least four or five companies of battle armor and enough heavy weapons to make the security detachment of, say, a medium-sized forward logistics base, piss their pants."

"Would they follow his orders to assault the depot?" Solace asked from Secondary Control.

Kyle shook his head, glancing at the link to the flag deck.

"Commander Snapes?"

"I'm... not sure, sir," the Intelligence Officer admitted. "But it looks like he and his Marine commander go a long way back. And, well... if he isn't going to surrender to Commonwealth authority, his Marines can either turn on him, or continue following orders."

"So one way or another, Captain Richardson plans on getting his resupply," Tobin rumbled. "That seems like it will provide us a useful opportunity."

"What's *Triumphant's* ETA?" Kyle asked Anderson.

"If they're planning on resupplying, they'll be heading for a zero-zero intercept," the younger man replied, "I make it just over five hours."

"And we're still nine and a half out, correct?" the Captain turned to Pendez.

"Yes, sir."

"Richardson can cause a lot of trouble in four hours, and still manage to evade anything except long-range missile fire," Kyle told Tobin quietly. "I wouldn't expect our missile salvos to penetrate a battleship's defenses, either."

"What about our starfighters?" the Admiral asked.

"If we launched right now, they'll get there *before Triumphant,*" Kyle replied. "The catch is that to keep their safety zones clear, a full fighter launch needs to take up a *lot* more space than *Avalon* does. It's not a question of if they'll be detected, but when."

"We can't let Richardson escape," Tobin told him firmly. "I won't tell you how to fight your ship, Captain, but that is the mission."

"Understood, sir." *Avalon's* Captain eyed the feed, studying the position of the ships and the depot. "The joker in the deck is still the question of what, if anything, is hiding behind the moon," he admitted. "I intend to keep Stanford's fighters aboard until we see how the depot responds to *Triumphant.*"

He turned to Anderson.

"I want Q-probes on route to the depot and on an intercept course for *Triumphant,*" Kyle ordered. "Do everything you can to keep them undetected – but we need to know what's going on *now,* not what was happening half an hour ago."

Tobin's face was calm, not giving any hints as to what the Vice Admiral was thinking when Kyle turned back to him.

"We'll get him, sir," the Captain told him.

07:00 January 14, 2736 ESMDT
DSC-078 Avalon, *Flight Control Center*

THERE WAS a feed from the carrier's sensors running in the Flight Control Center attached to the main flight deck. When Michael entered the room, every eye was focused on it, even though it didn't show anything exciting.

Triumphant continued her course towards the depot. No one at the base had taken any action beyond pulling the fighter patrols in and placing those twenty fighters between the orbiting platforms and the battleship.

With confirmation that his fighters wouldn't be called for immediately, Stanford had stepped out to get coffee and a shower. Reviewing the updates of the last half-hour, it had been a better use of time than waiting.

"How are we looking, Chief?" he asked Kalers quietly, stepping up next to his Acting Deck Chief.

"All the birds are locked and loaded," the older woman replied. "Avignon has his people in their birds. Rokos' are up next in an hour, barring the Captain ordering us into space."

"Let's keep an eye on everything," Michael replied. "By the time the Captain orders us into space, I want everybody already in their starfighters." He studied his implant feed for a moment. "Barring any change in affairs, let's assume we're taking the Group to Readiness Alpha in… three hours."

That would put the carrier six hours short of the depot, and the *Triumphant* two hours short. By then, *some* kind of reaction would have been seen from the depot – even no reaction would suggest that the base and the battleship had reached some agreement.

"What sort of operation are we anticipating, sir?" the Chief asked, pitching her voice so the rest of the Center couldn't hear her.

"Anti-shipping and boarding party cover," Michael replied. "We're going to go after *Triumphant*, and if they're playing nice with each other, whoever's behind that moon." He paused, then waved at one of the other figures in the room.

"Rokos, over here."

His Bravo Wing commander joined them in a moment.

"Since things aren't exciting right now, I'm guessing you're planning how to make my life exciting later?" the broad-shouldered officer asked.

"Exactly," Michael promised. "I'm tasking Bravo Wing for boarding party security," he told the Wing Commander. "One way or another, Major Norup's people will be hitting that facility. I want you to make sure they all get there. Chew on that, and let Chief Kalers know if you need any gear or munitions switched."

Without a very specific mission profile, it was rare for any of the Federation's starfighters to launch with anything other than Starfire missiles – the short-range missiles with their one-gigaton warheads being the weapon of choice for both anti-fighter and anti-shipping strikes. There *were*, however, more specialized munitions in *Avalon's* magazines.

"I will *definitely* want some Banshees," Rokos replied immediately. He glanced at Kalers. "I'll let you know how many in… fifteen minutes? Will that give you enough time?"

"I can't see the Marines launching in less than an hour," the Acting Chief replied. "I'll need forty-five minutes for the switchover, but, strangely, I already had a few dozen pallets of Banshees up for ease of loading."

The Banshee Seven was one of the most specialized munitions a starfighter could carry. It was the same size as a Starfire, but it was a MIRVed weapon with no less than *eighty* sub-munitions. While significantly shorter ranged than the anti-fighter missile, the Banshee's sub-munitions were smart anti-radiation weapons. Once deployed, each would seek a radar installation – such as those on the close-in defenses intended to shoot down boarding shuttles – and impact with the force of a half-ton or so of TNT.

"Good," Michael told them with a smile. "Unless there's something *real* nasty behind that moon, we are *not* leaving this system in Terran hands."

08:00 January 14, 2736 ESMDT
DSC-078 Avalon, Bridge

"WELL, *HELLO* THERE."

Kyle waited for several seconds, then cleared his throat and glared at his Tactical Officer.

"Would you care to share with the class, James?"

The redheaded officer's pale skin showed an embarrassed flush *very* clearly, as it turned out, and he quickly turned his attention to his Captain.

"Running the feed from Q-Probe Three," he said quickly. "I was angling Three around a bit to try to see around the moon, so it saw her first. Not too much of a difference though."

Kyle was about to ask him for more details when the feed from Q-Probe Three hit his implant. The familiar elongated egg shape of a Commonwealth warship was emerging from behind the moon. A single Terran squadron of ten *Scimitar* starfighters flew a high – low escort pattern as the ship set an intercept course for *Triumphant*.

"Well, I'd say our Captain Richardson wasn't being clear enough about his peaceful intentions for his friends," he said aloud. "What have we got on our newcomer?"

"Thousand meters long, twenty million tons, starfighter escort," his Tactical Officer reeled off in an instant. "Wrong shape to be a carrier, so unless the starfighters are from the base, that's a *Hercules* sir."

Avalon's Captain thought a command at his implant and zoomed in on the image.

"Definitely a *Hercules*, Commander Anderson," he said quietly. "You can't make out the details of her armament from this distance, but note the hull bulge pattern. Those are the blisters for her main guns – she's got a single set of three blisters around the middle, but a *Saint* has *two* sets of blisters, each a hundred meters from the center."

The junior officer blinked. "Of course. Why didn't I see that?" he asked.

"We got jumped by a *Hercules* at Hessian," Kyle pointed out. "The image, ah, stuck in my mind."

It was one of the very few images from that day he really remembered. The loss of his implant in that battle had cost him almost all of his memories from that day – his personal backup couldn't update from his starfighter.

"The question, I suppose, is just what our friend *Hercules* is planning on doing about *Triumphant?*" Tobin asked. The Admiral was watching the same feed as everyone else.

"I think he isn't certain himself," Solace observed. "If he *was* certain, he'd have all thirty of his fighters out and pulling a high speed attack run with his missiles right ahead of them. Instead, that looks like an intercept course – hard to say yet, but I think he's planning on pulling alongside."

That raised an interesting thought, and Kyle turned his gaze to the Vice Admiral.

"Sir, what do we do if the *Commonwealth* has arrested Richardson?"

"We are in position to retake the Alizon system," Tobin pointed out. "Unless they pick Richardson up and run straight for FTL, I think Richardson is going to end up in our custody anyway, don't you?"

After a moment's thought, Kyle returned his Admiral's grin coldly.

31

Alizon System
10:00 January 14, 2736 Earth Standard Meridian Date/Time
DSC-078 Avalon, *Bridge*

TRIUMPHANT WAS STILL an hour away from her destination, but she and the *Hercules* were rapidly approaching each other. Anderson had managed to sneak one of the Q-Com equipped probes in close to their intercept point, and Kyle watched with interest as the two Commonwealth warships approached.

The battleship was inbound towards the logistics depot at over eight thousand kilometers a second still, and the battlecruiser had reversed her acceleration half an hour ago and was rapidly building velocity towards the depot. They were two hundred thousand kilometers apart, the closing speed shrinking as their speeds came into alignment.

Neither ship had done anything noticeable yet. None of the defending ship's other twenty starfighters had been launched, and neither had done anything aggressive – though both had their electro-magnetic deflectors up. With the battleship-grade positron lances both ships carried, though, they were already in death range.

"What are they *doing*?" Kyle heard Solace wonder aloud.

"I'm not sure," he admitted, shaking his head. "My guess, though, is that whoever is in command of the battlecruiser is trying to talk Richardson into surrendering. Richardson... either hasn't made up his mind, or is playing a very dangerous game."

He flipped feeds to look up Stanford. The lack of visual data from the CAG's communicator warned him the other man was in his starfighter.

"Vice Commodore, are your fighters prepared to launch?" he asked.

"We are prepared and loaded," Stanford replied. "I have a Wing prepped to fly escort duty on Norup's Marines as well."

"Thanks, Michael," Kyle said quietly, and then flipped to that worthy.

"Major Norup, are your people ready to go?"

"I've got all four companies loaded in the shuttles, with First and Third in full battle armor," the Marine commander told him crisply. "Get us to the platforms, and we'll take control."

Both Kyle's starfighters and Marine assault shuttles could double *Avalon's* acceleration. The carrier herself had just made turnover and was still six hours away. If he launched his small craft, they could hit the depot in just over four hours.

Of course, his starfighters could make an *attack* pass, on *Triumphant* or the base, in a little over two – but they'd be moving at over thirty percent of lightspeed. A 'point three pass' was doable, but it was also risky and pushed the tiny spacecraft to their maximum capabilities.

Whatever happened over the next few minutes, Kyle was now confident that he could take control of the Alizon system and destroy the Commonwealth forces opposing him.

"The *Hercules* has launched shuttles, sir!" Anderson reported. "I'm reading... four ships, look like equivalents to our Marine assault craft." He paused, clearly reviewing data.

"They're only pulling two hundred and forty gravities, sir," he concluded. "I'd guess they came to a conclusion."

Kyle nodded. It seemed Captain Richardson had agreed to face Commonwealth justice. He smiled. It wasn't *quite* going to work out that way for the man, though. Given Fleet Admiral Walkingstick's reputation, all that was going to change was the brand name of the bullet.

"Holy shit!"

Richardson had apparently reached the same conclusion as Kyle.

The assault shuttles had crossed barely half of the distance between the two ships before someone on *Triumphant* pushed the button. Almost fifty light positron lances, each delivering ninety-kilotons-a-second of antimatter, lashed out into space. Four beams targeted each shuttle – and each of the *Hercules'* guardian starfighters.

But those beams were the side-show. At the same instant as the smaller craft died, eight one-megaton-a-second heavy positron lances fired – at a target that wasn't evading, whose ECM was down, whose bridge crew *knew* Captain Richardson and *Triumphant* had surrendered.

Even one hit would have been fatal – and none of them missed.

———

It was very quiet on *Avalon's* bridge. Kyle had taken his crew through two space battles, and they *understood*, in the bone-deep way only combat veterans could, how vulnerable the massive vessels that carried them were.

Watching seven thousand lives snuffed out in a moment of treachery was a shock to the system regardless.

"Sir," Anderson began, then coughed to clear his throat. "Sir," he repeated, "*Triumphant* has launched missiles at the depot. I'm reading less than twenty minutes to impact."

"Track their vectors," Kyle ordered. "Confirm their targets."

"They're… the missiles are targeted on the fighter launch platforms," his Tactical Officer replied quietly. "I *think* they were launched without warheads… they want to protect the rest of the facility."

At those speeds, a two ton capital missile would impact with thirty megatons of force – enough to rip through even an armored space station, but not enough to damage the rest of the depot.

"What do we do, sir?" Anderson asked.

"We wait," Kyle ordered harshly. "Remember that this is *our* system, and that depot is supporting the occupation on the surface. Every starfighter destroyed, every missile expended, makes *our* job easier.

"This kind of betrayal isn't something we want to watch," he said softly, making sure all of his people could hear him, "but our mission here is to take out *Triumphant* and liberate Alizon – and if the Commonwealth wants to shoot each other, I say we let them."

"Depot has picked up their launch and is returning fire," Anderson reported. "I'm not picking up any fighter launches though."

"They'll put everything into space they can," Stanford interjected. "But… if they didn't have everybody up, suited, and ready to go… a launch from a cold start can easily be thirty minutes."

"They don't *have* thirty minutes, CAG," the redheaded officer pointed out.

"If they weren't ready to launch, a lot of people are about to die," Kyle agreed. "And if they weren't, whoever was in command made a dangerous mistake."

His bridge crew seemed to accept that, slowly settling back into their tasks and tracking the two sets of missiles.

The depot really had depended on its starfighters and defending starships, he noted. *Triumphant* had fired twenty-four Stormwind capital ship missiles at the depot – and the stations had only fired sixteen back. Given that the Commonwealth generally designed their capital ships to handle at least half again their own missile strength, the depot's defenses weren't going to do much to the battleship.

"Captain Roberts," Tobin addressed him over a private link. "I really do hate to jog your shoulders in the middle of a fight, but what *is* your plan?"

"*Triumphant's* salvo will almost certainly remove the depot's starfighters as a factor," Kyle replied. "Once *Triumphant* is the only real threat on the board, I'll deploy Stanford's fighters. We'll need them to build up extra velocity to make sure they can *catch* her if she tries to run.

"There's a risk of detection," he admitted, "which is why I want to hold off on launching until *after Triumphant* has neutralized the defenses. I'm not sure how Richardson will react once he sees us, but I'd rather not fight both a battleship and a depot defense fighter group if I can avoid it."

Tobin nodded slowly.

"What if he runs, Captain?" he asked. "I am not prepared to lose our prey again."

"We only have so long before they're going to see us, sir," Kyle told him. "I'm surprised we haven't been detected yet, to be honest. Once the depot defenses are down, we will launch at *Triumphant.* If Richardson escapes…" he shrugged. "We still have a speed advantage. We can liberate Alizon today and bring him down tomorrow. It's worth the risk in my opinion."

The Vice Admiral looked like he was going to argue for a moment, but finally seemed to control himself and nodded again.

"Fight your ship, Captain," he ordered.

———

Triumphant's missiles struck home. There had never really been any doubt in Kyle's mind that they would, but it was still nerve-wracking to watch them hit. Anderson's assessment that the battleship hadn't loaded their warheads bore out, as while the explosions ripped through and gutted the six fighter launch platforms the impacts lacked gigaton-range antimatter reactions.

The depot had shot down twelve missiles, but that had still left two for each platform – and Stormwinds, like the Alliance's Jackhammers, linked together in a networked intelligence perfectly capable of making last minute target allocations.

Whoever had been in charge of the starfighters either had never taken them to full readiness status, or had stood them down after it appeared *Triumphant* was going to surrender. Across six stations, the defenders had only put another four squadrons worth of fighters into space in almost twenty minutes.

Sixty *Scimitar* fighters wasn't going to be enough to take down *Triumphant* – not unless they were well-trained, rigorously drilled, squadrons operating with comrades they knew and were well-prepared for the fight.

Kyle would have stacked any one of his Wings of forty-eight *Falcons* against *Triumphant* without hesitation, though the losses would be awful. The remaining defenders of Alizon's new logistics depot didn't stand a chance.

Triumphant herself had vanished into a ball of jamming as the defender's missiles closed, and even with the drones far closer than *Avalon* they couldn't pick out the moment the last missile died. There was a cascade of explosions as lasers and positron lances slashed the big missiles apart.

And in the middle of that cascade, the drone feed suddenly cut out. Then the second drone feed vanished.

"Anderson," Kyle snapped. "What happened to our drones?"

"They're gone, sir," the officer replied. "Give me a moment." He paused, reviewing data. "*Void*. Probe Three got confused by their ECM and misdirected their heat venting," he admitted softly. "They saw her, sir – and then picked up Probe Two on their active sweep. They know they're being watched."

The Q-probes were the stealthiest items in any Navy's inventory, but ninety-plus percent of that stealth boiled down to carefully directing their engines and heat venting *away* from their enemies. Once that had failed, they fell back on powerful ECM to stay alive in combat environments – but that ECM also made their *presence*, if not their location, obvious.

Anderson's Q-probes had died before they could bring their defense routines up, and without the probes in place, *Avalon* was now seeing everything as it was twenty-six minutes ago. They had *no* idea what *Triumphant* was doing in response to discovering their watchers.

"Can we say when they'll detect us?" Kyle demanded.

"No idea, sir," Anderson admitted. "They'll probably guess we're doing exactly what we're doing, and we are throwing off a *lot* of energy. If they take a close look, we'll be pretty obvious, sir. I'd guess they know by now."

"Understood," Kyle acknowledged. Well, he'd known the stealth trick wasn't going to work forever. *Avalon* was still almost half a billion kilometers from the depot – five and a half hours of careful deceleration for a zero-zero intercept.

"Stanford, Norup," he barked, opening channels to the two men. "Launch *now*. Don't worry about stealth – they know we're here.

"It looks like most of the defenses are down, but, Stanford, make sure Norup is covered all the way in. Those starfighters may still want to play."

"Rokos and his Wing are on the depot," the CAG replied. "I'll send Nguyen and Epsilon to back him up with those starfighters. The rest of us are going after the battleship."

"We're firing new probes now," Kyle told Stanford, with a commanding glance over at Anderson, "we'll relay data as we have it, but they won't be very far ahead of you for a while."

"I know the rodeo, Captain," Stanford replied. "We'll bring the bastard down."

"Good luck, CAG," Kyle said softly. "Seems we'll need more than I hoped!"

10:45 January 14, 2736 ESMDT
SFG-001 Actual – Falcon-C type command starfighter

IT WAS good to be back in space. There was little Michael found more frustrating than sitting on the carrier, watching other people make the decisions that would decide whether or not he and his people lived and died.

With all of his starfighters out and moving, however, he had a *lot* more control over how things would end.

"All right people," he told his flight crews. "Everybody but Bravo and Epsilon, set your course for *Triumphant*. Rokos, Nguyen – the Marines are in your tender hands. Try to get them to target in one piece?"

"I make no guarantees," Rokos intoned ominously. "Though I'll note that Major Norup owes me a beer."

"Then you'll want to be sure I survive to make good," the Marine commander replied. "We'll be fine, CAG. Go get *Triumphant*."

"Good luck, Major."

"*I'm* not the one charging a battleship in a tin can," Norup pointed out.

Michael really had no response to that, so he let the channel drop as the two groups of small craft separated. 'Tin can' was a more accurate description of his starfighter than he figured the Marine commander knew – tiny as the thirty-meter wedges of his ships were by the standard of modern spacecraft, they still massed about as much as the old wet navy destroyers that had first carried the nickname.

Depending on how *Triumphant* reacted, this could be a very short flight or long one. If the battleship set her course to engage *Avalon*, they'd be engaging in an hour and a half at almost a third of light-speed. If the battleship *ran*, they'd bring her down in about three.

It would be ten minutes before they knew for sure, though the time delay would drop as they closed – and perhaps more importantly, as the Q-Com-equipped probes fired ahead of them at a thousand gravities closed.

And… there were the Q-probes dying. What he was seeing on his scanners was still twenty-five minutes old, but it was now more recent than the last data from the dead probes. *Triumphant* continued on her course for a few minutes, though Michael winced as he saw the power readings from the scans she was sweeping space with.

Even at twenty-five light minutes, *that* was going to get a readable return off of *Avalon*. One way or another, the rogue battleship would know she was being hunted by the time the signal got back.

"What are they doing?" Kayla Arnolds, his gunner asked softly. "Are they… spinning?"

He was right, Michael realized as he reviewed the footage.

Triumphant had ceased to accelerate, turned so her longest side was facing *Avalon*, and begun slowly rotating.

"They're launching," the CAG said simply. "Find me the missiles, Kayla."

His command starfighter traded the third missile in each of its magazines for dramatically increased computer support. Linked into the systems via his implant, he almost *felt* the repeated reviews of the data with various levels of enhancement and different tools. The whole process took seconds.

There were almost certainly twenty-four missiles – a full salvo from the battleship – but they could only confirm fourteen of them. Four of *those* they only had vague locations on, and as Michael watched the computer downgraded one of them to 'probable' from 'likely'.

Then it blipped up six *new* missiles as the battleship rotated again – a reload cycle complete on all of her launchers.

"Keep an eye on those birds," he ordered. "I need an estimate of how many."

"They'll have to go live, won't they?" Arnolds asked. "We'll see them then."

"I dislike surprises, Lieutenant," Michael observed. "Keep them labeled on the feed, watch their course."

More missiles popped up. Not nearly enough for them to be detecting all of them, but as the minutes passed, Michael was detecting *dozens* of definite and probable missiles – none of which had fired their engines, and none of which were on a direct course for *Avalon*.

"What *are* they doing?" he asked aloud.

As if the universe was listening, the missiles finally activated their drives. His starfighter's computers dispassionately analyzed their numbers and course and gave him the most likely answer to his question.

Four full salvos, ninety-six missiles, activated their drives in a sequence carefully calculated to turn them into a single massive salvo. Their course arced away from *Avalon*, but his computers happily told him that they would almost certainly turn back, go ballistic, and make a final approach on the carrier from a direction his fighters could not intercept.

"Oh Starless Void," he cursed as he grasped the dilemma that Captain Richardson had left him with. If he pursued *Triumphant*, he could bring the battleship to bay long before they escaped into Alcubierre – but *Avalon* would have at best a fifty percent chance of stopping that many missiles.

He ran the vectors to be sure and sighed. *Triumphant's* commander had chosen his attack arc with care and skill – there was no line on which his fighters could catch the missiles and still have a chance of bringing the battleship to bay.

With two Wings detached to assault the depot, he only had three Wings – one hundred and forty-four fighters – left. He could, *maybe*, take *Triumphant* with one Wing, or stop the missiles with only one Wing... but to be certain of either...

"All fighters," he opened a channel to the ships in his attack force. "New course downloading, setup for missile intercept."

They could always catch *Triumphant* later – but if they lost *Avalon*, none of them got to go home.

11:30 January 14, 2736 ESMDT
DSC-78 Avalon, *Flag Deck*

DIMITRI LISTENED to the Vice Commodore's decision with disbelief. He understood the CAG's dilemma, but their mission was to catch *Triumphant*. He *had* to catch *Triumphant*.

"Captain Roberts," he snapped. "That salvo will go ballistic before it reaches us. How much danger are we seriously in?"

"Sir, they have enough ECM in play that we can't localize their vectors before they go ballistic," Roberts told him grimly. "With a fighter intercept, we're in no danger – *without* one, we'll localize the missiles when they bring their drives back up for terminal maneuvers. We'd have less than a minute to intercept the missiles.

"With that many birds, we're looking at a fifty percent chance of losing *Avalon*."

"If he goes after the missiles, we'll fail in our mission to catch *Triumphant*," Dimitri snarled at the other man.

"We will catch *Triumphant*," Roberts replied calmly. "Not today, perhaps, but we have a strategic speed advantage, and we have enough probes scattered around this system now that we'll know their destination when they jump.

"Given those conditions, the preservation of this ship takes tactical priority over catching *Triumphant* today," the Captain said flatly. "Ending our pursuit of *Triumphant* in mutual destruction has no purpose, Admiral."

Roberts, Dimitri reflected, wasn't thinking about their time limit. The Alliance might well pull *Avalon* back – or order them to hold Alizon! – if they didn't catch *Triumphant* today. If they could still pursue *Triumphant*, though, the Captain wasn't wrong.

"Damn it, Captain, you're supposed to be the aggressive wonder-boy," he snapped anyway. "You're the last man I expected to be a coward in the face of the enemy!"

"Aggression is about risk, sir," Roberts replied flatly. "It's about odds and probabilities, and knowing we can catch them later makes me perfectly willing to give up a ninety percent chance of catching *Triumphant* today to avoid a fifty percent of *losing Avalon*.

"I have no intention of dying for revenge today when we can live and have it tomorrow."

13:00 January 14, 2736 ESMDT
DSC-078 Avalon, *Bridge*

THE ENTIRE CONCEPT behind a missile strike with a ballistic phase was to use ECM and decoys to render the exact location of the missiles unpredictable. That way, they were almost impossible to destroy before they hit terminal range and brought their drives back up for their final attack runs.

Like most tactics, there was a counter-measure. In this case, using starfighters to intercept the missiles in their ballistic phase. While you couldn't locate the missiles accurately enough to shoot them down, you could bring starfighters in close enough that *they* could locate the missiles.

Kyle watched impassively as Stanford's fighters ripped through the missile swarm. The Stormwinds re-activated their ECM too late – a clear sign that the humans responsible for them weren't expecting them to survive at this point. A good missile jockey would have followed the starfighters' path and sent the lightspeed command to bring up the ECM early well before the attackers arrived.

"I show ninety-one missile kills, Captain," Stanford reported. "Can you confirm?"

Kyle glanced over at Anderson who flashed a thumbs up.

"We have the same, CAG," he told Stanford. "I'm pretty sure we can deal with five missiles."

"Want me to take off after *Triumphant*?"

Avalon's Captain looked at the geometry too and sighed.

"There's no point," he admitted. "Your velocity is all wrong at this point, you wouldn't even get close before they jump. Reinforce the depot strike," he ordered. "Let's make sure the Marines get in."

"Tally-ho, Captain."

Kyle focused his attention on the depot. They had a new Q-probe in the area, so he had real-time data on the defenders again. Those sixty starfighters continued to orbit, which surprised him. They might be outnumbered, but he refused to fault the Commonwealth Navy's will to fight.

"Sir, Wing Commander Rokos is on a channel for you."

"Link him in," he ordered.

"Captain, I'm receiving a lightspeed transmission from the depot," the Wing Commander told him. "They're requesting to speak with our CO, so I'm relaying to you.

"We are one hour from turkey shoot time," he noted. "Activating relay."

An image of a pale-skinned man with slightly pink eyes and pure white hair resolved itself on Kyle's implants. A small icon on the screen noted it was a recorded message, transmitted a little over five minutes beforehand – Rokos' fighters were still over five light minutes from their target.

"I am Captain John Paris of the Commonwealth Navy," the albino said calmly. "My people have completed their scans of their starfighters and confirmed what I presumed from the beginning.

"While the officers and men and women under my command are brave, their morale has been shattered by betrayal, and I am willing to admit when we face a superior foe. To avoid further loss of life on this already bloody day, I offer the unconditional surrender of the Alizon Logistics Depot, the shattered remnants of its defenses, and all forces on the surface of Alizon."

Paris sighed and bowed his head for a long moment before looking back up at the camera.

"I await the response of the Alliance High Commander," he said quietly.

Kyle checked that Tobin had received the message – for some strange reason, he didn't have an active link to the Vice Admiral right now – and then opened a link.

"Admiral."

"Captain."

From his frosty tone, Tobin hadn't quite forgotten their earlier argument.

"The depot has offered their surrender," Kyle said calmly. "How we proceed from here… is a strategic decision, sir."

Frost or not, that got a quirk that might have been the beginnings of a smile from the old Admiral.

"Then I shall speak to this Captain Paris. Stay on the channel, Captain."

Kyle watched as Tobin's people quickly and efficiently setup for the recording, and then the Admiral turned to face the camera, his most intimidating dark scowl settling onto his face.

"Captain Paris, I am Vice Admiral Tobin of the Castle Federation Space Navy," he rumbled. "Your surrender is accepted. My Marines will arrive in just under eighty minutes from your receipt of this message. Understand that any resistance to their arrival or their boarding will be met with maximum force.

"Enough blood has been shed this day," the big Vice Admiral told the Commonwealth base commander. "Your wisdom in avoiding further loss is noted. Once my Marines are aboard, you will be escorted to *Avalon* where my Captain and I will accept your surrender in person.

"Vice Admiral Tobin, out."

32

Alizon System
16:00 January 14, 2736 Earth Standard Meridian Date/Time
DSC-078 Avalon, *Bridge*

AFTER ALMOST SIXTEEN hours on the bridge, Kyle couldn't sit in his command chair anymore. His immobilized shoulder *hurt*, but it hurt somewhat less if he was standing, so he stood behind his chair with his hands carefully clasped across his torso.

He watched as Maria Pendez slowly and carefully brought *Avalon* to a halt, roughly five thousand kilometers from the Commonwealth logistics depot. Eight starfighters – Epsilon Wing's Third Squadron – made their approach from the depot, angling to land as the carrier continued to retrieve her starfighters.

"Get me Major Norup," he ordered. The Marines had been on station barely two hours – there was no way they had secured the entire facility yet.

It took a few minutes, but eventually the sallow face of the Marine commander appeared on Kyle's implant feeds.

"Captain Roberts," he greeted Kyle. "We're a little busy down here, so I hope this can be quick."

"It should be," Kyle promised. "I need an update on the status of the depot. How long until it's fully secured?"

"Captain Paris' people are being co-operative," Norup noted, "but we are talking almost twenty-five thousand military personnel across eight major and twenty-six minor platforms, plus the repair dock."

"I'm not asking for miracles, Major, just a timeline."

Norup shook his head.

"Between twelve and thirty-six hours is the best estimate I can give you, sir," he said. "I can guarantee we'll have the command facilities, any remaining defensive weapons, and the dock secured in a maximum of twelve hours."

"All right, Major," Kyle allowed. "I'm not going to argue with the professionals. We should be able to expect to take Captain Paris' surrender aboard *Avalon* by, say, oh eight hundred tomorrow morning?"

That gave the Marines sixteen hours to complete securing all of the systems necessary to control the Commonwealth base. It also meant they could complete the ceremony, return Paris and Norup's Marines to the base, and be on their way out of the system after *Triumphant* within twenty-four hours.

"We will also need to co-opt at least one platoon to coordinate with local forces on the surface," Kyle told the Major. "Details are shaky, but we have some communication with the remnants of the Alizon Guard. Commonwealth forces on the surface are being good so far, but we'll need to mobilize the locals if we're to detain and secure a fifty thousand strong occupation garrison."

From the slightly ill expression on Norup's face, the Marine battalion commander had been focused on securing the depot. While he probably hadn't forgotten about the five divisions of the Terran Commonwealth Army on the surface of Alizon, they hadn't been his priority.

"The Guard would be... very helpful with that," he agreed. "If we can coordinate with them and trust them to avoid retaliatory atrocities."

"Commonwealth Army occupation garrisons are usually *very* strictly disciplined," Kyle reminded him. "So far, they're sounding more 'get them off our planet' than 'kill them all,' but I want Marines on hand. Just in case."

"I'll see to it, Captain," Norup promised. "Anything else?"

"No. I suspect I'm going to have a doctor ordering me to sleep shortly," the Captain advised wryly, "but don't hesitate to reach out if you need anything from us. Commander Solace will be able to assist you if I'm out of communication."

"Thank you, sir," Norup said crisply. "We'll be in touch, sir."

The channel cut off. Kyle turned to Commander Anderson.

"James, what's the status of our mass-murdering friend?"

"We got a clean read when she brought up her Alcubierre-Stetson drive, sir," the tired looking officer replied. "Took us a bit to crunch the numbers, mostly because the destination looks strange. I'm not familiar with the system at all, but it's in our catalog as Barsoom. Inside Alliance borders, but shows as Commonwealth."

Kyle was about to start reviewing the information on Barsoom when Surgeon-Commander Cunningham called to give exactly the order he'd been expecting.

"Your brace is sending me all sorts of wonderful medical data, you know," Cunningham told him dryly. "Which means I can tell that if you *don't* get your ass either lying down, preferably asleep, or into my clinic, everything I did last night will be for nothing.

"Take a break, Captain. Doctor's orders."

Kyle shook his head at the Doctor – technically junior to him, but also the only man on the ship who could give him an order like that.

"I will, Commander," he promised. He turned to Anderson. "Commander Anderson, get together with Lieutenant Commander Snapes and pull together a briefing on Barsoom. I suspect the Admiral and I will need it."

18:00 January 14, 2736 ESMDT
DSC-078 Avalon, Vice Admiral Tobin's Office

"CONGRATULATIONS ON LIBERATING Alizon with only one ship, Admiral Tobin," Fleet Admiral Meredith Blake told Dimitri. The Federation's uniformed military commander looked almost cheerful compared to the last few times he'd seen her.

"We missed *Triumphant*," he admitted. That failure was far more important to him, even if everyone else regarded it as minor. "Liberating Alizon was, well, incidental."

"And still our first truly offensive victory of the war," she noted. "Have you made contact with the Alizoni government?"

"Captain Roberts has sent Marines to the surface to interface with the Alizon Guard," Dimitri told her. "We're hoping the Guard can put us in touch with whoever is left of the civilian government."

"Their emergency plans for this circumstance called for the civilian government to disappear into hidden underground bunkers along with the Guard High Command," Blake advised him. "Hopefully, President Ingolfson is still alive. Very sensible man, very competent."

"We can hope, ma'am. We have secured the orbitals," he continued. "My intent is to leave the Marines and a small force of starfighters and Navy personnel to support the Guard in securing the Commonwealth prisoners.

"We will be en route after *Triumphant* inside of twenty-four hours."

Blake was silent for a moment, a sour expression on her face he recognized as her marshaling the words to say something she knew a subordinate wouldn't like.

"Admiral, I've discussed this with Alliance High Command," she said quietly. "Don't get me wrong, *everyone* wants to see Captain Richardson take a long walk out a short airlock, but he's now unquestionably rogue by Commonwealth standards – and headed into Commonwealth space.

"We know Walkingstick. He's our enemy, but he's also an honorable man. He will do everything within his power to bring Richardson to justice, and we can now be certain Richardson will fight him. Walkingstick will lose ships and resources to bring *Triumphant* in."

She shook her head.

"Even if that wasn't the case, Dimitri," she told him gently, "holding Alizon would be more important than revenge. Destroying *Triumphant* won't bring back the dead, but protecting Alizon and providing the hammer to force the garrison to honor Paris' surrender will *save* lives.

"I am ordering you to remain in the Alizon system," Blake finished bluntly. "We have reinforced Kematian and the rest of your Battle Group is now en route to Alizon. They are twelve days away. You will oversee the security of the Alizon system until sufficient defenses can be set up."

"We cannot allow the devastation of an inhabited world to go unpunished!" Dimitri snapped, anger boiling through him at the thought. "Half a *billion* dead, Meredith! Even if the Commonwealth does punish him, then we show the galaxy we allow our *enemies* to punish crimes against *our* people."

"There is sentiment and there is practicality, Vice Admiral," the Federation Chief of Staff snapped. "I will leave half a billion unavenged to guarantee the safety of *three* billion."

"I do not agree with these orders," the Vice Admiral grounded out, but Blake simply shook her head.

"You have the privilege as an officer to disagree with your orders," she said calmly. "You do not have the privilege to disobey.

"Can you obey your orders, Admiral Tobin, or must I relieve you and place the fate of Alizon in Captain Roberts' capable hands?"

Dimitri swallowed his anger, letting it burn deep within him as he glared at the older, more senior, Admiral. He couldn't. He couldn't obey – he physically could *not* let Richardson go. Which left him only one real choice.

"I understand, ma'am," he lied. "I will make certain Alizon is secure."

"Thank you, Dimitri," Blake said quietly. "I know what you're feeling. But we can't lose one world trying to avenge another."

He nodded choppily and killed the connection.

THERE WAS VERY little breakable in his office, and it took Dimitri only a few minutes to work through the coffee cups, carafe and glasses scattered around the room. It made very little difference to his mood, and he found himself sitting cross-legged on the floor, staring blankly at the shards of ceramic.

Time and again, Commonwealth officers had gone too far. Logic insisted it was only a handful – less than half a dozen incidents in two wars – but Dimitri Tobin had been present for too many of them. Kematian was only the latest atrocity he'd seen with his own eyes.

The Commonwealth might well punish their own officers. Walking-stick might well take his fleet after *Triumphant* and bring down the battleship, perhaps even take losses the Alliance needed him to take in doing so.

But to leave the punishment of evil to those who enabled it stuck in Dimitri's throat. The souls of Kematian's dead didn't want their justice meted out by the very men whose actions had set their fate into motion.

Perhaps worse, if the Alliance allowed the Commonwealth to police crimes committed in their space, they surrendered a piece of the very sovereignty they fought for. They would lose some of their legitimacy in the eyes of both other governments and their own people.

Vice Admiral Dimitri Tobin could understand every single step in the perfectly logical chain that had brought Alliance High Command to the orders he'd been given. But he could not agree with them. He could not obey them.

As he searched for an answer, he began to clean up the debris of his rage. If he had it all cleaned away before he had anyone in his office, no one would ever know what had happened unless he told them.

He froze, his hands full of shards of glass, as the realization struck him. Carefully, ever-so-carefully, he finished cleaning the sharp pieces of glass and ceramic off the floor and then took a seat at his desk. No one else knew the orders he'd received.

It was still possible to carry out his mission – if he was truly prepared to sacrifice *everything*. Against half a billion murdered innocents, what choice did he have?

"Lieutenant Major Barsamian," he opened a channel to *Avalon's*

Ship's Marshal. "Have you made any progress in identifying our spy and assassin?"

The dark-skinned young woman in his implant feed looked up from her desk with tired eyes.

"Not yet, Admiral," she told him. "We have a lot of data to go over. It may be three or four days before I have enough for it be worthwhile to brief you and Captain Roberts."

"Major, are you telling me we have *no* idea who this agent is?" he asked. It was the response he'd expected, but he needed to get this on the record.

"Unfortunately, sir, that is exactly what I am telling you," she replied, her voice sharp.

"Lieutenant Major," he continued formally, "based on this newest incident, I see no option but to take the ship to Counter Intelligence Level One."

"Sir, that is Captain Roberts' decision…"

"Or mine if the risk is to the Battle Group," he reminded her. She pursed her lips sourly, but he knew he was right. With effectively a single ship 'Battle Group,' the line of just what the Admiral aboard could and couldn't do was very blurry.

"You will take the ship black," he ordered. "All communications to and from *Avalon* will go through my office, to be approved by my authorization code *only*. This is now a matter of the security of the Federation – and of Alizon."

"I understand, sir," Barsamian said quietly, bowing her head. "I will see to it."

She was true to her word. Less than five minutes later, the lockout appeared on his computer screen, requesting his personal authorization codes to confirm the complete shutdown of Q-Com communication with the rest of the universe.

He smiled.

The easiest step was complete. He wasn't, yet, committed – though as soon as *Avalon* left the Alizon system his career was over. No matter the price, he would make certain that *Triumphant* would not escape justice.

33

Alizon System
08:00 January 15, 2736 Earth Standard Meridian Date/Time
DSC-078 Avalon, *Main Flight Deck*

CAPTAIN JOHN PARIS was somewhat unsettling in person. The albino Commonwealth officer was extremely tall and gaunt – towering several centimeters over Kyle's own daunting height – which combined with his red eyes, pale skin, and almost translucent hair into an odd visage even by Federation standards.

Two Federation Marines had led the way off of the shuttle onto the flight deck where Kyle and Tobin were waiting. Another dozen from the platoon Norup had left aboard formed an honor guard around the two Federation officers.

Paris himself was escorted by a pair of burly, but unarmed, Commonwealth Marines in full dress uniform. Two more Federation Marines followed him, escorting a second Commonwealth officer, a redheaded and broad-shoulder woman with the paired gold bars of a Commander.

Kyle stepped forward as the prisoner paused in front of the honor guard, offering the man a firm salute.

"Welcome aboard *Avalon*, Captain Paris," he said calmly, reflecting again on the inevitable confusion of so many Alliance powers deciding a starship commander was an O-7. He and Paris had the same title, but he outranked the other man. With a nod, he led the man over to Tobin.

Reaching the Vice Admiral, Kyle rejoined his flag officer and formally introduced them.

"Captain John Paris of the Commonwealth Navy, this is Vice Admiral Dimitri Tobin of the Federation Space Navy."

"Admiral," Paris said with a sharp salute. "I hereby surrender my facility and personnel into your keeping."

"Thank you, Captain," Tobin replied calmly. "On the honor of the Federation, so long as your people cooperate, no one will be harmed."

"Thank you, Admiral," Paris replied. "I never expected to surrender my command to the Alliance," he said quietly, "but strangely, all I feel today is relief that you were here."

"We were in pursuit of *Triumphant*," Kyle noted. "Even so, we did not expect what he did."

"Commodore kaBhekuzulu knew about Kematian, obviously," the base commander said quietly. "He demanded Richardson's surrender. *Triumphant's* XO informed us he had Richardson in custody and would surrender the ship and Richardson so long as kaBhekuzulu guaranteed that no one other than Richardson would face the death penalty."

The skeletal Commonwealth officer shrugged, looking very tired.

"kaBhekuzulu agreed," he said simply. "The crisis appeared over, and we stood down to allow the *Triumphant* to be taken in. You saw what followed."

"You'll forgive me, Captain Paris, if I am more concerned about the hundreds of millions Richardson killed on Kematian than the thousands he killed here," Tobin said bluntly. "But do not worry. We will hunt Captain Richardson to the ends of the galaxy if need be."

Kyle managed to avoid making any noticeable response to that. Hopefully, the Admiral was exaggerating – there were limits to how far *Avalon* could go, or how long they could indulge in this pursuit.

"I must confess, Admiral," Paris replied, his voice very quiet, "that before I surrendered our facility to you I left a program in our surveillance network to inform Walkingstick of where *Triumphant* fled. Whether by your hand or by the Marshal's, Richardson will pay for his crimes."

Tobin grunted and gestured for the Marines to take Paris and his subordinate away. Once the prisoners had left, Major Norup exited the shuttle. The Marine was in an unmarked dark gray jumpsuit, the kind his people wore under body armor, and looked exhausted.

"Captain, Admiral," he saluted. "I beg leave to report we have secured approximately seventy five percent of the Commonwealth base. We have identified and sequestered slightly over eighty percent of Captain Paris' people – we're using one of the storage platforms to hold them all. It's been cleared of anything except food," he noted.

"Excellent work, Major," Kyle told him. For sixteen hours work in as large a facility as the Commonwealth had assembled here, that was almost a miracle.

"We have also managed to make contact with the command structure of the Alizon Guard," he reported. "My understanding is that President Ingolfson is alive, but buried *very* deep – both literally and metaphorically. He is expected to be in a position to speak with Admiral Tobin by later this morning.

"My people are coordinating efforts with the Guard, but so far, the Terrans are being cooperative. If," he finished with a wicked smile, "somewhat shocked at just how *many* intact, fully equipped, Guard units are still around."

"Well done indeed, Major," Tobin confirmed. "We're having a staff meeting on *Avalon's* next steps at oh nine hundred hours. It will impact your people, so I'd like you to be there."

"Yes, sir," was the disheveled Marine's only reply.

09:00 January 15, 2736 ESMDT
DSC-078 Avalon, *Flag Deck Conference Room*

DIMITRI TOOK a swallow of his coffee as he settled himself down at the end of the conference table, glancing around the room at the small group he'd gathered. If he failed to convince these five people of the validity of his plans and authority, he might well end up throwing his career away for nothing.

"Ladies, gentlemen," he began calmly. "It has been seventeen hours since *Triumphant* went faster than light. Since it will take us two hours to get clear enough to engage our own FTL drive, that means we are a minimum of nineteen hours behind Captain Richardson, and according to my math, we'll only make up four hours over the ten light years to Barsoom.

"We are under some pressure from High Command to bring *Triumphant* to heel and return to other duties," he lied. "I want to get us underway as soon as possible – I would very much like to have us underway by thirteen hundred hours. Giving Captain Richardson more than twenty hours in a system that is effectively defenseless makes my teeth itch."

"What about Alizon, sir?" Norup asked immediately. "The Guard may be doing the heavy lifting on the surface, but the Star Guard is functionally gone. Even if they have pilots, they have no starfighters or guardships."

"Remember, Major, that Captain Paris' surrender included the remaining starfighters," Dimitri reminded him, "While the flight crews did their jobs and wiped their systems, my understanding is that we have a copy of the *Scimitar's* flight and combat software. Vice Commodore?"

Stanford started, surprised, but nodded slowly.

"The *Scimitar* has been in service for years, and we've captured a few intact already," he agreed. "We have full copies of their software to use in our simulators. The Q-Coms won't work – we don't have updated Commonwealth codes and we're probably better off tearing the entangled particle arrays out of the ships for our own security – but we can give them control of the engines and weapons."

"The Alizoni should be able to come up with flight crews for sixty starfighters," the Admiral told his people. "As I understand it, the support ships we have left are capable of refuelling and rearming in space. They should be able to coopt some of the insystem clippers or civilian platforms to provide quarters for their crews, and we can leave… how many tugs would you be comfortable leaving, Captain Roberts?"

Avalon's Captain looked uncertain. Dimitri knew that Roberts had been aware of the original deadline, now expired, and hoped the man figured the Admiral was stretching his orders, not completely defying them.

"I'm not entirely comfortable only having eight ships for SAR," he admitted finally. "But we can leave four. The Commonwealth platform had enough Javelins aboard to provide functionally infinite reloads for the starfighters as well. From a planetary defense standpoint, though, sixty starfighters is a pretty sparse line to shield a world." The Captain paused. "*Triumphant* barely qualifies as a modern ship. We can probably spare one of Stanford's Wings."

"Agreed," Dimitri told him. "The rest of Battle Group Seventeen is already en route here and can reinforce the Star Guard and whichever Wing we leave behind. I can't see Walkingstick mobilizing an assault force and getting it here in the next twelve days."

He turned back to Norup.

"I have no intention of leaving the Alizon Guard in the lurch, either," he told the Major. "The truth is that we will not be attempting to board *Triumphant*," he admitted. "Outside of a small detachment – the platoon or so you've already left aboard should do – for onboard security and supporting Marshal Barsamian, I don't see any need for Marines.

"I intend to leave you and most of your battalion behind, quartered in the logistics base, with all of your assault shuttles. With you acting a fast response force, and the Commonwealth starfighters to provide a core force for the Star Guard, I believe the Alizoni should be able to secure their own system until BG Seventeen arrives."

"That… makes sense," the Major admitted with a sigh. "We can do that, sir."

"Admiral," Solace interjected, the first the dark-skinned executive officer had spoken so far. "We now know that Walkingstick knows exactly where Richardson was going from here. One of his main nodal forces is, well, only ten light years from Barsoom. He can have a ship – or even *multiple* ships – to Barsoom before we can get there.

"It's a Commonwealth system, sir. Can we really justify leaving one of *our* systems swinging in the breeze to charge off to protect a Commonwealth system from a Commonwealth Captain?" she asked bluntly.

"This system needs us, sir. This kind of decision is your prerogative as the flag officer on the scene – we need to at least consider whether or not pursuing *Triumphant* is really in the Alliance's best interests."

Damn, Solace was a clever woman. And a brave one too – Dimitri was sure several of the others had been thinking it, but Roberts' XO had been the one to put it forward. Of course, she was junior enough that no one would hold being devil's advocate against her.

"It's not our place to second-guess Alliance High Command," Sanchez snapped, Dimitri's Chief of Staff leaping to his defense. He wondered, for a moment, if she knew what he was doing. She was perhaps the only person on the ship who *might* have overheard something.

"It's not, Commander Sanchez," Dimitri agreed, but he forced a smile on his face as he looked at Solace. "However, as Commander Solace says, discussing and considering these sorts of points is the responsibility of a flag officer – or a ship commander," he added, nodding to Roberts, "on the scene.

"As it happens, Admiral Blake and I had this exact discussion." Though the sides hadn't been what he was trying to convince his people of. "High Command and I agree that we cannot risk the loss of face and sovereignty inherent in allowing the Commonwealth to exact justice for our dead. The Alliance has never allowed these atrocities to go without punishment at our hands, and we cannot change that policy now.

"*Triumphant* must – and *will* be hunted down and destroyed. We are the closest, and we will carry out this mission," he stated firmly. "Now, in regards to that, I believe Senior Fleet Commander Sanchez has prepared a briefing on the Barsoom system?"

He seemed to have won his case. His officers were nodding and turning their attention to the briefing. Despite everything, it seemed to have been an astonishingly easy lie to carry off.

"Barsoom," Sanchez began, "is a five planet system inside what has traditionally been Alliance space. It was scouted by ships from Earth around the same time as many of the planets that made up the first wave of colonization this far out, but deemed unsustainable for colonization."

A model of the star system appeared in the middle of the table. It was a stereotypical five planet system – two gas giants in distant orbits, an asteroid field of debris the gas giants had kept from forming into planets, a burnt rock in a super-fast orbit, and a heavy atmosphere hothouse world just too close to be habitable.

The third planet was the key. It was a reddish blue, an odd tinge, but one Dimitri knew tended to be found on barely habitable worlds.

"The system was named for Barsoom III's resemblance to what geologists believe Mars to have looked like tens or hundreds of millions of years ago. III has an atmosphere, even one breathable to humans. However, an extended weak period of the system star has resulted in most of the water on the planet being locked into the soil and a long-term die off of vegetation and animal life.

"Combined with a trio of large inner system cometary bodies, whose orbits are just fast enough to avoid being captured by Barsoom III but close enough in to strip atmosphere away every time they pass, the surveyors figured III would be uninhabitable by roughly Earth Standard Year three thousand and almost completely atmosphere-less by year four thousand.

"Since the area had many planets that could be inhabited without the massive intervention Barsoom would require, no one had any interest until the War ended," she said calmly. "At that point, the Commonwealth launched a government-sponsored terraforming operation. The three comets stealing Barsoom's atmosphere were destroyed or re-directed, and active warming efforts began.

"They have slowed the degradation and begun to re-stabilize the ecosystem. Current projections are to open colonization in about twenty years – at which point, the corp doing the terraforming stands to make an absolutely unimaginable amount of money."

"But we're pretty sure it was there as a listening post," Kyle pointed out.

"Exactly," Sanchez agreed. "To our knowledge, there is no military presence in the system, but there is a Commonwealth Intelligence facility and the terraforming base would be able to provide the *Triumphant* with all of her consumables except ammunition.

"And unless Walkingstick does send ships to its defense from Captain Paris' data, the system is completely defenseless."

11:00 January 15, 2736 ESMDT
DSC-078 Avalon, *Vice Admiral Tobin's Office*

"Sir, we finally have President Ingolfson for you," Dimitri was informed by the com operator. "He's requesting an immediate link-up."

"Put him through," he ordered. A momentary chill ran through him. If Ingolfson had an active Q-Com connection back to the Alliance, it was going to get a lot harder to pretend his orders were still to chase *Triumphant* very quickly.

His wallscreen dissolved from plain gray metal into the image of a heavily jowled blond man sitting at a cheap desk that could have fit in any office in the galaxy.

"Vice Admiral Tobin," the President of Alizon greeted him. "I'm glad to have the opportunity to thank you personally for your intervention. While the Commonwealth's occupation was not heavy, it is never... easy to rest under the hand of a foreign conqueror."

"We were in the area, Mister President," Dimitri told him. "But once we were here, we weren't going to leave the Commonwealth in charge."

It took almost a full second for Ingolfson to respond, and Dimitri checked quickly to confirm his impression – the President was speaking to him via an old-fashioned radio, not any kind of Q-Com.

Which made sense, as he'd have had to confirm any Q-Com communication himself.

Counter Intelligence Level One gave him complete control over the ship's interstellar communications. Technically, Captain Roberts should have been the one with the review, but Dimitri was perfectly willing to push the gray area of effectively having a 'Battle Group' of one ship.

"It's appreciated," Ingolfson eventually answered. "My understanding from my staff is that you do need to continue your original mission, correct? I've been briefed on Kematian."

"Exactly, Mister President," Dimitri confirmed. "We intend to be underway in approximately two hours. We don't intend to leave you defenseless, though I'm hoping you can contribute personnel if nothing else. Captain Roberts' people are just finishing re-booting the sixty *Scimitars* the Commonwealth has left behind.

"We'll be leaving one of our fighter Wings and those *Scimitars* behind. If you can provide flight crews for the *Scimitars*, plus hopefully some kind of quarters for our people, it would be appreciated."

Again, most of a second passed by, and then Ingolfson's face split in a wide grin.

"As it happens, Admiral," he said calmly, "several of the new stations being built in orbit under the Commonwealth's careful eye have interiors with a strange resemblance to our old orbital fighter bases. If we strip some redundant paneling off – which I'm assured will take only a few hours – they'll work perfectly.

"I won't pretend I wouldn't rather see *Avalon* in orbit," the Alizoni man admitted, "but I understand that sometimes the mission must take priority – and there is no question *Triumphant* must be destroyed."

"Are you in contact with Alliance High Command?" Dimitri asked carefully.

"No," Ingolfson replied. "When we assembled our emergency command bunker, we assumed that we would still have access to our own orbital switchboard array." He grimaced. "Given the Commonwealth's focus on interstellar communication as the reason for unification, I don't think they blew it up *intentionally*, but our Q-Com network went down with it."

He shrugged.

"Whether it was intentional or not, the Terrans took advantage of it," he continued. "They policed up every Q-Com unit they could find that linked to an Alliance switchboard. We're trying to find one, but I was honestly hoping we could borrow at least a block of entangled pairs from you."

Dimitri nodded slowly.

"Unfortunately, we're under an FTL communications lockdown due to evidence of a spy aboard," he told Ingolfson. "While I think we're *safe*, I'm not sure any block we could give you would be... uncompromised."

"Damn," the President cursed. "Given your time constraint, it doesn't seem worth the effort then," he allowed. "We'll find the ones the Commonwealth confiscated soon enough, I'm sure.

"I'll have Star Guard Command coordinate moving those starfighters into those concealed launch bases, and make arrangements for proper quarters for your people," Ingolfson concluded. "I'm sure you're busy with your departure preparations.

"But once again, Admiral, you have my thanks, and the thanks of the Alizoni people, for your efforts on our behalf. The name *Avalon* was in no risk of being forgotten here, but now... now I think she will once again be a legend to my people."

34

VICE ADMIRAL TOBIN'S deadline might not have been *necessary*, in the strictest sense, but it had at least been doable. With fifteen minutes to spare, Kyle sat on the bridge of his ship and watched the forty-eight starfighters of Wing Commander Lei Nguyen's Epsilon Wing gently boost across Alizon orbit.

The station they were headed for wasn't yet able to take them – or the sixty ex-Commonwealth starfighters orbiting it – aboard just yet, but the covert teams who'd snuck an entire fighter base into what they'd told the Commonwealth was a transshipment terminal assured him they'd be ready in less than an hour.

"All right, Maria," he told Fleet Commander Pendez. "That's the last item on the to-do list. Set your course for Barsoom, flank acceleration until we're clear for Alcubierre."

"Yes, sir," she replied crisply and hit a single button. The preloaded course activated, and *Avalon's* mighty engines flared to life.

Kyle watched the recently liberated planet drop away behind them and brooded. They'd done good work here, and he wasn't a fan of leaving the job half-done. While he agreed it was *unlikely* the Commonwealth could organize an attack to retake the system before the rest of Battle Group Seventeen arrived, leaving the planet half-defenseless didn't sit well with him.

Two hours to being able to warp space. Six days and four hours to Barsoom. But what then? Arriving in the system fifteen hours after *Triumphant*, it was entirely possible their visit to Barsoom would end up like their visit to KG-779 – barely in time to see the rogue battleship flee.

With a concealed sigh, he began to look up their orders. Just how far did High Command expect them to go to pursue Kematian's murderers? If they were willing to leave an Alliance world unprotected, then the deadline must have been released…

He barely prevented himself from sitting bolt upright in his chair as his attempt to access their orders hit a brick wall. He was locked out by the Admiral's seal – part of the Level One security?

As Captain, *Kyle* was supposed to control that. Poking at the locks, however, he'd rapidly confirmed that it had been done as a Battle Group Counter Intelligence lockdown, with Tobin as the only person with access. Kyle was unable to access communications on his own ship, and a sinking feeling took hold of his guts.

This whole trip was going to hell in a handbasket. First the assassination attempts, then the bombing of Kematian, then *more* assassination attempts – and now a mission of outright revenge, taken as black as the system could go.

It was a long way from what he'd hoped for in his first real command. Arguing with the Admiral was probably pointless.

He needed a drink.

14:40 January 15, 2736 ESMDT
DSC-078 Avalon, *Observation Deck*

"WHAT, are you making a habit of receiving wine bottles from thankful heads of state?" Stanford asked as he entered the observation deck and saw Kyle waiting for him with a bottle of wine.

"This one is mine," Kyle replied. "All I got from Ingolfson was the electronic equivalent of a 'thank you' card – the man is strangely busy for the head of government of a newly liberated planet."

"And one who we are basically leaving to the wolves with a pointy stick," Solace observed as she joined the two men.

The CAG glanced over at the Captain and the XO, and Kyle poured three glasses of wine with a wink at his friend.

"If you two are down here, who's flying this crate?" Stanford asked.

"Fleet Commander Maria Pendez is an extremely competent officer who is very able to hold down the watch on her own," Kyle said virtuously. "And if anything more dangerous than an Alcubierre-Stetson entrance comes up, and she somehow feels overly intimidated," he shrugged and tapped his temple, "I'm only a thought away."

Stanford shook his head and took the wine. Kyle knew the smaller man was more empathetic than he sometimes pretended and had probably guessed his Captain needed a drink and a friend.

"To Alizon," Kyle toasted, raising his glass to the other two officers. "May they stay well free of Terra's long shadow."

They drank. The wine Kyle had poached from the officer's lounge via the weight of the gold planet on his collar was not great, but it served the purpose today.

He realized with a minor start that it was the first time he'd ever seen his XO drink anything alcoholic at all. Something seemed to have shifted between him and Senior Fleet Commander Mira Solace at some point in the headlong pursuit of *Triumphant*. He wasn't entirely sure *what*, and he was pretty sure it wasn't something he should think on too hard.

She noticed him noticing the drink and winked at him.

"I'm not on duty, Kyle," she pointed out. "You can complain about my 'drunken ways' later."

He no longer had the ability to search and cross-reference reports at a thought he'd once had, but his implant interface bandwidth remained sufficient to match the clear quote with Captain Haliburt's evaluation report.

Kyle winced. *Now* he understood why she didn't drink in front of her Captain. In amidst all of the other specious accusations the first Captain she'd XOed under had leveled in that garbage report, he'd barely registered the alcoholism complaint.

"I never added those particular puzzle pieces together," he admitted aloud. "My apologies, Mira."

She chuckled softly and gestured for him to refill her glass.

"It took me a while, but I'm reasonably sure you're not Haliburt at this point," she noted.

"Speaking of… individuals of questionable judgment," Stanford interjected. "Am I the only one uncomfortable with leaving Alizon uncovered?"

"I wasn't just playing devil's advocate this morning," Solace pointed out. "This really is a situation where the Admiral should be using his own judgment and waiting.

"I want Richardson dead as much as anyone else," she continued, her eyes suddenly very dark and very flat, "but we can't leave an entire planet swinging in the breeze."

"High Command orders and even Admirals usually obey," Kyle reminded her. "But… Tobin wouldn't have disobeyed regardless. I'm not sure he's being entirely rational about *Triumphant*. This seems a lot more personal than it should be."

"We watched half a world die," Stanford said harshly. "I think it's a little Voids-cursed personal."

"No argument," Kyle agreed. "But with everything going on, I'm getting an uncomfortable itch between my shoulder blades – and not just because I'm sleeping on a mediocre cot in my office.

"Keep your eyes and ears open. Barsamian has half of the damn Marines on rotation watching *my* back, but our Terran agent went for Michael already."

He shook his head, eyeing his two key subordinates – and friends.

"With most of our Marines on Alizon, we can't put you two under guard, but Gods know I'd like to," he admitted. "If anything strange turns up, I need to know about it."

The other two exchanged a glance – a type of glance he was familiar with from being a battlecruiser CAG. It meant something had been discussed that the Captain *shouldn't* know… and that maybe the Captain now should.

"There's definitely been something strange going on," Solace admitted with a sigh. "We could never pin down anything solid, just rumors, but ever since the Admiral's staff came aboard…"

She laid out in precise detail everything they'd heard about Sanchez's sounding people out to Kyle's slowly growing sense of unease.

"You're right," he finally agreed, "I can't move on this. It's just rumors. What I *can* do is order you both to draw weapons from the Armory. Mira – find staff on the bridge watches you trust implicitly and encourage them to do the same. Michael – Rokos and some of the others at least have range time as well as known loyalties. I want you to start putting together a team out of your enlisted."

"What kind of team are we talking here?" Stanford asked slowly, carefully.

"A counter-mutiny team."

35

Deep Space, en route to Barsoom System
08:00 January 16, 2736 Earth Standard Meridian Date/Time
DSC-078 Avalon, *Flight Briefing Room*

THE PREFLIGHT BRIEFING room crowd Michael had gathered via conversations, in-system meeting invites, and other mostly quiet methods was sparser than he'd have liked. After a few minutes of soul-searching the previous day, he'd restricted himself almost entirely to old hands.

Key among the group were Wing Commander Russell Rokos and Master Chief Petty Officer Marshall Hammond. Rokos might have been the most junior Wing Commander in Starfighter Group Zero-Zero-One, but he was the most senior person in the room after Michael himself.

Hammond, on the other hand, even wounded was the most senior NCO in the Space Force aboard. He knew *everyone* in the Group. If there was someone Michael would trust to know who else to drag into their little 'team,' it would be Hammond.

"All right people," Michael said loudly, stepping up to the front of the room. As his people turned to him, almost every eye in the room went to him – and then to his hip. To his knowledge, no one in the room had *ever* seen him armed. He wasn't entirely comfortable with the seven millimeter automatic the Federation Navy and Space Force used as a standard sidearm, but he was at least qualified on the weapon.

"All right," he repeated. "As you may have guessed, this meeting isn't exactly on the books, and the selection criteria isn't particularly formal. For anyone who hasn't picked up on at least the first one, everyone in this room was at Tranquility."

That silenced the remaining conversations and fidgeting.

"You're here because *I* trust you, and the Captain trusts you," he said simply. "I'm sure the rumor mill has been working overtime on the ship for the last few weeks, so I'm going to give you some of the details behind those rumors.

"Firstly, yes, there was an attempt to assassinate me, and two attempts to murder Captain Roberts," Michael said bluntly. "This is why we're on a communications lockdown. The Captain and the Admiral both feel that we likely have a Commonwealth spy on board."

"Is that why you're armed?" Flight Lieutenant Ivan Kovalchick asked. The dark-haired young man looked nervous. Michael knew him well – Kovalchick had been under Michael's command the entirety of the younger man's career. Nervousness wouldn't stop him doing what he thought was right.

"The last attack on the Captain was the most blatant yet," Michael replied. "At this point, we face the possibility of our spy accelerating their actions and moving to direct attacks. We are, after all, five days from Barsoom."

"But you're not putting together this little conspiracy because of a spy," Rokos pointed out, the big Wing Commander leaning forward at the front of the room. "How much insanity is going *on* on this ship, boss?"

"Too much," the CAG told him. "We definitely have a spy aboard. We're also in complete communications lockdown under the Admiral's seal. We're on a mission that no one is even pretending isn't outright revenge anymore.

"Last, but by no means least, are the rumors coming to my ears of a potential mutiny."

There. He'd finally said it aloud, to his people. In a sense, saying that one word was crossing the Rubicon – once the senior officers of the ship started acting to curtail mutiny, a lot of questions would get asked when the dust settled.

"All we are going on is rumors," he carefully clarified, "but they're consistent and coming from all three services aboard *Avalon*. These rumors accused Senior Fleet Commander Sanchez of sounding out personnel about their loyalties, looking for people loyal to the Federation or the Admiral above the Captain.

"This is worrying as Void," Michael continued. "Perhaps more so because despite looking, and despite the rumors reaching our senior NCOs' ears," he nodded to Hammond, "getting more common, we have confirmed *nothing*.

"We took all of this, the rumors, our fears, our lack of evidence, to Captain Roberts yesterday. He feels… some degree of precaution is necessary.

"You are in this room because *I* trust you – and because you are rated in the use of shipboard small arms," he told them. "We have no idea what the mutineers plan might be – Void, we aren't even sure there is actually a mutiny.

"The immediate precaution is to prepare a small force of people we can trust and make sure they have the equipment they need," he gestured around the room. "Chief Hammond – with you on medical leave, I suspect you can sneak a few quiet meetings in without being noticed. I want you to coordinate with Kalers, the Gunny and the Bosun to have arms lockers added to the flight deck and locations of your choosing in Flight Country. The access codes are to be distributed to everyone in this room.

"The XO is pulling together a similar team of personnel from the shipboard side. Once we've established everything, we'll have you all added to a hidden com network in the ship's systems. If one of the senior officers or NCOs believes a mutiny has begun, we will transmit the code phrase 'Guinevere' over that network.

"Once you receive that message, we will need to draw arms and wait for instructions," Michael said in a rush of breath. "Hopefully, we will be in a position to coordinate efforts and neutralize any attempted mutiny quickly. If we cannot pass on instructions, I'll need this group to secure the flight deck and make certain that we remain in control of the starfighters."

The crowd in front of him was very quiet, and Michael scanned their faces. No one looked guilty, or unwilling – just shocked and concerned. Some fear. That was to be expected.

"I'm not going to order you to be involved in this," he told them quietly. "I'm not worried about anyone in this room joining a mutiny or even *warning* the mutineers, so if you want to just carry on… the door's behind you."

To his surprise, no one left.

11:00 January 16, 2736 ESMDT
DSC-078 Avalon, *Captain's Break-out Room*

Lieutenant Major Sirvard Barsamian, Kyle noted, was starting to look less nervous at giving presentations in the little conference room attached to the Captain's office. She faced the small gathering – Kyle, Solace, Tobin and Sanchez – calmly.

"We've reviewed all camera footage from the twelve hours prior to the attack on Captain Roberts," she told them quietly. "As I mentioned to the Captain before, the cameras in the section his quarters were shutdown prior to the attack, but I'd hoped to pick up footage of the drone somewhere else on the ship."

She shook her head with a frustrated expression.

"We've had no luck whatsoever," she admitted. "Whoever our attacker is, they appear to have *complete* access to many of our systems

– more complete than *I* have. I have to confess, sirs, that I have *no* idea how anyone could have this level of access.

"This isn't just viruses or access codes," Barsamian continued. "Even if someone had, say Captain Roberts' authorization codes, they couldn't pull this off without leaving traces. This is… someone with Command level codes, top-tier viral software, and a level of knowledge of the system architecture involved *no* Commonwealth agent should have. If Commonwealth Intelligence was this good, I'd expect the war to be over already!"

"So the surveillance footage is a bust," Kyle said. "That's… frustrating. What *do* you have, Lieutenant Major?"

"The drone itself, sir," she answered. "The computer core is useless. The damage that rendered it non-functional saved Captain Roberts' life, but also left us unable to extract any data. I have the drone under guard and my forensics team is going over it in detail.

"We already know it was manufactured in an auto-fabricator aboard *Avalon*," she warned them. "What we're trying to do, which will take time, is see if we can identify the exact fabricator that was used. While we have no record in the system of the drone being built, there are a number of things we can examine to try to identify our spy once we're looking at the source."

"Have you tried looking for other blank spots in the camera footage?" Solace asked.

"Unfortunately, it appears that whatever tool the spy is using is causing the footage to report as being present and functional to all searches – until someone actually tries to view the video, we can't tell it isn't there," the Ship's Marshal replied. "It's damned sneaky, and even full AI protocol defense programs are failing to find whatever is doing it."

"I get the feeling our spy is several steps ahead of us," Kyle said grumpily. "That's no reflection on you, Major. We're dealing with someone *very* professional and disturbingly well-informed on our systems and our counterintelligence procedures.

"We should have enough data to identify the fabricator inside the few next few days," Barsamian promised. "I wish I had more to tell you all. I expect to have a briefing of some kind before we reach Barsoom."

"Thank you, Major," Kyle replied. "Keep in close coordination with Master Sergeant Peng Wa and Senior Fleet Commander Solace," he ordered. "I don't want you carrying out any investigations without backup, do you hear me? This whole mess is making me twitchy."

He glanced over at Tobin and Sanchez.

"We have some ship business to discuss with the Marshal as well," he told them. "I'm sure you have other tasks to get to if you want to leave us to it."

Theoretically, even the ship's Captain couldn't dismiss the Admiral. In practice, however, even Admirals could take polite hints.

———

BY THE TIME Sanchez and Tobin had left, leaving Barsamian alone with Kyle and Solace, the Ship's Marshal's admirable calm at facing her superiors was starting to crack. She remained standing, straight-backed, but Kyle saw her gaze darting from side to side, like an animal for an escape.

"Take a seat, Lieutenant Major," he ordered. "This is in the order of a more… informal conversation than most. Coffee? Beer?"

"You realize absolutely *none* of your officers are going to accept a beer while on duty, right?" Solace asked him.

"Coffee, sir," Barsamian said quietly as she took the proffered seat. "What's going on?"

"I'll point out, Commander Solace, that the CAG does occasional-ly," Kyle told his XO. Nonetheless, he poured a new coffee for Barsamian and refreshed his and Solace's. There might be a mini-fridge stocked with beer in his office, but he didn't drink on duty any more than his staff did.

"That's because Michael can tell between when you're joking, when you're rewarding someone, and when you're about to hang someone out to dry," she pointed out. "The rest of us aren't quite so skilled yet."

Kyle shook his head at Solace, then returned his attention to Barsamian.

"I presume, Sirvard, that you've heard the rumors of certain individuals engaging in actions that could be… uncharitably considered precursors to mutiny," he stated. "I am now officially informing you that I have grounds for suspicion of mutiny."

Barsamian inhaled sharply, but Kyle nodded firmly. Once that status was declared and confirmed by the Executive Officer, what the Captain could order done expanded dramatically.

"What do you need me to do?" she asked levelly. That was impressive in and of itself, given the magnitude of Kyle's words.

"For the moment, keep an ear to the ground, and keep a weapon to hand," Kyle ordered. "Master Sergeant Wa is already aware of the situation. Make sure the Marines you trust are briefed, and aware of the concern.

"Our Commonwealth spy, aggravating as they are, gives us an excuse to post guards on key sections of the ship," he continued. "Use it. I want sentries on engineering, the bridge, and Secondary Control."

"What about the flight deck?"

"We have less than forty Marines aboard," Kyle pointed out. "I've asked the CAG to make sure the flight deck is secure."

The Marshal nodded, and he could see the wheels turning in her head as she planned.

"Sir, I have to ask," she said after a moment. "Have we considered the possibility this mutiny is linked to our spy?"

That literally stopped Kyle in mid-thought.

"It seems… unlikely," he admitted after a moment's consideration. "After all, while I'm not sure of the *reasons* rumor definitely places Commander Sanchez at the heart of this. If I had more than rumor, she'd be in the brig.

"Our spy seems unlikely to be a long-serving loyal Federation officer like Sanchez," he concluded. "I have no idea what bug is up her ass, but I don't think she's working for the Commonwealth."

"I understand, sir. But we do need to consider all possibilities. Given the level of expertise this agent has shown so far, it doesn't seem out of the question. In fact," Barsamian inhaled deeply, "we should consider the possibility these rumors were *started* by said agent to discredit Commander Sanchez and sow dissent amongst our senior command."

Kyle glanced to Solace.

"Mira?" he asked. "I am all too aware that Commander Sanchez hates my guts, for whatever reason, which may be biasing my opinion here."

"It's… possible," Solace admitted. From the sour expression on her face, the thought hadn't occurred to her either. "However, all of our preparations are defensive in nature," she pointed out. "We're not preemptively brigging Sanchez."

"You could, sir," Barsamian pointed out. "Even with only rumors, with a suspicion of mutiny we could arrest her and search her quarters and files. About the only thing we can't do is force her to submit to implant download."

Kyle sighed and shook his head.

"You didn't hear this, Major," he said quietly, "but the Admiral and I are… at somewhat of loggerheads over the continued pursuit of *Triumphant* and how he has handled the latest communication lockdown. Arresting his Chief of Staff would be *extremely* counter-productive to our working relationship at this point.

"If you find even the slightest scrap of evidence? She's going straight in the brig until we know more. But I need something *solid*. Something more concrete than lower decks rumor-mongering. Until then, all we can do is make preparations for a worst case scenario."

"I understand, sir," Barsamian nodded. She didn't look happy. "With your permission, then, I should get to it."

"Carry on, Major."

13:00 January 16, 2736 ESMDT
DSC-078 Avalon, *Vice Admiral Tobin's Office*

IT SEEMED dark in Dimitri's office. He'd turned the lights up as high as they could go, and it hurt his eyes to look at them, but everything still felt vaguely dim. Shadowy. Like a dark veil was draped over his gaze, even though everything seemed perfectly clear.

The paperwork and minutia of his job were on his computer, waiting for him, but he could barely muster up the energy to face them. The big Admiral paced his office. Ten steps one way. Ten steps the other. It wasn't a particularly large room, but he'd never noticed that before.

With a curse and a hand gesture, he cut the lights to a lower level, reducing the lighting in the room to match his mood. That only made the flashing red icon on the screen more obvious.

Right now, no messages could leave the buffer stack of *Avalon's* interstellar Q-Com array without Dimitri personally approving them. If that hadn't been the case, he never would have seen the message the warning icon was advising him he *must* release.

It was a Priority Alpha One communiqué. A recorded message, because the Joint Chiefs knew the ship was on communications lock-down, for Captain Roberts' eyes only. If Dimitri hadn't abused the strange situation with one ship under his direct command, he never would have seen it.

Priority Alpha One was reserved for either overriding orders or 'your position is about to come under attack'. Since *Avalon* was in FTL and untouchable to any force known by man, it could only be the former.

The specific exclusion of Vice Admiral Dimitri Tobin from a message being sent to the Captain of the ship could only mean one thing: Admiral Meredith Blake had almost certainly learned that *Avalon* had left the Alizon system.

An Alpha One message *excluding* Dimitri at this point could only contain one set of orders: for Captain Roberts to arrest him and turn the carrier around.

The admittance chime to his office sounded, and Dimitri froze like a panicked animal, his stare switching back and forth between the screen with its ominous warning and the door.

When the chime sounded again, he forced himself to calm down and hit the button dropping the message back into the buffer. He couldn't *delete* an Alpha One message – but he could make sure no one saw it until it was far too late.

"Enter," he ordered.

Senior Fleet Commander Judy Sanchez stepped through the door, the blond woman blinking in the dim light.

"Sir, we have a problem," she said bluntly as soon as the door closed behind her.

"Between the spy aboard, the mass murderer we're chasing, the system we just liberated, and the whole god-damn war, which exact problem do you mean?" he snapped.

"How about a new one?" Sanchez replied. "One where your flag captain is having paranoid delusions?"

Dimitri sighed. He knew his Chief of Staff didn't *like* Roberts, but the depths she seemed willing to plumb to try to discredit the man were starting to grate. If anyone on this ship had mental issues right now, it was probably Dimitri himself. He wasn't entirely sure.

"Commander, do you have *any* basis for this?" he asked bluntly. "You have spent far too much of your time since you arrived aboard this ship trying to denigrate Captain Roberts. Would you care to explain where this latest notion came from?"

"Sir, I have made no secret of my opinion of Captain Roberts," she said flatly. "But he's placed armed guards on the bridge and engineering. I was actively *denied* entrance to engineering by these guards."

"Commander, you do realize there is a spy aboard?" Dimitri reminded her. "I'm surprised we haven't had guards around the ship already – certainly that's entirely within Captain Roberts' discretion given the situation.

"It's also within his discretion to restrict access to the critical portions of the ship to the personnel assigned there. You have no need to be in engineering, Commander Sanchez – or on the bridge, for that matter.

"I can understand that being short-stopped by Marines is an unpleasant experience, Judy," he finished gently. "But I hardly see paranoid delusions in Captain Roberts taking reasonable precautions. Even if I found his actions unreasonable, Commander, the security of this ship is his responsibility – not mine, and most definitely *not yours*."

Sanchez had remained silent as he lectured her, but her eyes flashed and she glared at him as he spoke.

"Sir, your faith in Captain Roberts is blatantly misplaced," she told him. "The man is clearly out of his depth and unable to deal with the current situation. If things continue on this course, I cannot be sure I can keep you safe."

"I am concerned about the completion of our mission, Commander, not my safety," Dimitri told her. "Your concerns are noted, but I must warn you – if you 'continue on this course' you risk your career."

Of course, it was unlikely that when the dust settled, *he* would be able to save or destroy anyone's career. But Sanchez was already heading for a damning assessment report.

"I understand, sir," she grounded out. "I will... endeavor not to cause issues with the Captain. But I *will* keep an eye on this. That is, after all, part of my job."

36

Deep Space, en route to Barsoom System
05:00 January 20, 2736 Earth Standard Meridian Date/Time
DSC-078 Avalon, *CAG's Office*

MICHAEL HAD BEEN HAVING difficulty sleeping – something to do with nightmares about assassination attempts and watching worlds die. Normally, he'd see if Mason was awake so they could talk, but with the communication lockdown even that wasn't an option.

Which left him in his office three hours before his shift technically began, catching up on paperwork. He was still over a month away from having to provide assessment reports on any of his people, but getting them ready in advance never hurt.

It was also boring enough he was grateful, if surprised, when a com alert pinged.

"Vice Commodore Stanford," he answered, without bothering to even check who it was.

"I'm glad you're awake Commodore," Lieutenant Major Barsamian greeted him briskly. "I need to ask a favor."

"What do you need, Major?" he replied, wondering if any of his people had managed to get into serious trouble while the ship was in FTL.

"Put simply, sir, I need hands," she told him. "There are thirty-six Military Police and forty-seven Marines aboard *Avalon* at the moment. All of them are either currently asleep from pulling multiple shifts, or on guard duties I can't pull them away from.

"However, one of my forensics people was burning the midnight oil and has finally tracked down the source of the drone that tried to kill the Captain. The Captain was pretty clear that we shouldn't try to investigate anything without an armed escort, but I don't have one. And he told me you were handling security for the flight deck."

"So you're wondering if I have a few leg-breakers to spare?" Michael asked dryly.

"Yes, sir."

"I can rustle up a few boys with guns," he offered. "Where am I meeting you?"

"You, sir?"

"I'm not up at this time because I'm *busy*, Major," he pointed out. "Besides, you may end up needing a few more gold circles for firepower."

"Won't object, sir. We've identified the source as Auto-Fabricator Sixteen."

05:15 January 20, 2736 ESMDT
DSC-078 Avalon, *Auto-Fabricator Sixteen*

THE AUTO-FABRICATORS WERE SCATTERED throughout *Avalon's* hull. Michael was most familiar with the four attached to the flight deck that provided emergency parts for his starfighters, but he was aware that there were twenty or so in the ship.

Sixteen was buried deep in the lower half of the ship, down on Deck Fifteen and towards the engines. It was technically in engineering, but not anywhere near the main spaces containing the engines or zero point cells. It was in the section of the ship Michael tended to hear engineering crew refer to as 'the Dungeon' – and that the rest of the crew tended to forget existed.

He had collected four of the Specialists he'd inducted into Guinevere and drawn weapons from the arms locker before joining Barsamian. All were big guys – or gals, in one case – and cradled the shipboard security shotguns like they knew how to use them.

"Stun blasts, people," he reminded them as they met up with Barsamian and her tech. "If for some Void-cursed reason we actually have to shoot at someone, we want them *alive*."

"Of course, sir," Space Force Specialist First Class Anaru Tinker told his CAG. Tinker was a massive man, a shaven-headed tattooed individual who'd served on the old *Avalon* since before Michael had come aboard, and transferred over to the new ship with the fighter group. He looked almost insulted at the thought that he might shoot anyone he didn't fully intend to.

"I'm glad to see you," Barsamian told them. She gestured to the petite young woman next to her. "This is Corporal Filipa Kaczka, my forensics team lead."

Kaczka was a sallow-skinned woman of perhaps one hundred and fifty five centimeters. Like Tinker, her head was shaven, but where the big Space Force enlisted was covered in tattoos, a glitter of silver circuitry ran over the forensic tech's skin. Her augmentation clearly went significantly past the usual in-head implant and medical nanite suite.

"We've identified multiple serial number fragments inside the drone," she said calmly, her voice strangely vague as if her attention was only half on reality. "While an effort was made in the manufacture to prevent any intact serial numbers surviving, statistical extrapolation of the fragments, combined with analysis of several chemical markers, eventually enabled us to identify the source as this fabricator.

"Primarily, I will require access to the fabrication material log and the local physical backup of the video footage. We hope that our perpetrator is unaware of our breakthrough and we will not be accosted.

Given the degree of penetration demonstrated to date, this cannot be guaranteed."

"Hence asking for your help," Barsamian told Michael. "Let's go, Filipa."

The Marshal waved the golden badge of her office over the access panel for the auto-fabricator, which happily chirped acknowledgement of her authority and slid open.

The lights inside came up as Michael and the others entered, shining on a complex nightmare of computer screens, automatic arms, lathes, and other machines and tools the CAG couldn't name.

"Have at her, Corporal," he told Kaczka and stepped back to watch the door. The security shotgun weighed heavily against him – he *was* qualified on the weapon, but he'd last tested on it a long time ago. It had three separate magazines, each holding three shells. Right now, he had two loaded with stun blasts – 'shells' that contained one-shot electron lasers designed to disable a human without killing them – and the third loaded with flechettes.

He didn't want to have to fire the weapon at all, but he *really* didn't want to use that third magazine.

"The physical backup for the camera is missing," Kaczka's vague voice announced. "We've already checked records. The online records for this camera have no less than two hundred and seventy six hours of looped footage fed in at various periods over four weeks. There are also hundreds of hours where the fabricator is empty and unused which may contain looped footage we missed."

"At some point, the cameras on this ship are going to actually be of *use*," Barsamian half-snarled. "I'm getting sick of this garbage."

"Given the previously demonstrated capabilities of our spy, we did not expect useful camera footage," the forensics Corporal noted as she approached the main fabricator console. Instead of bringing up the screen or activating a hologram, she laid a visibly circuit-laced hand on the side of the console and paused.

"This is statistically improbable," she said after a moment. "The fabricator material logs do not exist."

"You mean there's no record of us?" Michael asked.

"No. The logs do not exist," Kaczka repeated. "There is no subtlety to this except that the alerts elsewhere in the system did not trigger. The entirety of the material usage log for this fabricator has been deleted, and the delete command wiped from the system.

"This should not be possible without high levels of access and sophisticated computer worms."

"Much the same as our agent has shown again and again," Barsamian concluded. She looked like she wanted to swear. "This spy has short-circuited every failsafe and every security measure aboard this ship. If Commonwealth Intelligence is this good, we are utterly outclassed in this war."

"None of this adds up," Michael pointed out. "If CI was this good, this war would already be *over* – plus, if their agent is this good, why are they wasting their time trying to off our senior officers? Just having this level of access on a Battle Group flagship is worth *Avalon's* weight in gold to their war effort."

He shook his head, looking at the clearly frustrated Barsamian and the not-quite-there Kaczka.

"You might be looking at this the wrong way," he thought aloud. "We keep thinking of it as a security problem, but the hardware is being circumvented as well. Perhaps we should look at an engineering solution?"

"What do you mean?" Barsamian asked.

"You identified the fabricator from fragments of the serial code," Michael noted. "My understanding of computers sucks, but I seem to recall that something isn't actually deleted unless you write over it with junk. There could still be retrievable fragments of data."

"I think we want to talk to Wong," he concluded. "If our enemy is beating us at every turn, we need to change the ground underneath them."

05:45 January 20, 2736 ESMDT
DSC-078 Avalon, *Chief Engineer's Office*

"You're all up very early," Wong told Stanford and his current collection of Space Force leg-breakers and Military Police as they entered his office. The room was surprisingly cluttered, with datachips and actual physical system parts scattered on every surface. "I presume there is something I can do to help you?"

A pair of engineering enlisted personnel stood guard outside the Chief Engineer's door, though they'd happily stood aside when they'd recognized the CAG. The two big Specialists weren't visibly armed, though Stanford made a mental note of a standard issue Navy duffel bag concealed under a bench only just out of reach.

"We had a breakthrough on identifying the source of the drone," Barsamian told him. She took a seat, gesturing Kaczka and Stanford forward as well.

Michael leaned on the back of a chair, and sent his Specialists outside to mingle with their engineering equivalents with a jerk of his head.

"We then ran into a problem," he added to Barsamian's explanation. "And I realized that we were going at at least some of this the wrong way around. Corporal Kaczka?"

"The fabricator logs for the unit used to manufacture the drone that attempted to assassinate Captain Roberts are missing," the strange Corporal announced. "Both the materials usage and the user logs have been completely deleted, turning the last week of my endeavors into a dead end.

"The Commonwealth agent is disturbingly capable and appears to have even greater access to our systems than we do," she said flatly. "Stanford suggested speaking to you. I am not sure what assistance you can provide that is outside my own skillset."

"I'm no forensic computer tech, if that's what you mean," Wong agreed, leaning back in his chair and eyeing his visitors. "If the logs were deleted and properly hashed – and I doubt our spy would suddenly become less than thoroughly competent – I would have no more success with the fabricator's computer than you."

"Then why…"

"What I *am*, Corporal Kaczka," the gaunt shaven-headed Chief

Engineer cut her off, "is a paranoid son of a bitch with direct access to all of the hardware on this ship."

Wong smiled coldly, his dark slanted eyes sending a chill down Stanford's spine.

"I may hide down in engineering – especially when we're pushing the drives like this – but I am not oblivious to the ship's affairs. Those two gentlemen outside didn't position themselves there without my suggestion, after all.

"What you have missed, Corporal, and what Vice Commodore Stanford was expecting me to have thought of, is the people involved here – not the software, not the hardware, the people.

"Auto-fabricators are the single most abusable and abused pieces of machinery on a warship. I've seen them used for everything from illegal weapons rings to assembling entire drug labs aboard ship.

"The people who abuse them are, sadly, almost always engineering personnel who know the systems inside and out. These are very intelligent men and women who are determined not to be found out. Fabricator logs get edited or go missing a *lot*, people," he finished calmly.

"And?" Michael prompted.

"And after getting caught up in an investigation that went on way too long and ended way too inconclusively back in the dawn of time when I was a mere Lieutenant Commander, I realized I needed to find a way to make sure that didn't happen again.

"So, since you ask so nicely," Wong continued with a cold smile, "it happens there is a hard, uneditable, backup being run on every single auto-fabricator on this ship. A backup that is *not* on the books and not otherwise linked to the ship's systems. Which fabricator did you say built that drone?"

Corporal Kaczka was actually *looking* at Wong. In the most of an hour since he'd met her, Michael hadn't seen the augmented tech actually directly look at a human being, and he mirrored Wong's smile.

"Auto-Fabricator Sixteen," the MP finally admitted.

Wong closed his eyes for a second, and one wall of his cluttered office flashed, the screen activated and covering the wall with hundreds of lines of text.

"Even with modification allowed, the fabricator logs are literally hundreds of thousands of lines of data," Wong warned. "The hard backup records every change, every step back to fix a typo, every edit as a separate item. Finding anything useful in here, well," he shrugged. "You have to know what you're looking for."

"May I interface?" Kaczka asked, her gaze now on the computer screen. Wong gave her a go-ahead gesture, and she stepped up to the wallscreen. Staring hard at the lines, the woman froze, her physical body stiffening almost completely as she dove into the data.

The screen flickered, the forensic tech allowing her data search to feed the screen as she worked. Michael wasn't going to pretend he could follow what she was doing, though. Sections of requests lit up, then data around them highlighted, de-highlighted, and then the screen jumped to another section of the code.

"The logs were deleted... three days ago," the forensic tech told them all, her voice even more vague than usual. "Via... a remote root override. Effective, but brute force. This backup would have prevented even a more subtle approach, but a cleaner removal of data may have prevented us looking."

"Why take the brute force approach then?" Michael asked.

"A subtler approach would have required physical access to the computer. Perhaps our agent either couldn't reach the system or was otherwise occupied and went for the fastest method? Now, I need to find the drone. With this quantity of data and the potential pattern manipulations, this will take some time."

The pattern of sections being highlighted, searched around, and discarded continued. It accelerated as Michael watched until each series of highlights was a blur concluded in under a second.

"There!" The screen froze, and Michael finally had a chance to see what was highlighted. It was a series of part numbers and command codes *he* certainly didn't recognize, but Kaczka clearly knew.

"That's the drone's manufacture," she concluded. "January tenth, oh four hundred twenty-six to oh five hundred thirty-eight. Middle of ship's night, it seems unlikely anyone would have happened over our agent.

"That coincides with one of our looped sections of camera footage for about four hours on either side," Kaczka admitted. "Given the area of the outage, potential candidates… exceed sixty."

"Who was the user?" Wong demanded. "It should tell us that."

The tech nodded, then froze mid-motion.

"That isn't possible," she said flatly.

"What isn't?"

"I'm validating," the Corporal said sharply. A moment later, she blinked and turned back to the officers in the room.

"Sirs, ma'am." The Military Policewoman's voice was very quiet. "The logged in user was Vice Admiral Dimitri Tobin. A lock was placed on that section of the log under his direct authorization code.

"The deletion was carried out three days ago using the same authorization code, remote from the flag deck."

Her eyes were less vague than they had been before, and Michael realized she looked utterly desperate. A junior MP did *not* want to say what that evidence pointed towards. Even Barsamian couldn't take that train of thought to its final conclusion.

There was only one man aboard who had any authority to judge the Admiral.

"We need to wake the Captain."

37

Deep Space, en route to Barsoom System
07:30 January 20, 2736 Earth Standard Meridian Date/Time
DSC-078 Avalon, *Flag Deck*

THERE WAS something ominous to the even boot-treads of the four Military Police and two Marine bodyguards following Kyle down the corridor to the flag deck. Behind them, each of the heavy security hatches slammed shut and sealed as Kyle ordered *Avalon* to cut the flag deck off.

He'd already sealed the off-duty staff reporting to the Admiral in their quarters. Procedure for the thankfully rare occasions where it was necessary to arrest a flag officer was clear: the entirely of their staff would be restricted to quarters until they could be interrogated and cleared of involvement.

The only members of Tobin's staff *not* so restricted at this point were the twenty-three people on the flag deck with Tobin. That included both his Chief of Staff and Intelligence Officer, and Kyle had to admit he was most concerned about Commander Sanchez.

Even if Tobin was everything they were afraid of, Sanchez's dislike for Kyle was going to make this messy.

"Sir," a voice sounded in his implant. As soon as they'd finished explaining the situation, he'd sent Senior Fleet Commander Wong and Corporal Kaczka to the Q-Com array. If Tobin was – *somehow* – the spy, he'd been the only one in control of *Avalon's* communication for weeks.

"We can't access the buffer stack yet," Wong informed him. "What I can confirm is that the Admiral has been sending a lot more messages than I would have expected for us being black. Encrypted and encoded messages sealed from normal visibility – even if someone had access to the stack – under his personal code. Um," the engineer paused and swallowed. "The outbound log was apparently secured against access. It just wiped and hashed itself."

"That is secondary," Kaczka interrupted. "Per your orders, I have accessed the inbound logs. Without an override, I am not able to view the contents of the messages, but there are *multiple* Alpha One priority messages in the buffer for you, Captain. He has archived them all."

Kyle closed his eyes as they reached the corridor outside the flag deck. He was trying to make sense of Tobin being the spy – of the Admiral being the one who'd tried to kill him. It didn't add up – but there was too much evidence. At this point, he had no choice but to leave it to the court-martial to sort out the truth.

Two Marines stood guard outside the nerve center of Tobin's operations. They were in body armor, similar to that worn by the six men and women following Kyle, but were armed only with sidearms. His escort were carrying full-size battle carbines – with electron laser attachments, in the hope that they could get through today without actually *killing* anyone.

"Sir," one Marine saluted. "What's going on?"

"Stand down, soldier," Kyle ordered. "Surrender your weapons to Marshal Barsamian. You're not in trouble, but I can't take chances today."

Barsamian stepped forward from the back of the pack of soldiers following him, holding her hand out to the two guards. With a visible swallow, the speaker slowly drew his sidearm and passed it to her. A moment later, the other followed suit.

Kyle paused in front of the doors, steadying himself to do something that would, if his staff were wrong, end his career.

"With me, then," he ordered softly and stepped forward.

For a few moments, no one reacted to the door opening or his entrance. Much like the warship's main bridge, the flag deck consisted of seats and consoles but most of the work was done via the implant network. Most of the people in the room weren't paying much attention to what was going on around them.

Vice Admiral Dimitri Tobin and his two staff officers, however, stood next to the big holo-display in the middle of the flag deck – an item completely missing from the bridge, where any necessary data was fed to everyone's implants – their heads together in discussion.

The MPs and Marines were in the room before anyone noticed, but by the time Kyle had crossed half the distance to the Admiral, the sudden presence of half a dozen armed soldiers had drawn attention. He *watched* the realization ripple around the room, techs and junior officers suddenly snapping into reality from their work and turning to look at him.

"Captain Roberts, what is the meaning of this?" Tobin turned and demanded. The big Admiral seemed surprised.

"Vice Admiral Dimitri Tobin. Under the authority granted to me under Article Ninety-One of the Federation Articles of Military Justice, I am placing you under arrest for treason, conspiracy, and attempted murder."

Even without looking, Kyle knew Barsamian's people had taken up careful positions covering the entire crowd. They were outnumbered by the flag deck staff, but they were also the only armed people in the room.

"What, wait, why?" Tobin spluttered, staring at Kyle in complete shock.

"I told you he was having paranoid delusions," Sanchez snapped, staring at the Captain with oddly calm eyes.

"Your command codes were used to manufacture the drone that attempted to murder me," Kyle replied. "While I personally find it hard to believe you would betray the Federation after your years of service, I have no choice but to act to protect this ship. You are under arrest. Your staff will be placed in preventative custody until we can complete interrogations."

A strange glaze seemed to settle over the Admiral's eyes as he glared at Kyle.

"You can't!" he snapped. "We need to complete the mission – we have to stop *Triumphant!*"

"*That* is apparently something I need to discuss with the Joint Chiefs," Kyle pointed out. "Apparently they've been trying to get ahold of me."

"No!" the Admiral bellowed. He turned abruptly in place. "Sanchez, *do* something!"

"Oh, thank you, sir," the Chief of Staff said with a vicious thin little smile. "All hands," she continued calmly, somehow completely over-riding Kyle's lockdown to transmit to the whole ship, "Bad Penny. I repeat, Bad Penny."

A moment later, a tiny pistol appeared in her hand and she opened fire. Kyle dove for cover as his Marines returned fire.

Weapons appeared around him, crude-looking submachine guns yanked from beneath consoles as his people were distracted. He rolled behind a console, firing his sidearm wildly. One of Sanchez's sensor operators went down – possibly his bullet, possibly one of the MPs.

He rose above the console, aiming towards Sanchez. She wasn't there, and then a cold metal feeling sank into the back of his head.

"Unless you want the dear Captain to have a new breathing hole, I suggest you *cease fire*," Sanchez snapped, and he realized there was a gun at the base of his skull.

"I suggest you drop the pistol, *Captain*," she hissed in his ear. "I'd hate to… *slip*."

07:40 January 20, 2736 ESMDT
DSC-078 Avalon, Flight Control

"Bad Penny. I repeat, Bad Penny."

The words echoing across the shipwide speakers in Sanchez's voice didn't meant anything to Michael in and of themselves – but he could *guess.*

"Guinevere," he sent on the special net they'd set up. "Guinevere, Guinevere, Guinevere – Sanchez is moving!"

He was grabbing for his sidearm when he found himself facing down the end of a crude-looking barrel. On the other end was Specialist Second Class John MacCarl – not a man he knew well, a fighter missile tech from Castle who'd been a new addition.

"Just stay still, CAG," MacCarl told him, his voice nervous. "Orders from the Admiral – we're taking control of the ship."

"Who's 'we'?" Michael demanded. "The Admiral doesn't have the authority to order a Voids-cursed mutiny, MacCarl."

"Bad Penny's just a precaution, not a mutiny," the Specialist told him. For all the man's apparent nervousness, the gun he held – product of an auto-fabricator, Michael guessed – stayed steadily trained on the CAG. "Means the Admiral's relieving Roberts. So we want to be sure no one does anything stupid."

There had only been six people in Flight Control with Michael. Another had produced a weapon at the same time as MacCarl and was keeping the others covered.

"Sorry, boss, but the Commander figured you'd be most likely to be a problem."

"Senior Commander Sanchez, I take it?" Michael asked, looking down the gun. "You do realize, MacCarl, that even *if* the Admiral has relieved Captain Roberts, what *you're* doing is still mutiny. The Admiral can't protect you from that. Even if everything you say is true, you're still going to hang if you don't stop this and hand me that Voids-cursed gun."

There might have been a moment of hesitation, but then MacCarl steadied his grip and gestured towards the door with the gun.

"Following orders, sir," he said bluntly. "Keep your hands where I can see them, we're going to…"

The big man spasmed, the gun spraying a burst of bullets into the wall where MacCarl had gestured as a Navy electron laser stungun hit him in the back and submachine gun slipped from nerveless fingers.

The other mutineer went down at the same time, the need to cover four people keeping his weapon from pointing directly at any of them.

"*Finally*," Wing Commander Rokos grumbled as he stepped out from behind the door. "Took long enough for the idiot to point the gun somewhere else."

Michael's heart started beating again as he looked down at the collapsed, still slightly twitching, form of the Specialist.

"Cuff them," he ordered the men who *hadn't* joined the mutineers. Turning back to Rokos, he realized the *other* shooter had been Kalers.

"Have you heard anything?"

"Nothing," Rokos replied. "Flight deck is secure," he reported crisply. "Seven mutineers including this pair." He paused, glancing at his fingernails as if pretending to be modest. "All taken alive, sir."

"Well done, Commander Rokos," Michael told him. "We have a team?"

"We have a team," his subordinate replied. "What's the plan, sir?"

Michael tried to reach Kyle for just that question. No response.

"The Captain appears to be jammed," he said quietly.

"Isn't just him," Kalers told him grimly. "Sanchez's announcement went out, then I got about half of yours and Commander Solace's 'Guinevere' announcement and everything cut out. Jamming field in effect across the whole ship."

"So we need to make sure everything's intact in person," Michael concluded aloud. "Rokos – keep half a dozen of our people, guard the flight deck. About the only thing someone could do with a starfighter right now is kill us all – but you know, I'm okay taking precautions against that."

He turned to Kalers.

"Chief, take another half dozen of our people and head down to engineering," he ordered. "Wong has a bunch of big guys and an actual Marine guard section but… let's be certain."

"Including us three, we've got twenty awake and present," Kalers told him.

"Twenty-four, sir," one of the Specialists who'd been manning Flight Control informed them. The others nodded as she spoke. "Not sure what the hell is going on, but we're with you."

"All right, you're with me," Michael told them and ordered the Flight Control arms locker to open. "We're heading to Secondary Control – if the Captain is out of communication, I need to find Commander Solace."

08:00 January 20, 2736 ESMDT
DSC-078 Avalon, *Secondary Control*

MICHAEL'S APPROACH to Secondary Control came to a halt when the sound of gunfire came echoing down the corridor. He gestured his collection of techs with guns to hold still as he crept forward, trying to get a feel for what was going on.

It wasn't pretty. There *had* been a pair of Marines guarding the entrance. Both were now dead, but they hadn't died alone. The mutineers had tried to rush the security door to take them out, and there were easily ten bodies scattered along the corridor.

The security door had been overridden half open, and the remaining quartet of mutineers were using it as cover to take pot-shots into the control room. Gunfire and electron laser beams replied, so presumably the crew inside had enough cover to keep it a stalemate.

"On my mark," Michael told his people, "stun them all. Though this lot may not feel it a mercy," he noted grimly. The dead Marines, if nothing else, would probably hang any survivors from this team.

"Mark."

He led the way, targeting the mutineer with the biggest-looking gun and firing into his back. The Navy-issue stun weapons weren't *perfect*, but a single blast of electricity was enough to put down most people.

None of the mutineers were from the small section of people a standard electron beam couldn't disable, and all four went down in spasming heaps. Michael approached the half-opened door carefully.

"It's Stanford," he shouted before exposing himself. "Is Solace there?"

"I'm here, CAG," the exec responded. "We've got injured – I don't suppose you have a medic with you?"

"Sadly not," he replied. "Fernandez – get your ass down to the Infirmary and get some people from Cunningham," he ordered one of his people. "If these *assholes* have picked a fight there, get back here and find help."

He stepped over the half-retracted door and into Secondary Control. The carrier's auxiliary command center was a mess. Consoles and screens were worse the wear for being used as cover, and too many people were injured. Now the shooting had stopped, one of the junior officers had grabbed a first aid kit and was seeing to the wounded as best she could.

"Do you have coms with anyone else?" he asked Solace as the tall black officer, looking much less elegant with a still-bleeding cut across her face and a security shotgun in her arms, unfolded from behind the command chair.

"We're hard-linked to the bridge and engineering," she told him. "Should be hard-linked to Flight Control and the flag deck, but those links seem to have been disabled."

"We're in control down in Flight," he replied. "We had no coms with anybody."

"All transmissions are jammed, and the ship network is down," Solace said grimly. "Apparently your team in engineering had even better timing than you did – Wong's people are all fine, and they've got a dozen mutineers in cuffs. He says the Drive is intact, no problems, and he's locked things down so no one is going to cause any problems with it.

"As for the bridge, Master Sergeant Wa was apparently *worried* about it," the XO said dryly. "Nobody told *me* she'd assigned an extra Marine to the duty – and had them standing by in a closet down in the corridor in god-damn *boarding armor*. The bridge is secure."

Michael winced. Boarding armor was about two steps up from regular powered battle armor – it wasn't nearly as maneuverable on a planet, as it was designed for vacuum and shipboard operations. It was also immune to any weapon that wouldn't breach the hull. There was no way the mutineers had expected it or had had anything capable of injuring a Marine in it.

"What about the flag deck?" he asked. "That's where Captain Roberts is, isn't it?"

"No contact," Solace admitted. "At this point, the flag deck is the last serious pressure point – I'd be worried about the armories, but Kyle locked them down before he went to arrest Tobin. I thought he was being paranoid."

"Apparently, Sanchez was preparing a fifth column for if Tobin relieved Roberts," Michael told her. "Now that we know Tobin was involved in everything…"

"Right. Let me talk to Sergeant Wa," the XO said quietly. "I need that Marine in the boarding armor."

08:30 January 20, 2736 ESMDT
DSC-078 Avalon, Flag Deck

Vice Admiral Dimitri Tobin looked around his flag deck and wondered where the hell everything had gone so wrong.

His Flag Captain and four Military Police were in handcuffs against the wall. Half a dozen people – his staff, MPs, Marines – were dead on the ground, and his Chief of Staff seemed to have taken over everything.

"You won't get away with this, Commander," Roberts said, his voice admirably calm for someone in cuffs and being watched by people with guns. "We knew about your mutiny."

"You heard the Admiral order it," she pointed out. "That makes it not a mutiny."

"The Admiral has already been relieved," the Captain replied. "He has no authority."

"Oh, don't worry, Captain," Sanchez said sweetly. "That little stunt of yours will only help hang you. I've been promised that on the *highest* authority."

"Tobin never did any of what his code was used for, did he?" Roberts asked conversationally. "It was you. It was *always* you. What did the Terrans offer you, Commander?"

Sanchez laughed, and Tobin looked at her desperately as leaned against the console.

"Is this true, Commander?" he demanded. "Did you try to kill the Captain?"

"I don't work for the Commonwealth, Captain," his Chief of Staff mocked Roberts. "No, there are those in the Federation who knew you were doomed to screw up. I was placed to make sure the damage was limited. My actions are approved and ordered by members of the Senate itself."

"You tried to assassinate the commander of a capital ship in the face of the enemy?" Tobin demanded. Suddenly, even his worry that they might not manage to catch *Triumphant* seemed small. His Chief of Staff was apparently a viper in their midst. If she wasn't Commonwealth... if she'd been sent by a *Senator*...

"My orders were to remove him before he did serious harm," Sanchez confirmed. "Utterly destroying his reputation and making his failures of judgement obvious to the public was preferred."

The Admiral noted that nobody in the room except Snapes looked remotely surprised by this, and remembered with a chill that *Sanchez* had picked most of his staff. Backed by the wealth and power commanded by any Senator, she'd easily hidden a private force inside his staff.

Lieutenant Commander Snapes, on the other hand, looked utterly horrified. The Intelligence Officer was edging towards Sanchez, and Tobin wondered just what she had in mind. He was starting to think he'd made one *hell* of a mistake by not checking into his new Chief of Staff's background more closely.

"Uh-uh," Sanchez snapped, her gun suddenly flipping around to point directly between Snapes' eyes. "Don't try it, Lisa. I *know* you guessed what I used to do. For every minute of training you've got, they gave me an hour. You don't stand a chance."

The room was dim. Startlingly, impossibly, dim. Tobin realized he was shivering, and it had nothing to do with the temperature. He'd screwed up. He'd screwed up *bad*. Nothing he'd done was going to catch *Triumphant* or avenge Kematian – but it might allow an insane operative on his ship to kill his Flag Captain and betray the honor of his Navy.

"What happens now, Sanchez?" he asked, and his voice seemed very distant.

"Once I've confirmed we're in control of the ship, we brig our idiot Captain, I make sure the records tie to our story, and then we go kill *Triumphant*," she promised him. "You'll have your revenge for Kematian, Admiral. A *Senator* will owe you. What's a few incompetents and idiots versus that?"

Nothing. And everything. And the honor of the Navy. The honor Tobin had wanted to serve with his revenge and had stained with his betrayal.

The gun was still focused on Snapes. Sanchez was perfectly willing to kill a loyal, competent officer for no other reason than that the woman was in her way.

Something snapped inside Dimitri Tobin, and he found himself charging across the bridge. Everything seemed to move in such slow motion, Sanchez shoving Snapes away and spinning to point the gun at him.

He hit her with full force. Tobin was twice the blond woman's size and he smashed her bodily into the console behind her. A moment later, he was flung to the side, gasping as his kidney seemed to explode in pain. A bladed hand slammed into his diaphragm, and suddenly he couldn't breathe.

Struggling to rise, he saw Lisa Snapes tackle Sanchez from behind. The spy – whoever she really was – had already grabbed her gun. An elbow slammed into Snapes' throat with a horrible crunching sound and the Intelligence Officer stumbled back.

Sanchez fired twice, and blood sprouted on Snapes' uniform. Struggling vainly to breathe, the Lieutenant Commander collapsed, clutching at her throat and chest as she died.

Leaving the other woman to drown in her own blood, Sanchez turned back to Tobin as he struggled to his feet. He was still having problems breathing, but his world had shrunk down to the woman who'd betrayed him and the gun in her hand.

"Damned shame," she said softly, raising the weapon again. "You weren't supposed to go down with him."

In the dimness filling the room in his mind, he barely registered the door snapping open. He saw Sanchez spin and fire – the bullets bouncing off a black metal monstrosity that filled the entire doorway. More bullets joined it as her allies opened fired as well.

Then the boarding suit opened fire. A pair of shoulder mounted electron lasers tracked the room, firing a single pulse at each individual with a weapon out.

The only result was a fusillade of return fire, and Tobin saw Sanchez grunt as electricity arced over her shipsuit without harming her – and pull another, larger, weapon from under one of the consoles. He didn't wait to see what it was.

Still struggling to breathe, he launched himself at her again. This time, she saw him coming and moved to sidestep – but he wasn't aiming at *her*.

He ripped the weapon from her hands and hit the deck – and then gunfire echoed through the flag deck again as the armored Marine opened up with the suit's battle rifle.

38

Deep Space, en route to Barsoom System
11:00 January 20, 2736 Earth Standard Meridian Date/Time
DSC-078 Avalon, *Captain's Office*

SIXTY-TWO DEAD.

That number was probably going to haunt Kyle for the rest of his life. Sanchez's mutiny had cost the lives of sixty-two of his crew – including the Chief of Staff herself, so they would never be entirely sure just what the hell had happened.

Sixty-two dead. One hundred and fourteen detained, including Vice Admiral Tobin. Kyle still had too many unanswered questions to allow the Admiral to wander free or to be in command of the ship.

His decision to prepare a counter-measure had made all the difference. Each of the teams Sanchez had pulled together had run into prepared and armed resistance. Wa's decision to dig out a full suit of boarding armor as part of those preparations had also paid dividends, especially after realizing most of the flag deck crew were compromised.

He shook his head and met his Executive Officer's gaze.

"Hell of a day," he told her. "I feel like an idiot for spending most of it in cuffs."

"That part could have gone better," Solace agreed. "But you're still in command and *Avalon* is still combat-capable. I think we can call that a win."

Kyle looked at the Alpha One icon rotating on his wallscreen.

"Fair enough," he allowed. "Shall we see what Command wanted that Tobin didn't want us to see?"

She made a go ahead gesture, and he activated the video, the most recent of *four* Alpha One recorded messages from Fleet Admiral Meredith Blake.

"Captain Roberts," the familiar gray-haired Admiral's face appeared on the wallscreen facing the two officers. "I feel like I'm sending these communiqués into the void. I am forced to presume you are not receiving them, but I have nothing else I can do from here.

"I do not know what you think is going on," she continued, "but your ship is *supposed* to be in the Alizon system. From my conversation with President Ingolfson of Alizon, no one on *Avalon* appears to be aware of this.

"Since I discussed these orders with Vice Admiral Tobin personally, I know *he* is, which forces me to the conclusion that the Admiral has knowingly disobeyed his orders and taken *Avalon* off on a damn fool mission of vengeance."

Blake shook her head, looking very old and very tired.

"Having to give this order once was bad enough," she said softly, "and now I've had to give it four times. Captain Kyle Roberts, you are ordered to relieve Vice Admiral Dimitri Tobin of duty and place him under arrest.

"You are then to immediately return to the Alizon system to await the remainder of Battle Group Seventeen.

"What the hell is going on aboard that ship, Roberts?"

The message ended and Kyle sighed, dropping his face into his hands.

"Well, isn't this a giant clusterfuck?" he demanded aloud.

"I'm glad we didn't release the coms lockdown before viewing this," Solace noted. "I probably have orders in the queue to relieve both you and Tobin. We need to report in."

Kyle didn't respond aloud to his XO, but he triggered a command that would try to open a communication on the same channel the communiqué had arrived on. The stylized castle and fourteen stars of the formal seal of the Castle Federation rotated on the screen for a few seconds, then a plain-uniformed dark-haired woman with the collar insignia of a Navy Commander appeared on screen.

"This is Commander Sonia Ardennes," she said crisply. "You have reached Fleet Admiral Blake's office. May I assist you?"

"Commander Ardennes," Kyle said quietly, "this is Captain Kyle Roberts of *Avalon* reporting in. I need to speak to the Fleet Admiral as soon as possible."

"Captain Roberts!" she exclaimed. "Hold on a moment – Admiral Blake is in a meeting but she left orders for if you made contact."

The screen returned to the logo. Now as it rotated, it switched between the seal of the Federation and the sword and rocket of the Castle Federation Space Navy.

They waited for several minutes, and then the screen resolved into the familiar image of the Castle Federation military's uniformed commanding officer.

"Well, you're alive at least," she snapped. "Report."

———

BLAKE WAITED PATIENTLY as Kyle and Solace laid out the sequence of events, their suspicions of Sanchez, and the details of the mutiny. When they finished, she was silent for a long moment.

"I assume you'll have a more formal report once things are more under control," she finally said. "This is going to take some digesting, Captain Roberts, Commander Solace. You are confident that Sanchez was not a Commonwealth spy?"

"Yes," Kyle confirmed quietly. "If she was, her level of access and skills would have been better used as a spy than as an assassin or agent provocateur. As a Battle Group Chief of Staff, she could have compromised massive swathes of our military operations.

"I... am forced to suspect she was an agent for more domestic employers. *She* said her orders came from members of the Senate... but the cameras were disabled so I have no record of that outside my people's implants."

"*That*, Captain, is the can-opener for a political shitstorm," Blake said bluntly. "You copy?"

"Yes, ma'am."

"I hate to ask this," she continued, "but I'll need two versions of your reports: one with *everything*, and one sanitized of all mention of Sanchez's motives. This is a time bomb I want to keep to myself for now, do you understand?"

"Yes, ma'am," Kyle agreed. He didn't like it, but he understood.

"How quickly can you return to the Alizon system, Captain?" Blake asked. "Ingolfson is hanging in the damn breeze, and the rest of Battle Group Seventeen is still over six days away."

He hesitated.

"Ma'am, we are almost five days away from Alizon," he reminded her. "It will take us as long to get back as it took us to get here, and..."

"And what, Captain?"

"We're barely a day from Barsoom, ma'am," Kyle said quietly. "We shouldn't have left Alizon, but it's not like there was no weight to Admiral Tobin's points. We're most of the way there, now – shouldn't we finish the job?"

Blake was silent, her eyes thoughtful.

"I'll confess, Captain, I am inclined to order you home simply because you are as close as you are due to Tobin disobeying orders," she admitted. "There may well be a major Commonwealth presence in the system engaging Richardson as well."

"I understand, Admiral," Kyle agreed. "My concern is also for my crew's morale," he told her. "We've been chasing *Triumphant* for weeks, and we've just taken the mother of all sucker punches. My people *need* a victory, Admiral Blake – and we *want Triumphant*."

"And if there is a Commonwealth force, Captain?"

"Then our actions will depend on the circumstances on our arrival," he replied. "If *Triumphant* is evading a Terran task group, we may be able to ambush and destroy her. Even the presence of a major

Commonwealth force does not preclude the completion of the mission."

"This is mad, Captain Roberts," Blake told him, but she'd relaxed and some of the worry had left her eyes and face. "Tobin's crazy quest for revenge has left a planet defenseless, and you want to finish the job?"

"If it were only Tobin's quest for revenge," Kyle said quietly, "we never would have made it this far."

"You're right, Captain," the Admiral allowed with a nod. "The entire Alliance wants to see Kematian's dead avenged, and as you pointed out, you're already too far away to make a difference to how long Alizon is defenseless.

"Very well, Captain Roberts. You are authorized to proceed to the Barsoom system. There, you are to exercise your own judgment over whether it is practical to engage and destroy *Triumphant*." She held up a cautionary finger. "*However*, Captain, under no circumstances are you to pursue *Triumphant* from Barsoom, or risk your vessel. Do you understand me?"

"Yes, Admiral."

"Then good luck, Captain."

12:00 January 20, 2736 ESMDT
DSC-078 Avalon, *Bridge*

THE BRIDGE HAD BEEN SPARED the worst of the conflict that had raged through the warship mere hours before. When a boarding suited Marine had appeared behind the mutineers and loomed over them in a metric ton of steel and ferro-carbonate armor, his polite request for surrender had been quickly granted.

It looked enough like the flag deck, which had resembled a butcher's shop by the time the same boarding suited Marine had finished their work, to still give Kyle shudders.

He concealed them as he stepped up to the command chair and

glanced around. Pendez and Anderson had been holding down the watch while he and Solace communicated with Command. His regular bridge watch was in place around them, men and women he knew he could trust. With almost a hundred and fifty members of his crew joining Sanchez's mutiny, it stood out that not *one* member of the bridge crew shifts had been among them.

"Thank you," he said softly. He didn't specify for what. He was certain he didn't need to.

Kyle took his seat, adjusting the chair to allow him to see most of his people and activated the all hands channel.

"Crew of *Avalon*," he greeted them. "I am reasonably confident that I can state that today has likely been one of the worst days of all of our lives – though I am debating its position versus flying *through* a battleship."

The chuckles that shocked from his bridge crew told him he'd hit the right tack. The last thing his crew needed today was an unending cascade of doom and gloom.

"Today, we were betrayed by our shipmates, those who we trusted and thought were our friends," he continued after a moment. "And now you find yourself looking at those around you and wondering who else you were wrong about. Who else might betray you?

"I have an answer for you on that, at least," he told them. "No-one. Less than three percent of this vessel's crew, Marines, or Space Force personnel, faced with someone who they could have easily believed truly had the authority to order this, joined in the mutiny.

"Many of those were deceived, or made an error in judgment, and truly thought they were doing the right thing," he continued. "Those who did *not* already betray us will not."

That was probably stretching the truth. After all, there had to have been a few people approached who hadn't joined, or the rumors that had reached his ears wouldn't have existed. Those people might not have joined up with Sanchez, but they'd certainly stayed quiet enough.

"I wish, in the aftermath of this morning, I had good news to give," he said quietly. "But it turns out we faced more than one betrayal. Officers and crew of *Avalon*, I am afraid this ship was never supposed to leave Alizon.

"Our orders from Alliance High Command were to guard Alizon and make sure the system we'd so fortuitously freed was protected until we could rebuild their defenses. Vice Admiral Dimitri Tobin chose to disobey those orders and *lie* to us about our mission."

Kyle paused, waiting for that to sink in.

"Sadly, this means that Vice Admiral Tobin, while uninvolved in the mutiny, will not be released from the brig," he said softly. "He has been relieved of command by Fleet Admiral Blake. And we, my crew, my pilots – my friends – were ordered back to Alizon."

He could only see the faces of his bridge crew, but even on those twenty faces he saw what he'd expected to see: disappointment, but also a determination to do their duty.

"However, as I pointed out to Admiral Blake, we are now barely thirty hours and counting from Barsoom – and five days from Alizon. We are close on the heels of one of the worst mass murderers in human history, and I'm not sure I have it in me to give up the hunt, no matter how solid, how pragmatic the reasons.

"Admiral Blake understands. The Alliance of Free Stars, the Castle Federation, our Navy and Space Force – these are not entities that can stand by while the innocent are slaughtered. Justice must be done one way, or another.

"We have been authorized to complete this final leg of the pursuit. We will bring *Triumphant* to bay in Barsoom, and we will either capture Captain Richardson for trial and execution, or we will destroy his ship with him aboard.

"Our orders are clear," he warned them. "We are not to pursue *Triumphant* beyond Barsoom. We are not to risk this ship against superior Commonwealth forces to engage her.

"I do not intend to disobey these orders – but I also do not intend to fail."

39

Deep Space, en route to Barsoom System
20:00 January 20, 2736 Earth Standard Meridian Date/Time
DSC-078 Avalon, *CAG's Office*

MICHAEL LEANED back in his chair with a small smile. Despite the beginning of the day, lifting the communication blackout was appearing to have a positive impact on morale. Certainly, his own morale had been boosted by the several messages waiting in the queue from Kelly Mason.

His girlfriend had settled well into her role as Executive Officer of the strike cruiser *Sunset*. That ship was assigned to the defense force securing the Tiāntáng system – one of Castle's daughter colonies, and on the opposite side of the capital from the Commonwealth.

The most dangerous thing Kelly Mason was facing was an occasional patrol of the uninhabited systems on the Federation's rimward frontier to make sure nothing untoward was happening in star systems rarely visited by man. Given the last few weeks aboard *Avalon*, Michael was guiltily *glad* she hadn't ended up serving as the XO for the big carrier.

His door chimed, and he glanced up.

"Enter."

As if summoned by his thought, Mira Solace stepped into his office. The elegant dark-skinned woman took a seat in front of his desk without asking and smiled slightly.

"Can I get you a drink?" he asked. "Something warm? It's been a hell of a day."

"Tea, please," she agreed. "You seem in a better mood this evening."

"Like most people, lifting the blackout has done me some good. Yourself?" He poured a cup of tea and passed it to her.

"I've been busy," Solace pointed out. "But yes, I did get to my back-log." The XO smirked, a surprisingly girlish expression on the normally serious officer's face. "My seventeen-going-on-thirty little sister left me a *long* message. Lots of stories about school, some chatter about a couple of boys in her classes – and a roughly five minute long lecture on just how *dreamy* the 'Stellar Fox' is and how lucky I am to be on his ship!"

Michael almost snorted tea as he laughed.

"Because his XO should be paying attention to how dreamy the Captain is," he observed as he cleaned up the mess he'd made. "Sib-lings, huh?"

"She's a teenager," Solace agreed with a shake of her head. "Things like 'chain of command' are meaningless to her still – and, God willing, will stay that way. Anna is *not* suited to the military."

"Neither was I at her age, looking back," Michael pointed out. "For that matter, given his family history, I don't think the Captain was planning on a military career at seventeen."

"And here we all are," she said softly, sipping her tea with unread-able eyes.

"Was there something you need, or was this just a visit?" Michael asked. She wasn't really interrupting, but it was rare for the Senior Fleet Commander to show up in his office without a reason of some kind.

"Yes," Solace replied, and sighed. "You know Kyle well, right?"

"I haven't known him *long*," Michael said slowly, wondering where this was going. "Only six months or so, really. But we've been through a *lot* of shit together in those six months."

"He has an… interesting personal reputation in the Navy," the XO said slowly. "The opposite of yours, in fact."

Oh. *That's* where this was going.

"He is interested in women," Michael pointed out. "Inasmuch as he's interested in anyone. You know about his son, right?"

"That wasn't…" Solace trailed off in mid-objection and smiled sheepishly. "Yes, I know about his son."

"Our dear Captain, having made an utter and complete mess of his first serious relationship, promptly decided he sucked at relationships and wasn't going to touch them again," the CAG explained, ignoring her objection as if she'd never said it.

"I see," the XO said primly.

"So, you and the Captain, huh?" Michael gently poked.

"Would be against regulations, so I doubt either of us would permit anything to happen," she said very precisely.

"But he won't be in your chain of command forever, and your sister isn't the only one making eyes at the war hero," he concluded.

"I am not 'making eyes' at my commanding officer!" she snapped, then smiled sheepishly again. "I… *may* be harboring possibly inappropriate notions about the man, but I am nothing if not patient."

Michael found himself having to clean up tea again, and he waved a warning finger at Solace.

"Patience would be the name of the game," he warned her. "While I wouldn't be surprised to discover that Kyle has had… professional companionship in the last ten years, he hasn't had a relationship since he joined the Navy."

She shook her head, sipping her tea.

"I can't believe I'm even thinking this," she admitted. "We work well together, damn it. The last thing I want to do is screw that up with a god-damn schoolgirl crush!"

"Why does everyone come to me for relationship advice?" Michael asked rhetorically. "Does something about my string of broken hearts and almost-ruined career suggest a great skill at this?"

"I'm not sure I'm even asking for advice here, Michael," Solace told him. "More… finding the lay of the land."

"Dangerous land, my dear," he replied. "Not just because he's your Captain – though Stars know that's enough! I suspect our dear Captain has more than a few landmines even a good friend hasn't seen."

She grunted, apparently lost in thought.

"Like I said, Michael, I can be patient," she pointed out. "If it's a crush fed by walking through hell together, then it will fade. If it's not… well, I didn't make it this far without knowing the tactics for dangerous ground."

21:00 January 20, 2736 ESMDT
DSC-078 Avalon, *Brig*

WITH EVERYTHING HAPPENING, it had been far too easy for Kyle to put off delivering the message from the Joint Chiefs to Tobin. Eventually, however, it had to be done, and he found himself in the brig – still half-expecting to meet Sirvard Barsamian in the office just outside.

The Ship's Marshal had not survived the flag deck. Another casualty of Tobin's failures as a commander. He sighed, straightened and stepped into the brig.

"How can I help you, sir?" a Military Police Corporal asked. The Asian-featured woman saluted crisply, but she kept her other hand on the shotgun slung over her body armor, and an eye on the hallway leading to the detention blocks.

"I need to speak with Tobin," Kyle told her.

"Cell A3," she replied immediately. "It's easy to pick out – it's the only one with a guard outside."

"Thank you, Corporal," *Avalon's* Captain said and heading down Corridor A – one of six blocks of twenty cells. The big carrier's brigs were almost full, though thankfully only four had been occupied before the mutiny.

As the Corporal had told him, only one of the twenty cell doors in Corridor A had a Marine outside. He wore body armor over his green-piped shipsuit and held a battle rifle at port arms across his chest.

"I need to speak with the prisoner, soldier," Kyle told him. A thought flipped an authorization code from his implant to the Marine's, and the man saluted and stepped aside.

The door slid open at a mental command and the Captain stepped into the cell.

It wasn't much of a room, basically a three meter cube. It had a bed, a console with a restricted entertainment library, and a Faraday cage layered into the walls that blocked implant transmissions.

Vice Admiral Dimitri Tobin sat on the bed. He was staring at the wall, though not blankly. Kyle recognized the stance of someone running through their implant's cyberneticaly perfect recall of events. The silicon remembered far more reliably than the neurons, though that also meant the loss of the silicon could be traumatizing.

Only a policy requiring shipboard backups for starfighter pilots had saved Kyle's own memories when his implant was lost.

Sighing, he coughed softly. Tobin blinked and looked up at him.

"You look very grim, Captain," the big Admiral rumbled softly. "You are not my executioner, and I sadly have little doubt I have earned whatever you are here to say. Do not fear hurting my *feelings*, Captain. That I have managed sufficiently on my own."

"I have reviewed the Alpha One communiqué from the Federation Joint Chiefs of Staff," Kyle told him, his voice formal. "I have also confirmed the situation with Fleet Admiral Blake.

"As of January Seventeenth, Twenty-Seven Thirty-Six, you are relieved of command of Battle Group Seventeen," he said flatly. "Investigation of your involvement or knowledge of Senior Fleet Commander Sanchez's mutiny will be carried out by qualified JD-Justice JAG personnel upon our rendezvous with the rest of the Battle Group at Alizon."

"There will need to be charges of incompetence laid as well as whatever they've already set their minds on," the big man said quietly.

"I should have seen and prevented Sanchez's plan. She was *my* Chief of Staff."

"I... cannot disagree, sir," Kyle said quietly. "But I will neither be responsible for the investigation nor sit on any Board or Court. I am far too close to this matter."

Tobin closed his eyes for a long moment. When he opened them again, he wouldn't meet the Captain's gaze.

"I failed you, Captain Roberts," he admitted. "I failed you, I lied to you, and I betrayed you. But please, *please*, tell me you didn't turn the ship around."

"We were never supposed to have left Alizon," Kyle pointed out. "Our orders have not been changed."

"Damn it all, Kyle – don't make me beg," Tobin said softly, desperately. "You *can't* let Richardson get away. We can't let so many deaths go unavenged."

"Our orders have not changed," Kyle repeated. "But I have been authorized to proceed to the Barsoom system. No one ever disagreed with you, Admiral. But revenge *couldn't* be our priority. But since you dragged us this far, it seems I will finish the job regardless."

"I will bring Richardson down, Dimitri," he promised very, very quietly. "You should never have done it, but you will not have sacrificed your career in vain."

40

A*VALON* ERUPTED into the Barsoom system in a blast of Cherenkov radiation, followed by full spectrum sensor sweeps. Emergence would temporarily emit as much energy as a small star, and Kyle saw no reason to pretend their entrance was stealthy.

"Get me a location on *Triumphant*," he ordered.

"Data coming in now," Commander Anderson replied. "We've got her – one light minute away and pushing for a zero gravity zone." He paused. "Sir, I'm reading two *Saint*-class battleships on my scopes. They're in hot pursuit of *Triumphant*."

"Show me," Kyle told him. His world spun for a moment, and then the tactical plot feeding his implants updated and he saw the three starships.

They'd arrived, it seemed, at the end of an hours-long game of cat and mouse – and the cats had definitely lost. The two *Saints* had a thirty gravity advantage over *Triumphant*, but they were ten million kilometers behind her with only a thousand kilometer a second advantage.

Triumphant was a little over two light minutes, almost thirty eight million kilometers, from reaching the zero gravity zone she was aiming for – a space cleared of debris by the motion of Barsoom's outer planets. She would reach that zone and bring up her Alcubierre-Stetson drive in sixty minutes.

At that point, the *Saints* would still be ten minutes from their own weapons range. Captain Richardson had escaped his pursuers again. Except…

Kyle had already put together a plan in his head. Now it was time to use *every* capability of his ship – including the ones they'd regarded as flaws.

"Commander Pendez," he said calmly. "I'm transmitting you a vector. I want us on that course at four hundred gravities until I give you new instructions. Once on our way, prepare a jump calculation to take us into FTL and drop us *here*."

He dropped a glowing sphere onto the tactical plot – at the exact point where *Triumphant* would be able to safely activate her Alcubierre drive.

"Sir, if we go to four hundred gravities…"

"We'll leave a trail of antimatter that'll light up the whole star system," Kyle confirmed. "That's what I want, Commander. Make it happen."

He flipped open another channel.

"Vice Commodore Stanford, are you ready to launch?"

"We are," his CAG confirmed. "But we're a long way away."

"I know. I'm arranging some cover, then we'll be leaving you behind to go say hi more closely. Do you follow?"

There was a long pause, during which the entire ship trembled as Pendez got her underway at a pace that would burn days' worth of fuel in minutes.

"I think so, sir," Stanford replied. "Initiating launch sequence. We'll be clear in forty seconds."

"Anderson, have they seen us yet?" Kyle asked.

"Should have just," he confirmed. "One minute till we see any reaction on their part."

"So let's see what happens," *Avalon's* Captain said with a smile. "We'll give Stanford that long to get clear."

"Sir, if we're leaving fighters and jumping in front of *Triumphant*…" Anderson hesitated. "I feel obligated to point out we don't match her firepower by a long shot without our fighters."

"But our deflectors are twice as strong as hers, which means we outrange her by half again," Kyle shook his head. "I'm not worried about engaging *Triumphant* in a ship-to-ship duel. It's those *Saints* whose guns scare me."

Seconds ticked away as *Avalon* burned through space – on a course *exactly* parallel-but-opposite to *Triumphant's.*

"All starfighters are away," Anderson reported. "They're flying *into* our exhaust trail?"

"The positrons carry a charge," Kyle pointed out. "They're not focused or under pressure, so they're not a significant threat to a ship with deflectors up. Makes a great shield."

"*I* can barely see them," the Tactical Officer whispered, his voice surprised.

"Sir, we're burning a day's worth of regular fuel every fifty-two seconds right now," Pendez pointed out. "When are we jumping?"

"Captain, transmission received from the Commonwealth ships!"

Kyle nodded and turned to his Navigator.

"Take us into FTL now, Maria," he ordered.

As the singularities and Stetson stabilization fields flickered into place around the carrier, the familiar distortions settling across his view, *Avalon's* Captain leaned back in his chair and nodded to his communications officer.

"Forward me their message."

The image of a dark-skinned man with Amerindian features in the red-sashed black uniform of the Commonwealth Navy, appeared on his implant feed. The stranger's hair was tied back in what appeared to be a shoulder-length braid, and his collar bore the single gold star of a Commodore – the Terran equivalent to Kyle's own rank.

"Federation warship, this is Commodore James Tecumseh aboard the battleship *Saint Anthony*," Tecumseh said calmly. "I can guess why you're here. I can *understand* why you're here.

"But this is Commonwealth space, and your presence is not welcome."

Tecumseh paused.

"We are in hot pursuit of *Triumphant*. I will permit you to witness the conclusion of this pursuit, but if you do not then withdraw from this system, I will have no choice but to engage and destroy your ship. Should *Triumphant* elude us, such an action would prevent me from pursuing Captain Richardson as he deserves.

"His actions are a stain on the honor of the Commonwealth Navy," the Terran Commodore concluded. "I would shed no blood today but his.

"Tecumseh, out."

Kyle smiled grimly.

"Time to emergence?"

"Five minutes and counting," Pendez replied.

"Let's see who counts as in hot pursuit then, shall we?" he murmured.

———

SIX MINUTES after disappearing from normal space, *Avalon* emerged again in a second burst of Cherenkov radiation. While they hadn't actually broken lightspeed in their micro-jump, the difference between the starship's regular acceleration of two hundred and fifty gravities and the estimated Alcubierre-Stetson drive acceleration of a hundred and thirty five *thousand* gravities still made short A-S hops useful.

Now, they were in *front* of *Triumphant* – emerging only a handful of kilometers from where Kyle estimated the rogue Commonwealth warship was planning on going FTL – with a vector directly towards her.

"Record for transmission to Commodore Tecumseh," Kyle ordered, then smiled calmly into the tiny camera pickup on his chair.

"Commodore Tecumseh, this is Captain Kyle Roberts aboard *Avalon*," he greeted the other officer calmly. "As you yourself said, I am in hot pursuit of *Triumphant* and have been since Captain Richardson launched antimatter warheads at an inhabited planet under the protection of the Alliance of Free Stars.

"My assessment is that your task group will not be able to intercept *Triumphant* before she escapes this system. *Avalon* will.

"You are welcome to bear witness to the fate of those who embrace atrocity as a weapon of war, and if you do not intervene we will leave this system with no further conflict. Captain Richardson's actions place him beyond the pale – and beyond the protection of the Commonwealth.

"I would shed no blood today but his," Kyle quoted back at the officer, and then killed the transmission.

"Do you really think that will work, Captain?" Solace asked over the link from Secondary Control. "Richardson may be a rogue, but standing back and watching us blow a Terran warship out of the sky is one hell of a pill for Tecumseh to swallow."

"It's a long shot," he admitted. "I call it seventy-thirty he fights. Be prepared for it."

"Sir, *Triumphant* is adjusting course," Anderson announced. "She's reversing her acceleration – they're falling back on Tecumseh's battle group."

"Richardson is thinking the same thing you are, Commander," he told Solace. "He stands a better chance in a Commonwealth brig than a shattered starship, so he'll play it up."

"Take us after her, Commander Pendez – flank acceleration."

"Oh thank god," his Navigator muttered. He chose to ignore that. The roughly two minutes they'd spent at four hundred gravities had served multiple purposes, but it had also burned through nearly five percent of the ship's total reaction mass reserve.

They were now almost two light minutes from *Triumphant* – over two and a half from *Saint Anthony* and her sister ship. With a combined velocity approaching three percent of lightspeed, however, that distance was going to evaporate quickly.

"Drones away," Anderson reported. "Assuming no change in profile, we'll have real-time information on *Triumphant* in roughly forty minutes. I'm staggering drone launches and acceleration profiles, we should be able to maintain real-time information indefinitely from that point."

"Thank you, Commander," Kyle replied.

The battleship was going to change acceleration eventually – if Richardson tried to run *through* Tecumseh's battle group and leave them to fight *Avalon,* it was unlikely to end well for the rogue Captain. Sometime in the next half an hour, he would start accelerating back towards the carrier.

Kyle had a guess, but sharing it with his crew would be embarrassing if he was wrong, so he watched the timer tick away the minutes

"Sir!" Anderson suddenly interrupted his thoughts with a shout. He saw what the Tactical Officer had seen almost instantly.

Saint Anthony was breaking off. Her course was exactly perpendicular to her previous path, pulling her away from the coming confrontation at over two kilometers a second squared.

"Do we have a message from our Terran friend?" he asked.

"Wait, watch the other ship," Anderson interrupted again, and Kyle looked at the tactical feed again with a sigh.

The second *Saint* remained on course for rendezvous with *Triumphant.*

"We have received a transmission from Commodore Tecumseh. Feeding it to you, Captain."

The Terran Commodore appeared on the screen, looking surprisingly calm for a man who had chosen to condemn an entire battleship to death.

"Captain Roberts," he said calmly. "You are correct in your tactical assessment. For the sake of the honor of the Commonwealth Navy, and to see these criminals brought to the justice their actions have earned, I am breaking off and leaving *Triumphant* to you.

"If you do not vacate the system upon the neutralization of Captain Richardson's vessel, I will take whatever actions are necessary to defend Barsoom. Until then, however, I am declaring a temporary cease fire in the interest of justice."

He paused, tilting his head slightly in the manner the vast majority of humans had acquired when receiving a voice transmission to their implant. The big dark-skinned Commodore sighed.

"I must also warn you that Captain Antioch of *Saint Augustine* has informed me my orders are illegal and is continuing on his course. While I will not engage you prior to *Triumphant's* destruction, I will also not permit you to fire on the *Saint Augustine*.

"Tecumseh, out."

———

"*TRIUMPHANT* HAS MADE TURNOVER," Anderson reported.

Kyle checked the time. Seventeen minutes after they'd started accelerating towards the *Saint Augustine* and still six million kilometers short of the other battleship. *Saint Anthony* had now separated two million kilometers from her sister ship, her velocity dropping as she fell back to defend Barsoom from any threat *Avalon* could make.

"Time to range for us, *Triumphant* and *Saint Augustine*?"

"We will range on *Triumphant* at two point one million kilometers in nineteen minutes, fifteen seconds," Anderson reported. "*Triumphant* will range on us at one point two million kilometers in nineteen minutes, fifty seconds. Passing velocity will exceed five percent of lightspeed."

Kyle nodded. *Triumphant* had one megaton lances to *Avalon's* seven hundred kiloton main guns, but the newer carrier's deflectors were over twice as powerful. He was sure the Commonwealth, like the Alliance, was looking to retrofit its older ships' deflectors – but they hadn't yet. Those thirty five seconds would almost certainly be enough to turn the battleship into scattered debris.

"And the *Saint Augustine*?" he asked quietly. The *Saint*-class battleship's deflectors were as strong as *Avalon's*, which meant he wouldn't range on them until much later.

"*Augustine* will range on us at one point two million kilometers… fifteen seconds after we can target *Triumphant*," Anderson said quietly. "She will be roughly two light seconds closer to us than *Triumphant* at that point. We will range on *her* at eight hundred and fifty thousand kilometers, forty-five seconds after she ranges on us."

"We won't live that long, Captain," Solace pointed out quietly. "What's your plan?"

"We carry on," Kyle ordered. "We make them think we're calling their bluff – and no matter what, we don't fire at *Augustine* first."

"Our only chance of taking her out without the starfighters is to launch missiles *now*," Anderson told him.

"Commander, do you really think you can get a nine missile salvo past the defenses of the *Triumphant*, let alone the *Saint Augustine*?" *Avalon's* Captain asked quietly. "Because if you can, feel free to open fire on *Triumphant*. We're in range."

"Why hasn't she launched on us then?" Solace asked.

"Richardson is saving his missiles," Kyle replied. "He can't have many left, and he's counting on *Saint Augustine* to cover for him today. Sadly, I suspect he's saving his missiles *for Saint Augustine*."

He felt more than saw the shiver that ran through his crew.

"They've got to be wondering the same thing about our fighters," Anderson realized. "It's a guessing game all around."

"Exactly," Kyle told him with bared teeth. "And so whether we all live or die comes down to who guessed better – me, or Captain Richardson."

"What about *Augustine*?" Solace asked.

"If Captain Antioch guesses right, he could change how this ends," Kyle acknowledged. "But he's already guessed wrong once today. I'm not discounting him, but he has shown his intuition to be… flawed."

"Sir, *Saint Augustine* is launching missiles!"

Captain Kyle Roberts nodded with a calm smile and leaned back in his command chair, eyeing the icons marking the thirty heavy missiles on his tactical feeds.

"So it begins," he murmured.

"You may return fire, Mister Anderson."

41

Barsoom System
20:15 January 21, 2736 Earth Standard Meridian Date/Time
DSC-078 Avalon, *Bridge*

TIMING WAS EVERYTHING. *Saint Augustine's* first missiles would reach *Avalon* over three minutes before she could range on *Triumphant.* Even faced with top-of-the-line capital ship missiles, the supercarrier could probably handle thirty missiles.

Saint Augustine's first missiles concerned him. The second salvo, fired a minute later, worried him a bit more.

The actual *problem* was that *Triumphant* had finally fired a missile salvo shortly after *Saint Augustine* had. Those twenty-four missiles would arrive alongside *Augustine's third* salvo. Without starfighters to play the first line of defense, Kyle wasn't at all sure his ship could take over *fifty* missiles.

"Hold your course, Commander Pendez," he ordered softly. "Commander Anderson, I'll take control of our missiles if you please. Focus on your defenses."

Kyle's gamble might still pay off, but that required them to still be *alive* when they reached positron lance range of *Triumphant*.

"Lieutenant Carter," he turned to his communication officer. "Any word from Commodore Tecumseh?"

"No, sir."

The commander of the Terran Task Group was apparently willing to stand back and watch. To be fair, Tecumseh was probably the smartest Terran officer in the system, which meant he *had* to be feeling paranoid about the absence of Kyle's fighters.

"First salvo impact in five minutes," Anderson reported. "I estimate a thirty-five second engagement window for active defense. Commander Solace," he turned to the XO on the intercom. "I'm passing control of the inner zone to Secondary Control."

"We're locked in here, Commander Anderson," she replied calmly. "You clean, we'll sweep."

Kyle left his subordinates to it. The light positron lances used for anti-fighter and anti-missile defense could start killing missiles at a million kilometers. The laser defense array had more coverage and more beams, but a lot less effective range.

He focused on that third combined salvo. The nine missile salvos that Anderson had launched weren't going to get through either battleship's defenses. Kyle had let his Tactical Officer launch them as much in reflex as anything else, but he still had a use for them.

"Impact in one minute, targeting with outer defenses."

Keeping a quarter of his mind on the immediate threat, *Avalon's* Captain directed his missiles carefully. Unlike the drones they could use to watch the battle, missiles didn't carry Q-Com systems – no one was going to put entangled particle arrays on something *designed* to be destroyed. An array large enough to be useful would increase the cost of a missile roughly a hundred-fold, leaving a single capital ship missile costing a third of the price of an entire starfighter.

Timing was everything.

Even as his subordinates fought to protect the carrier from the current attack, Kyle studied the enemy missiles, laid in the directions, and programmed his orders. A moment's thought sent a second salvo of missiles thundering out into space.

"First salvo is clear," Solace reported, her voice spiky with adrenaline. "Second salvo entering engagement range in twenty seconds. Third salvo in ninety seconds."

"Lance range in two minutes, thirty seconds," Anderson reported.

Kyle gave his final orders and returned his attention to the main plot. The inevitable natural 'jamming' effect of antimatter explosions was messing with their sensors now, with the cloud of radioactive debris from the first thirty missiles surrounding the big carrier.

"Second salvo entering range."

In the same instant *Saint Augustine's* second set of thirty missiles entered range of *Avalon's* defense, her *third* salvo interpenetrated with the nine missiles the carrier had fired back. The screen flashed with white light as all nine of Kyle's missiles shot closer to the Commonwealth missiles and detonated.

His subordinates wisely focused on their own work and Kyle studied the results. He'd lucked out – twelve missiles were gone, the Stormwinds not smart *enough* to avoid proximity kills without some kind of warning.

Even as he watched, though, the missiles spread apart – as did *Triumphant's*. His second salvo dove into the heart of *Triumphant's* salvo, but the missiles' simplistic but *fast* brains had reacted in time.

Only six missiles died this time, and Kyle leaned back in his chair as the remaining forty missiles charged in on his command.

"Second salvo clear," Solace reported grimly. "Third salvo entering range in thirty seconds. I confirm forty – repeat, four zero, missiles remaining." She met Kyle's gaze through the intercom. "We'll do what we can, sir."

The statue he'd accepted as his XO in time of stress was gone, and there was something in her eyes as she looked at him. He shook his head gently.

"No, Mira," he told her. "This is *Avalon*. We do what *no one else can!*"

There was a smile and a cheer on his people's lips as the enemy missiles charged into range.

———

KYLE WAS out of tricks now. No missiles left to use as sacrificial lambs. No aggressive suicide charge to shock and awe a second-rate enemy into submitting. No smart Alcubierre tricks to confound and surprise the foe.

Just one hole card he'd already played, and the sheer grit and skill of the crew of the deep space supercarrier *Avalon*. It would have to do.

Positron beams glittered across his tactical display as Anderson opened fire. Ghosts flickered around them as the Tactical Officer's subordinates unleashed the carrier's electronic warfare suite, tempting and tricking missiles away from their targets.

Seconds ticked by before the near-lightspeed weapons hit their targets. Missiles began to die. *Avalon's* forward broadsides mounted one hundred seventy-kiloton-per-second lances, and those weapons tore into the Terran missiles.

But those missiles had their own ECM. Ghosts flickered and appeared around the missiles, and the missiles themselves jerked and spiraled, throwing off Anderson's targeting programs and forcing misses.

A dozen missiles died. Then another dozen. Then sixteen missiles tore into the inner defense zone and the hundreds of small lasers mounted along *Avalon's* arrowhead hull opened fire.

Kyle held his breath. He wasn't the only one, and seconds passed in dead silence as *Avalon's* crew guided their ship from inside their implants. Missiles died, first in singles, then in pairs – a full *dozen* of the deadly weapons flashing apart in antimatter fire as Solace took them out with deadly precision.

Four made it through. Out of over a hundred capital ship missiles, costing millions of Commonwealth dollars apiece, four penetrated every active defense the supercarrier could throw at them.

They made it through every defense… and missed.

The carrier *lurched* as the missiles, fooled by ECM and the radiation clouds of their dead sisters, detonated well clear of her hull, waves of energy hammering into the warship's meters-thick ferro-carbon ceramic armor. The lights flickered, dimmed, and came back up.

The tactical feed didn't. A moment later, a fuzzy, mixed image appeared in Kyle's brain.

"Wong?" he snapped. "Where's our feed?"

"You're getting all you're getting," the Engineer replied bluntly. "Those blasts just melted every sensor array on our hull."

"We need those sensors to target the guns," Anderson said grimly. "Q-Com relay from the drones won't cut it – the bandwidth is enough for keeping an eye on people, but not for attack telemetry. Our drones are moving *fast* – we've got significant relativity impacts. The computers can adjust... but not fast enough to hit an evading target at two million kilometers."

"Damn," Kyle said mildly. "Prepare for random fire then," he told Anderson. "We may not hit them, but by the gods let's keep their eyes on..."

"Wait!" Anderson snapped. "*Augustine* just flipped and went to emergency decel. *Anthony* flipped as well – they're inbound. What the Void?!"

Captain Kyle Roberts glanced at the tactical display and ran the angles in his mind. A cold, savage smile grew on his face.

"It seems Commodore Tecumseh is *almost* paranoid enough," he said aloud. "He just spotted Stanford."

20:28 January 21, 2736 ESMDT
SFG-001 Actual – Falcon-C type command starfighter

IT WAS ALMOST a relief when the Commonwealth starships finally reacted to the starfighter group.

The expanding radiation cloud from *Avalon's* burst of emergency acceleration had covered and concealed Michael's people on their approach, but he'd *known* it couldn't last forever. Even if his gunner was estimating the antimatter left behind would keep annihilating itself for another twenty to thirty minutes, the further they got from the initial point, the more and more likely it was that almost *two hundred* antimatter drives would be picked up.

As they'd grown closer and closer, Michael had started to suspect that the two battleships he was targeting *had* to have seen him, and the whole thing was a trap, waiting to lure the starfighters in and annihilate them at a range where the starships could hit them and they couldn't return the favor.

Instead, they were almost *on top* of *Triumphant*, and only half a million kilometers from *Saint Augustine*, flying straight between the two starships at almost five percent of the speed of light. This was *insane*.

"All fighters," he snapped. "Random-walk to avoid fire, full missile salvo on *Augustine*. Close with *Triumphant* and *finish the son of a bitch*!"

Fitting actions to words, he twisted his starfighter into a spiral, narrowly dodging the first beam of the day as *Triumphant* finally realized the danger. *Saint Augustine* was trying to put distance between her and the starfighters, but with eight hundred Starfire missiles barrelling down on her, all she was doing was buying time.

Spiraling in towards *Triumphant*, Michael left the missiles to his gunner and spun up the positron lance. The six thousand ton starfighter vibrated gently as the zero point cell feeding the weapon fired up, pulsing power back into the fighter's grid and positrons into the capacitor banks for the weapon.

Now!

One hundred and ninety-two *Falcon* starfighters spun in space, dancing a pirouette of survival around the deadly beams of antimatter – and then fired their own lances.

Many missed. Some only contacted for fractions of a second. A handful struck and held, the beams burning clean through the battleship as they converted her own mass into devastatingly powerful explosives.

It took Michael Stanford's starfighters a mere eight seconds to cross their range envelope of *Triumphant*. When they left it, there was nothing left of the fifteen million ton battleship but radiation and debris.

Kematian was avenged.

———

MICHAEL HAD fractions of a second to process *Triumphant's* destruction. Even as their missiles struck home and his starfighters flashed by, *Saint Augustine* was firing on them. Her anti-fighter lances were targeting the swarm of missiles blasting in on her, but the battleship's main guns could *not* target missiles.

They were simply inefficient at targeting starfighters. Michael winced as he saw ships simply *disappear* as the massive, megaton-a-second, lances struck home on starfighters barely able to withstand laser hits.

Then the missiles struck home. Starfires were fighter-launched weapons, a tenth the size and even less of the capability of capital ship missiles. The secondary lances and laser arrays took a vicious harvest, and hundreds of missiles detonated, filling the space around *Saint Augustine* in radiation and debris.

But hundreds remained. At this range, their initial velocity provided most of their kinetic energy – and their antimatter warheads the vast majority of their impact.

The final explosion was over half a *teraton*… and once that terrible and tremendous star faded, it left nothing behind of the *Saint Augustine*.

"Captain Roberts, this is Vice Commodore Stanford," he said calmly, raising *Avalon* on the Q-Com. "We are adjusting course to rendezvous." He checked their relative velocity and winced. "It's… going to take a bit."

"We copy, CAG," Roberts replied. "We are vectoring to enable rendezvous. I make thirty-seven minutes to matched velocity."

Michael checked. It would still take time to bring the two groups of ships together safely once they'd matched velocities, but that would get them close enough to help defend the carrier.

"We lost six starfighters," he said quietly. "I have three pods on my scope, my Wing Commanders have already detailed retrieval teams."

"Understood, Vice Commodore."

"What about that last battleship, Captain?" Michael finally asked. The *Saint Anthony* was still heading for *Avalon*, though the vector the carrier was taking to rendezvous with the starfighters was helping keep her away. Unless the Terran ship actually turned away, though, she'd be able to bring *Avalon* to range before the starfighters would be in a position to assist.

"I'll let you know," Roberts replied. "It appears I have a call to make."

20:32 January 21, 2736 ESMDT
DSC-078 Avalon, *Bridge*

DROPPING THE CHANNEL TO STANFORD, Kyle took a moment to breathe a sigh of relief. Wong had been overly optimistic in his assessment. Not only were all of their sensors gone, but *all* of the missile launcher hatches were welded shut, along with half of the emitters for the main guns.

All easy enough to repair out of shipboard resources – *Avalon* could fix an astonishingly large amount of damage to herself given time – but not in the time they had. With no more starfighters aboard, and Stanford on a vector off to the gods' back acre, *Saint Anthony* was going to add a carrier to its kill sheet very quickly.

He smoothed his features, winked at the screen where Solace and the Secondary Control crew were watching, and activated the recorder in his chair.

"Commodore Tecumseh," he greeted the other man calmly. "I have completed my mission in Barsoom, but I see your vessel is on a course towards mine. Understand that I did not *choose* to engage *Saint Augustine*, but your Captain Antioch left me no choice.

"If you continue on this course, Commodore, remember that I retain a full Wing of *Falcon* starfighters aboard. Starfighters that have just thoroughly demonstrated their ability against a *Saint*-class battleship.

"I came here to avenge Kematian's dead. That is done. I have already shed more blood than I desired. Do not make me add yours to the total.

"For the honor of both our navy's and the safety of both our crews,

I offer you this one last chance. Break off, Commodore Tecumseh. Break off, and I will leave the Barsoom system with no further conflict. You have my word as an officer of the Castle Federation Space Navy, and as a fellow starship captain."

He ended the message and hit transmit.

"Kalers," he opened a channel to his Acting Deck Chief. "I want you to start running power to the launch tubes and moving ships into them."

"Sir, we don't have any ships *left*."

"Stick shuttles in them," Kyle ordered. "No crews, just make it damn clear to, say, a close-range Q-probe that we are preparing to launch ships. They won't be able to tell *what* we're loading unless the probe is inside the damn hangar."

The Deck Chief looked at him like he was crazy, then shrugged.

"This is why you're the Captain, Captain," she said, then cut the channel.

"Do you think he'll buy it?" Solace asked very softly on an implant-only channel no one else could hear.

"Thirty-seventy," he admitted. "And only that high because the Commodore didn't want to fight in the first place."

They waited. The distance between the two ships was well over a light minute again, even if there was no way *Avalon* could avoid engagement.

"Sir, Q-probes report *Saint Anthony* is breaking off her attack run," Anderson reported loudly.

Kyle had to check for himself. His Tactical Officer was right – the battleship had reversed her course, once again settling for a vector that would keep her between *Avalon* and the planet with its massive, expensive, terraforming machines.

He breathed a huge, obvious, sigh of relief – and then watched the bridge crew around him disintegrate into wild cheering.

"Message inbound from Tecumseh, sir!" Carter announced.

The now-familiar Amerindian features of the Terran Commodore appeared on the screen.

"I suspect, Captain Roberts, that a single Wing of your starfighters is no match for a fully prepared battleship," Tecumseh said bluntly.

"But you are correct in that Captain Richardson was a stain upon the honor of the Commonwealth. A stain I could not have removed without your aid.

"I will have my vengeance for Captain Antioch, Roberts, have no illusions about that," the Commodore continued. "But today... today the Commonwealth owes you a debt of honor. Leave this system, Captain Roberts. Today and today only, I will grant you that respect."

Kyle smiled. He'd done it. Somehow, against all odds, he'd done it.

42

Alizon System
16:00 January 28, 2736 Earth Standard Meridian Date/Time
DSC-078 Avalon, *Bridge*

KYLE MADE certain to be on the bridge when *Avalon* returned to the Alizon system. The Q-Com messages assuring him that the system was safe and that Battle Group Seventeen had arrived in his absence to secure the world were no substitute for seeing the sensor returns with his own eyes.

The three heavy capital ships orbiting above the liberated world were a welcome sight, a reassurance that despite having been lied to and led astray, the world he'd abandoned was safe.

"Scans confirm we have Battle Group Seventeen on our scopes," Commander Anderson reported. "I am reading IFFs for *Gravitas*, *Camerone* and *Zheng He*. Q-Com arrival alert has been transmitted."

"Thank you, Commander," Kyle told him, watching the three ships. In the back of his head, he tracked the automated interactions between his ship and the rest of the battle group. Data propagated around the ships as they began to feed their sensor data to *Avalon*, and notes flowed through his mind on each ship.

Including the fact that Battle Group Seventeen now had a new commanding officer – *Rear Admiral* Miriam Alstairs, formerly *Camerone's* Captain.

"Sir, incoming Q-Com transmission from the Rear Admiral," Kyle was informed.

"I'll take it in my office," he replied.

He took a moment to settle his mind after entering his office – he might have destroyed two battleships in exchange for the loss of six starfighters and eleven lives – two of the flight crew whose pods had successfully ejected had still died of injuries before rescue – but he'd also been duped into disobeying his orders and leaving Alizon effectively undefended.

"Captain Roberts," Miriam Alstairs greeted him once he opened the channel. "It's good to see you return – and once again victorious where many would have failed. Of course, this time, also in disobedience to your orders."

Kyle bowed his head.

"I was too… credulous, Admiral," he said quietly. "That Admiral Tobin cut us off from communication should have been a warning sign."

"It should have," Alstairs agreed. "And many will doubt the wisdom of continuing on after learning of Dimitri's treachery. Victory will cover some of those sins, Captain, but not all."

"I understand, ma'am."

"That said, I want you to realize that I am not moving the flag to *Camerone* to punish you or show a lack of confidence," she continued. "Quite the opposite. You are aware, I presume, that Admiral Tobin flew his flag from *Avalon* so as to keep an eye on his most inexperienced Captain?

"I don't think that will be necessary for me."

"I understand, ma'am," Kyle repeated. "Thank you for explaining."

"Oh, I'm not done with you yet, Captain," Alstairs said with a grin that could only be called mischievous. "The Joint Chiefs have informed that it would be weeks before they could get a new

Commanding Officer for *Camerone* out here, so I have a question for you.

"I've reviewed the assessments of Senior Fleet Commander Solace by her previous Captains. I suspect at least one is, well, bullshit. Traditionally you would not provide a review for three months, but I'm afraid I must ask your assessment of your Executive Officer."

"Ma'am, I am tempted to lie to you because I would vastly prefer to keep Commander Solace as my XO," he replied. "I suspect that in itself is enough, isn't it?"

"It is," she confirmed. The newly minted Rear Admiral sighed.

"I have Military Police standing by to remove Vice Admiral Tobin and your other prisoners from *Avalon*," Alstairs told him. "We have been provided basing facilities by the Alizoni, including a decent sized prison. I'm sure you want them off your ship as much as I do."

"Agreed, Admiral," Kyle admitted. "Tobin's actions I can understand and accept, even as they condemn him. The mutiny, though…"

"I've seen the unedited report," the Rear Admiral said. "I won't lie – that someone in the Castle Federation would stoop so low terrifies me, Kyle. Watch your back."

"I will, ma'am."

"Then I will see you when you make orbit. Travel safely, Captain Roberts."

20:00 January 28, 2736 ESMDT
DSC-078 Avalon, *Captain's Office*

"ENTER," Kyle instructed as the chime on his door sounded.

A moment later, Senior Fleet Commander – soon to be *Captain* – Mira Solace stepped in. She looked… hesitant. It wasn't an attitude he was used to seeing on her.

"I just received the notification from JD-Personnel, Captain," she said quietly. "I'm being promoted and transferred to command *Camerone*."

The words came out in a rush, and Kyle gave her his brightest smile. He was disappointed to lose her, but she deserved the command – deserved it more than he had when he was given *Avalon*.

"Congratulations," he told her. "I've served aboard *Last Stands*. They're good ships, and I've only heard the best from *Camerone*. And you'll get Battle Group Seventeen's tradition of the most junior Captain carrying the flag."

"It's a tradition now, is it?" she asked.

"Anything done twice in the military, Commander," Kyle reminded her.

"Sir – Kyle… I have an odd request," Solace said slowly.

"At this point, Mira, I've lost track of what I owe you," he told her. "We made a damn good team, and I'm sorry to see you go. You deserve it."

"My promotion and transfer officially take effect at noon tomorrow," she replied. "I… would like to be formally removed from my duties aboard *Avalon* immediately. It's… a personal matter."

Kyle considered. Solace was being oddly non-committal, looking down at her hands on the desk. It was an odd request, though hardly a difficult one. For sixteen hours or so, Solace would be 'between assignments on foreign post' and technically receive approximately ten percent less salary.

"You're not on shift before the transfer," he pointed out. "I can't see an issue, Mira." With a thought and a command in the system, the change was registered.

"You are officially no longer the Executive Officer of *Avalon*," he agreed. "Recorded and time stamped."

"Thank you, Kyle," Mira told him, and her eyes came up to meet his gaze. Something in them made him suddenly *very* aware he was still sleeping in his office and that the fold-out bed was in the corner.

"May I ask why?" he managed to choke out, but she was already on her feet and coming around the desk.

"Because as long as you were in my chain of command, Kyle, I couldn't do *this*."

The next thing he knew, she was kissing him. And since he *wasn't* in her chain of command anymore, he failed to come up with any objection before he stopped caring.

Niagara System – Commonwealth Space
08:00 January 29, 2736 ESMDT
BB-285 Saint Michael *– Marshal Walkingstick's Office*

Fleet Admiral James Calvin Walkingstick, Marshal of the Rimward Marches, liberator of New Dundee, and sworn servant of the Congress of the Terran Commonwealth, watched Commodore James Tecumseh enter his office with more patience than he suspected the officer expected.

"Have a seat, James," he ordered. "I'm not going to pretend this will be an easy meeting."

"Sir."

"Commodore, I will be blunt. You stood by and watched two Commonwealth battleships be destroyed, and then allowed their killer to escape without even attempting to pursue.

"You have not even attempted to justify this decision with questions of the balance of force, or even pretended this Captain Roberts' available starfighters were a major threat to your vessel.

"You have, in fact, justified this decision entirely in the context of the stain on the honor of the Commonwealth represented by Captain Richardson.

"Is my summary correct, Commodore?" he asked.

"Yes, sir," Tecumseh confirmed flatly.

"You do understand, Commodore, that permitting the destruction of *Saint Augustine* was very different than permitting the destruction of *Triumphant*?"

"Yes, sir."

"And you offer no further excuse?"

"It was already done, sir," Tecumseh said calmly. "Engaging *Avalon* would not have brought back the dead. And Captain Richardson's dishonor required… some repayment beyond his death."

"Suffice to say, Commodore, that the Commonwealth Navy does not agree with your assessment," Walkingstick told him bluntly. "You are relieved of command of *Saint Anthony*. You will report aboard Logistics Station Niagara Seven there to take up a yet-to-be-determined role in the Rimward Marches Logistics Command. Do you understand?"

"Yes, sir," Tecumseh replied crisply. He unwound half a twist. "Thank you, sir."

Walkingstick's lips quirked in what those very close to him would recognize as an honest smile. Tecumseh recognized that he could have been cashiered for his actions, but so long as Walkingstick *did* punish him, the Marshal could choose the Commodore's punishment.

"Dismissed, Commodore."

Tecumseh stood and Walkingstick could *see* the defeat in the man's stiff, Academy-perfect, posture. He made it six steps towards the door before Walkingstick hit a button on his desk.

"Commodore," he said calmly, his voice less harsh than before. Tecumseh paused, but did not turn around.

"Everything I have said is for the record and for the discipline of the Terran Commonwealth Navy," the Marshal of the Rimward Marches said very quietly. "Off the record, I am not certain I would have done differently.

"I know officers of your type, Commodore. Unwilling to bend. Determined to honor the ideals of Commonwealth above even the goal of Unity.

"You're goddamn pains in the ass," the man in charge of conquering the Alliance of Free Stars told the younger officer. "You're goddamn pains in the ass," he repeated, "and you represent the true heart and soul of this Navy.

"You *will* command again, Commodore Tecumseh. You have my word on that."

———

JOIN THE MAILING LIST

Love Glynn Stewart's books? Join the mailing list at

GLYNNSTEWART.COM/MAILING-LIST/

to know as soon as new books are released, special announcements, and a chance to win free paperbacks.

ABOUT THE AUTHOR

Glynn Stewart is the author of *Starship's Mage*, a bestselling science fiction and fantasy series where faster-than-light travel is possible–but only because of magic. His other works include science fiction series *Duchy of Terra, Castle Federation* and *Vigilante,* as well as the urban fantasy series *ONSET* and *Changeling Blood*.

Writing managed to liberate Glynn from a bleak future as an accountant. With his personality and hope for a high-tech future intact, he lives in Kitchener, Ontario with his partner, their cats, and an unstoppable writing habit.

VISIT GLYNNSTEWART.COM FOR NEW RELEASE UPDATES

facebook.com/glynnstewartauthor

OTHER BOOKS
BY GLYNN STEWART

For release announcements join the
mailing list or visit **GlynnStewart.com**

STARSHIP'S MAGE
Starship's Mage
Hand of Mars
Voice of Mars
Alien Arcana
Judgment of Mars
UnArcana Stars
Sword of Mars
Mountain of Mars
The Service of Mars
A Darker Magic
Mage-Commander (upcoming)

Starship's Mage: Red Falcon
Interstellar Mage
Mage-Provocateur
Agents of Mars

Pulsar Race: A Starship's Mage Universe Novella

DUCHY OF TERRA
The Terran Privateer
Duchess of Terra
Terra and Imperium
Darkness Beyond
Shield of Terra
Imperium Defiant
Relics of Eternity
Shadows of the Fall
Eyes of Tomorrow

SCATTERED STARS
Scattered Stars: Conviction
Conviction
Deception
Equilibrium
Fortitude (upcoming)

PEACEKEEPERS OF SOL
Raven's Peace
The Peacekeeper Initiative
Raven's Course
Drifter's Folly (upcoming)

EXILE
Exile
Refuge
Crusade
Ashen Stars: An Exile Novella

CASTLE FEDERATION
Space Carrier Avalon
Stellar Fox
Battle Group Avalon
Q-Ship Chameleon
Rimward Stars
Operation Medusa
A Question of Faith: A Castle Federation Novella

SCIENCE FICTION STAND ALONE NOVELLA
Excalibur Lost